MEINBALD

Juha Saarela

Contents

Dedication

~ i ~

I want to dedicate this book to my mother, who has always been there for me, not only on the sunny and glory days, but also in my times of trouble. Thank you for believing in me and my dreams.

I also dedicate this book to my late father, who helped and influenced not only me, but many people in his too-short time here on earth. I miss you more than words can say. I look forward to the day we meet again.

Acknowledgment

I want to acknowledge Markku Soikkeli, whose input was essential for me as a writer during my first authoring journey. Thank you Markku at Proosakuiskaaja for your dedication and encouragement!

Casper Williams with his team at Amazon Publishing Portal did an amazing job in translating this book from Finnish to English. I want to give you full acknowledgement of your diligence and patience in the process that took a long time, but was definitely worth it.

I also want to acknowledge the extraordinary debt I owe to these people in my life: First, my spouse - you truly have made my life complete and also made it possible for me to spend my leisure time working alone in my dungeon, diving into matters no-one ever knew even existed or at least saw any relevance in. And thank you, too, my beautiful daughters, you all, like your dear mother, give me love, joy and laughter, but above all, hope. Without these, I couldn't carry on. Thank you also Ellie, for you have not eaten my papers like you ate my presentation notes of a (now) meaningless webinar when you were just a puppy. We all love you, you furry cutie!

This book is based on compiling research of my own, which wouldn't have been possible without the due diligence of countless of writers, whose notes of historical events I was able to dig from the books and other writings documented on the

internet. I have listed my most important sources on
https://stiernkors.com/en/About-Meinbald/

Lastly, I want to thank Stiernkors, my publishing company, for
giving me the means to publish this novel, this all means so
much to me.

About the Author

Juha Saarela is a writer who makes his day job with information technology and knowledge, who over the years has become particularly interested in Finnish prehistory and history.

Saarela has worked, among other things, as a software engineer, entrepreneur, business manager and coach in the corporate world in Finland and internationally. In his works, he examines things not only in the distant past, but also in the near future, but above all here and now.

Saarela's historical debut novel "Meinbald" was published in Finnish in 2025. Books and writing are his way of fighting against oblivion and misinformation, ignorance and boredom.

Quotes

"Do not go outside yourself, but return to yourself. Truth resides within man, and if you find your nature changing, rise above yourself. But remember, as you ascend, that you are elevating yourself above your rational soul. Strive to reach the place where the true light of reason is kindled. For what would any good user of reason strive for, if not for the truth?"

Augustine, De Vera Religione 39, 72

"For the past no longer exists, and the future has not yet come. But the present, if it were always present and did not turn into the past, would no longer be time, but eternity. So, if the present is only time because it turns into the past, how can we then claim that it exists, when its only reason for being is that it will no longer exist?"

Augustine, Confessions XI.14, p. 421

"Actually, it cannot be said that there are three times: past, present, and future. Perhaps it would be more appropriate to say there are three tenses: the past present, the present present, and the future present. For these three things are somehow in the soul; I do not see them elsewhere. The present of the past is memory, the present of the present is perception, and the present of the future is expectation."

Augustine, Confessions XI.20, p. 429

Preface

The story of Meinbald came out of an inexplicable need of sorting out, where us modern-day Finns are coming from and how our forefathers were converted to Christianity. And how and from where did our country receive so many capable soldiers, that their descendants gave birth to a new warrior nobility into this eternal buffer between the east and the west. By chance, I had come across seals of two different men, a bishop and a nobleman, exactly similar to the one I found from a knightly order founded in Bohemia. The seals carry a star and a cross. After having researched into this strange coincident, I found many other random clues of historical Bohemia having quite many connections to the Eastern parts of medieval Sweden. I got into this subject so much that I decided to gather all the pieces to solve the puzzle, in order to see how life was lived here in north-eastern Europe 800 years ago. I could find puzzle pieces in historical literature, chronicles and annals, but also sagas, folklore, archeological studies and studies of ancient beliefs of Finnish and Norse people. However, quite early I had to face the fact that the historical sources are inadequate and so I needed some imagination and logical thinking to fill in the ever repeating gaps and blanks. That is how this life story you are about to read was born. Before diving into the story it makes sense to first have a short review of the world people were living in those days.

Pope Gregory IX encouraged Sweden and Denmark to crusade in the north and attempt to convert the Orthodox Slavic peoples of Eastern Europe, particularly in the republics of Pskov and Novgorod, to Western Roman Catholicism. In the north, the Pope requested that, for example, the Livonian Sword Brethren send troops to protect the Finns, who, from the Catholic Church's perspective as a "half-pagan nation," were in constant conflict with Novgorod, representing the Eastern Church. No clear evidence has survived to indicate whether the Livonians ever reached Finland, but it is known that the Finnish bishop, Thomas, was in close contact with the Livonian knights before he was suddenly excommunicated and forced to flee both the Livonians and the Finnish clergy to Gotland, Visby.

The Pope had several armed knightly orders in Europe, and although he was engaged in a power struggle with the Holy Roman Emperor, Frederick II, the German knights loyal to the Pope had been conducting bloody proselytizing campaigns in the Baltics for several decades. In their most recent victory, after over ten years of conquest, they subdued Estonia, with its last province, Saaremaa, falling to the Church in 1227.

In year 1200, the Western Christian world was led by Pope Innocent III, who had restored the Pope's secular power while ruling in Rome. Innocent interpreted that he was directly the vicar of Christ and, therefore higher than the kings, entitled to command them all. When he rose to lead the Catholic Church, Innocent III took charge of the most powerful organization of the Middle Ages.

The Church strongly resembled a great power, a supranational state: it had its own laws, legislators, courts, lawyers, prisons, and the best-organized and most efficient administrative apparatus in all of Europe at the time. Innocent III was the leader of all of Europe because, after the death of the Emperor of the Holy Roman Empire, he had no rival influential enough to challenge him.

The Pope's political advice was followed in France, England, Denmark, Hungary, and also in Bohemia. Innocent III started the Fourth Crusade in 1202, which lasted only two years, but led to events such as the sack of Constantinople and thus the separation of the Roman and Byzantine Churches, causing the Great Schism. East and West separated and never reunited. This famous predecessor of Honorius III focused on the Holy Land, aiming to reconquer it and enact spiritual reforms within the Church.

Unlike his predecessors, Honorius pursued his goals with gentleness rather than force. He knew that only one person could help him take back the Holy Land, and that person was his former student, Frederick II of Germany. In 1220, Frederick was elected Emperor of the Holy Roman Empire, and on November 22, the Pope crowned him on the condition that he participate in the Fifth Crusade.

However, Frederick II, the grandson of the famous Frederick Barbarossa, was in no rush to go on a crusade. Even his father, Emperor Henry VI, had wanted to make all his lands hereditary and had claimed that all Papal fiefs were the fiefs of the Emperor. Throughout the empire, there was a major conflict between the spiritual and secular leadership regarding matters of inheritance, ownership, and authority. This conflict created widespread uncertainty and restlessness among the people. Arguments erupted seemingly out of nowhere, often escalating into violence, which in turn caused further arguments, fear, and instability.

In Prague, the heart of Bohemia, the property of the Teutonic Knights was donated to a hospital founded by Agnes of Bohemia, the king's daughter. Pope Gregory IX confirmed the gift in 1236. The following year, 1237, the Livonian Order of the Sword merged with the Teutonic Order, becoming its own independent branch.

In 1238, the Pope formalized the new Order of the Red Star and Cross, under the Rule of St. Augustine, at the request of Agnes of Bohemia. It remains the only religious order originating from the Czech Republic and the only Catholic order founded by a woman in the world. In the Middle Ages, it excelled in charity, caring for the sick, and providing spiritual care.

The Order established a seminary in the Czech Republic, operated schools, and founded hospitals, acting as a small but influential part of the Holy Roman Empire. Despite its Bohemian roots, the Order cannot be described as exclusively Czech. It included Germans, Poles, Silesians, Moravians, and Walloons among its ranks, and its activities were closely tied to other Catholic orders.

Although the Order, aside from its founder St. Agnes, has not produced any other saints or blessed ones for the Catholic Church, it has made a deep and lasting impact in culture, education, and charity throughout Europe.

Alongside these "acts of spirit and philanthropy," much more was happening, often necessitating very different actions. The last pagans in Europe, such as the people of Courland, had to be converted and brought under the Pope's permanent protection.

Although no records of these actions have been preserved for posterity, it does not mean they did not happen, nor that they left no lasting traces on our understanding of history.

Many past events have also contributed to our ever-changing DNA inheritance. During that era, time was perceived differently. People were not yet enslaved by the clock, and time was primarily relative. It varied for soldiers, merchants, peasants, kings, and priests alike. Of course, the sun paced everyone, but daily rhythms were dictated by what tasks had to be done and under whose authority.

Chapter I
From Dresden To Prague

Dresden, in May Anno Domini 1220

The spring had progressed almost to summer. Sun was warming up the stones by the riverside, drying the roads so that dust clouds were rising as people moved on the sandy roads. Boots were changed to light sandals, as there hadn't been any rain in Dresden in over a month.

Udo and Konne, a merchant couple, had a baby boy in May 1220 and decided to name him Meinbald. The name came from Udo's family and originated from pre-Christian times. Udo and Konne were poor Christian merchants, enterprising and brave young Germans, whom life had happily brought together on the south bank of the Elbe in Dresden. People had begun to flow to the growing center on the site of an old Slavic fishing village as part of a large wave of German migration to the East.

For merchants, Dresden was an attractive border region, as the Elbe River acted as a busy trade route, leading numerous river ships to the developing center of Bohemia in Prague and back. The new parents were, of course, very happy and proud of their healthy baby boy.

In Dresden, in the spring of 1222, Udo and Konne were once again expecting a new addition to their family. It had rained the whole April, sludge covered the roads and it got stuck to the boots giving more sorrow to the family mothers, who had to be cleaning up all the time. Two-year-old Meinbald could already speak, but the parents were starting to run out of space. While a child's perception of the world was secure, the parents were plagued by worries and sorrows in their everyday lives.

"Konne, we won't be able to fit in this little house when the next child is born. I just heard, while in Hamburg, that quite a few people are planning to go east to the lands of the Slavs, now that the Church and the Emperor are working together again to expand the empire. Shouldn't we also go east?" Udo suggested.

"Well, you're right, Udo; the space will be even tighter when this new little one arrives," Konne replied. "Dresden has grown while we've been here, but we don't have enough wealth or income to rent a larger place or buy building materials for a bigger house."

"Yes, you know, somehow I feel that this border region isn't developing or calming down quickly enough, even though the Margrave has protected the area for a couple of decades."

Konne, holding Meinbald in her arms, listened to her husband and asked, "Well, why don't we move? But where would we settle?"

"I've heard many times from Bohemian merchants that the market there is huge, and there's a growing need for absolutely everything that can be transported by ship. Where there are people, there's always a need for clothes, fabrics, and consumables. So, let's go to Prague, the growing center of Bohemia!" Udo exclaimed, his enthusiasm growing.

Excitement and faith in a better future begain to take hold of their moods. Since they had agreed so easily, it didn't take long for the family to make plans to move from Dresden to Prague. Udo wrote to the Prague Council and received permission to practice his trade, along with his wife, under the protection of the Prague town fortress.

The move took place conveniently by traveling along the Elbe on a riverboat, which accommodated all the worldly possessions of the small family. A river barge transported the family to the newly built river port near the Prague marketplace in just three days.

The new landscapes and the unfamiliar people of Bohemia caused some unease in Konne, but Udo was a bit more relaxed about the unknown. They settled in the German district along the Vltava River, just west of the center of Prague. With only about 2,000–3,000 inhabitants, Prague was still a small town, but nevertheless, it was one of the centers of the Holy Roman Empire. Ottokar I, who had sworn loyalty to the Emperor, reigned as the King of Bohemia.

Last day of August, AD 1222

Meinbald's little sister was born in Prague on a hot August afternoon. The midwife, who had come from a monastery in Prague, had asked a couple of German ladies from the neighborhood to assist her before beginning her sweaty work.

While Udo primarily acted as Meinbald's nurse, the women helped bring the child into the world. Udo focused entirely on his son, calming himself in the process. Still, he couldn't help but feel anxious at times, as it was common for either the child, the mother, or – at worst - both to be lost in childbirth. Thankfully, Konne received excellent care, and both she and the new baby survived the delivery unharmed.

As the evening faded, the family was filled with gratitude for their circumstances and their healthy baby girl. Four weeks later, the girl was baptized at Prague Cathedral and given the name Kunigunde.

The siblings grew up together under the tender care of their mother and father. Bohemia had a growing and strong German community, as migration from the west had brought many families to Prague. As a result, the children had close friends their age, and playing with the children of other German families was really joyful in the backyards and nearby woods. Meinbald and his neighbor Fridrik played together almost every day.

Whether they were pretending to be merchants, riding horses, or waging play wars against the older boys, they always sticked together. Kunigunde was often included in their games, even before she was old enough to play.

Usually, her role was to be the maiden who had to be rescued or protected, while Fridrik and Meinbald played the valiant heroes. There were plenty of heroes to admire, emperors, kings, saints, and great knights, about whom the children heared bedtime stories from their parents.

AD 1227-1228

In 1227, Gregory IX was elected as the new Pope, continuing the tradition of asserting papal supremacy, as his predecessor

Honorius III and his uncle Innocent III had done. Like his predecessor, Gregory challenged the authority of Emperor Frederick II, ruler of Sicily and Germany. The Sixth Crusade, in 1228, was the first crusade not organized by direct papal order. Frederick II lead the expedition toward Syria, but due to a plague epidemic, his fleet had to return to Italy at the outset of the journey. This gave the Pope a reason to excommunicate Frederick from the church. Nevertheless, Frederick set out again for Syria and arrived in Acre in September 1228.

Acre, the nominal capital of the Kingdom of Jerusalem, was divided in opinion regarding Frederick. His army and much of the nobility supported him, but the patriarch, the Templars, and many ordinary citizens did not. This division reflected the broader European split between supporters of the Pope and those of the Holy Roman Empire.

Despite opposition, Frederick united the city and entered Jerusalem as king. Through diplomatic means, he achieved significant successes, reclaiming Jerusalem, Nazareth, and Bethlehem. However, the Pope, having lost control of these territories, refused to acknowledge Frederick's methods, insisting that Muslims should be fought, not negotiated with.

For ordinary people, the power struggle between secular and ecclesiastical authority forced them to choose sides. Princes and their vassals leaned toward the Emperor, while bishops aligned with the Pope. At lower levels of society, priests, peasants, and merchants often sided with their Local Feudal Lord.

In 1228, King Ottokar I's eldest son, Wenceslaus, took the throne of Bohemia, ruling alongside his father. During these years of tension and division, Udo went daily to the Prague fortress to sell imported German goods. He quickly learned that, unlike in Dresden, here in Prague, it was essential to appear loyal to the Pope. The Bohemians were more likely to buy his goods if they believed he shared their disdain for the Emperor.

"Mein Gott, what kind of emperor do we have?" Udo exclaimed, sometimes intentionally, to attract the attention of potential customers.

Once a year, Udo traveled along the Vltava and Elbe Rivers, stopping in Dresden and occasionally venturing further to Magdeburg or even Berlin. In each port, he seeked out goods that he believed would sell well in Prague and negotiated trade deals with suppliers. These trips took about two weeks, and Udo always returned home in good spirits, proud of the successful deals he had made. The river merchants brought back more cargo to the Bohemian market, keeping business thriving.

Meanwhile, Konne cared for Meinbald and Kunigunde at home, managing the household and the family's finances. Occasionally, local Bohemian children insulted Meinbald and Kunigunde, calling them "low German scum" and telling them to return to where they came from. Konne calmly reassured her children, explaining that such people are just ignorant and that their opinions should not be taken seriously.

By the age of seven, he could already read and write. Konne taught both him and little Kunigunde not only writing but also arithmetic. The children proved to be quick learners, and their parents, of course, considered them talented in both languages and mathematics.

At the age of nine, he begun helping his father with the family's business, and within a few years, he took over the record-keeping for their goods and finances. He also became a skilled negotiator, often bargaining hard with the riverboat merchants. Sometimes, Udo had to step in with a laugh when he saw that his son had driven too tough a bargain, leaving the middleman merchant with no margin left.

Kunigunde, though gentler, was just as sharp when it came to negotiating with suppliers of fabric and yarn.

Udo taught his son: "Son, don't be too harsh or cruel. Let the other side feel they've won something too. If you feel someone has wronged you by asking too much or lying, it's fine to stand your ground. But remember, they have families to support as well. And son, always help someone in need if you have the means.

Even if you don't like their ways, it's important to show kindness and help when you can."

He listened and learned compassion, fairness, justice, and tolerance from his father, striving to live by these values.

March, AD 1230

Old King Ottokar I passed away and Wenceslaus was crowned king. Together with their parents, Meinbald and Kunigunde visited Prague Castle to sell goods in a shop located on the edge of the central square. Naturally, it's an exciting experience for them, and they had plenty of customers to serve. While there, the children witnessed King Wenceslaus I himself, riding across the square with his guards. Just the year before, in 1231, Wenceslaus had granted the city's merchants new privileges.

After the royal entourage passed, a group of noblewomen and their escorts arrived at the square, walking proudly through the stalls and shops. Soon, they came to Udo and Konne's store. Kunigunde and Meinbald greeted the women with humble nods and bows.

"Welcome to our store, honorable ladies," Kunigunde said confidently. "How may I be of service to you?"

"May I see what fabrics you sell?" a young woman asked, dressed simply but elegantly, standing out from the others. Meinbald quickly realized that she was the most important of the group, as the other women fell silent when she spoke and that they made room for her.

"Of course," Kunigunde replied. "Please, come inside. We offer silk from the East, as well as wool and linen fabrics from northern Germany and Scotland."

"You are sweet children," the woman said warmly. "I'm Agnes. What's your name?" she asked, looking at Kunigunde.

"Kunigunde," the girl replied, now a bit shy.

"Lovely name!" Agnes smiled and then turned to Meinbald. "And you, young man, what's your name?"

"I am Meinbald, Your Highness. Our parents, Udo and Konne, own this shop, and they warmly welcome you inside to view our humble but high-quality fabrics."

Once inside, Konne greeted the guests warmly and started showing the fabrics to the women. Konne was visibly surprised when Agnes expressed interest in purchasing their entire stock of linen. She explained that it is intended for a new monastery under construction, where the sick and needy will be cared for.

"Would it be possible for my servants to collect the fabrics this afternoon?" Agnes asked. "Let's settle the deal now. At what price, dear lady, would you sell your stock?"

A deal was made, and when they returned home, the children excitedly told Udo about what had happened in his absence while he was overseeing goods at the Vltava merchant ship docks.

"Did you say the woman introduced herself as Agnes?" Udo asked, astonished. "That's the king's sister!"

"It can't be true!" the family exclaimed in unison.

Udo went on to explain what Konne had already heard: Agnes, the king's sister, refused to marry Emperor Frederick II and instead devoted her life to Christ. She was currently building a monastery on the eastern bank of the Vltava River.

"Oh, what a joyous day!" Udo said, beaming with pride. "Udo and Konne from Dresden delivering linen to the royal Abbess of Bohemia!"

The joy in the family is immeasurable. In the months that follow, their warehouses emptied as business continued to boom, driving their success even further. Udo's journeys became more frequent, and the family's standard of living rised. There was no shortage of food or resources in their home, and their confidence grew along with their prosperity.

"We will become prosperous burghers of Prague!" Udo declared, a sentiment shared by Konne and the children.

Life in Prague moved forward in these work-filled atmospheres slowly and steadily until the 4th of January arrived. Udo woke Konne in distress in the middle of the night.

"Wake up, Konne! Fire! We have to save the children in the courtyard; we can't get to the front door because the whole house is on fire and smoke is everywhere!"

In the children's room, Meinbald was already awake; he had heard a rustling outside and was now also waking up Kunigunde.

"Kuni, let's go out through the window; let's go wherever we can, but now let's go!"

Konne and Udo could not get to the children's room without going through the hut. Udo shouted to Konne: "You open the window and leave through it. I'll go into the children's room!"

"No, Udo, I'll come with you. I won't leave my children!"

Udo threw the door open, and they plunged into the scorching heat as flames licked the roof and walls of the hut. They couldn't know that the children had already left thru the window. When Udo got to the door of the adjacent Children's Room, it wouldn't open because the broken ceiling rafter had fallen and pushed the door from the inside. Konne saw how a burning fireball fell from the roof of the hut onto Udo.

"Udo!! Konne tried to scream, but the smoke muffled the voice into a mere squeak."

Outside, Meinbald and Kunigunde were distressed and at a loss; what to do, where are their beloved parents? He ran around to the side of the home to see the whole house in flames, as well as Fridrik's apartment next door.

And when he looked around, he realized that the entire German quarters were in open flames. He was also worried about Kuni, whom he left alone in the courtyard, so he returned and luckily found his sister dangerously close to the burning household.

"Kuni! Get out of there quickly! Come here, away from the flames!"

Kunigunde woke up as if from hibernation, got up from the ground and ran to him. Leaning on each other, the siblings got out of the burning yard to safety. Then their strength ran out, and they threw themselves on the ground to lie down.

The bishop of Prague himself arrived with his men, but the fire was already so far that extinguishing it was an impossible task. The men concentrated their energy to save those still alive from the reach of the fire. There were a few survivors here and there, and they were all quickly carried into the horse-drawn carriage of the bishop's rescue carriages. Meinbald and Kunigunde were also found unconscious but alive. The carriages rushed the children to the monastery hospital.

At the monastery, Abbediss Agnes herself took the children under her special protection, because she recognized and remembered them well.

"Dear children, our Lord has taken your parents to him. The fact that you appear before me saved is a sign from our Lord that I have to answer for you in the future." Agnes told the children about her background and that of her family.

"All of us Ottokar's children, including my brother Vencelaus, are descended from the legendary Přemysl, the founder of Prague. In the beginning, several centuries ago, he was just a poor ploughman, a peasant whom Queen Libuše had caught her eye.

Libuše was the youngest daughter of the then-Czech ruler, Kroki. She was the wisest of the three sisters, and although her sister Kazi was a healer and Teta a knower, she had the gift of seeing the future. Krok chose Libuše as his successor to rule, or as it was said at the time, to judge people. Libuše came out on a rock high above the Vltava and prophesied: *"I see before me a great city whose glory touches the stars."* He ordered a castle and a city called Prague to be built there.

Although he proved to be a wise chief, the male part of the tribe was unhappy that their ruler was a woman and demanded that he marry her, but she was in love with the ploughman, Přemysl. Therefore, he related a vision in which he saw a farmer with a broken sandal eating from an iron table. He instructed his advisers to search for this man by letting the horse loose at the crossing; they followed it to the village of Stadice and found Přemysl exactly as he had said, eating, using an iron plow as a makeshift table.

After finding Přemysl, the men brought him to the princely palace, where Libuše married him. The Přemysl plowman thus became a ruler. He was also said to have removed the peasant's sandals before donning his royal robe when he was found and told the councilors to bring the shoes with them and keep them as a reminder to the people that the peasant had risen to the highest rank. He also wanted to remind his followers to be humble, remember their origins and stand up for the peasants.

This is why every new king of Bohemia, after receiving the crown, shows the people sandals."

The children listened intently to this wonderful story of Agnes; it somehow made them calm down and accept what happened as a fact: They were now orphans, and their parents were no longer there. But they didn't have to worry because this royal sister in black said she'll take care of them.

Of course, Agnes didn't tell her children everything, just like no parent who wants to save their children from unnecessary shocks. If she had told how her father Otakar I had already arranged her marriage when she was only eight years old, it would have been completely irresponsible of her. However, this was what really had been done to her.

According to the custom of the time, she had been promised to the son of Emperor Frederick II, the ten-year-old Henry, who had just been crowned king of Germany. For the duration of the engagement, Agnes was sent to grow up in Babenberg at Duke Leopold's court. However, Leopold wanted to marry his own daughter to Henrik, so Agnes and Henrik's engagement was broken off after six years of engagement. Agnes had become a valuable political pawn. Because of what happened, her father went to war against the Babenbergs and planned to marry Agnes to Henry III of England. At this point, Emperor Frederick II used his right of veto and wanted to marry Agnes himself. However, Agnes herself had had enough of being a pawn; arranged marriages were over as far as she was concerned. She decided to dedicate her life to prayers and spiritual work and sought the support of Pope Grekorius IX for this. So she rejected Fredrik, who is known to have said in disappointment:

"If she had left me for a mortal man, I would have demanded revenge with my sword, but now I cannot attack my rival suitor, my winner, because instead of me, she chose herself the king of the kingdom of heaven."

Prague, AD 1233 - 1235

The years to come would show the children that Agnes did indeed care for them - she fed, clothed and cared for them as if they were her own. Agnes also loved to tell the children stories in the evenings. They were usually not fairy tales but wonderful true stories that she had come across in her life and that she wanted to share as lessons for people. One evening, she told the following story:

A rich and noble knight lived in the town of Assisi in Umbria. He had a pious and good consort named Torculana. One day Torculana was praying in the church, and as she knelt before the crucified image, a voice spoke to from on high: Torculana. You will give birth to a wonderful light that will shine over the whole world.

Torculana became happy and went home. And after a little while, a daughter was born, and they named her Clara. And this child was good and pious, and did not need beautiful clothes or jewelry like others of his age. When she was growing up as a girl, she heard of Francis of Assisi, who was a holy and pious man. Clara wanted to see this holy man, and when Francis of Assisi heard about Clara, he went to her and began to teach and talk to her about God. One day, Francis of Assisi said to Clara:

"Now it is Palm Sunday; dress in your best and go to church, and in the evening, you will have to leave your father's house forever."

Clara did so, fled her home in the evening and went to the convent of Portiuncula. There, her long hair was cut and she changed her precious gown into a penitent's skirt. When her father and friends found out where she was, they went looking for her. And they found her in the church, where Francis of Assisi had hidden her, and they called her, and besought her to return home. But she answered to them: "No one can wean me from the service of my God."

Then Clara founded her own nunnery and was blessed by the Pope. Countesses and duchesses came to her convent when they heard about her pious life. Clara was humble and helpful to everyone, and even though she was the abbess, she washed the sisters' feet and ministered to them.

One night during the fast, she wanted to feed the sisters who had been fasting for many days. And she told the cooking sister to bring them food, but she had nothing to give. Then St. Clara covered the table with her own hands and knelt down by it, praying that God would send someone to bring them bread and two fish. And at the same time a woman entered the gate of the monastery, whose face shone like the sun, carrying a basket on her head. She gave the basket to the gatekeeper and said: "Give this to St. Clara."

"Who sent this?"

"She does know who the sender is", the woman replied.

After saying that, the woman disappeared. The sister took the basket to Clara and told her what the woman had said. Clara opened the basket, and saw that there were the two fish and the bread. They all praised God for his mercy and ate until they were satisfied.

"Children, I have met this Saint Clara. I am constantly in contact with her by letter; she has given me a model that I want to follow with her own example. This monastery, of which I am the abbess, is my way of following the path indicated by St. Clara. Maybe one day I, like Clara, will come across a real miracle. I believe in it, kids. Please, dear children, you should believe, too, that when you do enough good around you, when you humble yourself, when you act selflessly towards other people when you help the poor and the sick, then you can witness the miracle of our Lord that comes to you, just like it happened to my friend Clara."

Just like St. Clara, Agnes also devoted herself completely to monastic life, caring for the sick and disadvantaged, and she also often wrote letters to the Pope.

Agnes wanted to do something to control and calm the unrest of the time - she suggested to the Pope that a new order be founded in connection with the Bohemian hospital, whose mission would be to civilize and calm the restless people. She had seen that you can only get so far with just good deeds, but in order to get all the way, you also had to be ready to use strength to defeat the evil forces that were against you.

One morning, Agnes called Meinbald and Kunigunde to her in the hospital. "My dear children", Agnes started gently. "You are both very dear to me, almost as if I were your mother, although I can't say that, don't get me wrong. Now, however, the time has come for me to introduce you to what I consider to be the right doctrine. Kunigunde, my sweet girl, I want you to become one of our sisters here in the monastery. You will give your life to our Holy Lord Jesus Christ as his follower and work with your fellow sisters as a nurse for the weak in this hospital. You spend a beautiful, peaceful, monastic life with the nuns.

As Abbess, I will continue to be like your mother, but I have other children here, your sisters. Meinbald, my brave boy, I want to offer you the best school that all Bohemia, indeed the whole Christian world, has to offer its men. That is why I want you to join the new order that the Pope has just at my request allowed us to establish here in connection with the hospital."

"Really? What does that mean?" he asked, anticipating that in the future, they would see each other less often, but Agnes' words showed that this was a once-in-a-lifetime opportunity for him.

"You start the education of a cavalry soldier or knight as an apprentice. You will be taught by older monk brothers who have dedicated themselves to the rules of Saint Augustine of the brotherhood, and they have also been to the Holy Land on a crusade. The monks of this order treat not only physical injuries but also the mental ailments of the sick and wounded."

"We understand your will, holy mother", started Kunigunde, "but will my brother and I see you and each other in the future?"

"Of course, you'll see, don't worry, and I'm not going to disappear from your life either. And, of course, you can meet each other, even every day, because such brave siblings cannot be separated from each other even in the name of our Lord."

The children were brought to meet their new guardians. Kunigunde was taken to a convent by a young nun named Gertrud, and Meinbald was taken care of by the German knight Hartvig.

He learned to use a sword already at the age of 13 and he saw and heared a lot about the distress and suffering of people. A lot for a boy at his age. With him, there were five other boys of German background as apprentices of the older knights: Fridrik, his childhood friend, who had also lost his parents in the German quarter fire; Konrad "Kort" Bitscher, whose family came from the Alps; moved to Prague. He got the additional name "Buck" partly because of his Alpine origin. The name also seemed appropriate in that he pushed through every situation and never wavered in his faith.

The next apprentice was named Klas, "Fläming" – Flemish. He was very serious and withdrawn by nature, but in his military skills, he showed great hardness. Then followed Otto, who turned out to be the most skilled swordsman of the group very early in their training - he got the nickname "Swerdh," sword. Next in line was Lydeke, who liked to read and he read a lot. He was skilled in literary skills, so the gang christened him "Teen." At the tail end came Gödecke, originating from Vienna, Austria. He was always a good-natured, singing kid, thus earning the nickname " Fincke" - "Finch."

The boys were trained to work as one unit, as they were united by the same language, which was also used by the learned men of the Teutonic Knights who had arrived in Prague. Knight Hartvig had been specifically sent by the Teutonic Knights to train boys into men and knights. Grandmaster Albert nurtured his own connections with other brotherhoods; he, too, was a fluent, learned monk and soldier. He had crusade experience, as he participated in Emperor Frederick's Sixth Crusade together with a few knight brothers who returned from Egypt to Prague. Their families were from here.

Life in the monastery was very disciplined; everything follows the rules of St. Augustine, and the apprentices were taught manners using very austere teaching procedures. There were a few knights working as trainers from the Order of St. John because their hospital actually served as a model for the entire brotherhood.

The brothers of St. John's and the Teutonic Knights told the students stories, e.g., from the Crusades to the Holy Land. Hartvig told the legends that were most interesting to Germans; for example, he told about Friedrich Barbarossa, who had died during the crusade by drowning in a river, became a saint and shut himself up in a mountain.

"Young brothers! It is said that Friedrich is not dead but is asleep with his knights inside Mount Kyffhäuser in Thuringia, and when the ravens stop flying around the mountain, Friedrich wakes up and restores Germany to its ancient greatness. His red beard has grown through the table he sits at. His eyes are half closed in sleep, but now and then, he sends the boy out to see if the ravens have stopped flying."

Meinbald listened to stories with others, he was really interested in them. After hearing Barbarossa's story, he couldn't keep quiet but opened his verbal coffin.

"Brothers, I have heard a very similar story from Mother Agnes. She once told us a story about St. Wenceslaus, who was a Bohemian prince 300 years ago. His father, Vratislav, had been brought up as a Christian, even though his mother, Drahomíra, was the daughter of a pagan chieftain.

Wenceslaus's father died when he was a child, and he was raised by his Christian grandmother, Saint Ludmila. The mother is said to have strangled Saint Ludmila in her anger. Wenceslaus became prince at the age of 18, banished his mother, and began to spread Christianity in Bohemia.

Brother of Wenceslaus murdered him on the way to church;

his body was dismembered and buried at the scene of the murder. Three years later, brother Boleslav repented of his act and moved the relics to St. Vitus Cathedral.

According to the story, Wenceslaus also sleeps in the mountain; he sleeps in Blanik mountain inside with his knights and is ready to defend the country when enemies threaten it."

Everyone, including Hartvig, listened to Meinbald's story in complete silence, almost in a trance.

"Meinbald, thank you for telling us this story; it does make me wonder in my mind, could it be a coincidence that both great princes are locked up in the mountain and did not ascend to heaven when they died, like all other mortals? This is remarkable, very remarkable", said Hartvig. "But now, young brothers, it's time to go to dinner together!"

Meinbald and Kunigunde met each other every week. This was thanks to Agnes, Agnes herself was often in the monastery talking to her young protégés and asking about their week with interest. Quite often, Agnes also wanted to tell them a story; she had enough of them for every trip.

One Friday, when they got together again, Agnes told how she had kept in touch with her half-sister, Queen Dagmar of Denmark, by letter but lost contact when she had died in childbirth at the young age of only 25.

Agnes told how she had read in Dagmar's last letter that the three-year-old Valdemar the Younger was being raised to be the next king of Denmark. When she heard the news a few years later that her father Valdemar had married Berengaria of Portugal as his next queen, Agnes had a vision that Valdemar would die young. So it happened that Valdemar died in 1231.

This new Bohemian Order founded by Agnes received official status from the Pope, it took its name from the coat of arms of its first Grand Master Albert's family, the Brothers of the Red Star and Cross. Albert came from a noble family that had served the Premyslid rulers for centuries. King Wenceslaus I, Agnes' brother, hosted and graced the celebration with his presence. Wenceslaus gave the opening speech of the celebration.

"Dear invited guests, Knights of the Red Star and Cross and students. I have been following your training and life in the monastery with great interest since my dear sister invited you here to us in Prague. I have been able to state that your skills and knowledge, both in spirit and in physical endeavors, are first-class and unparalleled. I am filled with great respect and pride to be able to work with you in times to come, both in war and in peace. Please, our table is set, today we will enjoy a festive meal in your honor. Let no one leave here today without first filling their bellies!"

"My king, thank you for your hospitality and your beautiful words. We are the only order in Bohemia and in the whole world founded by a woman, our beloved King, the sister of Yours, abbess Agnes. So let's drink the first toast in honor of our Lord Jesus Christ, the second in honor of abbess Agnes, and today, exceptionally, only the third in honor of your majesty", Albert responded with a twinkle in his eye in his reply speech in the king's castle.

After the celebratory dinner, Bishop Bernhard delivered a celebratory mass in the St. Vitus Cathedral next to the Castle, to the mass dedicated to the Holy Virgin Mary, all the citizens of Prague were invited. The knights in their best suits of armor stood in front, the apprentices behind them. The Mass started with a hymn associated with the name of St. Adalbert, the second martyred bishop of Prague:

Hospodine pomiluj ny

Hospodine, pomiluj ny,

Jezu Kriste, pomiluj ny,

ty Spase všeho míra,

spasiž ny, i uslyšiž,

Hospodine, hlasy nášě;

daj nám všém, Hospodine,

žizň a mír v zemi;

žizň a mír v zemi.

Krleš, Krleš, Krleš!

O Domine, miserere

O Domine, miserere,

Iesu Christe, miserere,

Salus es totius mundi,

salva nos et percipe,

o Domine, voces nostras;

da cunctis, o Domine,

panem, pacem terrae;

panem, pacem terrae.

Kyrie eleison!

Agnes was shown deep favor and respect when she rose to address the brothers of the new order.

"Brothers of the Red Star and Cross! You have a great task ahead of you. You must protect the weak and the sick and fight against the heretical and aggressive forces that threaten us Christians. You are our heavenly father's sword and shield here on earth. All around you, you will encounter hatred, terror, heathen customs, war, hunger, pain and disease - and yet, in the name of our holy Father, I know you will not bow before these enemies of ours. You will ensure that the kingdom of heaven wins here on earth. You take care of the injured like your brothers in the Order of St John, but you also fight like them, like the Knights Templar, and you always find the right path that leads us all to our Father's home in the end. Remember in the moment of danger, sometimes even when despair arises in your mind, remember then that your sisters in the monastery will pray for you and take care of you all, and if you receive an invitation to your Father, they will anoint you for your last journey. So be men of peace and pacify this restless country and all the countries around it in the name of our Lord Christ."

Agnes' speech had a deep effect on Meinbald and the other men. They now clearly knew their tasks and were ready, come what may. When leaving the mass, no one spoke a word, but a devout silence prevailed among the brothers. Not even Finch was singing or whistling, he was also silent for once.

In the following years, the order carried out, among other things, the extermination and deportation of those who had fallen under the church curse in the Bohemian region.

Witchcraft and pagan customs were determined to be eradicated once and for all from the entire territory of the empire.

For the young brothers, this meant short, refreshing detention trips in between constant combat training, hospital shifts and moments of devotion. Imprisoned heretics were interrogated, even tortured, in order to make them confess and abandon their pagan ways. If someone who had already received a church curse was caught a second time for heresy, according to the rules of the church, the unequivocal consequence was a death sentence.

Quite often, the interrogations ended with a verdict of acquittal handed down by the inquisitor council. Many who had already received a church curse for heresy, who did not want to end up with this harsh fate, decided to flee Bohemia, mostly towards the north.

Chapter II
Bohemia repels the Mongols

In Bohemia, AD 1240 - 1241

Eastern Europe was shadowed by a great threat, which had made people look for shelters and prepare themselves for the coming distress and suffering. The Mongols had destroyed Kievan Rus in 1240 and continued their attack to the west. In 1241 they headed to Hungary. The Mongol Empire had an effective network of spies and was likely aware of the disunity in Europe caused by the constant feuding between Emperor Frederick II and the Pope. However, Bela IV of Hungary, Venceslaus I of Bohemia, Henry II the Pious of Silesia and three other princes who came to power in Poland after its disintegration, as well as a number of lesser influential people, knew how to expect an attack. They had formed an alliance against the Mongols, following the Tatars' avalanche and destruction from city to city.

King Wenceslaus called also the knights to arms in 1241. He had received confirmation that the Saxons were sending a strong army from Dresden to Legnica. Wenceslaus rode with his troops to Legnica as well. Duke Henry, the husband of Agnes and Wenceslaus's sister, Anna, had retreated there with his army after the Mongols had destroyed Wroclaw, one of the last Polish cities. Meinbald quickly managed to visit the hospital to say goodbye to his sister and Agnes. Kunigunde seemed a little nervous, but Agnes was her calm self as they wished him good luck on his journey.

When the Mongols had arrived in Legnica on 9 April 1241, Wenceslaus was only a day's journey away with his troops. The number of forces of Henry II of Silesia would have increased to about five thousand if they had waited in the fortress for another day. However, Henrik was unaware of this and decided to engage in battle before reinforcements arrived. Henry had apparently divided his army into four divisions, the first of which consisted of Bavarian gold diggers and other peasants, the second of Greater Poland troops, the third of Opole and the troops of the Teutonic Knights, and the fourth Henry's own Silesian troops and mercenaries.

The Mongols apparently launched a surprise attack, luring their opponents into an ambush. A favored tactic for the Mongols was to feign flight, which the next enemy would be surrounded by. Henry sent his cavalry after the Mongols, apparently thinking that he was facing a relatively small army. In this case, however, the Mongol flanks appeared, which isolated the cavalry from the rest of Henry's troops.

According to battle descriptions, the Mongols also used smoke to confuse their enemies, which miraculously spread over the entire battlefield. Most of Henry's army was killed. The few who were spared now confusedly told the course of events.

Saxon and Thuringian troops also arrived at the Legnica battlefield to witness this terrible sight. To count the dead, the Mongols had cut off the ears of each corpse. Later, it was said that after the Battle of Legnica, they had taken nine sacks of loose ears with them. There were corpses all over the battlefield in large piles.

Henrik had also fallen; his head had been raised on a pole, and the headless body had to be retrieved from the field long after Wenceslaus' troops had already moved on. It was only when Anna gave the information that her husband had six toes on his left foot as a sign that Henrik's body was found and identified.

Meinbald closely observed how Wenceslaus I acted when he immediately took charge of the situation in Lenica. He gathered the commanders of the Saxons and Thuringians and Grandmaster Albert for a consultation. The gentlemen didn't have a long meeting when Albert already arrived at the row of knight brothers to address his men.

"Brothers, Brothers! We will immediately ride with the Thuringians to Klodzko. We were tasked by our king, Wenceslaus, to protect the city and its inhabitants from such a similar terrible destruction. The Saxons, together with brother Merbot's strike group, set off in pursuit towards Wroclaw, following the enemy's movements. Wenceslaus himself goes inland with his life guards to organize the defense. We keep daily communication with the Saxons and our king's troops. No time, brothers, let's act! Let's immediately group into marching sections, destination Klodzko. I act as marshal, and my deputy marshal is brother Hartvig."

After riding for a day, they reached a road leading to the mountains, and since both men and horses needed rest and food, they set up a tented camp before dark. The journey continued in the morning and before midday, they had already arrived in Klodzko. The city opened its iron gate to them, and the townspeople gladly welcomed the knights to defend them.

By then, the Mongol forces had split into two, one led by Tsingis' grandsons Batu and Subutai, who had planned an invasion of Hungary. The second army was led by Baidar and Kadan and they had destroyed everything in their path through Silesia and Moravia. Approaching Bohemia, these forces encountered mountains, and their vanguard saw that the defenses of the Kingdom of Bohemia were set up in mountainous terrain, making it impossible for the Mongols to use their cavalry effectively. This deterred them from attacking, and they decided to retreat to and around the town of Othmachau.

From there, however, they sent part of their forces to attack the strategically located town of Klodzko on their way to the mountain passes towards Bohemia.

The approaching Mongols were spotted in the morning, which obviously aroused great concern among the defenders of Klodzko. The squad was not impossibly large, but they had siege engines and catapults with them. In addition, they seemed to know how to use Greek fire as soon as a curtain of ominous smoke rised around them.

It was not long before the first strange fireball already flew over the city wall. It hit the ground with a thud and rolled quickly towards the stone wall of the building. Fortunately, the wall held up and stopped the rolling fireball. More fireballs would come; this time, they hit the wall and exploded on impact.

A small group attacked and broke through the holeshot in the city wall. Merbot and his troops arrived with the Saxons to help, and together they defeated the besiegers to the dispersion of the Mongol army. Many Mongol men fell, and those who survived ran away.

Merbot conveyed the information that only a part of the crowd was here, the larger part had started advancing towards the town of Olmuetz. After receiving the information, Grandmaster Albert was more serious than usual. He decided to speak his mind directly to his troops right away.

"Brothers! We must not stay here in Klodzko to celebrate our easy defense victory. I have just received information that a much larger body of Tatars is marching towards Olmuetz, intending to besiege the fortress and exterminate all the inhabitants. Brethren, some of you already know, but I will now tell you all: my brother Divish, who died a year ago while serving as supreme marshal of the Bohemian troops, has founded that fortress of Sternberg north of Olmuetz, and he swore to protect the inhabitants of the city all his life.

Now, that he has passed away, that duty of protection has become a duty of honor for his entire family, so also for me, who also come from that small village of Divishau. Divish's son Zdeslav is only six years old; he and his mother cannot be responsible for the protection of the city because they now quickly need protection from the best warriors in Bohemia, that being us. Get ready for the march at once; in two days, we will be in Olmuetz unless we catch the Tatars before then!"

The marching divisions set off briskly, with the cavalry under fast, hardy horses that had been allowed to rest within the walls of Klodzko for a couple of days. Slower horse-drawn carriages followed the cavalry, carrying gunners and supply troops.

After a day of riding, the knights led by Albert arrived in the small village of Štíty, which really had nothing but a church, a blacksmith's workshop, an inn, and a couple of local stables. The peasants of the stables had the pleasure and honor of exchanging new horses for the knights so that they could continue at full speed on horseback, leaving their own horses to rest.

As the morning dawned, they broke up their night camp and left. In the evening, near Olmuetz, Albert stopped the troops with his sign. They saw how a huge Mongol army was massing for the siege of Olmuetz. However, they still hadn't had time to start battering the city walls with their catapults. Albert invited the leaders of the equestrian departments to him.

"Dear brothers, let us go under the cover of the darkness of the coming night to find out where the command of the troops keeps its yurt. Let's attack the enemy only in the morning. Have you understood? Meinbald, do the men in the platoon you lead also understand this?"

"Of course, we are young and eager, but we know how to hold our horses and pants dry, waiting for the right moment, brother Albert," he replied.

"Good, because you young people can see better in the dark than us old people, so take a few of your men, with whom you will carefully patrol the front of the camp. You request information about the location of the leaders in the camp, we make an attack plan based on them. Do you have any questions, Meinbald?"

"No, brother Albert, my mission is clear."

He took Kort, Klas, and Otto with him and left Fridrik in charge during the scouting trip. They left in light gear, without ring shirts, without protection, so that they could advance quickly and silently toward the camp.

The Mongols guarded the road routes, so they used trees, bushes, and ditches as their cover as they advanced. Bonfires had been lit in the camp, the flames of which illuminated and fluttered here and there. Klas knew how to advance very purposefully and cunningly past the guards; he lead the patrol, Meinbald advanced second, Otto behind him, and Kort last.

After advancing a good distance, they found guarded yurts where the commanders camped.

"This is a clear command post," Meinbald whispered to Klas and Kort.

The men discreetly returned to their own camp and reported to Albert. The plan was to attack the command tents directly with cavalry at dawn. At the same time, Austrian auxiliaries requested by Wenceslaus would attack the sites of the besieging forces.

Meinbald got to lead the group because he knew the route. All the knights were now dressed in full armor up to the helmets with the help of the armor bearers. They rode quietly well all the way to within sight of the lead yurts until they were spotted.

At that point, Albert commanded the entire knight division to charge, and they attacked with their lances straight towards the tents. The Mongols were really confused to see that they were being attacked.

From inside the yurts, the bodyguards came out, ready to sacrifice their lives to receive the incoming onslaught. That's what most of them only could do. The brothers of the Red Star and Cross stroke like lightning from a clear sky into the Mongol horde. Every collision knocked a man to the ground permanently. They took another charge and stroke again.

A great disunity arised among the Mongols. Meinbald saw through his visor from his horse how the two generals, Baidar and Kadan, decided to run away. It was not worth leaving the fight after them because there were still enough Mongols to strike.

Finally, he dismounted and caught the commander of the Mongol left-wing army. This commander found his situation hopeless, and was captured alive and imprisoned. The knighthood was victorious in its surprise attack. The Mongols either left on horseback or ran away after their generals. Albert ordered Hartvig to take a detachment of men to chase them.

"But brother Hartvig, take care that you don't suffer the fate of Henry of Silesia!" Albert shouted. The knights who remained on the battlefield calmed down the situation when every Mongol was either killed or captured.

Merbot and Albert immediately thanked Meinbald for his bravery on the battlefield. They begun to treat the wounded and collect bodies to be buried in mass graves, which some of the infantry dug at the site.

Hartvig and his troops returned unharmed in a couple of days. He reported that they had escorted the Mongols to the border and saw that they had continued their full march towards the south.

Bohemia, led by Wenceslaus, remained one of the few kingdoms in Eastern Europe that were never plundered by the Mongols.

Most of the kingdoms around it, such as Poland and Moravia, were completely destroyed. Bohemia's success was such that several chroniclers of the time sent messages to Emperor Frederick II about the victorious defense of Wenceslaus.

After failed attempts, Baidar and Kadan continued their raids into Moravia via the Moravian Gate into the March River valley towards the Danube before finally turning south to join Batu and Subutai in Hungary.

June 15, AD 1241

Wenceslaus granted a number of privileges to the knighthood led by Albert as thanks for their excellent work in defending Bohemia against the Mongols. In practice, the entire brotherhood got full tax exemption, the grand master got the right to tax, and the cavalry soldiers got the right to act as battle commanders in the name of the king, similar to the military commanders of the upper noble class.

Bishop Mikuláš and Grand Master Albert received these privileges. The bishop got a tenth of the tax revenue, the church got five-tenths, and the brotherhood itself got four-tenths.

The noble lords of Bohemia were not too pleased with this Wenceslaus tribute to the knights of the spirit, as they felt that it belittled their achievements on the battlefield. Wenceslaus' son Otakar was the future king, and the noble princes began to poison his mind and turn him against his father, seeking to advance their own interests through him.

This did not go unnoticed by Meinbald and the brothers, and they also warned Grand Master Albert, who knew diplomacy and thus was able to keep King Wenceslaus up to date. Bishop Mikuláš from Reisenburg was also a skilled diplomat and knew how to side with the reigning king without closing the doors to the king's son, who would one day become the next king.

In the spring of 1242, Albert ordered Merbot to travel to burned Wroclaw to establish and lead the new Silesian Commandery of the Red Star and Cross. The following years included a lot of recovery and medical care but also a lot of research and learning about the new ways and techniques of warfare brought by the Mongols, such as gunpowder and explosives.

The Mongols had shown how easy to conquer undefended cities and trade routes could be. Thus, defense capabilities began to be purposefully built, and the importance of the armed branch in the knighthood was only emphasized. Movable sections began to be planned for trade routes to protect traders. Merchants also began to form unions. In the north, the great Hanseatic League arose, which seized control of the most important trade routes. The rebuilt Wroclaw also joined the Hanseatic League in due time.

Brother Konrad, who had been working with Albert since the trip to the Holy Land, was building his own policy in the direction of Bishop Mikuláš and, through him, the Pope. He clearly strived for the bishop's favor, riding on the common achievements of the entire brotherhood, and at every turn, he tried to take credit from achievements of others. He clearly did not understand his vanity or how the other monk brothers saw through him. Meinbald also thought that Konrad, who was called "Cockroach" among the brothers, turned out to be quite an unpleasant guy.

"Why does Albert put up with this?" Asked brother Konrad, "the Bock", when the two of them were doing their shift at the monastery's armory.

"To be honest, I've wondered that myself, but you can't know what they've experienced together on the Holy Land Crusade. I don't think Albert can possibly be so blind that he wouldn't understand what a Slytherin that Cockroach is."

"Where was he when our Department fought against the Mongols in Klodzko? He was nowhere to be seen on the battlefield, but when the victory came, he appeared out of nowhere to rant about how he was behind the whole victory. Albert, on the other hand, was himself among the rest of us, fighting against the Tatars."

"Meinbald, sometimes I wish you would just call me Kort or even Bock so that no one accidentally confuses me with that cockroach."

"That's fine, Bock, just leave this to me," he said and smiled approvingly.

First day of April, AD 1245

In April, the time to departure to the world had come. Meinbald was tasked with protecting the Elbe trade route. Before leaving, Kunigunde and Meinbald wanted to say goodbye to each other.

"My brother, please write me about your journey," Kuni asked with tears in her eyes.

"Nothing out of the ordinary happens in the monastery, but it would be nice to hear what the world brings to you."

"My sister, you are my only family member. Of course, I am writing to you. Our connection will not be broken, I promise."

His platoon left Prague on riverboats along the Vltava, heading for the Elbe. The ships pulled behind them rafts loaded with full loads of horses and trade goods. Along the Elbe, the journey continued to Dresden, where they stopped by the port to refresh themselves.

Meinbald thought quietly to himself about his parents, with whom he left here for Prague as a small child. The thoughts felt too painful, the corners of the eyes got wet, so it was best not to say anything out loud. *"It feels like it's been forever, and I don't really remember anything from the whole time"*

Dresden was a lively place; the trade route had increased the population, and it was nice to watch the happy interactions between people while they spend their breaks in the harbor. The men paid attention to the fact that their leader was less talkative than usual and they gave him space to immerse himself in his thoughts. When they finally set off to continue their journey, there was still more than a thousand miles to the port of Cuxhaven, north of the market town of Hamburg. So there was plenty of time for the exchange of ideas.

The Elbe was impressive; on its long journey to the sea, it was winding, and sometimes the wide channel seemed to crawl, while in narrower places, its speed accelerated.

The ferry stopped in almost every town, and merchants exchanged cargo for another until they continued their journey. Meinbald's men saw a lot of dealings, sometimes a bit of mischief and sometimes, of course, some good deeds.

In a port, when the merchant had made sales and purchases, he noticed that he had received boxes of hay instead of barter. In his distress, he immediately told Meinbald about it and showed the boxes he opened.

"Men! The recent merchant was a scoundrel; let's catch him and bring him to account for his fraud!" Meinbald shouted and, setting an example himself, jumped into the first barge to pick up the horses.

Kort and Fridrik were right behind him, following suit. They saddled and harnessed their horses and then set off riding in the direction they saw the rogue trader's cart going. After riding the river, the carts were already visible; you couldn't help but recognize them because the boxes of exchange goods were marked with the barge merchant's stamp. Kort, Fridrik and Meinbald easily caught the thief and stopped him.

After seeing the armed knights in their ring shirts, the merchant guessed that he had been caught in his deception and didn't even try to resist. They tied the man up and turned back to port. At the port, the man was handed over to the port guards, who were allowed to take care of the thief to be sentenced by a local judge.

"Brethren," Meinbald started, "look, there is a man who will receive the judgment he deserves. He will most likely be hanged for his actions. If he had taken only a little money, he would certainly have been able to continue his miserable life single-handedly, but since he condescended to cheat another merchant of a whole cargo while still fleeing the scene, he can have no future but to be hanged. Or maybe the hangman will cut his neck with an axe."

The brothers were very quiet and stared at the man who, staring at the ground, had lost all hope. The trade ferry and rafts left the platform, and their journey continued.

"Thank you, brother Meinbald", the merchant said. "Thank you for getting my cargo back, which I can sell in the next ports. If that large part of my property had gone, my family and I would have been devastated. Then I myself would probably have preferred a quick death sentence rather than watching our lives slowly sink into misery and destruction, hanging loose with a debt pile."

Gödeke decided to break the dark silence of brothers:

"Come on, brothers, the day's good work is done, so let's rejoice and gratefully admire the landscapes flowing before us, the likes of which we haven't even seen before! Otto, you are the wizard of the fraternity at swordsmanship, but can you swing your jaws and tell us again the story of how you got Brother Hartvig to surrender to you during our first combat training?"

Otto didn't have to say anything because everyone remembered it like it was yesterday, and everyone started laughing out loud. A happy chatter started, and a happy feeling of unity took over the mood. Gödecke, who liked to entertain others, even sang a happy song.

In the next port, the merchant got the majority of his cargo sold, this time getting completely reasonable payment commitments and good trade goods in return.

The merchant was so happy that he gave alms to the poor housewives staying at the port, which could be described as princely from a poor person's point of view. And so the journey continued; the ports, merchants, and goods were buzzing while the brothers took care that safety was not disturbed.

From that day onwards, when they reached the port, they always knew how to place guards in visible places and they even always kept two horses saddled on the barge waiting for the task. By doing this, they prevented injustices experienced by merchants and got to spend a much more peaceful trip themselves.

First day of May, AD 1245

Finally arriving in Cuxhaven, many of the knights saw the sea for the first time, the Atlantic, or the North Sea, as it was called. It made many a young man's imagination run wild and his sense of adventure rise. On the other hand, a long river trip had been enough to fulfill the biggest ship travel dreams, and many also understood that traveling at sea was much more rocking than smooth sailing along the river.

Meinbald had the main responsibility for ensuring that the fraternity itself followed its own rules. Gödecke, who came from Austria, was called "Finch" in a brotherly way because he was the bird of joy and the joker of the group. He also liked to sing happy songs that easily got stuck in his head. Due to his cheerful nature, Gödecke also attracted women. Cuxhaven and Hamburg were full of happy women practicing the world's oldest profession. So it happened that one evening in the port guard of Cuxhaven, Gödecke fell and made sin. His watchman, Kort, came in the morning to report to him what had happened. Meinbald knew that he had to punish Gödecke, even if he didn't want to. Namely, he appreciated Gödecke's happy singing and the atmosphere he always brought to their midst.

He dug out the notes he had made during his training. The code of St. Augustine was very familiar to the brotherhood, after all, everyone had gone through it in their training. "However, it was good to see how it went", he thought and read aloud to himself:

"In Chapter IV of the Code, About Protection, Chastity and Fraternal Correction

You can rest your gaze on some women, but you can't fix it on any woman. It is not forbidden to look at women when you are out and about, but it is sinful to lust after them or want them to lust after you. Coveting desires do not arise alone from a mere thought or passionate feeling but are mutually awakened by a fixed gaze.

So if you see a lustful look in your brother's eyes, you must warn him.

So that evil does not take hold of him. If he repeatedly looks at her lustfully, even after warnings, he must be treated like a wounded brother. He needs to be reported to 2 – 3 others so that he is not accused based on just one opinion. If he denies these charges and does not confess his sin, his action must first be brought to the notice of the commander before it is communicated to all others. If he admits and corrects his actions in private, there is no need to bring the matter to the attention of others at all, and he can continue his service normally. On the other hand, if he does not confess, he must be condemned in front of everyone, and he must be expelled from the brotherhood if he does not agree to the punishment that is imposed on him by the priest or commander.

This is also the way to act in other crimes than just fixing one's eyes on a woman: the crime must be detected, repelled or made known, proven, and finally punished - all out of love for man and hatred for sin.

But if anyone goes so far in wrongdoing as to secretly receive letters from any woman or any small gifts, you should show mercy and pray for him if he confesses this of his own free will. But if the crime is discovered and he is found guilty, he must be punished more severely according to the priest's or superior's judgment."

Meinbald addressed Gödecke, who admitted his sins and asked that he would punish him so that he could atone for his sins and continue his service with them. The brothers agreed that Gödecke took extra night shifts for two weeks, allowing the other brothers to sleep soundly. This is how a practical tradesman worked.

First day of May AD 1246

Meinbald had communicated weekly to the grandmaster via carrier pigeon. One morning, a pigeon flew in with a message that they could leave for Cölln-Berlin, first by going along the Elbe, then the Havel River, through Potsdam, turning to the Spree River. Slow and calm travel was therefore ahead, and the familiar safety provisioning of travelers at the same time.

The men would have liked to go along the Elbe to Magdeburg, but they had to turn from the Elbe and march overland to the Havel River, annoyingly close to the city, which had been founded by Charlemagne himself, fortified by Henry the Fowler and which was a famous central place of trade and administration in the empire.

The border county of Brandenburg, a principality formed by Albrekt the Bear 90 years earlier, part of the German Empire, welcomed the Knights of Bohemia to the bustle of people. Compared to not only Magdeburg but also Prague, Berlin was an even smaller growth center on the north bank of the river Spree.

Cölln, which was growing on the southern bank, was founded about seven years earlier than Berlin, but Berlin had nevertheless overtaken these twin cities in terms of growth. Both Berlin and Cölln had been granted independent city rights, so the area had a growing number of merchants and soldiers. The city wall was being built, as well as many buildings inside the walls.

Meinbald led his men along the main street covered with wooden planks. The clatter of horses' hooves echoed off the gables of the houses.

As the men walked slowly forward, they noticed that the ends of all the houses faced the street. Right next to each other, mostly two-story buildings were built, with the lower floor having a stone frame and the upper floor having a wooden frame.

The closer they went to the center, the more often they saw shopkeepers and workmen lifting goods from pallets directly from the street with the hoist crane at the end of the house to the warehouse upstairs.

In addition to these merchant houses, there were also numerous sheds and stables. The peasants were most obviously staying in their countryside surrounding the central wall, as the last farmhouse they had seen had been passed ages ago.

Finally, they began to approach the place where he had purposefully headed – the town hall square. In addition to the town hall, next to the market, there was the guild house of merchants and craftsmen, the church of St. Nicholas and next to it, the house and stables of the Teutonic Knights.

Meinbald arrived as ordered to report to the Order's house for protection. He was received by a bearded man slightly older than him.

"Greetings, Sir Knight. I am Johannes from Blankenfeld, responsible for the fortification of Berlin and Cölln. Who are you, and what are you doing here in Berlin?"

"I am Meinbald, a member of the Brotherhood of the Red Star and Cross from Bohemia. We received orders from our Grand Master to arrive here to protect the trade route between Hamburg and Berlin, Your Grace Lord Fortress Master."

"Ah, well, you arrived quickly. I imagined it would take weeks from Bohemia to send troops here, but here you are. Great! Have you had lunch yet?"

"We haven't had time; we just arrived, and I came here first, according to my orders, to register, sir knight."

"You can call me Johannes. Let's leave out the formalities. I am happy that I can invite you to dinner at my family's home on that side of Cölln."

"To your home, Sir Johannes? Don't you belong to the Order of Knights?"

"Right, it can be confusing for you. I really understand, but agreeing to a vow of celibacy and familylessness would have been impossible for me since I already have a wife and two children. We live over there behind the wooden bridge in our townhome. However, because of my war experience, I was asked for this position and I considered accepting the position with the condition that I can continue as a family man. The Landmaster was granted an exception by the papal legate to agree to my condition, and so here I am, the master in charge of the walls and defense of Berlin and Cölln, Burgermeister. I want to protect people and peaceful commerce. I'm not as warlike as I was when I was a young man."

Meinbald felt that they got along so well and were on the same wavelength as Johannes that he accepted the dinner invitation with gratitude. During dinner, he also got to know Johannes' wife, Grete, and their children, 5-year-old Johannes and 3-year-old Hans. The kitchen servant served the men dessert at Johannes' request in the backyard garden while Grete retreated with her children indoors.

"You are a rich and lucky man, Johannes. Thank you for inviting me to dinner and introducing me to your family. Your children are great little men and such funny pranksters!"

"Thank you, brother Meinbald, thank you for your beautiful words. But listen, luck is not evenly distributed in this world. And this job of mine isn't always so festive either. Five years ago, when we had just arrived here, and Grete was on her last days waiting for Johannes junior, I had to take care of doing excruciating things as soon as I arrived at my post. The frontier count had just captured three young Jewish men who had been caught near Maria's church. Wafer had been stolen from the church, and it was said that it was found in the possession of imprisoned Jewish youths.

After spending three days in the dungeon and two nights in the torture chamber, they had reportedly confessed to the Frontier Count's men that their intention had been to desecrate Christ's body by cutting up the wafer.

The bishop sentenced these men to death by burning. I was given the dubious honor of overseeing their execution with my men. We took those Jewish youths to a high hill, collected a pile, and burned them while the people, the bishop, and the Dominican monks watched the service.

Today, that hill is called Judenberg. Every time I see Jews or hear someone mention that name, even in passing, I shudder and don't sleep the next night."

"Whoa, you've had to experience quite a bit of responsibility, Johannes." he sighed and continued: "But you just carried out the bishop's sentence. If you hadn't done it, someone else would have. And that action of the young people was a conscious blow against the church. If they had not been executed, the church would have given the message that Christ's body could be desecrated".

"I still don't understand how stealing a loaf of bread can suddenly be equated with desecrating the body of Christ, our Lord!"

"Communion is a holy sacrament instituted by our Lord Jesus Christ himself. He himself has said that his body is present in unleavened bread, which is broken in his memory and enjoyed at communion. Whoever takes away this bread takes away the body. He who intends to cut the bread and slice it, therefore, intends to slice and dishonor the body of Christ. There is no way this can be allowed."

"Yes, I understand that, but anyone who is tortured for two nights is ready to confess to anything. So those who are being tortured will do anything to get out of the torture; it's obvious now."

"You are right about that, Johannes. But it wasn't you or your men torturing them. Your hands were not stained, and you are not guilty of anything, but either the men who confessed or those who tortured them into false confessions. Remember that whenever you start to feel anxious about this."

"Thank you, brother Meinbald. Your words are wise, and I will remember what you just said in the future. Listen, if that helps me sleep better, if I can be more at peace with the thought, I owe you a big debt of gratitude." Johannes was already visibly relieved.

Men becoming friends was also obvious to Grete, so he continued to receive dinner invitations. Meinbald and his men were tasked for the coming months to protect the trade route on the long journey from Hamburg here to Berlin. The Elbe, therefore, became very familiar to the men; the journey was mostly made by riverboat, sometimes on foot and sometimes on horses.

Meinbald himself saw up close how the organizations run by the mayor worked, and he got to know rich, powerful businessmen. The big movement of German expansion to the east had started, and the Hanseatic League acted as a central engine and operator of this change. He also saw how the entire chain worked. Sometimes, the contrast between the miserable and the hungry and the rich and the full made him stop to think and wonder if such a world really was according to God's will and if man could change it.

Meinbald was still the Grandmaster's trusted man. He had taken care of the department's financial affairs and the collection and distribution of rewards. He asked for help with this - he asked Lydeke to record the records required by the economy, focusing himself only on command correspondence and directing the group.

The Teutonic Order worked closely with the bourgeois; after all, the entire order was founded and financed by the Hanseatic League in the beginning. From this, he adopted the market fees and also took the model of lending money, making the financing run very efficiently. After a while, they no longer depended solely on funding from Bohemia.

Moving between the marketplaces of Berlin and Hamburg, he couldn't avoid hearing important news. It was said that Lübeck was expanding its fleet sailing to the north, because the trade route to the east was getting wider. Riga, Danzig, Königsburg, and Reval on the southern shore of the Gulf of Finland were the Hanseatic places on the route on the way to the Neva River, from which the import route was already open for furs and honey.

Furs were also obtained from Sweden, but the Swedes wanted to expand to the east, and for that, they had already taken over the old harbor of the Finns, Tavastians and Slavs - Turku by the river Aura.

The furs on that market were of remarkably good quality and many people thought that more of them should flow through Lübeck all the way to Berlin.

In Berlin, his department grew, and more horsemen and swordsmen joined the party. Some had a background from other knights, some from merchants and some even from noble families. Someone told a rumor they had heard about the upcoming northern crusade and how the Pope had declared that in addition to the Baltics, which had been christened "Saint Mary's land," Finland would also be the destination, where the fight against the enemies of the faith had the same benefits as in the Holy Land.

Knight Rheinhard, who had served in Lithuania, told how the Estonians had also been a very cruel and fierce warlike people; their last chief, Lembitu, had fallen in battle, and after that, Estonia had finally bowed to the power of the Pope. It was said that men wrestle with bears in Finland, and that bears are also worshiped as gods, as well as a large animal, a wild northern primordial bull with a multi-thorn crown on its head.

"It is a strange and wonderful country; it has held its ground for centuries also against the Nordmanns; neither the pagan Vikings nor Saint Olaf took over Finland. The Swedes have tried, but they themselves are still such a new Christian kingdom that they need help in conquering the country", Rheinhard stated. "They still don't have order or inner peace, but their construction has already started", he continued.

Meinbald remembered hearing a story from the monastic brothers, according to which centuries ago, when the land of Lower Saxony had been conquered and converted to Christianity, the king chief of the tribe named Widukind had managed to escape to the North with his close bodyguards. From the land of the Danes, he ordered some of his men to ask for auxiliaries from Finland with the help of the Frisian fleet. According to the story, Charlemagne himself had been at this conquest and ordered the last Irminsul tree in Lower Saxony to be destroyed. However, Widukind's fleet had taken with it saplings of the tree and spread them here and there on the coasts of the northern sea, strengthening paganism among the nations.

Chapter III
Life in Finland

Upper Satakunta, Tavast land, AD 1180 – 1199

Girmund was an ancient Germanic name meaning "spear guard". Before the beginning of the 13th century, a man of this name lived among a tribe that called itself the Water People in Tavast land, in the ancient province of Satakunta. Even as a child, Girmund aroused admiration in others with his extraordinary abilities. In his harsh home near Lake Pyhäjärvi, he grew up to be a brave and skilled warrior.

He, who was called the Lord of the Veil, had come from afar to Finland, disembarked on the holy land of Kalanti, wandered from there along the wilderness and along the banks of the river Kokemäenvirta far into Tavast land, and came to the shore of a beautiful lake called Pyhäjärvi in early spring.

The man had been walking along the ice when it suddenly gave way under his feet, and the Lord of the Veil fell into the ice. The story of a stranger who was rescued from the ice on the Hinsala River spread widely among the water people. He spoke a strange language that someone knew as Latin.

Great humility, love, and the desire to serve were transmitted from him despite the fact that no one understood what he said. Little by little, this missionary learned the language of the water people because one of the inhabitants knew Swedish and thus could teach the stranger the language of her own people word for word.

After learning enough of the language, the Lord of the Veil said that he was a man of the cross - he recited fragments of Christianity and urged the people to be baptized so that their sins would be washed away. He sang songs in Latin to the great delight of the water people. They were clearly a people with a strong singing tradition, inclined to poems, songs, and spells.

Girmund, who had grown up to be the chief of his village and tribe, heard that there was a monk preaching some new faith. He didn't like what he heard at all because, in his opinion, the old gods should be respected, and the monk's new doctrine was mocking the old gods.

It is said that the monk had already baptized many people into the new faith. Girmund confronted the monk and urged him to give up his faith and side with them, the Tavastian water people. If he did this, he would save his life.

"How could I deny my Lord and my God? I won't give up even if I get as much silver as that silver drops on the surface of Lake Pyhäjärvi during the rain", answered the monk to Girmund.

"Then die of hunger, a man of Kiesus, because you are so inflexible," said Girmund, whom the people called Kirmu in their local language. Lord of the Veil was captured and taken to a small rocky island at Lake Pyhäjärvi and left there to starve to death. Kirmu's comrade in arms, Urth, insisted that the monk would at least not die of thirst in the middle of the lake.

However, during the coming week, local people who had already been baptized into Christianity secretly took food to the monk, past the guards set by Kirmu, and saved him from starvation. They also eventually smuggled him into a secret sauna to continue his teaching and proselytizing work.

At the end of the week, the people of water had gathered in large numbers for a feast, where Urth arrived cursing and saying that the monk had disappeared from the island. Someone thought he had drowned, but Girmund knew that suicide was the greatest crime for believers in Christ. Girmund had had all the routes and boats guarded, so he was at a loss.

"This is remarkable! So, is there any power greater than anger?" He shouted, raising his hands to the sky.

"The power of the White Christ surpasses the power of anger and the sword"; a voice was then heard from the crowd. There were many friends of the Lord of the Veil in the crowd. Girmund flinched. Kirmu's lover, Annikki, noticed her fiancé's face turning pale, grabbed him by the arm and asked: "Do you know, Kirmu, what could overcome anger and death?"

"Annikki, who loves Kirmu?" he answered.

"Say, dear Kirmu, Aren't you afraid of death?"

Kirmu said that he fights even in fever when anger is raging, for duty and honor. Then, there is no fear of death.

The people of water returned home with mixed feelings, but in the secret sauna, there were nightly devotional moments where the Lord of the Veil taught and preached.

The time soon came, however, when white bonfires were lit from several castle mountains as a sign that the people had to prepare for war. The Novgorod troops had not been persuaded to stay away from their plundering expedition in

Tavast land, so it was time for the men of Tavastia to attack Novgorod.

Kirmu's old father said to his son: "You should take the life of that " Fish from Kalanti" that swims away from Sakaselkä's island. Do it before you go."

"I'm going to get the Lord of the Veil, and I'm going to crush him so that everyone feels it in their spines!" Kirmu shouted. Kirmu and his young cocky warriors began a general search. The search did not yield results at first, but then someone noticed a stream of people going to the secret sauna. A monk was found preaching there, and Kirmu was informed of the hiding place of the Lord of the Veil.

When Kirmu heard this, he took Kaakila's gallant Urth and Osmo the Karelian with him, and together they rowed to Hinsala, finding the place of the secret sauna.

After rushing inside, they found the monk, took him with them, and rowed him to Sakasela on the same island where they had left him earlier. There, they nailed him to a cross on an alder tree growing on a bank.

There were no cries of pain, no pleas for mercy; in a quiet voice, the monk mumbled the Pater Noster, and, in the language of the water, people asked his Savior to forgive Kirmu and his men.

Astonished by the monk's behavior, the men were silent for a long time until Kirmu raised his sword up towards the sky and shouted so that the entire back of the lake rang out:

In Kaakilanahti, the water people were ready for a military expedition to Russia with other men from Tavast land. The moment of departure had come.

Crying, the wives hugged their husbands and promised to take care of the choirs and work. Children hung around their fathers' necks, and young maidens dared to reveal the secrets of their hearts to the youths they liked.

The Laplandian girl, Jaanu's beautiful Annikki, in her blue dress and colorful capes, entered In front of Kirmu, rose to her toes, and attached a bundle of flowers to his chest.

"I always remember this blue maid on my trips, and when I return, I will hold her in my arms," Kirmu whispered.

Our old uncle Jaanu, who is Lapland's great archer, has to represent the Lapps of this region on your joint military expedition. He will be your constant gunman and serviceman, assured Annikki.

Girmund was also joined by Osmo, the Karelian who knew Russian, Tarkka's daughter Mielikki and Kaakila's gallant Urth. The groups got into their boats and started rowing.

The trip was headed from inland along the waters of Vanaja towards the Gulf of Finland, from there along the coast to the mouth of the Neva River and along the route of the East Road to distant Novgorod.

The Tavastian people, who were isolated and lived in their large forests or on the shores of inland lakes, had lagged behind in general development compared to the Karelians or the Novgorodian-Russians. These had converted to the Greek-Catholic faith and entered the sphere of Byzantine civilization.

The people of Tavast land achieved easy victories at first when they pushed against the borderland people, but when they had to fight against organized Novgorodian troops deeper inland, they were mercilessly defeated.

After a brave but hopeless fight, only Girmund, Jaanu's uncle, and Osmo the Karelian were left together with Mielikki when they had to flee to the watery marshes of Russia.

The constant hunger, tension, and emptiness of the forests had made Girmund so weak that he was nothing more than a shadow. He was struck with a feverish cough, and the others had to carry him so that they could hobble forward.

Girmund's faith in the old gods began to waver. Eventually, they found locals who fed and helped them, but then they were enslaved by a Boyar.

After receiving care, food, and drink, Girmund slowly regained his strength and became Boyar's best servant. After seeing how the grace and life of the Christians, in general, worked so much better in Novgorod than in their pagan Tavast land, also Girmund finally converted to Christianity. In particular, the fact that the Christians had taken him into their care, even though he had come here as an enemy with the firm intention of destroying them, had left a deep impression on Girmund.

After many twists and turns and an incredible coincidence, they were all freed and were able to return from Novgorod back to Tavast land. There, Girmund and Annikki and Osmo and Mielikki were married, and the first church in Vesilahti was started to be built in Vesaniemi.

The clashes and raids described, along with the increasing interest in the Finnish region as an excellent source of furs, led to the emergence of increasingly organised armies from both the east and the west during the course of the century. These forces directed their attacks towards the Finnish territory. It seems that Häme (Tavastia) was considered the final area worth conquering, caught in the pressure between the Eastern and Western Churches and the rising and expanding kingdoms in both directions.

Pagan nature religion had developed over the first millennium AD, influenced by Germanic traditions from Scandinavia and Central Europe. Nature held a close relationship with the people of the Merovingian era, and all supernatural beliefs were naturally tied to it. Nature provided harvests or, during years of famine, failed to do so. Agriculture and animal husbandry had reached the northern lands thousands of years earlier.

Ancestors and spirits of the dead were worshipped, for example, in sacred groves, and there was belief in various beings such as spirits, elves, goblins, and deities like Ukko,

Tapio, Ilmarinen, Lemminkäinen, and Turisas.

Sacred groves, known as *hiisi*, often contained a holy tree or bush, and sometimes sacrificial stones with cup-like depressions were used for offerings. Grain, bread, and milk were brought as sacrifices to gods, ancestors, or other entities.

Seers were the elders and wisest members of the community, often living near sacred groves in connection with villages. They knew spells and could, for instance, stop bleeding or cure illnesses. Witches also knew spells and magic but used their abilities to harm enemies, whereas seers sought to assist their community members.

Villages had an elder, leader, or king, and similarly, provinces had their rulers. Secular matters were addressed in *käräjät* (assemblies, like norse tings), where village leaders decided on common issues, such as resolving disputes, punishing criminals, and organising warfare. Blood feuds and family honour were central motivators.

From the 12th century onwards, missionaries venturing into the Finnish peninsula encountered these ancient customs and beliefs, and the new religion they preached began to merge with them among the population. The memory left behind by figures like Kirmu-Karmu and Hunnun Herra is just one testament to this blending. Another story from that era that has endured is the tale of Saint Henry, a bishop who, according to legend, met a violent end at the axe of a peasant named Lalli. Although the story was only recorded in the early 14th century, it still reflects the same clashes of worlds and the persistent mistrust Finns felt towards the coercive measures introduced by outsiders, such as episcopal taxes.

The tribes living in the Finnish peninsula and its surrounding areas included the Tavastians, Finns, Karelians, Sámi, Ingrians, and Bjarmians. Despite their shared Finno-Ugric ancestry, these tribes spoke slightly distinct languages and often harboured mutual suspicions. At times, they engaged in wars and raids against one another.

AD 1200 - 1230

By the 1200s, Christianity had spread and rooted itself sporadically across the Finnish mainland, with a somewhat more established presence along the coast facing Sweden. Christianity and paganism coexisted among the Finnish people, though not always peacefully. From the perspective of the Western Roman Church, Finland was seen as the "last frontier", a buffer zone that needed to be integrated into the Church's domain.

Missionaries from this frontier were also sent to convert the pagans in Estonia, as evidenced by the mention of a priest named Pietari Kaukovalta in the Chronicle of Henry of Livonia. Kaukovalta, alongside a monk named Otto from the Order of the Swordbrothers, converted pagans in Estonia. At this time, the Kingdom of Sweden was still forming, too weak and fragmented to manage its neighbouring territories on its own, thus requiring the Church's supernatural organisation to help with the governance of both Swedish and Finnish regions.

In a letter dated January 23, 1229, Pope Gregory IX authorised the transfer of the Finnish bishopric from Nousiainen to a more suitable location in Turku, on the Koroistenniemi peninsula. In 1231, the Pope enacted foundational laws regarding the ecclesiastical inquisition, thus establishing the inquisition as a papal legal institution.

Gregory IX also adopted the imperial regulations of Emperor Frederick II, which had been applied to persecute heretics, though the use of torture was omitted. In 1232, the inquisition was practically handed over to the Dominicans, who were the majority of the inquisitors appointed by Gregory IX. They acted as both accusers and judges in matters related to the Church's laws.

Emperor Frederick II of the Holy Roman Empire did not extend his influence to the north but focused on the Holy Land and Mediterranean regions. Despite being excommunicated by the Pope and even declared the Antichrist, Frederick II provided protection for the Dominican order within his empire:

"Furthermore, we wish to inform all that we have authorised the prior of the Dominicans in Würzburg and the brothers to act on matters of faith against heretics in Germany, and that they are under the special protection of the Emperor and the Empire."

-    Excerpt from Emperor Frederick II's declaration of 1232.

The Dominicans had already arrived in the Nordic countries in 1221. Their habit was white, with black cloaks and head coverings, which led them to be called the "black brothers." The monastery established in Lund in 1221 was known as the Monastery of the Black Brothers or the Dominican convent of St. Mary Magdalene.

Finland was a part of the ongoing struggle between East and West, not only over the spread of religions but also regarding the economic benefits to be gained. Finland's bishop, Thomas, was the first military-political figure in this context, wielding both a cross and a sword.

Albert von Buxhövden, the bishop of Riga, had already been building an independent ecclesiastical state in Livonia between 1200 and 1220, with the help of the Knights of the Sword. Bishop Thomas followed Albert's path, attempting to create a similar ecclesiastical state in Finland with the aid of the Order of the Sword and the German Order of Knights, hoping to rule over both secular and ecclesiastical matters in the region.

In 1227, when a Novgorodian fleet, led by Prince Yaroslav, sailed to Tavastia to convert the Karelians to the Greek Orthodox faith, Bishop Thomas led a retaliatory raid with a 2,000-strong Finnish force the following year. Later, when Novgorod sent another army, which advanced deep into Tavastia with support from Karelian forces, the Tavastian people saw that even the Karelians had become Christians.

This caused confusion among the Tavastian people, who were still strongly adherent to their ancient Kalevala beliefs, and they began to question which form of Christianity they were supposed to embrace, and at what cost. This also sparked the thought: Was either form of Christianity any better than the Kalevala faith that had been practiced by their ancestors for centuries?

The Dominicans used their inquisitorial power in Finland, and under Bishop Thomas, the Church began to destroy the pagan sacred groves of the Tavastian people, sacred sites known as hiisi. Nothing could be a greater provocation to a nature-based religion. The Kalevan boys rose up in armed resistance.

Pope Gregory IX's bull, issued on December 9, 1237, describes a great rebellion by the Tavastian people. Although the Tavast land had been forced into Christianity for decades, they had rejected it and directed brutal violence towards Christians.

Newborn children were killed, adults were disembowelled and sacrificed to evil spirits, some were run around trees until they died, priests had their eyes gouged out, and they were burned at the stake.

According to the bull, this was caused by incitement from the Tavastia's malicious neighbours. The propaganda does not mention Novgorod by name, nor does it hint that the provocation might have been self-inflicted. According to the Pope's bull, Christians from Sweden and nearby islands were to prepare for a holy war against the Tavastian people. Of course, the Pope and his bishops had their own personal goals of creating alliances between Church and state at the empire's borders.

Looking at this situation in a broader context, we see how it fits into the larger narrative of the era. The period approaching the mid-1200s in Finland and the Baltic Sea region was marked by turbulence for many reasons. It would be incorrect to portray the Finns as a peaceful, impoverished people who were unaware of the outside world. In fact, looking just a couple of decades back into the written history surrounding Finland, one can see how events followed each other and how the situation around the Baltic Sea heated up.

In a letter from 1216, Pope Innocent III confirmed to Swedish King Erik Knutsson the ownership of the land "taken from the pagans", undoubtedly referring to Finland. This question was primarily based on the achievements of King Knut Eriksson, the father of Erik Knutsson. However, at the time, Sweden only controlled Southwestern Finland. The Pope granted the Swedish king the right to appoint a bishop for Finland.

The key message of the letter was that the Pope specifically recognised Sweden's right to the lands it had conquered in Finland. Earlier, the Pope had transferred responsibility for the entire Northern mission area from the archbishop of Hamburg-Bremen to the Danish bishop Anders Sunesen in Lund, much to the dismay of the region's German-speaking inhabitants.

Therefore, as the Germans succeeded in the Baltic region, having subjugated Livonia and penetrated into Estonia, Denmark rushed to claim its share. In 1219, King Valdemar of Denmark, a rival to Swedish King John Sverkersson, began military operations to conquer Estonia and won a battle near the Estonian town of Rävala.

The fierce competition for control of the Estonian Crusader front led to forced baptisms and made Finland's eastern neighbours, primarily the Novgorodians, restless. The Pope's 1221 decree banning the sale of weapons to pagans, likely aimed at the Karelians, who were threatening the "new growth of Christianity in Finland," was a sign of this.

The western crusader front in Finland was therefore in a defensive position, while Novgorod began to adopt the forced conversion methods of the Western Crusaders. In 1227, Prince Yaroslav ordered mass baptisms in Karelia. "It was a near thing that not all people were baptised," boasted the Novgorod Chronicle. The goal was to strengthen Karelia's ties to Novgorod, which likely became more solidified.

ThomasThomasIn the winter of 1226–1227, the Novgorodians, under the leadership of Prince Yaroslav, launched an invasion of Tavastia, which, according to the chronicle, was nearly completely conquered, meaning it was subjected to the forced baptisms described earlier. To defend his diocese, Bishop Thomas appealed to the Pope for guarantees of protection. The following year, the people of Tavastia recovered from their forced baptisms and retaliated by launching a raid as far as Lake Ladoga and Aunus. At the same time, the Karelians were being baptized from Novgorod.

In these circumstances, Thomas worked to secure further papal support for his diocese. On January 21, 1229, Pope Gregory IX sent a letter to the Bishop of Linköping, informing him that he had placed the Bishop of Finland, the clergy, and the people under the protection of the Apostolic See. The letter also authorized the bishop to oversee this protection. Additionally, Thomas obtained a papal decree imposing a trade embargo on Novgorod in the Baltic Sea. The Pope renewed the embargo, specifying that it applied to the Russians. At the same time, the Bishop, clergy, and people of Finland were placed under apostolic protection. The intention was to forbid any actions that could disrupt the Finnish crusade's efforts against the Russians and the pagans. The enforcement of the papal decree was entrusted to churchmen close to the trade power of Gotland, as Gotland traders were known to treat business matters as purely commercial and benefit from arms trading with Novgorod and its allies.

AD 1232 - 1239

As the resistance of the pagans grew stronger due to the violent methods of missionary work, a new idea emerged among churchmen: negotiating with the leaders of the pagan nations could yield better results than conquest. However, this new approach led to conflict with the secular rulers who had been carrying out the crusades.

In Finland, direct papal control became evident in 1232 when Baldwin of Aulnes was appointed papal legate for both Livonia and Finland. Without his consent, negotiating peace or truces with the Russians or pagans was forbidden.

Bishop Thomas sought to bring Tavastia under the ecclesiastical control of the church and may have used the Livonian Brothers of the Sword to assist in missionary work. Initially, this strategy appeared to work well, but by 1236–1237, the people of Tavastia resisted.

The cause of the uprising was likely either the harsh tactics of the sword-brothers or the church taxes and other burdens placed upon them. Missionary preachers had ventured into the interior of Finland and achieved some success with their proclamations. However, the leaders and people of Tavastia had decided to abandon the new faith at a local assembly, and almost everyone had been baptized.

Now, however, they had grown tired of the bishop's tax, which was set at four marten pelts per bow, and became discontented with the fact that they could no longer burn their dead, abandon their infants, or practice their beloved blood vengeance. As a result, they defiantly washed away their baptisms in the waters of Lake Katumajärvi and drove the missionaries away.

To quell the rebellion, Bishop Thomas sought support from Sweden, and he succeeded in obtaining a papal crusade bull from the Archbishop of Uppsala in 1237. King Erik XI of Sweden had recently regained the throne after the death of Knut Long.

The young and ambitious Birger of the Bjälbo family married Erik's sister Ingeborg in the same year, thus securing the support of the Bjälbo clan for Erik's reign. At the time, Birger's older cousin, Ulf Fase, served as the jarl of Sweden.

While the exact methods used by Thomas are unclear, he managed to calm the Tavastian rebels with Swedish support and easily reconverted them to the "true faith." Perhaps he promised to leave sacred groves in peace? Birger had been involved in the campaign with Ulf Fase, during which they had captured the fort of Hakoisten on the Janakkala hill fairly easily.

The Swedes primarily sought to establish a foothold at the mouth of the Neva River to control the entire eastern trade route. In 1240, the Swedes launched a military campaign to the Neva, with the Tavastian people also participating. Bishop Thomas was also involved in this campaign.ThomasThomasThomasThomas

#

July, AD 1240

In the West, Novgorod's growing activity toward the west was seen as a source of unrest. Only a direct strike on Novgorod's innermost areas of interest could bring a decisive success in the missionary work and secure control over the Neva trade route. This opportunity seemed to present itself as Russia was weakened by the advancing Tatar hordes in its heartland.

Papal legate Wilhelm of Modena tried to rally Western forces for cooperation, but this effort was not entirely successful. Fortunately for the Novgorodians, they had the opportunity to confront the attacking forces from both sides of the Gulf of Finland separately. In the summer of 1240, Prince Alexander Yaroslavich won a victory over the northern group at the Neva River. This group included a fleet led by the Swedish jarl, along with bishops, forces from Southwest Finland and Tavastia, and apparently some volunteers from Ingermanland. The Western Finns fought against Novgorod, while the Eastern Finns fought as allies of Novgorod.

According to an old Russian account, an Ingrian tribal chief near the mouth of the Neva was the first to bring news of the western invaders' approach. This chief, named Pelkoinen, had been baptized and given the Christian name Filip. On a previous punitive and destructive raid against Tavastia, the former Novgorodian prince, Jaroslav, had left Greek Catholic priests behind the Kymijoki River to convert the areas of Virolahti and Valkeala to his faith. These priests did not use the sword in their missionary work, so the people of Tavastia could hardly have failed to notice the difference between the representatives of the two churches.

Thus, while a crusade was preached in Sweden, Norway, and Finland by papal order against the Tavastian people, and a large fleet was assembled in Turku, the campaign did not target the Tavast land, but rather the root of all evil, Novgorod. Interestingly, many Tavastians were involved in the campaign. They had the best local knowledge, not only from numerous military campaigns but also from commercial connections with the Novgorodian territories.

The essential question was whether they participated in the campaign as pagans or as Christians, something the Tavastians likely pondered themselves.

The fleet sailed up the Neva River to the mouth of the Inger River, landing troops on both sides of the river. Pelkoinen brought Prince Alexander Nevsky, the son of Jaroslav, the news of the enemy landing.

The information was so crucial that Alexander did not have time to request reinforcements from his father in Kyiv. He ordered Pelkoinen to keep the news secret, and with a small force composed of Novgorodians, Ladogans, and Ingrians, mainly Finnish tribes, he unexpectedly attacked the enemy camp on Sunday, July 15, 1240, at six o'clock in the morning.

According to the account, it became a "terrible massacre for the Romans," with a vast number of Romans struck down, and "the king himself" (actually the jarl, Ulf Fase) was dealt a blow to the face by Pelkoinen with a sword.

At the same time, a miracle occurred: when Alexander had defeated the king on one side of the Inger River, on the other side, where his army could not reach, a large number of bodies lay lifeless on the ground, apparently slain by the angel of God.

The rest of the invaders fled in shame, and the bodies of the dead were gathered onto three ships of the victorious leaders, but all drowned at sea. Some were buried in pits, countless bodies thrown in, and that same night, the invaders fled.

As a sailor and chief of the coastal guard, Pelkoinen was familiar with the ships and observed their crew landing and setting up the leaders' tents on the other side of the river. He also watched the "Swedes" and "Jäms" (likely referring to groups from Häme) establish their camps on the other side of the river. He deduced that this group from Southwest Finland and Tavastia secured the eastern shore while the Swedes remained on the western shore, sending out guards to watch over the Tavastians, whom they considered untrustworthy. Pelkoinen advised Alexander to launch an attack on the leaders' tents, leaving the Finnish forces on the other side of the river undisturbed.

The result was as expected. Early on Sunday morning, the Finnish battle cry rang out from the Ladogans and Ingrians, and the gilded dome of the leaders' tent was among the first to fall, the tent collapsing on the leaders, who, wounded, tried to flee to their ships. The surprise and confusion were complete. The wounded required so much attention and effort that, during the day-long battle, the Swedes and Norwegians were driven into the river. The boldest of the attackers, swimming on pieces of wood, tried to reach the ships anchored in the Neva.

The familiar battle cry "Hakkaa päälle!" (Strike them down!) roused the Finns, primarily the Tavastian guards, who turned on their own forces, completing the destruction of the Swedes and returning to their ships. This campaign, more than any other, gave Birger the reason to launch what became known as the "second crusade" to Finland, to conquer Tavast land and punish the Tavastian people.

After the defeat and their retreat as a broken force, Birger began to devise a foolproof plan to make a great conquest. The next crusade would not end in defeat; he would convert the Tavastian people and permanently claim them for Sweden. After all, he was the brother-in-law of King Erik, and his children would be first in line for the throne if Erik left no sons.

Bishop Thomas's dream of a grand ecclesiastical state was shattered by the Ingrian Filip Pelkoinen. But in Birger, a desire to own Finland and Tavastians in their stubborn, rebellious, and defiant form had been awakened.

From this point on, Birger no longer trusted Bishop Thomas at all, as Thomas had sided with the Tavastians on the same side of the river, holding both sword and cross, and had failed to prevent the Tavastians from attacking their guards and slaughtering them. Thomas, it seemed, did not understand the mindset or language of the land he was supposed to lead.

AD 1241 - 1247

Thomas resigned or was dismissed from his position in 1245 and withdrew to Gotland to spend his retirement, leaving the Bishopric of Finland vacant for several years. Contrary to canon law, the secular authority of Sweden appointed a relative of King Erik, Bero, as the Bishop of Finland in 1248. This occurred under the guidance of Birger, after the conquest of Tavastia.

The Swedish and German Hanseatic connections to the trading ports along the Finnish coast had been established for centuries. However, the situation in the interior was now very unstable, and the availability of furs, for example, had declined as a result.

Prince Alexander, who had completed his victory in 1242 by also defeating the German invasion on the ice of Lake Peipus, had earned the honorary title of Nevski (from the River Neva) in Russia. The Battle of Neva was a turning point, as it halted the progress of Western forces toward the heartlands of Russia and the Orthodox Church, while also sealing the division of the Finnish tribes. Alexander, alongside his father Jaroslav, had also managed to form an alliance with the fearsome Mongols, or Tatars.

The Tatars destroyed all other Russian cities, but the Republic of Novgorod became a more or less submissive part of the Golden Horde. Alexander and the Tatars also sent an army up the White Sea, invading the area the Norwegians called

Bjarmia. The Bjärms, fantastically rich from trade dating back to the Viking era, had built hill forts like other Finnish tribes but could not defend against the overwhelming force of their wild enemies. Eventually, some of them fled westward, some to Norway, but most stayed behind as a subjugated people. The Bjärms were effectively erased from the map, and no references to them exist after 1240.

At the same time, in Sweden, the Bjälbo family, related to Erik, was fighting for power against the Sverker family. Violence and raiding were rampant in Svea.

After rising to become Duke Erik's jarl in 1247, Birger began suppressing a tax rebellion in Uppland. Holmger Knutsson, the son of the late Knut the Long, had come of age and was naturally seeking the crown he believed was his.

Erik's heavily armoured cavalry and Holmger's Uppland warriors met in battle at Sparrsätra, north of Enköping in Uppland. Following Erik's victory, the Svea of Uppland lost their semi-aristocratic status and began paying taxes to the king. Holmger fled, but he was soon captured by the king and jarl further north in Gästrikland, where he was executed.

The papal legate William of Modena, on his way back from Norway, arrived in the quieter region of Eastern Gothenland to meet not only the church leaders but also Duke Birger, offering to mediate peace between the factions. In March 1248, a peace agreement was reached in Skänninge, where Sweden was formally integrated into the Catholic community.

Birger's ledung fleet also visited the shores of Estonia, where Birger remarked on the chaos of the "crusading" in the region, observing how Christians were fighting other Christians. Bloody wars were being fought along the Baltic coast, and might made right; church fathers and kings directed the fate of nations, not gods, though they were often invoked to justify and legitimise terrible deeds.

The Hanseatic League sought to manage trade from the Baltic to Novgorod. Although Novgorod was not part of the Hanseatic League, it was a vital trading hub. Furs, salt, hides, and other goods flowed in shiploads.

Novgorod had maintained connections with Finland and Scandinavia since its founding. The legendary Rurik, the founder of Kievan Rus, had actually come from Finnish lands, meaning deep-rooted connections to Russia had existed for centuries.

Very little is known about Finland and its history before the 1200s. It has always been a borderland, a dividing line between east and west, with no written records surviving.

Various mythical interpretations of Finland's history have often come from outside the country. Based on historical experience, Finns know that any conqueror, whether from the east or west, has rewritten history to reflect the "truth" that best suited them.

The Swedish Erik Chronicle, written in the 14th century, describes how King Erik the Holy conquered Finland and converted it to Christianity. This same chronicle also includes a brief account of Birger's "second crusade," mentioning how the pagans either accepted baptism or lost their lives, and thus the Christians triumphed. In his famous work The Conquest of Finland, Russian court master K.F. Ordin, published in 1889, argued that before the Swedish conquests, not only Karelia but also Tavastia had been part of Novgorod's territory. He was followed by Soviet historians, particularly I.P.

Saskolski in Leningrad and V. Pasuto in Moscow.

Saskolski developed a theory that Novgorod's influence on the Finnish peninsula was unique, primarily involving tribute; Novgorod had not brought any permanent fortifications with garrisons to Finland. However, this tribute extended not only to Karelia but also to Tavastia.

In fact, Novgorod had fought several battles against the Swedes in Western Finland but lost them. In his biography of Alexander Nevsky, Pasuto included a map of Novgorod, marking Sweden's eastern border at Lake Päijänne, with Tavastia placed just northwest of that border. According to this map, Sweden did not conquer a "cultural Finnish people" but a part of Novgorod's trading state, what is referred to as its "Vadja fifth."

Whether true or not, invaders from both east and west would have realised that they didn't even need to burn the Finns' own historical texts because there were none.

The Finns' own truth, however, was impossible to burn or erase; it was hidden but spread and lived on stubbornly like a peat fire in the Kalevala tradition, in songs and poems passed down from generation to generation, despite earthly and spiritual powers.

Chapter IV
Kaukomieli

In Tavastia, AD 1248

Kaukomieli, whose name means a far-sighted person, was a good chief. He knew that the world around him was changing, that the old ways and the independent, centuries-long barter and hunting economy, eternal looting and quarrels with neighboring tribes, blood feuds protecting the honor of the family and clan, and polygamy would soon be all things of the past. A new order was coming to replace them, which the church fathers and earthly great princes together were to bring here, even to the last final frontiers.

He was a Christian himself. His family had been Christian for as long as he knew - at least two hundred years. He was called "Kuningas", a king. His grandfather, also named Kaukomieli, had already made peace with the Swedes a hundred years ago when they had come with King Erik's army and Bishop Henrik's Latin spells to convert the pagan Finns to Christianity. After that, the trade was doing well again. Furs, fish and Väinölä's long-distance imports traveled smoothly from Kokemajoki river or Aura river to Turku, all the way to Lake Mälaren, the Christian center in Sigtuna.

After the previously flourishing marketplace in Birka was destroyed, the center of trade had moved to Sigtuna for a couple of centuries. But in 1187, the Karelians and Estonians had destroyed all of Sigtuna. The power of Novgorod rose from the east and took more hold, coming closer every year. In 1200, when Kaukomieli was born, there was already more trade in Turku, Finland, with ships from Lübeck and Frisians. Trade goods arriving in Turku had to pay customs to the Swedish crown, which had taken a permanent foothold in the territory of Finland proper.

Collecting taxes in Eura and Kokemäki had been Kaukomieli's father's main task. The taxes belonged to him, the vassal, but he paid part of them to the church. Farming was the main means of livelihood of the vassal king, but he was a large landowner of his time because he could afford to support his servants as well. In return for taxes, the local chief provided his tribe with protection and law enforcement.

Kaukomieli had already learned to read and write as a child. He had also been the court boy of the Swedish king Erik X for 5 years, from the age of 12 to 16. He had learned the customs and languages used at court easily. Father Faravid also had a head for languages, so the skill ran in the family.

He was fluent in Norwegian and Swedish as well as in Latin and German. When conversing with different people, he could smoothly switch from one language to another on the fly. This was a bit confusing for those who knew only one language, but the skill gave the ruler a significant advantage.

Even the names were often changed from one language to another in speech. For example, Faravid is the Norwegian equivalent of Kaukomieli.

The king of a small trading center in Vanaja, the heart of Tavast land, named Satatieto, and the king of Satakunta, Kaukomieli, agreed on marriage deals for their children in the spring of

1220. Kaukomieli, son of Kaukomieli and Kyllikki, daughter of Satatieto, got married in midsummer. In keeping with the spirit of the times, these marriage deals aimed to unite the Tavastian people under one king. Kyllikki's and Kaukomieli's firstborn, a girl who was baptized Elin, was born in the year 1225 on a sunny June morning in Satakunta, on the Kaukola farm.

Elin's grandfather, King Kaukomieli, died in Eura when Elin was four years old. He was seriously wounded while defending Satakunta in the winter of 1227 when the Novgorodians came to forcibly baptize the Tavastian people. At that time, the young father, Kaukomieli, also fought for his tribe. He had to become the head of Satakunta at a young age, inheriting his father's position and duties. The following year, they had a son, Matti, who was baptized as a Christian by Thomas, who was the bishop of Finland at the time.

As a vassal ruler, Kaukomieli acted especially as a protector of the northern fur trade and an organizer of taxation. He strove to be a friend of merchants on both sides of the Gulf of Bothnia, or Pohja, respecting long traditions. Hundreds had been a Germanic form of government that spread to these latitudes hundreds of years ago, and both Uppland and Sata-Tavast land had always raised hundreds of men for battle when necessary. There had been enough battles over the centuries whenever a neighboring tribe had gone plundering, trying their luck, since the Viking times.

Defending southern Finland against enemies required fortresses suitable for defense. Over the centuries, they had been built on almost every suitable steep rock and hill that could be found next to a settlement. Blacksmiths knew how to skillfully forge iron made from lake ore. Iron was used to make weapons and shields such as swords, spearheads, and shield caps. Likewise, it was used to make tools needed for earthwork and the iron frames, hinges, and hinges of buildings.

Kaukomieli held the Kokemäenjoki fortress in Harjavalta as his main administrative seat, living in the Kokemäki manor. Although the people of Satakunta called him "King," he was a Western Christian but not a royal ruler. However, Kaukomieli did have his own decentralized "Court" in a way, because he commanded several Hundreds through their chiefs.

"Antero, my closest chief, this spring, we get to brandish our swords again. I am worried about my son Matti. He is still so young and wild that he does not understand fearing for his life."

"King Kaukomieli, don't give way to your worries when it comes to Matti. He is a skilled sword, bow, and spear user", Antero, leader of Kaukomiel's bodyguard, answered.

"Yes, you are right. However, for some reason, I am more worried about him than about my firstborn, Elin. I'm sure that whatever happens, Elin will be fine because she is so warm and gentle. It's funny; I have many sharp children and a whole great tribe of wonderful free souls, but I'm just worried about my second oldest son, who is already a grown man and knows how to defend himself and defeat his enemies. I don't know why that is. Maybe I'm afraid that he won't recognize who is a friend and who is an enemy and that he will be taken advantage of."

"Wise king, it's sometimes difficult for anyone. But as long as you're in charge, we have nothing to worry about. You know who is on whose side."

"Don't flatter, Antero. You know I don't like it. We've been through so much together that you need to know that. I am no longer so young and immortal that I would imagine that I am the one who always guides us from victory to victory."

"It's clear that guidance must come from God and not from man. So leave it to the gods."

"I would leave it, but which one? Which of them is on our side? Even the experts are tight-lipped about this and can't say anything. It's good that you, Antero, said that. I guess I'll decide that, too."

In the spring of 1248, a cold wind blowed from the northeast, from the Arctic Ocean, which moved the cold air masses to the heart of Tavast land and Satakunta. In April, the snow covers, which already had melted once, had a new arrival. "Spring will come with a swing," knew all the expert wizards of the provinces.

Kaukomieli, on the other hand, knew that both the East and the West were now coming with armed forces to conquer Tavast land at the dawn of spring. So they had to prepare again for new hostilities and choose their allies carefully.

Chapter V
Northland

At Berlin in April AD 1248

Earl Birger had sent a crusade invitation to the free mercenaries of the Holy Roman Empire and to the knights under the command of the Church. The invitation was sent through the papal legate, William of Modena. The purpose of the campaign was to defend Finland's Christians and cleanse the rest of the pagans in the North.

The invitation referred directly to the fact that with a successful campaign, there would be land and mammon for the participating soldiers. Originally, the Pope himself had sent a letter of exhortation to the Swedes, and now Birger, as a man of action, in good cooperation with the Catholic Church, was going to implement this exhortation.

The time was right; there were plenty of hungry mercenaries and military knights. An order had also come to the Grand Master of the Order of the Red Star and Cross, through the Bishop of Prague, to send five ships' worth of troops, who would not only carry weapons but also take care of the wounded.

Meinbald received the order from the Grand Master. The messenger had ridden tirelessly for three days, changing horses at inns, and finally reached him with his troops in Berlin.

Brother Meinbald,

Pope Innocent IV, our spiritual father, has assigned the following Holy mission to our brotherhood:

"Your department is going to the North to support Sweden's young secular power as it embarks on the Holy War against the pagans in Finland. The Teutonic Order also sends a section to support this Holy Journey, the goal of which is to convert even the last pagans to followers of our Lord Jesus Christ.

You act as the trip leader for our fraternity. Head from Berlin to Lübeck, and from there by ship north towards Finland. Get ready for tough battles. I have received word from the Grand Master of the Teutonic Knights that the heretics of Novgorod have conquered the heathen lands and are subjecting them to their own taxation and heresy.

Tell all your brothers who are strong in faith that the Holy Father has promised that if you fall or are wounded on this trip, you will get a safe place with our Heavenly Father. This trip has the same blessings and benefits as on previous crusades to the Holy Land.

You keep the war diary of your troops, acting as the marshal of our brotherhood on your journey and battles. You establish a field hospital to treat the wounded as needed in the battles you face. You, your deputy marshal Fridrik and I keep in touch by letter; the supply connection is maintained during the operation with the help of ships equipped by the Lübeck burghers. My messenger will give you the payment order I wrote, which you can exchange for money at the Knights Templar base in Berlin and use them to buy more men, equipment, horses and hay for the men and oats for the horses. I am also sending a small first batch of bandages and care supplies from here in Prague directly to the ship waiting for you in the port of Lübeck. You take care of replenishing the supplies and your hospital organization using local Christians.

It was mid-April, and spring was already starting to feel warm in Berlin. He realized that he had to act quickly, so he held a consultation with Brother Fridrik immediately.

"Meinbald, this means we can say goodbye to these boring trade route security patrols. We're getting down to business again!" Fridrik gloated like a little boy in knight games.

"Yes, now, instead of the Tatars of the eastern steppes, we get to face the pagans of the north and convert them to Christianity. This is a wonderful mission blessed by our Lord, so let's get down to business, Deputy Marshal," he stated with a carefree chuckle.

After exchanging the money order for money, Meinbald immediately started recruiting. His first thought was that here in Berlin there was a good chance of getting the department up to full strength. While recruiting veterans of the Teutonic Knights from Berlin, he heard that there were many young mercenaries heading north in Lübeck.

It was a perfect fit because Meinbald, like an experienced merchant, had calculated that he could acquire five ships and ship 20 men and 10 war horses per ship. It was more difficult to find enough willing travelers from Berlin because they had been recruiting for Baltic tours for twenty years.

Most Baltic veterans said frankly that they were not interested when they had already seen enough bloodshed and that it was better to send younger men to the harsh conditions in the north anyway. So they set off on the march with barely a section, heading straight to Lübeck.

At Lübeck the twentieth of April, AD 1248

In Lübeck, it turned out that the information was correct; there were many young men pretending to be heroes in the harbor near the ships. First, Meinbald walked to the shipowners' guild house and secured four seaworthy cogs to transport his troops. The fifth ship, his future command ship, had already been booked and loaded in port by Albert.

He set up his recruiting office in the port next to their cargo hold and ordered Otto and Lydeke to walk around the local taverns, telling them that crusaders are being recruited here. Meinbald himself accepted eager recruits one at a time. A group of men had noticed that the recruitment activity had started and so the line started to gather for meeting him. The first to speak to him was a large man who introduced himself:

"Lord Dominus, I am Dietrich; I would like to enlist in your army."

"Your profession?"

"I am a carpenter, sir knight. I have worked on house buildings and fortress sites as well as church sites. I'm used to carving with an ax and a cleaver, and I don't mind carving anything other than wood. Because of my big size, my friends call me "Balk." Partly it is also due to the fact that my father's family originates from the village of Balk in Friesland."

"Alright, so Dietrich Balk." Meinbald dipped his quill in ink and wrote down the first name, adding a few notes to himself.

"Good, you have been recruited, and from now on, you belong to the armed crew of the Brotherhood of the Red Star and the Cross, and you obey the commands of your superiors. Questions?"

"No, thank you, Lord Dominus. I am grateful to be able to join this crusade. My late uncle Hermann organized the Teutonic Order's sword mission in the Baltics. He was the country master of Prussia and Livonia. He died ten years ago, but I feel that now it is my turn to be involved in the conversion of the Gentiles."

"Okay, thanks for telling me, this is very interesting. Go over there to the left, Do you see that sturdy knight? Make sure with him that you get equipment of sufficient size for your trip, we are ready to equip even big men."

Meinbald noticed that a line of men had already gathered behind them. After Dietrich Balk walked off, he raised his voice so that everyone could hear:

"When you come in front of me, just tell me your name, your profession, and your weapon-handling skills. If I accept you to join us on the crusade, I will direct you forward. Our ships can accommodate many more men. If you can't make it to the trip now, you can wait for the next shipment with us, which will be organized in a couple of weeks. Next!"

Now, two men stepped in front of him at the same time. The other took a step closer, having time to introduce himself first.

"I am Magnus, lord knight. I am a blacksmith by trade and a very good one at that. I can also use the swords and axes I have forged. I have used a shield when fighting bandits. Most of them ran away when they saw how they were met by a blacksmith tougher than themselves."

"All right, Magnus. You have been recruited and henceforth belong to the armed men of the Brotherhood of the Red Star and Cross and obey the commands of your superiors. Questions?"

"No, thank you, Lord Knight."

"Follow that big brother-in-arms of yours over there, and we'll equip you with a hero's cloak." "Magnus, the Hero," he wrote down the name in the Men's List.

"Next!"

"Ulf, Sir Knight. I'm a carpenter, I carve houses. I haven't used a sword, but I can swing an ax in battles as well. That Magnus you just hired and I have fought against bandits and thugs here in Lübeck."

"Alright, Ulf Axe. You have been recruited and henceforth belong to the armed crew of the Brotherhood of the Red Star and Cross and obey the commands of your superiors. Questions?"

"No, thank you, Sir Knight."

"Follow your friend, and we'll give you a decent battle ax and a shield." "Next!"

This way, during the morning, Meinbald was able to recruit his full fleet and when they all had been equipped, it was dinner time. The Order offered its new crew the first meal together, after which he gave a short speech to the entire group they had gathered.

"Men, listen up! I am Meinbald, marshal on this crusade. I was appointed by Grand Master Albert of the Order of the Red Star and Cross. My deputy marshal is Fridrik. If I am wounded or fall, Fridrik here, he will take command."

"All of us knight brothers have gone through long and hard military training and have also fought against the brutal Tatars, repelling their attempted coups in Bohemia. Martial art is one thing; internal discipline is another. In our fraternity, we strictly follow the code of St. Augustine. Our one basic task is to treat the sick and wounded in the best possible way. In Prague, where our fraternity is from, we have a hospital that has sent a shipload of treatment and dressing supplies along with our trip. We will take care of all the wounded on this trip, Christians as well as pagans of false faith, because that is our basic task written in the rules of our brotherhood. If you get wounded, you can count on being treated at the field hospital and not left on the field to run out of breath and die.

Each of you also gets to take turns treating wounded brothers-in-arms and enemies. Yes, you will also tend to our wounded enemies. We start from the fact that the unbeliever is also a fellow human being and we should help all people who are in need. You will see that this is a good principle, the observance of which will make you blessed. Brother Kort, this man next to me, is the priest of our group, and you can get help from him in spiritual matters.

If your earthly journey comes to an end on this trip, you will be blessed and the heavenly congregation will receive you with joy, rejoicing in your sacrifice. This has been promised by our Holy Father Pope Innocent himself.

You enlisted men now; you come from different backgrounds, so you don't all know our rules or our ways of fighting, but you will learn them.

On the upcoming ship sail, we will go through the basic training, which we will deepen by practicing when we stop in Visby on the island of Gotland. It is extremely important that we train you into skilled fighters as quickly and efficiently as possible because the coming crusade will require that we know how to work well together in order to dispel even the most powerful heathen forces. Tomorrow, our journey begins.

The wake-up call is at the time of the rooster crowing in the morning. Sleep well and gather your strength for the upcoming trip."

Little did Meinbald know what they would be facing with these men, and what they would become; these fortune hunters collected from gutters and harbor taverns.

After his speech, the troops were organized to spend the night in a tent camp built in the port area. The marshal himself retired to his command tent in good time. At first, he felt like he didn't want to sleep, but finally he fell asleep.

The dream he had during the night felt so real. In the dream there were Finnish wild tribes who were dressed like pagan tribes and who spoke a strange witch-like language. Savages wrestled with bears and worshiped the great crown-headed primordial bull.

The dragon familiar from his childhood dreams returned again to fan its flames. Only this made him realize that he was dreaming and this was not real. He tried to wake up but couldn't. The whole night just had to be used for preliminary battles, oh St. George! Finland's future warrior nobility had to be created.

In the morning, when the rooster crowed, Fridrik blowed his horn to wake up and so all ten tents were dismantled and carried to the ships along with other equipment.

Meinbald and Fridrik walked to the Hansa-equipped command ship, which was already loaded with bandages and a field hospital tent ordered by Albert.

"This is where it starts, my brother, the journey towards the great unknown", he said to Fridrik.

Fridrik answered a little restlessly. "It's a shame that Finch went to another ship. He could lighten the mood."

"You speak the truth, brother Fridrik - perhaps we can hum some song that he has played for us on our many trips along the Elbe. Blow the horn, and then the two of us start to sing that song we learned in Hamburg and let's sing it so loud that we get the others to join us."

This is what they did, and in no time at all, the whole ship was hollering in polyphony with the same shrill rattling that was familiar to anyone who had wandered into any of the German region's taverns. And because the entire lead ship was singing, the song caught on to the next ship, then the next, until the entire fleet of five ships, which plowed its way across the Baltic Sea to the north, sang like there was no tomorrow.

You could imagine that the priest of the group would even protest and disapprove of not singing a hymn, but Kort sang along and enjoyed how all the unnecessary fear, worry and anxiety faded away from his mind. They managed to sing about twenty verses, after which each of the ships exploded into loud laughter.

At Visby on April 25, AD 1248

In the town of Visby, on the island of Gotland, the naval forces stopped at the port and held a day-long maintenance break. Meinbald walked to the Dominican monastery to meet Bishop Thomas to ask a little about the conditions in Finland. He was directed to the door of the chamber at the end of the narrow corridor.

Priori knocked on the door, and Thomas invited them in. After the introductions, Thomas told Meinbald his own story, how he had been the bishop of Finland but got beaten in Neva and betrayed by the Tavastian people.

"I feel that they stabbed me in the back. First, they converted to Christianity, but then next, they murdered the Swedish guards and turned to the Novgorodians again.

Absolutely incomprehensible! I tried to talk sense into them, but they refused to listen. However, I got a ride to Turku on the Tavastian captain's ship.

As a result of the events, I incurred the wrath of both the earl of Sweden and the squires of Livonia because, from their point of view, I was responsible for the betrayal and their abandonment on the battlefield."

"All my life I have done my work in good cooperation with your compatriots, Meinbald. That's why I came here to spend my last days, Visby is a Hanseatic city and full of well-behaved, friendly people who know German. This Dominican monastery is my last home; I feel that I am well taken care of here."

Thomas also revealed how there was currently no bishop in Finland and that he expected that Sweden was now filling this power vacuum.

"Meinbald, you should be on your guard and aware that even though the already Christian people in Finland want my successor to be raised from among them, that probably won't happen. Lord Birger has his own family in Sweden available for this seat."

Thomas had been in contact not only through the Visby Dominicans directly with the Pope, but also with the Dominican monastery founded by the Danes in Lund right from 1222. Now, he was sure that the information he had gotten through Lund was correct and that Sweden was being unified. According to reports, Birger had a strong plan, which included establishing a Dominican monastery in Finland, whose founder would be from Birger's close circle.

"Lord Birger of Bjälbo comes from a family that wants to take the entire Swedish crown for themselves. They don't avoid any means, and the church is just a way for them to get ahead in their quest for power. Remember this, Meinbald. And also remember who you are ultimately loyal to."

"I have received my orders from the Pope, who says that this crusade is God's will. Only to our Lord, I am faithful."

He also got tips from Thomas about the encounters between the Novgorodians and background information about their influence among the Finnish tribes.

Thomas had a very rough map of the local defense fortifications. He had gone on conversion trips in Tavast land with the help of the Sword Brethren but had not been able to get them to convert completely to the Western faith.

Thomas told how they, together with Bishop Hermann of Tartu, started the construction of the first fortress in Finland. A stone cellar had already been built in Ratzeburg, and the first protective pilings had already been driven in when suddenly all the Sword Brothers had to retreat back to Reval because the Tavastians had attacked and driven them off their land.

"Good luck on your journey! The competition between Rome and Byzantium continues", Thomas stated, as Meinbald bid him farewell.

May was approaching, but he noticed that the air in the north was a little cooler than in Lübeck. The men spent the rest of the day in Visby practicing military skills. The next morning, after the sun had risen, the ships sailed towards Stockholm.

Ingarö Island, April 27, AD 1248

Preparations for the war and training for combat continued on the island of Ingarö off Stockholm. Meinbald left the supervision of the training to Fridrik and attended to seek Lord Birger's company himself. Birger was clearly a very important lord because even getting to meet him required going through several prefaces.

The commander of the troops of the Teutonic Knights, who held their quarters in Idalen on the southern shore of the island of Ingarö, was the first that he found. Commander directed him to ride a couple of miles to the north, where Birger's command tent could be found. He was received politely by the Swedish knights. He had clearly already been expected there.

The men did not directly have a common language, so a local interpreter was used. Meinbald introduced himself to the reception committee saying that, according to the letter of order he had received, he was coming to report with his full military detachment to the command of Earl Birger.

The eldest of the gentlemen introduced himself and the others:

"I'm Bengt, the military marshal of Birger, the Earl of the Kingdom of Sweden. These younger gentlemen with me are my son and my armor bearer, Kettil. Next to him is young Sir Gregers, the Earl's own son, then junker Nils Sigridsson, Sune Ille's armor bearer, and here on the left are Olof Drake and Karl Ulv. Together, the four of us form Birger's ladder of command for the military forces. Herzlich Willkommen, Meinbald. Our Lord Birger has already been waiting for you; come with me, and I will introduce you to him."

They walked together towards Birger's command tent, outside of which were two guards armed with spears. He remembered how, as a child, he had been afraid when meeting Wenceslaus for the first time, even though Agnes had been with him and Kunigunde as an apron.

But he had been only human, and Meinbald hadn't felt any fear when meeting royals for many years, so this kind of earl from the north was hardly an odd case either. A red-haired man a little older than him immediately walked up to him to shake his hand.

"You must be Meinbald? I am Birger, you must have heard of me, just as I have received word from the Pope himself that you are coming. Welcome."

"Thank you, Lord Birger. Yes, I have heard a lot of good things about you. According to the Pope's command and the letter of command I received from my Grand Master Albert, I have assembled the army which I brought with me to assist your Grace in the Holy War in the East."

"Exactly, it's great that you arrived so soon. I would have known to miss you only a week from now, but now that you are already here, I have the best feeling that this joint effort of ours will have a very favorable wind." he quietly noted to himself how Birger's subordinates had told him the exact opposite; this indicated that their words couldn't be completely trusted - at least not yet.

"You can camp for the time being near the landing place of your ships", Birger continues. "You may continue to equip and train until we have held all necessary consultations and created a plan to carry out our joint campaign."

He went through in his mind how Birger seemed to be just as accustomed to a military commander as Wenceslaus in the battles against the Mongols. They exchanged a few meaningless pleasantries until Birger allowed him to exit back to camp.

When Meinbald bowed his head and made a turn towards the door of the tent, he noticed how a beautiful young lady had appeared behind him. He let his eyes rest on the girl's charms for a moment, and he noticed how the girl also looked at him deep in the eyes. The rules of his order flashed through his mind, and he had to force his gaze away from her lovely, deep blue eyes, turning his gaze to the ground.

"Meine Dame", he greeted the maiden. She nodded, accepting the compliment, and then looked questioningly at Birger.

"Father, who is this stranger, and what language does he speak?"

"My daughter, let me introduce you to each other"

"Sir Meinbald, Land Marshal of the Order of the Red Star and Cross sent by the Pope, may I introduce you my daughter, Hildegard. Hildegard, this is Meinbald, Commander of the Order of the Red Star and Cross." His and Hildegard's eyes met again, and a warm smile appeared on both of their faces.

"Miss Hildegard, it's a pleasure to meet you."

"The same, Sir Meinbald, indeed the same", Hildegard replied.

He nodded to Birger and forced himself to leave, even though he wanted to stay. While returning on his horse, he noticed how Dominican monks in their black robes were walking with the bishop. Sigtuna monastery had been founded ten years earlier, in the year of the Tavast land rebellion. When he returned to the camp, he remembered that the Pope had also sent Dominicans in a ship after them, and indeed, the ship had been seen even before turning into the Stockholm fjord, but now it was nowhere to be seen.

He waited in the camp for a couple of days, watching the training of the new men, until he received a letter of invitation from the messenger for a meeting at Birger's command tent.

In the meeting, they introduced themselves and got to know other department commanders. Birger personally introduced

Meinbald to everyone. A new acquaintance, whom he had not met before since he had arrived, was called John Teet. Birger mentioned he was "Scottish," a tight-lipped but greedy mercenary - and revealed that he's on very good terms with him. The men shook hands.

John spoke a strange language that Meinbald did not understand, but Birger's interpreter did and translated Scottish as fluently as German and Swedish. John told him that he was a former Knight Templar and that he had been in the service of King Valdemar of Denmark when Denmark had conquered Estonia and founded town of Reval. When it was his turn to introduce himself, he said briefly:

"I am Meinbald, Marshal of the Order of the Red Star and Cross from Bohemia. I fought in King Wenceslaus' army against the Mongols, and we repelled their invasion of Bohemia. I have come from the Pope's command to support your Holy War, and I bring with me bandages. We will establish a field hospital where we can treat the wounded in future battles." When the interpreter translated this into Swedish, there were many happy comments, and Birger himself stated:

"It is absolutely wonderful that our ecclesiastical father has sent his best professional soldiers, even troops capable of field care, here to support us! This will surely increase the desire and courage of all of us to give our all to conquer those stubborn, misguided bastards and drive the damned heretical Novgorodians out of our lands!"

The consultation continued in the afternoon with getting to know each other, and the distribution of orders were arranged for the next morning.

In the distribution of orders, the war plan presented by Birger was reviewed. There were three attack routes: The first was the northern route, along the Kokemäki River, to Tavast land.

"I shall assign you, Meinbald, with your section to this offensive path. The province of Satakunta, which the river cuts through, is very peaceful and favorable for us. For years, merchant ships have sailed up the river to the trading post, which bears the name "Koggimäki" – the Cog Hill. The name comes from the ships of the Hanseatic League. I believe that since you know German, you can form a good alliance with the locals, and together, you can continue the attack inland, all the way to the waters of Vanaja. Do you have any questions, Marshal Meinbald?"

"I do have one proposal and a related question, Lord Birger. Can we keep a messaging connection with pigeons? We have a flock of pigeons that have been trained all the way in Bohemia. Do you have already trained pigeons?"

"That's a great idea, yes we have them. Watch with Marshal Bengt that the pigeons learn to recognize the baskets, we can fly pigeons already when we move to Turku."

"Great, we'll look into it together", he answered and looked at Bengt, who also nodded, acknowledging that the matter was agreed.

"Good. Then another route, from the south to the Tavastian Kukinjoki to the north", Birger continued.

"This route of attack is taken by you, Teet. You get your squires and mercenaries from Reval, and after crossing the

Gulf of Finland, you sail straight up the river to the inland. We have used that route many times. After crossing a couple of isthmuses, you can go up the river to a small lake, next to which is the fort I built. You are waiting there for my troops; we will head there with the knights commanded by Bengt by land route. When we meet there, estimated to be about five days later, we will continue by boat, sailing together up to lake Vanaja, by which the Tavastian people live and cultivate their pagan land. So we will strike right into their heart from both the West and the South and put an end to their persistent heathenism forever."

At the beginning of May they left. The largest army that Christian Sweden had ever seen was moving as a naval force through Mariehamn to Taivassalo, where a church base had been established a hundred years earlier.

Meinbald marvelled at the archipelago sea after Mariehamn; he had never seen anything like this before *"How long will this puzzle and maze continue?"*

Finally, as they approached the port on the mainland, he noticed that the Dominicans from the Visby monastery had sailed straight here. Their ship lied empty on the ropes in the harbor as his ships docked.

Birger introduced Bishop Bero to him, quickly urging the men to agree on the necessary arrangements for the conversion of the Gentiles.

"From Bero, you will get Dominican friars on your way, who are prepared to convert the pagans as soon as you have disarmed them. Remember, if they don't convert, you'd better let them out of their misery. Know that this heathen nation loves treachery and revenge, so if you kill the father, kill their children as well. You shouldn't kill mothers. As a rule, women are not vengeful. Of course, there are exceptions; use your judgment.

Now, organize your troops and food supply, and then leave as soon as possible for the northern attack route. You should keep in constant contact with Bengt so that we know how and where the fronts are advancing and where we shall meet. You will set up your field hospital only where we face the enemy together. I swear that's when it's really needed. I have seen for myself how the bastards slaughtered my best military guard on the Neva River years ago. My daughter Hildegard is joining, Sir Meinbald, on your journey. She knows how to bind wounds and she has been taught by my mother in herbal secrets. You protect the honor of the maiden in your brotherhood, and you know how to deal with nuns, too, don't you?"

"Yes, Lord Earl, your word is our law. We are protecting the Hildegard maiden from the pagans, and it is great to have her on our journey who knows northern herbs."

Chapter VI
Sons of Kaleva

Early May, AD 1248

Meinbald's five ships sailed up the coast of the Gulf of Bothnia. A new pilot had boarded the leading ship in Taivassalo, who knew the coast of the Gulf of Bothnia in addition to the archipelago route.

Thanks to the southwest wind, they were able to move forward rather hastily. The pilot had followed the coast to the north all day since their departure. The spring sun had been giving daylight for quite a long time, although it had not significantly warmed up yet.

The pilot steered the leading cog closer to the shore seeking shelter as the evening darkened. They dropped anchors side by side on the sheltered shore of the bay. He examined the map and concluded that tomorrow they would already be on the trade river, as long as they left as soon as the morning broke, to continue sailing.

Karl Ulv, a member of Bengt's leadership ladder, was also on his flagship. He approached to talk to him.

"Herr Marshal, I know German, so I will be happy to act as your interpreter when you need one."

"Herr Karl, it's great that you know German. My Swedish skills are pretty much non-existent. Of course, many of your words are very similar to the words we use, but it is still difficult to understand and follow the conversation at times. We definitely need to keep in touch a lot, because the better we understand the situation, the better we can avoid unnecessary misunderstandings with the locals and we can avoid unnecessary casualties."

"It's great that you say that, that's exactly what I think! We Swedes have been trading with the Tavastian people for a long time. There are already many people living on their shores who know our language and have even married into our families."

Meinbald and Karl seemed to get along so well that their conversation did not want to end at all, until darkness fell and it was bed time.

In the morning, the journey continued at the time of rooster crowing. The pilot continued to guide the lead ship, following the coast up to the north. In the afternoon, he steered the ship and the entire fleet following it through a narrow strait and then turned to starboard towards the shore.

The crew woke up and started to look at the beach in front of them, which, as they approached, revealed itself as a large river estuary. The air was cool, and even though the sun had just been shining from a partly cloudy sky at sea, in the river estuary, it suddenly started to rain in big, moist flakes. Meinbald pulled on a cowhide jacket so as not to get completely soaked.

Hildegard, whom he had taken to his own ship to protect her, tried to find words he could understand. He spoke German and also understood Czech, but he couldn't understand

Swedish without an interpreter. Knight Karl came to their aid to interpret:

"Miss Hildegard would like to know if this river is the old trading river of the Tavastian people", Karl translated.

"Yes, this should be it. This castle at the mouth of the river is the landmark I was looking for," he replied and showed them both the map he had gotten from Thomas. After unrolling the map scroll, he immediately realized that it was a bad idea, because map paper got wet quickly in this weather. So, he quickly wrapped the map back in the leather protective tube.

Past the fortress at river Kokemajoki, the ships continued along the river inland without stopping. The ships floated slowly up the river past the castle by rowing. A few spear guards were seen on the walls, not making a move, just staring at the fleet that had suddenly appeared in front of them from the sea.

"They don't go out to raise an alarm or attack. So, let's just go forward," Meinbald commanded the rowers.

After a short rowing journey, they were met by a settlement in a place where the upstream of the river started to become too big for the rowers. The ships were anchored on the south bank of the river, and the cargo was unloaded. Their landing was noticed, and a group of people quickly started approaching the shore. He tried to see from a distance whether they had weapons in their hands.

"Keep your weapons hidden, but within reach," he commanded.

When the crowd was close enough to make out their faces, he let out a sigh of relief. Their hands were empty, and their expressions showed no hostility. Instead, the crowd seemed friendly, and the elder of the crowd spread his arms wide open and begun to speak in an audible voice. Meinbald didn't understand the words, but their tone was gentle and calm. These local people spoke Swedish, so Hildegard could converse with them, as well as the two Swedish knights Sune and Karl who came along. Meinbald understood enough of Hildegard's words and gestures that, from here on, they had to continue on horseback or using the smaller boats of the locals, which they happily offered to travelers. Karl translated into German and confirmed his understanding.

"Are they Christians?"

"Yes, these people are baptized Christians, and they told us that their leader sits higher up by this river. They urged us to go to him."

Meinbald paused for a moment before ordering the knights to mount and the horsemen to take the spare horses with them as well.

The knights jumped on their horses, the men-at-arms took light riverboats which the locals called "haapios", to carry them above the rapids, from where they continued their journey by rowing.

May 10th AD 1248

In Janakkala's fortress Hakoinen, Birger's forces had a bigger battle with the Novgorod detachment. Hakoinen's was burned. Teet and his boatmen arrived to help, along with the Knights of the Sword and mercenaries.

Some of his men had been there already ten years ago, when they had been driven away by the Tavastian rascals. However, there were also completely new men, such as Asser, who had moved from Constantinople to Danish-ruled Reval. He had joined a group of a few former Knights Templar when they had decided to go north to seek new adventures.

After meeting Teet in Estonia by chance, Asser and the other badass of the party, Berlhold, decided to join him. They had heard from Teet that the Swedes were now seeking the lordship of Tavastia and the removal of Novgorod from the region permanently. Their decision to join was greatly helped when Teet mentioned that the profits would pay handsome fees, possibly also in land.

In Hakoinen, all the Novgorodians left to fight were killed. However, a large part of them retreated through the forests to the south. Bengt sent a small shock detachment after them to make sure the enemy didn't mass and strike their rear. Olof Drake and two horsemen rode after the enemy.

Kokemäenjoki, May 16, Anno Domini 1248

Meinbald and Lydeke had been flying carrier pigeons every day with Birger and his marshal Bengt. There were 14 pigeons in each loft, and they were flown daily, whenever the lofts moved, so that the pigeons could follow the familiar loft and return to it to be fed.

When one wanted to send a message, the pigeon in the messenger queue was left unfed. This was how it changes varnish. Today, Bengt had time to send the pigeon first, and it arrived with a message. Lydeke opened the message and read, "16.5.1248, Hackois fortress. Yesterday, Olof Drake and his men returned, saying that the Novgorodians are coming back with reinforcements to attack our rear. We were grouped in the terrain of the burnt fort, well prepared. We destroyed the enemy's vanguard and repulsed the entire attack, driving the rest of the reinforcements to the ground. Now we gather our strength overnight, and tomorrow we continue north. Report enemy contact immediately if you receive one. With good luck, we will meet soon somewhere in the heart of Tavastia. On behalf of Jarl Birger, Marshal Bengt."

All of Meinbald's troops landed on Koggemäki. There was a big iron chain in front, which prevented progress to the upper reaches of the river. The local chief and his men calmly waited for the knights and men-at-arms to advance along the river and its banks.

Meinbald and Fridrik stopped to stand alert on the riverbank when the chief and his entourage came to meet them. The crowd was armed, but the gray-haired, moustached, moose-skin-clad chief extended his unarmed arms to them and smiled broadly.

"You're not Swedish? Are you Saxman?" the captain asked, speaking Finnish.

"Sachsmann, Ich?" Nein! "Ich bin aus Böhm. Ich heisse Meinbald. I am on the crusade blessed by Pope Innocentius, bringing the salvation message of our true Lord and his son Jesus, the Christ, here to a land occupied by false believers. Who are you, and are you prepared to receive our gospel by becoming a Christian?"

"Ich bin Faravid, the Far-sighted," Kaukomieli answered in German so that he had no trouble understanding him. The old man laughed out loud and continued, "I have been a Christian all my life. I was baptized and accepted into our Lord's church when I was just a couple of weeks old little baby."

After hearing his name, Kaukomieli starts calling him in Finnish "Mielivalta".

The gentlemen got along well; Kaukomieli knew German quite well. Meinbald thought that he would like to learn a little Finnish, especially since he had seen Kaukomieli's beautiful daughter, Elin. He found it a bit difficult to say the matter out loud, but he concluded that the ancient customs found to work in the Baltics also worked here.

"Chief Kaukomieli. I demand hostages from you. And not just anyone, but I want you to give me ten of your closest warriors to fight with us against the heretics. I have heard that there are Novgorodians here, and I want you to know that we are going to defeat them and drive them out of here. I also insist that your eldest son be among those ten. Your daughter is very beautiful and charming. I would like to see her free and laughing and enjoying her brother's company in the future, when our journey together is finished, and we release the hostages we took back to you."

Kaukomieli clearly had not expected such a direct demand. He thought quietly to himself for a moment and then stated, "It's fine. I understand the old ways perhaps even more than you think. Since you ask me to give my son Matti to you, know these two things: One, he has already achieved the rank of centurion at a young age and he will show everyone how brave Kaleva's boys really can be. Two, in order to hand him over to you, I will join that battle group of yours myself. You do not know our ways or our defenses, but I assure you that it would be of more use to all of us to go inland with you, than to send one of my men to fight for me, and stay here to fear whether you will return in one piece, or whether my wife will make a hack of me too, if you do not return. So let's go together to Vesilahti, where Matti is now leading his men."

His knights jumped on the horses, but the squires, gunmen, priests, and monks headed from Koggemäki along the waterways on river boats to Tavast land. Meinbald and Kaukomieli and their men advanced on horses because it was much faster.

"This is a very friendly chief. I wouldn't have dreamt of advancing towards the pagan territory under the guidance of a Christian local chief" he thought as they rode along the river.

Vesilahti, May 18. AD 1248

The Novgorodians had recruited Karelians with them for their own crusade. They had made it as far as Narva in Vesilahti, where Matti's Hundred ("satakunta" in Finnish) of Pirkka confronted them. The Novgorodians had camped at the marketplace that had been formed as a result of the fur trade, located near the shore of Lake Pyhäjärvi ("Pyhä järvi" means Wholy lake). Matti, son of Kaukomieli led his troops from the front. They attacked the unprepared Novgorodian army with surprise superiority right at dawn.

The battle was bloody, and as the name "satakunta" suggests; there were about hundred men of Pirkka, and about twice as many of their enemies. Suddenly the camp exploded into full chaos. Matti found the command tent and cut the head of chief Jaroslav swiftly with his sword.

Matti had warriors, among others, descendants of Osmo the Karelian, who had settled to lands of Pirkka. They attacked the Karelians and disarmed everyone they caught alive. Some of the Karelians fled with the Novgorodians towards Lake Pyhäjärvi.

Meanwhile, Meinbald and Kaukomieli had advanced along the banks of the Kokemäki river as far as Kaukola farm in Sastamala. Kaukomieli suggested that they set up camp for the night in Kaukola, which was his farm. It suited him well.

At the campfire, Kaukomieli suggested, "Brother Meinbald, I would like us to go meet our seer, who lives here close to Kaukola's sacred grove Hiisi."

"I've never met a seer before, so it fits perfectly. I'm looking forward to hearing what he says"

Shaman Vehnäpää, an old man with a gray beard, lied down on the floor and began to chant a spell. He fell into trance and predicted death to the Karelians and Novgorodians, but also to some Tavastians.

"Many people loose their heads!" he shouted. "The cruel horsemen of distant steppes have come with them! But the Swedes, the Saxons, and the Pirkkas will win together. Kaleva's ridges will protect them, and Tavastia will see a different fait than was the fait of the poor folks of Väinölä."

Kaukomieli translated the seers words briefly to him. He also explained him the locals' religion and gods, "Our seers know how to travel in both the overworld and the underworld, just like our numerous gods do. They can go there to learn about future events or spells that can affect them. Ukko is our overlord, and his wife is Rauni. Tapio is the Finnish god of the forest and hunting. Blacksmith Ilmarinen, the forger of the sky, is the god of weather and atmosphere. It was his wind which hastily blew your boat here from the Åland Sea. Some of our people still completely believe in the old gods, some believe only in the Christian God, and some fluently in both."

"What do you believe in, Kaukomieli?" he asked directly.

"I believe what my seer tells me. And as for gods, well, I already said that I am a Christian."

The next morning, they continued on horseback further inland. Kaukomieli knew how to lead the riders along the fastest route. The waterway they had followed stretched as far as the eye could see, cutting through the flat landscape of wide fields and small forested islets.

"We should turn straight east after the next open field," said Kaukomieli. "The waterway curves farther north until it reaches a long stretch of rapids. Don't worry, Mielivalta. Antero's guide will tell the boat convoy behind us when it's time to come ashore and carry their boats over the land ridge to the small stream flowing into Lake Pyhäjärvi."

The horsemen turned away from the water route and headed from the open fields toward the rolling forest terrain. The path ahead grew narrower and more difficult with each step. Soon, they had to dismount and continue on foot, leading their horses.

"There's a swamp ahead that we must cross. It's the only swamp on our route, and I know its paths well, so there's no need to worry," Kaukomieli reassured them.

So they marched onward until a wide, boggy marsh opened before them. A wooden, plank-reinforced path cut through the swamp.

"We have plenty of these swamps here, Mielivalta," Kaukomieli remarked. "You have to watch where you step and where you lead your steed, so it doesn't sink into the bog's eye."

"At least here, we don't have to fear an enemy cavalry charge," Meinbald thought to himself.

After a long, exhausting, damp, and sweat-filled crossing that demanded constant focus, they finally reached dry land again and could mount their horses. The terrain, however, was still so rough that they had to proceed with great caution and at a slow pace.

Eventually, by evening, they reached the top of a hill, where they set up camp for the night. The hill stood by a long but rather narrow lake.

"We'll cross that lake tomorrow morning by raft, and then continue our journey on horseback. We'll reach Vesilahti by early afternoon," Kaukomieli said with determination.

Meinbald wondered a little at the old man's haste but thought it was simply the eagerness to see his son. It was time to make a fire and lie down to rest; exhaustion weighed heavily on them, though the light still felt strangely bright.

Chapter VII
Novgorod retreats

May 20th, AD 1248

The sun was shining very brightly from a cloudless sky, giving its warmth in the afternoon so that sweat drops fell from crusaders' backs and foreheads. The weather in inner land was shiny and calm, leaving the winds from the coast just a distant memory.

Meinbald, Kaukomieli and their men arrived in the village of Narva when the battle was already over. Matti had won, and the remaining two boats full of men retreated rapidly towards lake Päijänne, where they had come from.

Matti and Meinbald met on the battlefield in the Novgorod camp.

Many Karelians and Novgorodians had fallen, about three times as many as the Pirkka-men were laying dead on the ground. Blood-covered Matti was surprised by his father's presence, but after he had explained the situation, he understood that it was best for him to yield as a hostage to Herr Meinbald, according to tradition. Matti handed his sword to this crusader, who was about eight years older than him. He accepted the sword, admiring its skillful forging.

"Ulfberht," he read the inscription on the sword.

"I've heard of these mythical swords, but I've never seen one before, and now, suddenly, I'm holding one in my hand! Matti, you must earn my trust with your actions, and you will get your wonderful sword back soon, do you understand?"

"I understand," Matti answered in German and nodded his head down.

The pursuit had to be started, and they had to make sure that the Novgorodians were not seeking new forces and troops to attack again. Matti told that he had men in a nearby fortress who took care of protecting the women and children, so they had to go in pursuit themselves. They rode their horses to Castle Rock, where the scouts told them that the Novgorodians had landed and were camping at the upper reaches of rapid Kuokkalankoski. No other troops had been seen, and no new signal fires had been lit.

Meinbald stated: "We will wait to see where they will go in the morning. Matti, ask your guards to keep an eye on them all night and notify me immediately if they make a departure. I want to follow where they're going; I'm sure they'll be applying for reinforcements."

Matti translateds his instructions into Finnish. He also seemed to understand German well, even if he didn't really like to speak it himself, like his father.

Kaukomieli told about Girmund, a chief locals called "Kirmu", who had finally converted to Christianity and had lived here before. Before his conversion, he had fought for years against the priests and soldiers of Novgorod. He had even been to Novgorod on a revenge trip with his friend Urth. Urth had lived in this very castle mansion.

The "Moisios" were the master's estates. There was even a manor near here. The "Hiisis" were the farms of the sorcerers; there were fewer of them, but there was one in front of the long narrow water way, "Hiidenvuolle". In between there was the Kuokkalankoski rapid.

Bishop Thomas began to label the Hiisi and the seers as evil and had their sacred groves razed to the ground. After all, the people of Kaleva did not allow that but washed away their baptism and turned against Thomas's church and men. Thomas had to call the Sword Brothers to his aid, but they were quickly defeated and had to retreat from Tavastia.

Kaukomieli told how the Germans had been visiting here in the north for hundreds of years. His own trading places, like, Eura and Koggimäki, had seen many generations of Saxons before him, and he had inherited all this information from his parents. In fact, his own father, the late Satakunta king Kaukomieli, had once said that they, too, were descended from the Saxons. That's why the language had been passed down well in the family until today.

Meinbald recalled a story from more than 400 years ago, which he had heard from the monk brothers in Bohemia:

"Widukind defended the independence of the Saxons against Charlemagne until the year 777 of the Lord. Finally, he suffered a defeat, Widukind was imprisoned, and he converted to Christianity. Henri the Fowler's wife, Mathilde, was a descendant of Widukind; she even had a brother of the same name. Their child, Otto, became Emperor Otto I. Henry of Saxony made Wenceslaus the Holy, the Duke of Bohemia, pay tribute to himself, i.e., Wenceslaus' Bohemia became a vassal of Saxony."

One of Henry's daughters, Adelheid, was married to the Duke of Bohemia, but she died very young in childbirth. She was buried in Prague Castle. Agnes had told about her, and he had visited her grave as a child, together with his sister Kunigunde.

"We have also heard about the old Visukinttu here", Kaukomieli said.

"Some of the Low Saxons have claimed that some of his men came here from Denmark and that they claimed some lands for themselves. But such men have not been seen here! Traveling preachers have instead said that Visukinttu is the devil, i.e., the main devil himself."

"Listen, Kaukomieli, I too have heard about those men who visited here from Denmark. Help was sought here for Widukind's last battle, and Irminsul seedlings were brought here, which were planted here and there on the coasts. Your sacred groves, where you worship your gods, they are likely to date back to that time. The Low Saxons brought the trees here, and they also brought your pagan beliefs."

"Be quiet, young man. We have had groves for several centuries, and our gods and our deceased have lived here long before Visukinttu... But now that I think about it, you might be right with that idea of yours, Mielivalta, my friend — we may have many roots in common, not only in the trees you speak of but also in us humans. In terms of names, we have a lot of Germunds, Gertrudes, and other Saxons."

"A hundred years ago, my grandfather set out through Lapland to take revenge on the Karelians of Väinö for their raids with three Hundreds of Satakunta's best warriors. They allied themselves with the Norwegians in the Lapland fells, crossed them together and struck hard among the Karelian robbers."

"The military campaigns with the Norwegians have always been smooth and favorable; with the Swedes, it has played out so that we have had to bear the heaviest responsibilities. But we have gotten along with both neighboring tribes and, in the end, have always agreed on how the trade is taxed and distributed. The Swedes and Norwegians have also tried to attack and rob us here in the past, but after all, that has ended very quickly when they have gotten a blow to their noses."

"Well, last summer, some Karelians came into exile from the east of their country. They told me that my old enemy, Aleksander Nevski, had attacked their hilltop castles along the Väinö river. Or the 'river of Vjiena,' as the Russians call it. Alexander had a large army of horsemen from the steppes, Tatars, and cavalry with him, and they had shown no mercy to Väinölä's people."

"Some had dug themselves into hiding in forests and earthen pits, hoping to stay where they were, but many males and their families had fled to the west, some to the south, and some to the north to the Norwegian lands, some all the way to King Harald's court."

"After all, they had been trading for centuries, and Jomali, whom they worshiped, had protected them from the greatest destruction, even though some Norwegians had robbed them. Now, however, all that power of theirs have been defeated, their wealth looted, and their homes destroyed."

"The Silver Road, which led far from Mesopotamia all the way to the river Väinö and the sea, has now been taken over by the Novgorodians all the way up to the northern sea."

"Then, even our seers saw that this did not stop here but that we had to start equipping ourselves. One of the people from

Väinönheim, who escaped from the hands of the Novgorodians, told me that Alexander Nevski, the great warlord and Russian hero, had gone to the Golden Horde and finally all the way to the Mongol Horde in order to gain the favor of the Grand Khan of the Tatars and apparently succeeded.

A year passed, so here we are; the Novgorodians have replaced their Tatar hordes with the Karelians they subjugated, and they were able to strike here right into our heartlands. Looting is now being done in the name of their Byzantine Church, and they are trying to convert us 'Jems,' as they call us, under their faith."

"Oh, have the Mongols struck here in the north as well? In the south, in Poland and Moravia, they also sowed destruction and devastation. But they didn't get to Bohemia because we, the troops of King Wenceslaus, repulsed them. The Tatars went to Hungary, from which they suddenly withdrew, leaving all of Europe in peace."

"It's great to hear that you've had contact with those savages of the steppes and that you've managed to beat them. Frankly, I doubt that we and the Swedes would be able to do the same for them, although the Swedish knights are a very magnificent sight with their shiny shields and breastplates. Our warriors are brave, but deterrence and protection are very lacking. The Tatars also have firearms with them, explosive bullets that tear holes in the fortresses."

"Yes, we also saw them in Moravia, and we are studying such a firearm that resembles Greek fire."

Kaukomieli told that by no means were all the chiefs and kings here as sympathetic to the Germans or Swedes as he was. For example, by Lake Vanajavesi in Sääksenmäki there lived King Ragvald, who was called "Rapo" by the locals. He would never surrender without a fight if they tried to force him to kneel to some otherworldly power.

With the Novgorodians, on the other hand, Rapo was a good match. For example, those Novgorods that Matti had driven away had made it all the way to Vesilahti without having a single signal fire lit. If even one had been lit, they would have had no chance of getting through Hiidenvuolle or past Pirunlinna. Now, instead, they had managed to completely surprise the men of Pirkka.

In the morning, Meinbald's division crossed Kuokkalankoski, following the Novgorod division, which included some Karelians. The Russian boats retreated to Hiidenvuolle, getting his boats on their heels.

He wanted to follow the squad so that they would maintain line of sight but were not in striking range until the time was right. So, he gathered the horses to a river ferry.

Chapter VIII
Battle of Sääksenmäki

May 21, AD 1248

The spring sun was still shining from a cloudless sky and warming, driving away the coolness of the night well before midday. The Tavastian men, women and children of the Sääksenmäki had all taken refuge in the wooden escape fortress of the local king, Rapo. The fortress had been built on top of a steep hill called Rapolanvuori. The fortress guards saw how down on lake Vanajanselkä the two Novgorod boats landed, grouping up to take on the Swedish troops approaching from the south along Vanajanselkä.

The two ships of the Novgorodians had landed at a small peninsula, with a land connection to Rapolanvuori. The other half of the detachment landed on the cape on the southern shore of Vanaja.

Meinbald and Kaukomieli were just sailing and rowing along the lake shore from the west to see when the beaching took place. He made a quick decision and commanded:

"I will take my boat over there to the castle hill; we will land and strike the enemy with the full force of our knights. Kaukomieli, you take your boat and knock out that enemy division on the right!"

Kaukomieli showed that he understood and yelled, "Let's do it! They will become hacks because they are not covering their backs. Remember, Mielivalta, that you have the largest fortress in this country in your back, and its commander is not as friendly to you as I am!"

Meinbald made a bold attack on the Novgorod detachment. The knights stroke six men dead until the rest lowered their swords and surrendered. Kaukomieli hit the other department grouped in Jylhänniemi just as effectively. No man could escape. They took nine prisoners.

When Birger's fleet was close enough to hear the sounds of battle, they turned their course and landed. From there on, they advanced on horseback towards the fortress.

#

Birger's troops advanced towards Rapolanlinna. They knew what they were doing because they had already conquered several fortresses on the way. Fortresses Hakoinen, Kiianlinna, Palvaanlinna, Hakovuori, Aulanko and Tenhola had already all surrendered, and Birger's force had not lost a single man. The blood on their clothes had been spilled from Novgorodians and some few Tavastians who had not unconditionally renounced their paganism and accepted the baptism of Christianity.

After finishng the enemy section on the shore, his knights put on their armor, as they only had been wearing light equipment during the boat journey. Putting on the ring shirt and protectors required the help of another man, so they worked in pairs. After getting his own and helping Fridrik's gear on, Meinbald sent a messenger back with orders to set up a field hospital in the immediate vicinity of their landing site. Finally, he also put on his helmet.

His own breathing sounded heavy in his ears. The mesh limited visibility so that he had to turn his head to see his teammate when giving the marching order.

"Brother Fridrik, let's ride after the Swedes now; the battle awaits. Blow your horn so that even the stern will know that we have contact with the Gentiles."

Birger rode as the third of his armored cavalry division towards the southern gate of the fortress, where the road arose steeply. The steepness forced them to dismount only 20 meters before the gate. Birger's Finnish interpreter, riding in front, shouted:

"Rapo and the people of the castle! Earl Birger Magnusson of the Swedish Empire has arrived to free you from your pagan ways once and for all. Open your gate and surrender to receive God's grace and blessing. We came to baptize you into our Lord's church!"

Rapo climbed up to the rampart of the gate himself and shouted back:

"Tell your master that free men and women live here who will not accept anything from you. Go on your journeys, and leave us alone. Novgorod had already baptized all those of us who wanted to abandon the old gods and convert to the faith of the Lord of the Cross."

After hearing the interpretation, Birger ordered the archers following on foot to straighten their bows and to aim at the firing holes of the fortress. He knew the Finns' defensive tactics and was in no rush to get any closer to the goal.

Meinbald's men arrived on horseback, as did Kaukomieli's men of Pirkka. Kaukomieli greeted Birger politely and asked to say a few words to this king of Sääksenmäki. Birger was amazed that Kaukomieli introduced himself as Faravid and that he spoke intelligible Swedish.

"Var så god," Birger stated and pointed towards the gate.

"Ragvald, listen to me! I'm Kaukomieli, the Far-Minded, and I'm called the king of Satakunta. You are known even among our bravest men of Pirkka as an unyielding warrior who shows no mercy to his enemies. Now, hear what I have to say to you!"

"Kaukomieli, I've heard of you too, and we've met at least twice, in Kokkimäki and most recently in Vanaintaa. You've always been more of a merchant than a warrior, so I guess I shouldn't be surprised that you fraternize with these Swedes. What do you want to say to me, you Kauppo of Satakunta, you con man of Kokkimäki, and what do you say to my tribe who has fled these enemies of my people you brought to my gate here before our castle, which is, as you probably know, an impregnable refuge shaped by our ancient gods and protected by our wizards?"

"I tell you, Ragvald, king of Rapola, if you have any sense in your head, you will now open your gate and receive us in peace. You don't want to clash with these gentlemen; you see how their gear is shiny and sturdy compared to your leather guards! Your arrows will not penetrate the armor these knights wear."

Ragvald thought for a moment and then ordered his men to open the gates, showing them the agreed attack sign at the same time. The gate was stormed by a heavily equipped detachment of six horsemen with their swords ready to strike down anyone who came their way.

"To arms!" Kaukomieli commanded and drew his sword. He nimbly turned aside in front of the first attacking horseman.

Meinbald quickly pushed Birger aside and parried the swinging sword strike with his own sword.

"Mein Gott! Novgorodians! Men, charge on!"

His monk brothers acted as they were used to. Kort, Klas and Otto also parried the blows quickly with their swords. Dietrich knocked one of the men off his horse with his axe. The horse also fell at the same time, letting out a big squeal.

Kaukomieli's and Matti's men from Pirkka pulled out their swords and prepared to receive the attack farther back, lower down. Birger's Swedish knights also raised their shields and swords to be ready. There was no one from them to protect Birger in front and the Swedes knew that nothing good would come of it unless they showed their skills now and slayed the enemy.

Kaukomieli's men got a couple of riders dropped; the remaining three got through to the Swedes. Unbridled fighting and disunity ensued. Meinbald's men ran in through the gate, Kort first, followed by Klas and Otto. He advanced in the middle of the crowd, followed by Dietrich, Gödecke and Lydeke. Kort got some boiled water down his neck, but luckily, most of it missed his eyes, so he didn't become completely incapacitated.

Behind him, Otto Schwerd, true to his nickname, let his sword sing and swing and hit the first gatekeeper to death. Ignoring his slight pain, Kort charged towards the King, because he had a plan to end this fight in a very short time. Kort got up the ladder in no time fighting with Rapo's bodyguard at the same time. The guard made a mistake in his protection, and Kort used the moment to stab the man directly in the chest with his sword and killed him. Rapo was still on the rampart of the gate, but after realizing that that crazy German was still going to come over, he decided to go down the second ladder while he still could. But a surprise awaited him below: Meinbald had anticipated the move and threatened now Ragvald's neck directly with his sword blade.

"Put down your weapon and surrender, he said in a calm but audible voice." Ragvald stopped and, after thinking for a moment, dropped his sword on the ground.

"Command your men further away; also, tell the Novgorodians to lay down their weapons. RIGHT NOW!" Kaukomieli, who had arrived, translated Meinbald's sentences into Finnish for Ragvald.

Ragvald obeyed and quickly calmed down the situation with his order. Gödecke climbed up to the rampart of the gate after Kort and shouted happily: "This war was over very quickly! The King and his men have surrendered to us!"

The Novgorodians, with their horses, were repulsed and knocked down from their steeds. The survivors were captured and now the Swedish knights also rushed in through the gate. The armed guards inside the fortress were quickly disarmed and forced to their knees on the ground.

There were even more Novgorodians and Karelians hidden in the protective moat in the middle of the hill fortress. Some of them retreated from the back gate to their ships in Vanaja to escape after seeing the superiority of the enemy. Some of the men dispersed to the nearby woods to gather strength for another attack. However, no one noticed this until the guards left on the boat by Kaukomieli saw two ships full of men rowing and sounded the alarm by blowing a horn. Matti and Meinbald's hastily gathered strike group plannned to go on a chase together with horses and ships. Meinbald left Fridrik with the command:

"Brother Fridrik, you act as marshal now; take the horn, the flag and the men in your command. We catch the fleeing Novgorodians. They must not be able to assemble auxiliaries for a new attack."

"Brother Meinbald, I accept the task with a heavy heart. Don't kill yourselves, but come back safe - remember what happened to Henry of Silesia when the Mongols pretended to escape."

"Meinbald, I will come with you", Kaukomieli intervened. "I know the waterways and have been to the lands of the Karelians. Matti, my son, don't teach your father how to fight. Of course, I've been through wars when I was young. And the last time, when you were just a little boy, I was on the Neva river with my men on a military expedition led by Bishop Thomas." Soon the chasing group was already riding to the boats.

Fridrik blew the horn as a signal, gathering the men around him. He wasn't yet at all sure that this would be over so easily.

"Men, Meinbald went in pursuit with a strike group, but now we have to make sure that the fortress is not going to be attacked through, say, our backs. Kort, you take the first ward and go to the north side of the fortress. Klas, you take the second section and deploy to the defense east of the south gate. Division Three will come with me. We will set up camp on the forecourt of the south gate of the fort."

Chapter IX
The End Of Paganism In Tavastia

Tavastia, in the afternoon of May 21, AD 1248

Escaped Karelians rowed along Lake Vanaja for their lives. Meinbald's and Kaukomieli's boats chased after them about half a mile behind. The spotter sitting on the prow saw how the Karelians turned between shore and island to a new lake back.

The Karelians went ashore and carried the boats over the isthmus to launch them back in the water. Meinbald, Kaukomieli, and Gerhard, a German knight who had joined them, followed ashore and jumped on their horses to catch up with the fleeing boats by land. They rode at full gallop to the thin isthmus between lakes Hauhonselkä and Roine, just to see how the Karelians had managed to continue their escape journey to great Roine.

Through Hauho, they continued on their horses to the narrows between Roine and Pyhäjärvi but could only watch from the shore as the Karelians rowed towards yet another lake. While the rowers had to sweat through lakes, the trio of riders could travel more calmly, following the boats. Kaukomieli told Meinbald:

"From Ormajärvi, it is a couple of miles march to Lammi hill fortress, from where you can reach lake Pääjärvi. From the side of the Mustijoki, which leaves the eastern end of the main lake, there is also a land march of a mile to the river, which leads to Lahdenpohja, from where you can then go all the way to the sea along the river Kymijoki. Alternatively, from Pääjärvi, you can also go down river Teuronjoki through rapid Hämeenkoski, and skirting the northern shore of Valkjärvi, there is a two-mile land march to river Äväntjoki, from which you can go directly to the sea. River Teuronjoki flows into Lake Kernaalanjärvi, from where you can directly reach Vanaintaka. Hakoinen hill fortress and all nearby fortresses up to Rapola and even Vesilahti are part of one large network of waterways, Lammi fortress as well."

Meinbald listens and thinks...

"How similar their use of river routes is, but here, those marshes and lakes and the rivers which connect them are criss-crossing everywhere, by thousands!"

At Sääksmäki, in the afternoon of May 21, AD 1248

Teet and his men went to patrol the terrain near the castle in pairs in different directions. The Swedish knights commanded by Bengt took over the fort's guards. Fridrik had received an order from Bengt to stay with his men as protection troops in a camp to be established in the immediate vicinity of the castle. The duty of these security forces was also to transport the wounded for treatment to the field hospital established on the shore of Lake Vanajavesi.

In Vanaja, on the afternoon of May 21, AD 1248

Meinbald decided to share Kaukomieli with the updates he had heard from Teet in Rapola.

"Birger's fleet came up the river you mentioned, led by Teet, and the light boats were marched to another river, from which they then descended to Kernaala. Birger and the cavalry, on the other hand, came directly from Turku on the road leading to Tavastia. They met in Hakoinen the Novgorodians, who had captured the fortress, reportedly using the same route."

"The Karelians knew how to guide these routes all the way to Vesilahti," Kaukomieli thinks aloud. "The Novgorodians and the Karelians are allied, and they are trying to get Finland's hook taxes for themselves. You Saxons have allied with the Swedes, and you are aiming for the same, to get the taxes for yourself and the trade routes under your control."

"The Hakoinen fortress was burned to the ground, and the Novgorodians were executed while some fled," Meinbald said as if he hadn't heard the recent nasty comment. After all, he was here on a mission blessed by the Holy Father himself, for God's sake and not for any earthly tax.

"The people of Tavastia have once again turned the other cheek to the new conqueror and, this time, accepted the baptism of Western Roman Christianity — that is, those for whom their own life is more important than the customs of their ancestors," Kaukomieli said wistfully.

Rapo had the same destiny as Estonia's Chieftain Lembitu; he lost his life. Remembering how chief Kauppo from Livland had also lost his life in the same skirmish, even though he was an ally of the Saxons, Kaukomieli continued, "Mielivalta, if I don't return from this trip, promise me that you will take care of my family, marry my daughter Elin, and consider Matti as your own brother. I'm not afraid to go even as far as Novgorod with you, as long as I know that my descendants will have a secure future, whatever happened to me. I'm already an old man compared to you."

Kaukomieli stared deep into his eyes as if seeing directly into his soul. Meinbald thought quietly for a moment before opening his verbal chest:

"Clearly, that old man is more civilized than I could have imagined; he knows German and Swedish and apparently knows the events and history of the Northland much better than I do. But he can't know the rules of our brotherhood, because he offers me, the guardian of the rules and the commander of my troop, to take his daughter as my spouse."

He said calmly, "Kaukomieli, I will not take you to Novgorod, but we will evict them from here, from the whole territory of this marshy land. As for your offer of your daughter, I find her very attractive and I promise you that I consider her and Matti very close friends. We'll come back to this in more detail when we both come back from this chase unscathed."

"We ride directly to Lammi Linnanmäki fortress, Meinbald. If it is in the possession of our people, we will get additional troops from there to receive these fleeing Byzantine robbers," suggests Kaukomieli.

"And if Lammi has surrendered to the Novgorodians, we will have time to cut off this group from joining them."

"You talk wise, old man, let's go!" he answered and spurred his horse into a gallop. The trio rode towards the fortress.

At Sääksmäki, in the afternoon of May 21, AD 1248

Meanwhile, on Sääksenmäki, John Teet's men continued to rake the surroundings of Rapola fortress. One patrolling duo also had a dog, a German shepherd as a tracker. They watched as the dog had clearly found a track.

"Dog on the trail!" one of the horsemen shouted.

"Men, follow my voice; we have a dog following a trail!"

It wasn't long before the dog reached one Novgorod and latched onto his leg. When Teet and the knights, following the dog, reached the man, they were attacked by a five-strong group of men armed with footbows and swords. Teet commanded the men to protect themselves with their shields, but one of his knights got an arrow directly to the chest and died on the spot. They also had foot archers further back who had had time to regroup and were now shooting at the attackers.

Two attackers were hit and fell. This was enough, the initiative turned to Teet and he attacked himself the central attacker with his horse, striking a hard blow with his sword, which the enemy could barely parry. Asser followed him riding and slaught the enemy on the right to the ground.

Teet stopped his horse because the terrain was too hilly and forested for maneuvering. He quickly dismounted, and attacked at the man, striking him hard with his sword, finally finding his weakness. Striking also with his shield, he managed to stagger him enough to buy time to strike his sword into his defenseless neck.

Blood spurted out from the gurgling man's neck as he fell to the ground to remain still. Meanwhile, the other knights fought on horseback, striking the remaining opponents to the ground with their swords.

In the meantime, a larger detachment of Novgorodians had managed to return back towards the south gate of the fortress. Antero, who was vigilantly scouting the front terrain of the camp to be set up south of Rapola, saw movement ahead. He sent his men to take a message to the camp that the enemy was here preparing to attack with a large force.

Antero avoided contact with the enemy, burrowing into a hole in a large rock to hide. He saw Karelians, Novgorodians, and Lappish archers moving together in a large mass of infantry across his hiding place.

At the camp, Fridrik and Karl received Antero's messenger. He told Karl in Swedish:

"Enemy spotted ahead about a mile away; there were a lot of them, and they were heading here to the fort on foot."

"How many?" Fridrik asked after hearing Karl's helpful translation.

"Several tens, maybe a single hundred," answered the messenger.

"Heretics tend to attack from several different sides at the same time, so word of this must be sent to Bengt and Birger immediately. Lydeke! Message by pigeon: The enemy is approaching from the south a mile away, following the water. Alert Klas' and Kort's front departments with the help of messengers. Frederick."

"Writing and sending," Lydeke replied and after a short while, he let the pigeon fly.

In Tavastia, in the afternoon of May 21, AD 1248

Kaukomieli, Gerhard, and Meinbald arrived at Lammi's hillfort. Kaukomieli shouted:

"Open the gates! I am Kaukomieli from Satakunta, and I come to report the enemy's movements." The gates of the fortress were opened, and the chief of the fortress appeared.

"Kaukomieli! You are most welcome, although I greatly wonder why the war signal fires don't burn, but instead you come with this message. I'm Kaleva. Do you remember when we met in Turku and traveled together all the way to the Neva seven summers ago?"

"Kaleva, greetings! It's a pleasure to see you as the head of the fort. In Rapola, a Russian "brother" had spoken softly to Rapo and made him switch sides, have you not been brainwashed?"

"Don't talk rubbish, old man. I wouldn't be inclined to do that at my age; a Rusky is a Rusky, you know that." So, the gentlemen were on the same side. Kaukomieli introduced Meinbald to Kaleva:

"This here is my future son-in-law, Mielivalta, a German knight from Bohemia, commander of the Brothers of the Cross and a brave man." He greeted kindly by extending his open hand, getting Kaleva to do the same.

"Listen, my brother, we only have a moment to think about how we will receive the horde of Novgorodians and Karelians who are about to come here, who are on the run after making a raid deep into our Tavastia," Kaukomieli explained, to launch rapid creation of tactics.

The people of Novgorod chose the route from Ormajärvi to Pääjärvi just as Kaukomieli had predicted. In the middle of the narrow waterway leaving Ormajärvi, after eye contact with Linnamäki, one of the boats went ashore, and the crew left carrying the boat forward.

Kaukomieli, Meinbald, Gerhard, Kaleva, and six of his warriors had prepared to ambush the Novgorodians moving by boat just before entering the Main Lake. They raised the chain and cut off the passage in front of the boat. Kaleva's men threw tow hooks, which they used to pull the boat to the shore. The Novgorodians in the boat couldn't even try to resist their capture; they were exhausted from rowing. When the men were being chained on the shore of the lake, one of Kaleva's men warned that a missing group of Novgorodians was rowing away in the middle of Pääjärvi.

Kaukomieli and Meinbald followed them. When the middle of Lake Pääjärvi had been crossed, and the Novgorod boat had completely disappeared from sight into Mustijoki river, Kaukomieli said: "Mielivalta, my friend! There's no way we can catch them anymore. By the time we have exhausted ourselves by trying to catch up during the coming isthmus crossing and we reach Lahdenpohja with the men from the boat, exhausted, they will no longer be seen, and we will have no way of finding out where they have headed on the big island-strewn Päijänne. They practically escaped, Mielivalta. Let's save our strength and let them run as far as Novgorod."

"Damn!" he exclaimed in frustration, knowing the old man was right. "Stop! Let us turn back; our main troops await their leader, and we must continue unwearied on this Holy mission."

Fridrik's knights and men-at-arms on all three sides of the fortress had received the word and were well prepared to meet the enemies. In the fort, Birger's bodyguard troops, commanded by Gregers, had climbed the stilts and were also looking carefully to the west in case enemy troops might come across the lake in boats.

There were no boats to be seen anywhere; everything looked very calm, too. Then suddenly, the horns started blowing on the south, east, and north sides of the fortress as a sign of enemy contact.

Kort was on the north side of the fortress, where the cut-down, uneven, broken terrain made cavalry charges very ineffective. After thinking about a quick battle tactic together with Hermann, Kort commanded all eight knights, counting himself, to dismount and line up in the front line. They grouped up in such a way that in a row, every other was a knight, and every other was an armed infantryman. The Novgorodians and Karelians were grouped at the edge of the clearing and the forest.

Loud commands were heard, and for a moment, the sky was filled with arrows which were soon to rain down on their necks.

"Shields!" Kort shouted, preparing himself to receive the rain of arrows.

The enemy started its attack. They didn't come as a cavalry charge either, but advanced slowly at first by marching and then running.

"Men, slowly ahead!" Kort shouted.

The troops met in the middle of the down-cut glade and stroke each other for their lives. Dietrich, being a large man, worked with his full shoulders strength and stroke dozens of warriors to the ground with his axe. He threw his shield to the ground and took a sword in his other hand. He spinned and danced like an angel of death among enemies, and men fell around him.

Herman, on the other hand, was more careful but precise. In terms of swordsmanship, he was superior to the Novgorodians and Karelians, so it wasn't difficult for him to defeat every single enemy he encountered in a duel.

The same applied to Kort. With his sword in front, he slashed from one man to the next, and always a new unbeliever was destined to taste his blade. At Klas' eastern defence block the terrain was open, and the large open fields of Sääksenmäki opened up in front of the troops. Enemy grouping was easy to spot from a distance.

"At a quick estimate, there are about a hundred men," Klas spoke his mind out loud.

"I would estimate the same amount, at most two hundred," Gödeke answered. His voice had lost its characteristic tone of happy song, which had given him his nickname Finch.

"Men! We charge the enemy with horses before they know how to spread out into a line in the open field. Men-at-arms, you will follow us, marching close to us until we come within assault range."

Klas, Gödeke, and six other knights mount their horses and rode calmly towards the enemy. Armed warriors like Ulf and Magnus followed as infantry.

Fridrik was on the south side of the fortress with his men, ready to face the enemy in the hilly forest terrain. They were stationed on top of a hill, so when approaching them, the enemy had to climb up, unable to charge on horseback. While waiting for the battle touch, Fridrik tried to calm his men and his own mind too:

"Brothers, you surely remember the traces of the Battle of Legnica. The Tartars had a reputation for being ferocious, but they didn't do well for us at Olmuetz at all when we used the mountains to our advantage. There are not so steep mountains here, but even a smaller hillock gives us a lot of advantages, even though there are more unbelievers in number."

The enemy section spread out under the hill in a row about a hundred meters long and started to climb up to hit its enemy.

"Let's attack!" Fridrik shouted and targets the first Novgorod when he is about ten meters away from him. Fridrik is also not overshadowed by his brothers in his fighting skills, so the first blow brings a sure hit, and the enemy falls to the ground. Then to the next one.

"Don't let them go so they can't encircle us!" Fridrik shouted.

Lydeke had also managed to kill his first opponent. He fetched the next one from the left side of the previous one. The enemies tried to attack Lydeke as a group at once, but Otto noticed this and rushed to help. He's the most skilled swordsman in the entire fraternity, so it only took him a couple of hits per man before he had already struck down six foes.

"Lydeke, let's go over there and attack the next ones!" he shouted, getting Lydeke with him towards a group of adversaries gathered twenty meters further to the left. After they were finished with them, they moved further on. Many knights and men-at-arms fought equally bravely, inflicting defeat on the heretics.

Klas's knights approached the Novgorodians, followed by the infantry of men-at-arms. After they had reached striking distance, Klas commanded his horsemen to charge. They struck in the middle of the spreading enemy group and knocked down about ten cavalry men.

"Tatars!" shouted Gödecke as they rode after Klas to the left, turning to regroup for another attack. Magnus ran with Ulf behind him, leading the infantry men, about ten meters from the enemy front.

"Give me a couple of Tatars!" Magnus shouted, preparing to attack the men of the steppes with his sword drawn.

Ulf ran to the side and lifted his ax up, ready to strike. The men-at-arms were all caught up to their enemy in an instant and fought man-to-man, witnessing fear and even terror on their adversaries' faces.

The Tatars were used to being the ones who sow terror; for them, this was a new, strange situation. In disbelief, they struck again and again, each time a new tier of men meeting their fate on the field.

There was fierce fighting on all three fronts, with neither side showing signs of retreating or surrendering. However, fighting in full gear was exhausting, and there were still at least four times as many foes as them. So Fridrik finally blew his horn to signal retreat, to which both Klas and Kort responded with their own signal.

They retreated to the fort, bringing their troops to cover, each three of them from their own sectors. The enemy tried to follow closely behind, but the gates were closed, and Finnish crossbow archers shot a shower of arrows at their necks, forcing them to stop. Novgorodians, Karelians, Tatars, and Lapps began to besiege the fortress.

"No wonder there were so many of them; there are also archers from Karelians and Lappish!" yelled Mielinoita, the commander of the Sääksmäkelians. They had decided to show new loyalty to Lord Birger and thus got their crossbows back from them.

Fridrik's men were thirsty after fighting, covered in blood, with the enemies on the front. The Finnish women brought them fresh water from the fortress's own well and also served them rye bread, on which they had spread a thick layer of freshly churned butter. Fighters were hungry so they ate to gather their strength back.

At Lammi, in the evening of May 21, AD 1248

In the evening, three exhausted men from boats arrived at the camp at the Lammi fortress. Horses and prisoners of war with their guards were also dragged in a barge, and the prisoners were thrown into a guarded dungeon.

Inside the Lammi fortress, Kaukomieli asked:

"Have you ever been to a sauna, Mielivalta?"

"What is it?"

"In the sauna, you can heat up that stubborn sweat and wash it off. Come, let's go together. I'll show you, Mielivalta, how to bath and clean up here in Tavastia."

He recalled the rules of Father Augustine: *A brother should never deny himself the opportunity to bathe if it is good for his health.*

"Yes, let's go, old man. You go ahead since you have bathed there before. Sauna? That was it?"

"Yes. SAUNA."

Together with Kaukomieli and Matti, they walked in front of the log sauna building to undress. Kaukomieli opened the sauna door, and Meinbald followed him into the darkness. Matti followed and closed the door. Only a little light shines through a small window. With it, however, they know how to navigate and get up onto the benches.

He sits next to the men, wondering what has happened. The knights and men-at-arms who arrived by boat also sit on the benches timidly.

However, the mind calms down in the warm darkness of the sauna. Kaukomieli takes a wooden ladle and uses it to throw water on the stove. There is a loud hissing and steaming sound; the stove is clearly very hot.

"Accept the warmth of the bath, Mielivalta. Breathe through your mouth so your nose doesn't burn. Breathe easy; you have nothing to worry about here."

He does this and relaxes.

"This is great, really great. Sauna. Steam."

Matti takes a whisk of birch from the lower bench, dips it in water, and starts to lash himself on the back. Meinbald notices how the hot air begins to burn his skin with each blow.

"Take bath whisk too, and do the same. You will notice how it cleans and smoothens your skin, Mielivalta!"

Kaukomieli encourages him and throws more steam on the stove. Again, a loud hissing fills the darkness.

In Sääksmäki, evening of May 21, AD 1248

In Sääksmäki there has been a different kind of bath — a blood bath.

Antero had gone around Rapola through the forests from the east side to reach Matti's Pirkka warriors who had arrived to north side. They had heard the sounds of battle as they approached from the north, so they had spread out to surround the besiegers, who were completely unprepared for another ring of siege.

In the afternoon, just before the besiegers had prepared their first siege machine ready to fire, arrows began raining, shot from behind their troops, cutting them down. Each time a new group of men was ordered to ready the slings or ballistas, they had to lower their shields, and a new deadly rain wiped out their intentions.

The besieging forces also tried in disarray to attack the fort with part of their strength, and with part against the outer siege ring. This only cost them more men, and the enemy was worn down to quite a small number.

The Novgorodians, Tatars, and Karelians made a desperate attack on the northern gate of the fortress before dark. The sentries set by Fridrik were awake and sounded the alarm by blowing their horns. A huge final battle ensued, which could only have one kind of ending.

The blockade forces were killed almost to the last man. Some of the Lapland archers managed to sneak through the second blockade ring thanks to the darkness, as the Pirkka warriors didn't want to shoot at their comrades. Only a very small group of Karelians surrendered and were captured.

Fridrik told his men that together with the Pirkkas, they had saved the Tavastians in the Sääksmäki fortress and Birger, with his life guard, from certain destruction. "Brothers, we have real brothers in arms here," Fridrik said, patting Antero on the shoulders.

Antero understood the gesture well and knew enough German to answer with a smile that he agreed.

At Lammi, in the afternoon of May 21, AD 1248

After the whisk lashing and several splashes of löyly, the gentlemen go downstairs to wash themselves. The water is warm, and it washes away all the sweat. Only the good smell of birch remains on the skin. They go outside, dry their bodies on linen, and get dressed. It feels like being born again.

"Drink beer so you don't pass out," says Kaukomieli, handing him a tankard of ale.

He drinks. The beer is strong. *It's starting to go to my head. Gotta get philosophical,* he thinks.

"Kaukomieli, do you and your tribe brothers have a soul? Do you know what it is?" he asks simply.

"You forget, Brother Mielivalta, that Matti and I are just as

Christian as you. We know the human soul, although we didn't have a name for it until the Novgorodian brothers, or the Swedish and Norwegian brothers, came to baptize us already hundreds of years ago. Saint Olav of Norway visited here with his axes. Before these conversions, we spoke of *man* and *mind*. Of course, the wife has a mind, too — and that, sometimes, is quite changing, hot or cold!"

Kaukomieli laughs, hoisting from the tankard, then grows thoughtful, "War is fought with luck, not with the boldness of a warrior nor with the roughness of a man."

"Do you know Saint Augustine and his thoughts?" he asks. "He was a wise man, and we follow the rules he wrote in our brotherhood. Augustine lived hundreds of years ago. He wrote wisely about the human mind and soul. According to him, we are surrounded by reality, but each of us has our own separate mind, with its own space — a mental palace where we can search our memories and gaze with the eyes of our soul towards God."

"I haven't heard of this Akustiinus, but we have had wise men too. We had Steady-Old Väinämöinen, knower of all ages. He went down to Tuonela and dived into giant Antero Vipunen's belly to seek lost verses, which he then sang to build and complete a ship without touching it with his hands."

Kaukomieli shouts to Matti in Finnish:

"Väinö surely had a palace in his mind when he took and sang the ship, *Perrkele!*"

"What is that *Perrkele*, some god of yours?" he asks, astonished at the strange word.

"No, just Satan himself. He is the biblical main devil nowadays. We shout the old word when we want to emphasize what we're talking about. Don't worry — it's just stubborn talk, a habit with us. But each of us have little devils in our heads from time to time, telling us to do bad things and drink spirits," Kaukomieli explains, taking a sip from the tankard.

"Verdammt…" he whispered quietly. "You have no soul, no matter how Christian you are."

"It is pretty is to die in a war, beautiful to clang of swords", Matti threw his own philosophy into the conversation, translating it into German on the fly — to Meinbald's great surprise.

"Listen, Brother Mielivalta," Kaukomieli said more seriously than before. "I want to confess something to you. I have known Lord Birger and his character for years. I was with him at Neva, on the military expedition which he and Bishop Thomas organized to convert the Novgorodians. We sailed there together from Turku, where we had agreed to meet. I wondered if Birger remembered me, but luckily, today, I could see that he didn't."

"Why do you say that?" Meinbald asked, curious.

"Well, that trip went badly. We had hardly reached the Neva estuary when we noticed we were being watched. Birger had ordered his Swedish guards to keep an eye on us. That was quite an insult — because only *ledungs* from our coast had set off, none from our heartlands. The men of my *ledung* were only Ala-Satakunta men from Eura. Ragvald and his men weren't there, nor anyone from town of Vanai or the shores of Vanaja.

"At that time, I lost my trust in Birger. When we came to the river Inkereenjoki, we landed on the east bank, while the Swedes, led by Ulf Fase, Birger's cousin, pitched their tents on the west bank. We had hardly set our camp when a boatload of Birger's men rowed to our side, boarded our camp, and stayed to watch our activities.

"Since I know Swedish, I asked them what they were doing. They said young Birger of Bjälbo had ordered them to make sure our troops did not fraternize with the enemy. I disliked this rudeness and silently ordered Antero and my guards to be ready if the Swedes turned their weapons on us."

"I also sent Uolevi, my messenger, to rake the woods for enemies. In the evening he returned, saying they had met some Ingers, who told them they planned to attack Ulf Fase and Birger's side in the morning, leaving us alone.

"I wondered whether to warn the Swedes, but because I was so annoyed by their arrogance, I decided not to. I told Antero that in the morning we'd see if we had to kill those Swedes or if they'd run away when the attack started. And so, as dawn broke, there was a cry of '*Hakkaa päälle!*' in clear Finnish. It was clear no Finn would attack other Finns.

"The Swedes misunderstood, drew swords against us, and fled. After that, we could do nothing but retreat back where we came from, leaving the Swedes to their luck.

"You must wonder, Brother Meinbald, why I tell you this?"

"Well, I don't deny, that is what I wonder. Why do you, wise old man?"

"I have seen your soul. You are honest and capable. That's the kind of man I want to have in my family, not as an enemy. Do you understand as a Saxon, Meinbald, that blood is thicker than water?"

"I understand," he replied. "And what you said opened my eyes regarding Birger. He sacrificed his men knowingly — though he must also understand that blood is thicker than water."

"Good. Keep your eyes on your back with him too. And take my daughter as your wife."

"Elin is very beautiful. If it only were possible, I would take her. But I am a warrior monk. I cannot take a wife."

"Right? So you can kill other Christians, but you cannot marry? Doesn't it sound like something is not right there? Well, let's see how things go, Brother Mielivalta. Let's see," Kaukomieli concluded enigmatically.

Meinbald remained speechless and thoughtful. After the sauna and a drunken *sahtihaarikka*, the men slept deeply. The journey continued early next morning back to Rapola.

Sääksmäki, late evening, May 21, AD 1248

Meanwhile, in Rapola, Birger's men were baptizing the pagans into Christianity. They coldly cut off the heads of those who refused. Rapo and his son and grandson were the first to die, ensuring no male line remained to seek revenge. All surrendered Novgorodians were also executed. Even Rapo's wife refused baptism, spitting in the baptizer's face. She too was killed on the spot. King Ragvald's, or Rapo's head was speared and Birgers squire had to carry it so that everybody could see it.

It was easy to convert the surviving women, young people, and children. The bodies of the dead were buried on the south side of the hillfort, in an insignificant place. Rapo's headless corps was thrown into the bottom of the pit, which had been dug by the Tavastians. No memory or monument of these heathen dead remains was allowed. The Pope's organization had decided how to tame and convert unbelievers. Dominican monks knew how to work very effectively in conversion.

Moments exactly like this show, how single deeds become entangled together with the greater network of historical events. Sääksmäki had not only a large fortress but also sacred groves and cup-stones where the Tavastian people sacrificed to ancestors, to the *People of the Forest*, for success and favorable winds in their lives. A new sanctuary — a church, had to be built here to erase the old ways.

Cup-stones could also be found in southern Hattula. The Dominicans mapped such sites along their route. Church organization was well developed, planned for the long term. Europe was already one to two centuries ahead in this process. Monks had recorded methods from Bohemia in the 9th century. Generation by generation, step by step, old habits were erased and replaced them with new ones.

A century later, a relic — a piece of Jesus' wooden cross from Holy land — would be moved to Hattula's new church. It was claimed, that the piece really was wood of Jesus' crusifiction wood. Fragments of the cross were widely distributed to churches across Europe in the Middle Ages. This relic drew annual pilgrimage, for it was believed to cure pain and suffering. Hattula's church of the Holy Cross is mentioned first time as a place of pilgrimage in documents from early 15th century.

Modern research has mapped that so many "Holy Cross" fragments were distributed across Europe that they would amount to a shipload of wood. Another miracle — like the five loaves and two fish feeding thousands in Galilee.

Another relic is said to rest in Cologne Cathedral — the remains of the three Wise Men: Caspar, Melchior, and Balthasar. According to legend, Empress Helena brought them from the Holy Land to Constantinople. Constantine gave them to Milan in 334. Frederick Barbarossa later seized them and gave them to Cologne in 1164.

This began Cologne's rise as a pilgrimage center. To honor the relics, construction of a new cathedral began in 1248 — at the same as time the last pagan North was conquered and its conversion began.

The "Three Crowns" of the Wise Men also became Sweden's national emblem — though only centuries later, with Albrekt of Mecklenburg.

When viewing all this from the comfort of a modern welfare state — where everyone's beliefs are their private beliefs, and most of religion's power has been diminished by science — one must ask:

Were the Christians of that time truly spiritually higher than the pagans they scorned?

Pagans worshiped the supernatural in nature and their ancestors, yet they left their dead in peace — burned them to ash or buried them in earth.

Perhaps that question itself is misplaced. Whether or not they were, the Christians still won. Paganism in Tavast land receded into oblivion with the generations. Thus the church gained its permanent foothold, and secular and ecclesiastical powers joined their hands as victors.

Chapter X
Birger's Thanks

May 22nd, AD 1248

After returning back to Rapola, Meinbald, Matti and Kaukomieli witnessed a really wild vision. The field hospital set up near Vanaja shore was full of wounded men who moaned in pain and mourned their lost arms or legs. Hildegard and the Dominican friars, together with Meinbald's men, treated the wounded.

Hildegard toiled at the foot of hill Sääksenmäki in the field hospital. The wounded were brought to him to be bandaged. Hildegard was helped by two monk brothers who had left Stockholm with her. She had brought herbs that were ready to use. He spread them on the wounds, recited a short spell or prayer taught by his mother, and then gave the wounded person a potion she had made from herbs, which she knew would intoxicate and thus relieve the patient's condition.

The complaint was loud; the drugged wounded soldiers did not understand anything of this world, but the pain still beat through for a while before the herbal potion numbed the sensory nerves.

"Mother, help, I can't take it! Please let me go…"

"Mutter, Vater, Gott! Ich bin kaput..."

"Mom! Hjälp Mor, jag… orkar inte"

Every now and then, it happened that one of the wailing sounds suddenly stopped. Hildegard knew that the patient had passed away and called the monk brothers to give the last blessing. Technically, it may have come too late, but no one was pointing that out. The Dominican friars oversaw who would be buried in the Christian grave and who would be taken to the heathen heap. They treated everyone with the same piety and let God decide who would survive and whom he would call to him.

Meinbald went to see how Hildegard was doing and wanted to praise how effective and skilled a healer he saw. That woman was like an angel who hovered over men and gave them her sweet bliss. Since there were no words, he showed his fondness and admiration with gestures. He bowed his head in reverence, joining his hands in thanks.

Hildegard understood the gesture and was clearly taken that Warlord Meinbald came to notice her modest contribution. She sent a flying kiss back as a thank you. It really hit him like a thorn in the face, but in a good way. Confused in his thoughts, he left the field hospital to join the management of the situation up in the fort.

Bodies were lying in heaps near the gate of the fortress, as well as inside the fortress. "Lappish archers", Matti shouted to his father.

"Yes, apparently, they have also entered into an alliance with the Novgorodians, just like the Karelians", replied Kaukomieli. "Oh, those wretched apostates"!

In front of the gate, Meinbald was still examining the piles of corpses, noticing that, in addition to the Novgorodians, a large number of Tatars had also met their end here. He looked up to see Fridrik beside him, greeting his brother and commander.

"Brother Fridrik! Glad to see you're okay! Apparently, you crushed these heretics here. Did we have a lot of casualties?"

"Three men-at-arms and two knights were killed fom us, roughly the same amount from the Swedes and the Sword Knights, maybe a little more", Fridrik answered modestly. "I haven't counted the wounded, but roughly, I would say that about a quarter of our men were taken to the field hospital."

Birger and his relative Bishop Bero, who had joined the party as Birger's trusted spiritual advisor and chaplain, came to praise Meinbald profusely. They said that more Novgorodians had come in heaps after their departure, but since he had left this excellent vice-marshal Fridrik with his troops in charge of the defense of the fortress, they, together with the Swedes of Bengt and Teet's knights, had succeeded in repulsing these huge hordes of the enemy.

Birger's marshal, Bengt, was a little upset when he heard his master praising Meinbald's troops, but he could honestly admit that without them, they would have been left underdogs.

"Meinbald, thank you also for the information you sent via pigeon from Vesilahti; we were well aware of the enemy's movements in the north, although this scale of the clash here in the Sääksenmäki fortress came as a complete surprise. We haven't seen anything similar on our ledung trips before. Pigeons are really great messengers!"

In the evening, by the campfire, the soldiers enjoyed the sahti brought from Lammi, offered by Kaukomieli and Matti. It was so strong that in no time, the warrior forces commanded by Bengt and John Teet appeared to be anything but well-organized. The same could be said about some of Meinbald's men, but he knew how to hold his own now.

Bengt came to talk to Meinbald, with Kaukomieli acting as an interpreter.

"Brother Meinbald, Let me tell you about our great leader, Lord Birger. He is of the great Bjälbo family, now he is the second biggest chief in the land of Sweden, but soon, he will be the biggest. This victory we brought him sealed his greatness. His mother, the great Ingrid Ylva, has seen it. She knows how to look into the future. She has had the gifts of a seer all his life. Even now, although she is already old, she knows white magic. Once, she conjured the whole of Sweden full of knights from the feathers of a feather pillow! Isn't it wonderful!"

Kaukomieli could barely contain his smile when he interpreted the drunken Bengt's words to Meinbald.

"Mein Gott! Kaukomieli, my dear friend", he stated, "these children of Svea live even further back in their old heathen ways than you do."

"Meinbald, my boy, I'm relieved that you now see it too. Isn't this our strong magic potion, Ukko's sahti, a wonderful drink? It gets the truth out of the mouth of even a raw male! Not to mention a mama's boy," grins Kaukomieli.

"What is he saying?" Bengt asked, turning to Kaukomieli for a translation of their conversation.

"He greatly admires the wonderful abilities of your leader's mother and hopes that they have been passed on to the son as well. Now, Herr Meinbald retires to his tent to sleep. Perhaps you should do the same, Marshal", Kaukomieli replied.

On the way to his tent, Meinbald ran into a drunken John Teet, who grabbed him with both hands. Teet's eyes were blurry, and his mouth was rapidly blurting out words that he didn't understand. Taking the man by the wrists, he calmed him down.

"Calm down, good man. Sahti is the drink of wise people. What's wrong with you?"

Reason returned to John Teet's eyes. He pulled away his grip and left the place regretfully. Or so he at least explained that incomprehensible gabble to himself on the way to the tent. *"It was best to go to bed now before this all turned into a full-on fight."*

Sääksmäki, May 23, AD 1248

After the battle of Sääksenmäki and the subsequent events, Meinbald built very good relations not only with the secular power of Sweden but also with the spiritual power because Bero was appointed bishop of Finland immediately after the expedition calmed down. Birger thanked Kaukomieli:

"Faravid, our old vassal - without your help, Ragvald's plot would not have been revealed right from the start and I myself would perhaps be there among the corpses."

"Well, my lord Birger, the first attack of the Novgorodians was repelled by my son Matti already at Vesilahti, at the mouth of the little Narvajoki river. From that counterattack given by Matti and the brave Pirkka warriors, their plot began to unravel, and it became clear to them that they would not be able to convert the people of Satakunta, who had already professed the Roman faith for more than a century and had even gone to Novgorod to fight for it."

"Oh, this young Herr Matts was the driving force behind your whole chase and the Primus motor? Congratulations, Herr Matts, many congratulations on your bravery!" Birger said and patted Matti on the shoulder.

"I'll make sure that you in Satakunta can continue your taxation as before, it won't be interfered with as long as I continue as king. I understood from Brother Meinbald that he has taken Matts hostage in exchange for your loyalty."

"Yes, and I have given Matts into Meinbald's custody to show our loyalty."

"Well, fine, I'll gladly take Matts with me to Stockholm, where he can get to know other courtiers, the closest men to the King of Sweden will teach him, he does already know a little Swedish like you, does he not?"

"Yes, he can speak and I will gladly give my beloved son to the court of the King of Sweden as proof of my loyalty", Kaukomieli said, thinking that he is lucky that Birger doesn't remember him from Neva.

Birger left Bero to organize the affairs of the church. Birger saw Meinbald as a reliable man who could be entrusted with a lot of responsibility for the affairs of the new part of the kingdom in the future.

"Very soon I have to return to take care of government affairs in Sweden", stated Birger. "Meinbald, you stay in Turku with Bero to take care of practical matters. Fortification must be started immediately in order to avoid surprise attacks by the Novgorodians here in the backwoods of Tavastia. Order one of your men to look into it here"

He thought for just a moment.

"As an experienced castle master, Dietrich Balk gets to handle this responsible position; building a castle is like a child's play for him!"

"Good", stated Birger. He put his hand over Meinbald's shoulder and led him a little to the side from the others.

"Meinbald, I want you to marry my daughter Hildegard. That way I can trust that you and your men will remain loyal servants of Svea."

"My lord Birger, haven't you heard that all of us cross-brothers follow the rule of St. Augustine, which forbids us to take a wife? Your daughter is very attractive, and I would gladly take her as my wife if it were possible, but as the commander of my troop, I must set an example and follow without compromise these strict rules of ours, for the observance of which I bear the main responsibility on our expedition."

"Oh, I really didn't know this. I admire your uncompromisingness, Brother Meinbald", Birger stated thoughtfully. "Let's at least organize a proper party in honor of the success of the military expedition when we get to Turku, I guess your regulations allow you to celebrate with us?"

"Yes, of course, and we will be happy to celebrate this great victory with you", he replied and respectfully lowered his head.

"Excellent, good then. I want to be absolutely sure that everyone who participates in the administration of our expanded empire is extremely loyal to us, not only pursuing their own interests, and can be completely trusted in every matter.

Especially the collection of tithes, the storing and carrying of grain and funds to the crown and the church are matters I leave to no one but You, Meinbald, I trust you and your most faithful men to do it. You get two tithes from the bishop's tithe. The bishop distributes the rest to his church here in Finland. You send the tithe of the crown to King Erik's Chancellor of the Treasury in Stockholm."

He left Dietrich, Ulf, Magnus and about twenty men to build a fortress called Tavastehus Castle. Dietrich took responsibility for the management of the fortification work and he gave Magnus as his first task to organize the surrendered Tavastian men for forced labor.

Magnus set out to map the bedrock of the nearby area, looking for the best place for a quarry site. He had already decided to forge himself some chisels, hammers and horseshoes as a model in a local blacksmith's workshop.

Birger's convoy deviated from its march to fortress of Mantereenlinna, where both fortresses of Hakoinen and Aulanko could be seen. Lake Katumajärvi was near the castle. Bero explained to Meinbald how the Tavastian people washed away their baptism in this lake. It had been given to them during the time of Bishop Thomas. They hadn't gotten further than that then, unlike now, ten years later. Now, the whole of Tavast land was kneeling before Birger. He listened to Bero, thinking at the same time: *"I want to take care of the taxes myself, I have the best control over money matters among my brothers."*

Kaukomieli invited Meinbald and Birger to visit Niemenpää, his Kyllikki wife's home farm nearby. Antero, with his life guards and Matti, with his pirkka warriors, ensured safety and set up guards along the banks of the two rivers, big and small Hiidenjoki and on the Niemenpää village road. A negotiation was held in Niemenpää, where Birger was to strengthen the future position of Kaukomieli and Matti in Tavastia, Satakunta and Pirkanmaa.

Kyllikki welcomed the guests as a proud hostess. She was wearing the traditional outfit of a noblewoman with capes, knives and buckles. She commanded the maids to offer beer and rye bread to the guests seated at the table inside the manor house.

Kaukomieli opened the conversation by saying in clear Swedish:

"I myself gave the order to all the fortresses in Tavast land to open their doors to you. All the castles free from Novgorod obeyed my order. My son Matti was the first to beat the Novgorodians and Karelians who had invaded the country.

You got a warning from us at Sääksmäki. We have not raised our swords against you but have welcomed you and gone together to smite the heretics of the East who besieged you at Rapola. We prevented your starvation by striking your besiegers to the back with the strength of our best Pirkka warriors. Because of all this, I expect you to maintain my position at the head of my tribe and accept the loyalty of my clan for centuries to come."

Bero noted that the fields were well-tended here. He mentioned this casually as a compliment, as it were. He continued:

"Lord Birger and I are of the opinion that since you have shown us and King Erik of Sweden obedience and true faith in our God, we consider that the papal church will collect the tax tithe from you in the future, in the same way as you have collected the Finnish tax before.

The church builds a monastery here and more churches around the country, teaching the people Christian doctrines and making sure that there is no return to paganism. We are happy to say that we have here such an experienced and strong chief, whose family has shown us loyalty for a hundred years.

The fact that you will pay the tax to us in the future will, in our opinion, prevent you from being tempted to turn to the sledge of the disbelievers of eastern Novgorod in the future. In the future, you can also collect tax from the people of Lapland all the way to the Arctic Ocean. Their loyalty is apparently very shaky and it is necessary to make sure with a heavy hand that they do not ally themselves with the Novgorodians or the Karelians in the future.

Regarding the Karelians, we also have further plans, but with this successful trip we wanted to make sure that we will not be disappointed by the support of the Tavastian tribe again, as happened in Neva ten years ago." Now Birger opened his verbal chest:

"Bero, I and King Erik will gladly take the people of Tavastia under our protection, but it requires your absolute obedience in return. Since you have shown by your actions that you are worthy of our trust, Herr Faravid, we feel that we can leave you to your previous position. However, you have to accept these tax payment changes, just as the powerful men of Uppland had to accept them. If you can promise it, we will leave the responsibility of collecting taxes to Herr Meinbald and his men here and leave Tavastia peacefully."

Kaukomieli raised his beer mug saying: "I accept these changes, and I am happy to continue serving the King of Sweden here in Tavastia. Skål, gentlemen!"

From Niemenpää, the gentlemen's paths diverged, Matti and Meinbald and their men continued with Birger's convoy towards Turku, and Kaukomieli and Antero returned to Kokemäki along the southern route together with Matti's Hundred. This was to ensure that there were no more enemies hiding along the access roads in Lower Satakunta.

After riding less than a mile, Meinbald shouted to Fridrik: "I forgot to tell Kaukomieli an important thing. You take command of the troops; I will ride to them and then come after you!"

"That's clear", said Fridrik, and didn't add anything, even though he was once again worried about letting his brother Meinbald run after Kaukomieli's convoy alone.

The journey of Birger's convoy continued for three days, and they saw no signs of Novgorod on the way. In the small villages of Tavastia, they were received with respect; in every village, there was a brave village elder who welcomed the conquerors by offering rye bread, butter, milk and fresh water to the military convoy. In a couple of places, they also offered sahti, but Birger forbid it; it was not appropriate to intoxicade his soldiers anymore.

Chapter XI
Brotherhood of Arms

Tavastia, May 24, AD 1248

Meinbald caught Kaukomieli's convoy after riding after them for about an hour. It wasn't too hard to follow the tracks of a large army. He had left his armor and helmet for his own convoy to carry, so he moved very quickly in the spring-misty landscape.

"Kaukomieli, I want to talk to you about a few things in private."

"Yes, that's fine, I always have time for you Mielivalta", Kaukomieli replied and halted his horse.

He signaled to Antero that the group would continue on their way, while he stayed by the cart path.

"Did you come to ask for my daughter?" Kaukomieli asked and winked with a laugh. "You already took my son and handed him over to Sweden. But Matti got into good company."

"Not yet", he replied, partly surprised by his own choice of words. "I came to talk about what you discussed with Birger and Bero in Niemenpää. You said something that made me think, and I wish we could talk now, after all we've been through, man to man."

"Aha, I think I know what you're talking about. Yes, you understand, Meinbald, that I couldn't tell you everything until I was sure that you or one of your men wouldn't screw things up for the Swedes. I myself wanted to tell directly and secure my own place under the new regime. I did this because I see it as the best for the Tavastian tribe, that I can continue as long as I live. I have quite a legacy to carry on my shoulders, and if my head was cut off before I have passed that legacy on to the next, it would be a great loss to our entire tribe."

"Well, I can understand that very well, and I'm not surprised at all. But, if I may ask, dear King, I think I understood so much of your speech, although you spoke Swedish, that you said that you gave orders to the forts to surrender to Birger?"

"Yes, that's what I said and that's what I did."

"It was done wisely, but how the hell did you manage? You have been with me non-stop since we met on Koggimäki. We rode and rowed the boat for long stretches, fought together and even slept next to each other. And how did the Pirkka warriors know how to come after us to Sääksmäki to break the siege ring? Didn't Matti leave them in Vesilahti?"

"You have a lot of questions, son. But, since we are now talking man to man, and since I trust you, I will gladly tell you, if you promise that everything I say now will remain just between us."

"Of course, I respect your friendship, and I don't want to break your trust in any way. Or put your son Matti's life in danger."

"Good! Well, listen when I tell you. I was informed of your arrival here already two weeks before you disembarked at Koggimäki."

"How the hell? At that point, we hadn't even made a war plan with Birger."

"Well, the truth is that lord Birger had already done it well in advance, before you even met. I have scouts, trusted men who are in good terms and close to him. I also knew Birger's father, Magnus Minnesköld, as well as his uncle Charles the Deaf and Birger the Smiley. Their father Bengt, that is Birger's paternal grandfather, was nicknamed Stupid by his contemporaries. Birger is by no means like his grandfather, he is cold but sharp. So keep your guard up when dealing with him, keep your friends close, but your enemies even closer, Mielivalta."

"So you know it all better than I thought. And did you say you knew we're coming?"

"Yes, and I knew how to prepare for the fact that you will come along three routes: Kukinjoki, Härkätie and Kokemajoki. We planned a suitable reception for all those routes. We were without an ally, because the Novgorodians, Tatars and Karelians had also decided to come and stay with us for a longer time. This army we defeated together was no ordinary small group of marauders, they even had throwing machines with them. They were going to do the same to us now as they had done to the people of Bjarmia earlier, to beat us so badly that we would either flee or completely submit to their tax authority."

"So you didn't know how to expect the Novgorodians from the east?"

"As far as they are concerned, we have also been on the lookout for a long enough time that I knew of course, I told you before, that those Bjarmians who had escaped from the Väinönjoki river told us what had happened there. With the help of the Karelians and our soothsayers, we got some vague information, after all we have long-term friends there as well, but they didn't know exactly the routes or schedules of the arrivals, like our scouts from the west. And so Novgorod got deep inland. Ragvald had been leaning more in their direction for years, so he had to know, he probably had been involved in planning the whole attack."

"Sir Kaukomieli, I have to admit that I had a completely wrong picture of this situation. I thought when we left here far to the north that we would meet hordes of heathens here, whom we would convert to Christianity by the sword. Then the first chief I met, You, said right after we shook hands that you were already a Christian. And then it turns out that there are Byzantine Christians here, like those Karelians and Novgorodians. Even the Pope himself called them heretics in my letter of instruction. After all, they believe in the same Christ, and are here to spread their own true doctrine, just like us."

"Yes, For us, protecting our own home is more important than going to conquer other countries. Our Karelian brothers have strayed from this holy principle, but we Tavastian people still adhere to it, no matter what religion we identify with."

"Speaking of your own home, thank you again for inviting me to your home in Niemenpää. You have a nice farm and good fields, and more than enough cattle."

"It is indeed my wife Kyllikki's home, which I am hosting there in Tavast land. Kyllikki was born in Niemenpää, his father Satatieto was king of Vanaja. Our fathers arranged the marriage of me and Kyllikki, and our wedding took place in the year of the Lord 1220. It was a great time, through our family, Tavast land and Satakunta were united, we had guests from both tribes at our wedding. Later my father Kaukomieli died in Eura in 1229. He was seriously wounded while defending Satakunta in the winter of 1227, when the Novgorodians came to forcefully baptize us under the leadership of Prince Yaroslav. For a couple of years he persevered single-handedly, but then winter came, the frost took away his strength. Kaukomieli was the king of Satakunta, a Lapland wanderer, known for his courage. He was known in Norway and Sweden as Faravid, especially the Norwegians valued him as a brave man.”

“My father-in-law Satatieto was, as his name suggests, a wise man. Unfortunately, he died in 1236, when Bishop Thomas, in turn, tried to convert the heart of Tavast land with the of Sword Brethen. I came here after hearing about this with my men from Satakunta, as did Ragvald with the Sääksmäkelians. Together we were able to beat the Sword Knights and evict Thomas and his men from Tavast land, they had to retreat to Turku. We didn't follow them there, because the Swedes and Saxons there would have been too tough opponents together. But then, 12 years ago, Kyllikki and I moved to Niemenpää and took over the ownership of the farm. Matti and Elin were born in Kaukola, but they grew up in Niemenpää. When I became the head of Tavast land after the death of Satatieto, Ragvald didn't take it well. We didn't hold hostilities, but he didn't show any submission or acknowledge my kingship either. I am the vassal king of Sweden in Satakunta, in Tavast land everyone except Ragvald has understood that very well. Well, now Rapo is no longer an obstacle, so the whole of Tavastia can much rather bow to Sweden than to Novgorod. And Thomas, whom you also met in Gotland, his men captured one of Novgorods during the campaign to river Neva. They tortured the man to get information about the enemy, but he died in their hands. Later it turned out that this man had Curonian relatives, one of whom was in the Knights of Livonia. He filed a complaint about Thomas' actions and eventually the Pope removed him from his post."

"Mielivalta, now I'm going to tell you something you can't tell anyone. Will you promise to keep your mouth shut?"

"You can trust me, I won't say a word."

"Do you remember when I told you while we were having a sauna at Lammi, how my men had to kill the guards that Birger had set for us on the Neva?"

"Of course I remember."

"Well, that wasn't quite the whole truth, you see, Birger's cousin, Sir Karl, who is also familiar to you, he surrendered to us and did not raise his weapon against us. So I took him with us when we went back to Tavast land."

"So he is close to your friend Birger", Meinbald stated. "How on earth did he manage to come back unscathed and keep Birger's trust?"

"Well, after I had agreed on a secret correspondence with him after his return to Sweden, we took him from Turku to Stockholm and I told him that my men had found him walking hungry in the forest, running away from the Tavastians. It went perfectly. By returning Karl unharmed to Birger, I proved myself a loyal vassal of the good King Erik, and Karl owed me his life's eternal debt of gratitude. I also knew his father, Carl the Deaf, who is Birger's uncle."

"Thank you for sharing this, Kaukomieli, now I understand you better and how this has come to be. You've done a great job of organizing things, considering how difficult cross-pressure you've been from both the East and the West!”

“Thank you, I myself have nothing else in mind, other than trying to lead Sata-Tavast land to a good new home, in good hands, before I will be buried in Kaukola. As a young boy, I myself have been a pawn in the court of the King of Sweden, just like my own son will now be. Back then the king was Erik Knutsson, the father of the current King Erik. Erik died suddenly of a fever in 1216, and Erik the Moss Tongue was born in the same year only after his father's death.”

“Why did you call him moss tongue?”

“His speech is a little slurred, it's been like that ever since he learned to speak, and besides, he's always limped on one leg. But he is exceptionally wise for a young king. He lets Birger do the dirty work and he himself is a very understanding and gentle ruler. I like him. Even the pope himself would have wanted him to be king earlier, but then, in 1219, Johan Sverkersson was crowned king. Johan’s mother was Ingegerd, daughter of Birger Brosa, a cousin of the current earl. The only good thing I can say about Johan is that he let me return to my home when he didn't want to keep Erik's courtiers with him. Johan died in 1222 without an heir, so he remained the last king of the Sverker family. However, Earl Birger's mother, Ingrid Ylva, is also descended from the Sverker family. If Erik the Moss Tongue dies without an heir, what we have in that earl is a very stubborn power seeker who can still bring the Sverker family back to power. I'd bet a few squirrels' skins that this will happen!”

“You mentioned Kaukola earlier, is that where your father's family is from?”

"No, it's my mother's birthplace. We actually have quite a few places where my family can claim to be from - Kaukola in Sastamala, Kokemäki castle, Eura castle for example. Now, when I start to decide where I should be buried, I still have to take into account not only Niemenpää, which we inherited from Satatieto, but also the old fortress and house of Lammi."

"So you tend to bury your deceased in the land of either your father's or your mother's birthplace?"

"Yes, our mother's home can just as well come into question. Our region has also had female warriors and queens for a long time. Kyllikki has already informed me that he should be buried next to his father in Niemenpää. I myself have ended up in that Kaukola actually because my children were born there, the Novgorodians won't conquer it and also because probably the Swedes don't want it for themselves either. I myself was born in Eura, where we are now on our way. Are you coming with us?"

"Thanks for the invitation, but Fridrik leads my troop in my absence, but he tends to worry if I'm gone too long."

"You know each other well and you trust him like your own brother?"

"Yes, that's what he actually is, not only a knight brother, but also just like my own brother. Listen, I'll also be happy to tell you my own background, if you can listen?"

"Of course, I'm very interested."

He told Kaukomieli about his birth in Dresden, playing with Fridrik in Prague and the deaths of both their parents in a fire. Sister Agnes' kindness towards him and his sister Kunigunde was praised by Meinbald. "Oh do you have a sister who is also alive, but you don't see her anymore?"

"I hope that one day we could still meet each other, because she is my only surviving family in this world."

"Oh, yes, my boy, you will definitely still see him, I also have enough visionary gifts that I can confirm that for you."

"Thank you, Kaukomieli. You know, for some reason I believe you, even though you didn't fall into a trance in that ground. I feel that a very strong connection has developed between us over the past few weeks. Is it okay for you that we keep in touch, also in ways other than just tax collection?"

"Mielivalta, I feel exactly the same, it fits perfectly. Do you also keep in touch with Matti? He needs his older brother's support, because he is not used to visiting Sweden and court life may therefore arouse a lot of wonder and questions in him."

"Of course, I'll write to Matti in Stockholm, and also to you in Niemenpää or Kokemäki. I'll send my men to get our ships in a few weeks, as long as we first go over with the Swedes where they will be most needed in the future. The ships belong to Hansa, and they must be sent back to Lübeck as soon as possible."

"But, you shouldn't send them empty, but with commercial cargo", Kaukomieli noticed the practical possibility.

"Well, that's the right topic for our first joint affair! Let's write about it, goodbye now, Kaukomieli. And don't worry about your son Matti, I'll take care of him. You take care of your beautiful daughter Elin!" he said as he mounted his horse to gallop back towards his own troops.

"Goodbye, thank you for coming to discuss these important matters, Meinbald!"

Riding back, he thought with satisfaction:

"How did I manage to form a working alliance with such a wise and important chief. We became brothers in arms during this campaign. We are all brothers in arms, we brothers of the knighthood, the Swedes led by Birger, the sword brothers of John Teet and the Kaukomieli hundreds in Tavastia."

After riding for about an hour, he caught up with his closest brother Fridrik and his troops from taking a break in the march. Fridrik was visibly relieved to see brother Meinbald return safely.

"You didn't get ambushed", Fridrik stated.

"Not at all, my brother, I met our new friends very piecefully", he dismissed his brother's worries.

Chapter XII
Wealth, Love And Fine Offices

In Turku, the first of June, AD 1248

In Turku, Bengt and Gregers' task was to establish a permanent garrison and organize the management of the fortification works at the mouth of river Aurajoki on the island. Both of them really had a burning desire to return to their home Sweden, so they asked Meinbald if any of his men would be eager to take on the task. He paused for a moment, understanding the unsaid, he thought that it was best to take this given responsibility to his own regiment.

"Lydeke is exactly the right man for this job. He keeps the stone walls and rows of fortresses straight as well as the books and scrolls."

Together with Lydeke, he also organized taxation in the official building of the Swedish crown built next to Turku's market square. The bailiffs collected the taxes from their county, Lydeke became a self-righting bailiff of the Turku castle county.

In Tavastia, Dietrich Balk worked as a bailiff, who also managed the fortification works. Kaukomieli and Matti also took care of the office of the bailiffs, Kaukomieli continuing as Satakunta's local vassal, king, and Matti as the head of Upper Satakunta, who had received even more extensive rights to tax the Lapps as a thank you from Birger.

As for Satakunta, the taxes were transferred to the Kokemäki river fortress, from where they were easily delivered along the river and by sea to Turku and further to Stockholm. The bishop of Finland was entitled to the bishop's tithe, of which he distributed a portion to the clergy.

Meinbald sent a copy of the diary he kept about the events of the campaign to the Grand Master. He enclosed a letter in which he asked for instructions regarding further tasks, writing also that his men were already thinking about how long their command under Birger would continue. However, there was no answer, even though weeks had passed.

In Turku, the second of June, AD 1248

Birger hosted a big end-of-war party in the crown house next to the market square. For years, he had been planning the conquest of the whole of Tavastia, so he had no difficulty in creating a small additional plot to his plan, with which he would ensure the obedience of the German knights to the crown in Finland in the future. Birger has already sent a messenger ahead of him before he left Tavastia, that the best wines, the best songs and the best free or free-spirited women should be brought to Turku. There were enough of them in Stockholm after Birger's appointment as earl.

The monk brothers, who were strong in spirit, the armed knights of the Pope, had no idea what was planned for their destiny. The festivities began with Birger's speech of thanks and praise and a toast, to which sufficient additional percentages had already been ensured for the knights by adding a splash of brandy to the Rhine valley wine.

So Meinbald unwittingly got himself drunk, even though it was against the rules of the soul brothers. Many other comrades-in-arms did also unwittingly break the rules. Soon after his speech, Birger noticed that the atmosphere has risen to the ceiling, so to speak, and gave the signal to invite "Sweden's best girls" into the ballroom. The marching in of the girls, their glowing blond hairs shining, their beautiful smiles and joyful gurgles made everyone stare at them in awe. As if the whole maneuver had been rehearsed in advance, each maiden walked straight up to the knight of her choice and kissed them right on the mouth. Hildegard marched in the lead and chose Meinbald, who was very receptive to her. The Swedish and German knights each received the undying favor of their own women.

"Meinbald, we don't have a common language, but today I want us to speak a language that we both understand. I want you, Meinbald. I want you to take me today and make it hard, Hildegard whispered in his ear."

His mind only picked a word here and there, but the whole body understood the matter. He felt how the whisper in his ear made his breathing hard and his penis stiffen. He kissed the girl on the mouth, she opened her lips and pushed her tongue into his mouth. His eyes widened with lust. He grabbed Hildegard in his arms and took her with him to the stable. In the stable, Hildegard grabbed him by the crotch and squeezed hard on his stiffened penis. Meinbald, panting, pulled off his woman's skirt, took off her panties and thrusted his fingers into Hildegard's hot, moist vagina. Hildegard screamed in her lust and he took off his pants, sat down on the grass to lie on top of the woman, who was spread out with her legs, and thrusted into her. The love-making was fiercely rhythmic and he came very quickly, launching into Hildegard. Everything happened so fast and at a feverishly accelerating pace that neither of them really knew what had just happened. After resting for a while, they wanted more of this.

Hildegard and Meinbald spent a hot night in the stable. In the morning, he regretted deeply, and it seemed that many other "Brothers" did also when they woke up next to their own maiden. Fridrik, Kort and Lydeke had also joined the stable with their ladies. Some had gone elsewhere, some were excited to stay under the table in the party space. At least Asser, Berlhold and Klaus woke up happy in the morning from the party space.

The next day, when the tormenting self-recrimination had been seen and heard even more strongly, especially among the Brotherhood of the Red Star and the Cross, Meinbald decided to deal with the matter jointly with the men.

"Brothers! I confess to you that I, too, have broken our rule as regards restraint towards women. I know and see that many of you are experiencing the same pains of sin as I am. That is why I have asked Bishop Bero to forgive us of our sins today so that we can continue our mission as a brotherhood here in Finland."

Bero, apparently aware of Birger's plan, declared:

"With the authorization of the Holy Father, Pope Innocentius, I can tell you that you can atone for your sins by marrying your maiden. The Holy Father himself has told me in his letter that here in the North he has changed your rules so that you can continue as servants of your brotherhood as married men, as long as you also show loyalty not only to your wife but also to the Swedish crown and serve the crown until the end of your earthly life. This is God's will, which I and the holy father hereby convey to you."

Rejoicing broke out among the brothers as if they had been freed from all the evil they had ever done! Meinbald also felt a wave of relief flowing through him, although he was somewhat suspicious of the motives of Bero's message:

"It is very strange that the holy pope sets conditions like this, as far as obedience to the Swedish crown is concerned. And it is clearly impossible that this message has not already been made before this blunder of theirs. So this smacks strongly of a completely planned plot."

"Well, it's better to just go along with the special rules of the north like this, Hildegard is very sweet and living with a wife is certainly a great privilege that would never be possible to brothers in the south," he finally told to himself.

Asser and Berlholt calmly followed this strange ritual. They had equally found love here in the middle of the last heathen land, but they were just plain happy.

In Turku, the twenty-first of June, AD 1248

Hildegard and Meinbald were to be married on June 21st at Nousiainen Church, Bero of course would marry them. As a wedding gift and dowry, Birger had arranged for them a farm in Rusko, ten miles north of Turku.

The couple happily settled down in a new log mansion built for them in Rusko. Here, Meinbald and Hildegard set up a home, which he considered his base while he would stay in the eastern land to take care of tax matters, the protection of German merchants and the affairs of the "Brothers of the cross."

He had delegated the accommodation of the soldiers to Fridrik, whom he had appointed as accommodation master. As Finland's country master of the Order of the Red Star and Cross, he took care of e.g. financial affairs on behalf of the Order in Finland. As the bailiff for the crown, he had the supervision and implementation responsibility for taxation in Finland.

Fridrik organized a camp on an island at the mouth of river Aurajoki in Turku to accommodate German troops. He started the construction of the garrison very quickly, knowing that in these latitudes the winter would be cold and the conditions change quickly anyway.

July was very warm and sunny, and so was August. Just when Meinbald was already a little used to the white nights of the North, they started to get dark again during August. When September arrived, the rains came and the air cooled down appreciably. It was time to start using the furs of the Pirkka people provided by Matti, to survive in the cold.

In October, almost half a year after he had sent the letter to the Grand Master, the answer finally came with the ship courier of the Hanseatic League. It turned out that Grandmaster Albert had died and brother Konrad had been appointed as his successor, who had now written to him about the matter himself. "Konrad!" He couldn't stand this man, but he couldn't help but tell his brothers about the information he had received. The knights gathered every Monday for a joint consultation around worldly matters after a Sunday spent with spiritual ones.

"Cockroach as our grandmaster! What a disgrace!"

"Listen up brothers! We have taken an oath to follow Augustine's rules and we will follow them, even if we are led by a person like Cockroach. After all, he too could have repented, who are we to judge him?" Meinbald asked and made the brotherhood calm down.

Winter was coming. The first snow fell in November. Night frosts had been cooling the weather for many weeks. Meinbald, Fridrik, Kort, Klas, Lydeke, Otto and the whole crew were all equally unaccustomed to this dark, freezing cold winter. The shingles were burned in shingles nailed between the wall logs for a little light, logs split in the summer were burned in ovens and stoves for heating. The locals' outright frenzy to cut large piles of logs had somewhat puzzled them in the summer and even in the fall, but now the fraternity was very satisfied that they themselves had followed their example and started their own log cutting on due time.

Correspondence with Konrad turned out to be - well, sticky like a cockroach. Konrad did not note the achievements of Meinbald's troops, and he did not give any thanks, but on the contrary accused them of waste when he asked Konrad to send more supplies and money orders for the brotherhood's growing expenses. From all this, he, as a seasoned tradesman, concluded that he shouldn't waste his time fighting with that sticky cockroach man.

Instead, he decided to seek the favor of the Swedes in order to get the financial and material resources he needed from them. The Hanseatic League had also proven to be a very good, reliable partner, and what's best, it seemed that the Swedes and the Hanseatic League were looking very well in the same direction about Finland, at least for now.

In anticipation of Christmas, the last Hanseatic ship brought with its cargo gift packages addressed to the brotherhood. This is how they continued the legacy of St. Nicholas. The ship also brought letters, one of them was from Matti.

"It's gratifying that brother Matti writes to me - and apparently, he also knows how to write in German like his father", he thought after reading the first few lines. In the letter, Matti told how he had learned a lot about the customs of Swedish soldiers and administrators, and how he enjoyed learning new things. He also sent warm greetings from his sister Elin, he wrote that Elin had often mentioned in her letters, admiring his courage and skills. Meinbald was delighted by the greetings but felt a small sting inside remembering that he "had to" get married.

"Gentiles had polygamy, at least in Bohemia, but how can it be the case here?", he muttered to himself. *"However, it doesn't seem to be a good idea, it is forbidden in Christianity. And I don't think I'll get an exception to that rule from the Pope like we got to the brotherhood's celibacy rule",* he smiled to himself.

There were very few connections to Sweden in the dead of winter. A few skiers cross the sea, which was all frozen. The men of the south had never seen such a freezing sea before. It only seemed to emphasize the harsh long winter in the North and increase their isolation.

In Turku at the beginning of May, AD 1249

In the spring of 1249, in May, messenger on the first ship from Stockholm delivered Meinbald an official, sealed letter. It was a letter of appointment from Erik XI, who appointed him as marshal in charge of Finnish affairs. He asked Hildegard to translate the letter, because even though he and Hildegard had already found a common language during the winter, mostly

Swedish, he still didn't understand written Swedish. "Marshall? Marshal of Finland? Why not, I guess I can do that", he pondered.

"Congratulations, my brave, handsome husband! You will be a good Marshall to the eastern land. I remember how my father said that the military administration needs to be renewed, instead of the old earl system, new positions of the crown are needed. You are now the office holder, the first, supreme military leader of Finland!"

Meinbald sent some of his men back to Bohemia, or at least to Lübeck, from where they would travel to wherever they came from. This was because the northern coldness was too much for some and the strange language and strange mind of its people for some. According to his interpretation, some people were homesick, which the inactivity of winter had brought upon them. His most loyal men who still remained in this northern strange land were Fridrik, Kort, Klas, Otto, Lydeke, Herman and Gödecke. Staying here was self-evident for them because their leader Meinbald stayed too. But besides these brothers of cross, also many others remained, e.g. Asser, Berlholt, Dietrich, Magnus and of course Ulf. All of them also just happened to have another common factor, other than just loyalty to Meinbald: They all had happened to fall deeply in love with a Finnish or Swedish girl they "had found."

He continued his correspondence with Birger in the spring, after the ice had melted from the Baltic Sea. He clarified which powers were associated with Marshall's position and presented Birger the organization he needed.

"The Swedes follow good governance and are open to new ways of working, that's a good thing", he thought when reading Birger's reply letter.

Fortunately, their knight training had also covered the structure of the king's troops, and he could also ask for more information if he wanted, for example from Bohemia by writing to Cockroach. That's what he decided to do as well.

He was ordered to lead several fortress building projects, for which he needed fortress masters, castle wardens and garrison. He presented his knight brothers as castle wardens and judges, adding that, of course, Swedish knights who were willing to move to the new eastern land were needed. Birger liked his presentation, added only a few of his own names, and introduced the management structure to Erik. The King confirmed the presentation.

Among the common people, the king was called "Moss Tongue", because his speech was a bit slurred and he had been lame on one leg since birth. However, Birger and Erik seemed to get along well, they had mutual respect. King Erik invited Meinbald to his court for a presentation visit in July.

In July, he sailed on a Hanseatic ship to Stockholm following the king's invitation. The new Marshall had to introduce himself, and since he had familiarized himself with Swedish court etiquette, he was also prepared to present a counter invitation to the king for an inspection visit to Eastland in August.

The Germans brought more reinforcements from Lübeck, the Hanseatic League for the fur trade, and the church to inculcate the faith of the Western Church. However, this was only a small portion of the flow of people that was starting to come from Sweden.

Swedes started a real wave of immigration, whole family groups moved to settle here permanently, usually to live near the coast. Soldiers also moved with their families to fortresses or apartments built near them. They always had to report to the land marshal after arriving in the country. Meinbald very quickly appointed Lydeke as his scribe and deputy marshal, because he was not interested in receiving every single Swedish soldier who came to the country.

Stone castles and churches were now being built, that's why master masons from Germany were needed here. Several of them arrived already in June. Meinbald decided to go with one of the new master masons to Tavastia to check the progress of the fortifications at the same time. Tax collection in Tavast land also needed to be inspected and planned.

"At the same time, it's nice to see Kaukomieli and Matti again ", he thought. Lydeke was glad to stay to take care of the fortress in the Aurajoki estuary and receive the arrivals in the country.

Hildegard didn't want to go with him to the wild hinterland but preferred to stay in Turku, which she considered to be a bit of a remote trading place. Stockholm, too, was only a very new, free city founded by his father, but it would grow to be a much bigger and grander place than this village. *"Maybe Meinbald and I will move there when father's plans progress"*, Hildegard thought. He had lots of office trips in the coming summers and winters, repeating every lunar cycle.

In the North AD 1250 - 1256

King Abel of Denmark ruled from 1250 to 1252 and at that time there was peace in the Baltic Sea and trade with the Hanseatic cities grew. However, Abel fell on a campaign against the Frisians in 1252. His successor was his younger brother Kristoffer I.

1250 Erik X I of Sweden died and eight days later Birger Jarl's son Valdemar was elected as the new king of Sweden. However, Birger was the one who practically ruled the entire kingdom, as Valdemar was a minor. Meinbald sent a congratulatory letter to Valdemar via Birger by pigeon, pledging allegiance to the new king.

In AD 1251 Birger bloodily defeated a coup attempt led by Holmger's brother Filip – Holmger had been killed in Uppland AD 1247. Philip was allied with Denmark and invaded Sweden with Danish and German mercenaries. The troops led by Birger met the attackers at Herrevadsbro in Västmanland.

Bishop Magnus of Västerås is said to have made the attackers lay down their weapons with his peace declaration and proceeded to negotiate peace. However, Birger did not even negotiate for peace but had the attackers executed and confiscated their property. After the event, no one dared to stand against the earl.

In the same year, Birger concluded a trade agreement with the Hanseatic League of Lübeck. While preparing a favorable basis for the agreement, Birger invited Meinbald to Stockholm to give him advice.

Birger knew his son-in-law's story as the son of a German merchant. Birger's cousin Karl Ulv, whom he of course remembered well, was also there. He also knew German and acted as Birger's interpreter. Birger greeted Meinbald warmly and got straight to the point:

"I want Stockholm to become a successful, growing trading city. We invite and attract a lot of German traders here by giving exemption from taxes and customs duties. All they have to do in return is obey our laws and call themselves Swedes.

You, Meinbald certainly have an insight into what kind of views German merchants might have on this."

"Your majesty, dear father - King Otakar I of Bohemia made a very similar trade agreement with the Saxons when my own parents also moved to Prague to trade there. If our home had not burned down in Prague in a great fire, I would certainly be there now as a merchant, as my father and mother were."

"For the German merchants, the main thing is certainly that they want a safe peaceful place to trade and the protection of the king, not only here, but also on the whole route up to here north. Visby in Gotland is certainly an important stopover on the way here. Together with the Germans, the Danes have already built quite a lot of fortifications and a town in Visby. Look at what's there and make Stockholm at least twice the size of Visby. This way you ensure that traders prefer to visit Stockholm rather than Visby."

Karl, Birger and Meinbald discussed the different aspects during the afternoon so long that Birger finally stated that all the necessary points had been covered. The scribe had kept a record of the conversation, so the gentlemen could now return to draw up the contract document after he left for home.

Before he boarded his ship back to Turku, Karl escorted Meinbald through Stockholm Island, where Birger had built a stilt fortress. Stockholm, a fortified island in the middle of the long, narrow waterway connecting the Baltic Sea and Lake Mälaren, was a location ingeniously chosen for military strategy. It was deep enough inland, it was surrounded by water bodies, so the advance of the enemies was difficult and laborious, to say the least.

The sea was close, but not right next to the area, so the cold winds from the sea did not blow like they did right next to the coast. It was a good place for a trading post. Since the Viking Age, ships had sailed deep into lake Mälaren, sometimes in good faith to the island of Björkö, to the trading post of Birka, sometimes on raids and extermination trips to Sigtuuna.

It made sense to build a lock in this narrowness, where friendly merchants could stay to trade and where hostile enemies could be repelled. It improved the perceived security inland.

"Herr Birger wants to go immediately to the castle of Alsnö in the island of Adelsö, to draw up the final agreement. So we head west from here, while you return to Eastland."

"We still need a lot of stonemasons and masons here, Karl. Wooden forts can be burned, so they are no longer used in the German Empire. Even in Berlin, a stone wall was built around the entire city years ago. Ask the brothers from Order of St John or the Teutonic Knights where they can get the best stone masons here in the first place."

"Good point, we haven't had time to deal with that yet, but it must be taken into account soon. Castles and monasteries are needed here. Thank you, Meinbald", Karl replied and after that, they said goodbye to each other.

In Eastland

In the spring of 1252, in May, Hildegard gave birth to Meinbald's firstborn son, who was named Magnus. Hildegard wanted to name the boy after his grandfather Magnus Minnesköld, and he had no dissenting opinion. *"Magnus, the Great, no better name for a boy."* Happiness bloomed for a while in the young family. Hildegard, like Gregers, were Birger's own illegitimate children, they were full siblings. They had no official status in the Swedish court, but their lives seemed to be on the right track, as Birger steered the newly united kingdom.

Gregers received large fiefdoms in Västmanland from his half brother King Valdemar, where he established his own manor. Hildegard, on the other hand, was doing well in Eastland, Finland, where she traveled weekly between Rusko and Turku.

Hildegard later traveled to Tavastia after Meinbald, because she had heard a malicious rumor circulating in Turku that he had a local fiance in Tavastia. Similarly, it was rumored that his own brother Gregers was also inclined to polygamy like his father, and that he had already had time to have a child with one of Tavastian housemaids. This was all too much for Hildegard... She had suffered throughout her childhood with the knowledge that her father had another, official wife, although father Birger was seen at her and her mother's home very often.

Somehow, the fact that Gregers continued on the same line, was easy for her to understand, but the fact that Meinbald had also engaged a local woman in addition to her, that information was just too much. She was furious and decides to confront the couple in the sin itself.

"How can a man who calls himself a Christian, leading a Christian brotherhood of knights, break the holy rules of Christianity and marriage in such an insidious way?" There was a storm in Hildegard's head, when she packed Magnus and herself into travel wagons to Tavastia.

When Hildegard then actually found his husband together with Elin at Kaukomieli's and Kyllikki's home in Niemenpää, her worst fear seemed to have come true and she decided to stand her ground.

A huge, mainly Swedish-language verbal sparring and raging fight ensued. Elin had to defend herself against Hildegard who shouted insults and attacked her, punching and kicking her. After losing the fistfight, Hildegard seemed to calm down and lifted the little Magnus she had been carrying before the fight escalated, back into her arms.

For a moment it seemed that the situation had calmed down, but to everyone's surprise, Hildegard decided to take her own life by drowning in river Hiidenjoki. She left Magnus on the ground and walked straight to the river without saying a word. Meinbald ran after her to dive and save her, but he was forced to find the current of the river too strong.

The shock was great for everyone. Hildegard's lifeless body was only found late in the evening in the lower reaches of Hiidenjoki. Meinbald was broken by grief and weakened by self-recriminations.

There was no option: A message of condolence had to be sent to Birger, Gregers, Bero, and other relatives of Hildegard. In his letter, Meinbald directly asked for help in organizing the funeral, he seemed to have no strength at all. Birger quickly replied to the message that he, Hildegard's mother and Gregers only wanted to hold a small, intimate funeral, the arrangements of which would be taken care of by Bishop Bero. In his own letter, Meinbald had not mentioned a single word about Elin, but only wrote that an accident befell them on the way to Tavastia.

The funeral would be held in Church at Nousiainen, Bishop Bero will deliver the blessing. Meinbald felt like he was walking in a fog as he carried little Magnus in his arms and they entered the church to bury his spouse and Magnus's mother.

Elin had travelled with him to Rusko, taking care of Magnus as best she could, but she didn't dare to come to church. Birger, Gregers and Hildegard's mother attended the funeral. Birger mourned his daughter, of course, but also took part in Meinbald's grief.

Eventually life went on, but slowly. Then one day in late autumn, Elin told him that she was pregnant. He hurried to ask Kaukomieli for Elin's hand in marriage.

"I've been waiting for this day, Kaukomieli confessed, "I knew that you two would still end up together. Of course, you'll get Elin, and we'll have a really decent wedding, the Pirkka men and other hundred-clans can see to it that you're at least a week in peace!"

Their wedding was celebrated in Niemenpää and it lasted almost a week, with all the bride-robbings and old Kalevala traditions like bear commemoriations.

They had barely recovered from their weddings when he received an invitation to participate in a hunting trip to Uppland. The summons was delivered by a messenger who told his commander was the noble Sir John Teet. Remembering good manners, Meinbald immediately responded affirmatively to the invitation and announced his new brother-in-law Matti and his knight brothers Fridrik and Kort as his own party for the trip.

The trip was otherwise quite successful, but the behavior of the host of the hunting party left some room to improve. John Teet invited him to the same hunting ground with him to wait for deer and elk to be driven toward them with hunting bows. During the waiting, Teet started to ask information from him about his affairs. He had learned Swedish, so an interpreter was no longer needed.

"Herr Meinbald, you are a brother of the Bohemian Order? I used to be a Knight Templar, if you remember. I once left the brotherhood because I wanted to serve the earthly power more than the heavenly one. But if I understood correctly, you are still a member of your order?"

"Yes, that's right. I work as the country marshal of the order here in North."

"But you are already married for the second time, isn't breaking your vow of celibacy a problem for you?"

"Regarding that, my brothers and I have special permission from the Pope himself, Herr Teet."

" I see... But does that permission also cover meddling with the local heathen chief's daughter?"

Meinbald got completely fired up by such a rude question.

"Listen, Herr Teet, if you invited me here on a hunting trip just to make fun of me and my spouse, let me tell you that I won't listen to that. I also don't understand what you want to aim for with your actions like this."

"My apologies, Herr Meinbald, I just wondered when I heard from Lord Birger how you had first married his daughter and then, barely having buried her, you have now already had time to take another wife. Is your loyalty to the Swedish crown or the pagans?"

"Are you asking this for yourself or for someone else?"

"You know that Lord Birger and I are on good terms. I want to make sure that the interests of the kingdom and the crown are still uppermost in your heart."

"I'm sorry, Herr Teet, I was too hasty. You may tell Birger that my allegiance is still entirely to the Crown and the Church. As a sign of that, I shoot and give the first catch to Birger. In fact, I hope you personally take it to him when you go back to Stockholm."

"Really? Are you serious?"

"Yes... Now, Sir, let's shut up. If we continue this conversation, not a single animal will come this way"

Agonizing silence followed. Finally, the growl of an approaching animal started from the bush, and in a moment a large bull elk appeared in front of them with horns like two big shovels on its head. Meinbald fired his bow, as did Teet. The animal finally fell loudly to the ground after having run twenty meters past them. When the men go to the elk, they found only one arrow in the carcass, straight through the elk's heart.

"Exactly where I was aiming at", John Teet rejoiced.

"My lord, this arrow is mine", Meinbald stated and pulled the arrow out of the animal's chest. "I have made a cross on these arrows of mine, see? You can pick your own arrow from among the wildflowers."

"I see… Well, but I'd be happy to take this crown head to Lord Birger in Stockholm. Happy hunting, Mr. Meinbald", Teet said and left to get his servant, leaving him to drain the blood from the animal. The remaining hunt was more relaxed, the gentlemen no longer sought each other's company. Kort and Fridrik noted Meinbald's irritability. After the hunt, on the way home on the ship, Kort dared to ask:

"Brother Meinbald, what happened? You are just like a different man, and you don't seem at all satisfied, even though we got a decent catch."

"Brother Kort, our host insulted me and Elin as soon as we were left alone at the beginning of the hunt. I can't understand what he wanted to achieve with this."

"Aha, it sounds like this Herr Teet is very upset about your position and achievements, Meinbald. He's jealous of you, if I'm not mistaken. He would want to be in your place and not just a poor mercenary of Earl Birger."

"Yes, that's what it seems, when you think about it for a moment. Absolutely. Thank you, Buck."

"Teet is quite a nuisance", says Fridrik, who had been listening to the conversation thoughtfully. "Did he realize that he also insulted Matti's sister?"

"He didn't get it. He obviously didn't realize that Matti, the king's courtier, was Elin's brother. Or then he's even more ruthless than I could have imagined."

On April 21, 1253, Elin gave birth in Rusko to a daughter, who was baptized and named Mielikki. Elin was visibly happy taking care of her first child. Elin also acted as a surrogate mother for Magnus as best she could and raised him as if he were her own. Life was suddenly very demanding with two small children, but Elin coped bravely and she also got support from her sisters and mother Kyllikki.

Kaukomieli invited Meinbald to seed work in Niemenpää in May.

"Just go, you can join Ukonvakat", said Elin.

"What is that?" He asks his wife.

"You'll see then, just go now, we'll do well here with the children. I would come myself, but it's not suitable with small children because they drink beer there."

He traveled alone to Niemenpää. It felt strange to ride without Elin, family, even without his knight brothers. "But this is also exciting", he thought to himself.

"However, I can't wait to stop by Tavast Castle first, because I have to talk to Dietrich and the men and see how the masons got the castle built."

He arrived at the castle after three days and two long nights. Dietrich Balk was a little surprised to see him here, when he suddenly gallopped into the castle yard on his horse.

"You have to make that gate narrower and lower, so that no one can just ride in here", he pointed out as his first words, "Greetings, fortress master Balk!" he grinned.

Men clapped hands and patted each other on the shoulder.

"This is a pleasant surprise, my lord Meinbald! What brings you here to the backwoods of Tavastia without warning? The Tatar horde isn't after you, is it?"

"No, I'm coming to visit my father-in-law to Niemenpää for spring sowing, he answered without hesitation."

"A-ha, well that's great, then please do share your sowing experiences with us too. Here, we've had local rye bread and barley beer, but I've often wondered how to get any grain to grow in such a short growing season here in the north."

"Well, Dietrich, you can actually come with me, and you'll see for yourself, I'm sure my father-in-law will be happy to accept the extra men for the sowing work. Take two or three men with you."

"Your word is my law, noble knight", replied Dietrich. He took Magnus the Hero, Ulf the Ax, and Knight Berlholt with him. Berlholt had also stayed in Tavastia with a few men from Teet's department, such as Asser.

In Niemenpää, Kaukomieli welcomed the men with joy.

"Welcome, dear son-in-law! And it's good that you brought fortress men with you, because now we can get the plows moving and the grain in the furrow in record time!" And so they did. But before starting the work, Kaukomieli spoke out the sowing verse:

"Hag below the ground, Lad at the bottom of the field!

I have no shortage of people, the field does not belittle the legacy.

Give us hundreds of branches and forks, Thousands of noses in those,

From my sowing, from my plough, From my efforts,

Over the envious man, by the heart of the good-natured,

against the mind of the evil!"

Meinbald had done plowing and sowing work in Bohemia, so he was familiar with using a plow. He also recalled the story told by Agnes according to which the entire royal Premysl family of Bohemia had descended from a peasant, a ploughman, who had dined on an iron plough. Dietrich was, as a big man, almost equivalent to one horse, as he pulled the plow which Ulf steered.

Magnus, who had worked as a blacksmith in Lübeck, also proved to be very competent in organizing the sowing work. There was something in him that even Kaukomieli's own workers respected, even though they didn't understand his language and he didsn't speak Finnish very well yet. Matti also got along well with Magnus, as did Kaukomieli.

"Where are your bodyguards, Oh, father-in-law?" he asked, because he didn't see Antero anywhere.

"They have their own sowing jobs on the coast", replied Kaukomieli, "I always give my men a day off for sowing, hoping that the Russians will also sow and not attack here."

"Yes, well thought out, they really have to eat too..."

There were so many workers that the entire sowing job was done in half a day.

"Now the work is done and we are leaving for Niemenpää's courtyard", Kaukomieli stated in an audible voice. "It's our turn to hold Ukko's party this year, the Vakka party. So all the men and women from Vanaja village join us. Meinbald, tell your men too that you are welcome and that there's plenty of beer available!"

On the way, Matti explained to Meinbald that Ukko's party was a centuries-old rite that they celebrated every spring, sacrificing to Ukko to get rain after sowing. The bushel keeper called the party, made the beer, and stored the food and drinks to be sacrificed at the feast in the Ukko's bushel, "Vakka".

People started arriving in the yard here and there, all men and women who had done their sowing. The early summer sun shone from a cloudless sky. Matti, Kaukomieli, and men have carried the chairs and benches from the hut to the yard. Hostess Kyllikki and the maids offered bread and brought everyone a large cup of beer.

Kaukomieli got in front of the party, in the middle of the yard, to pray:

> *"Oh Ukko the overlord*
>
> *Father,ruler of the sky*
>
> *Lift the cloud from the northwest*
>
> *Another soon from the northeast*
>
> *Push them together side to side*
>
> *Let them gallop on top of each other*
>
> *Sprinkle water from your clouds*
>
> *To the new crop to grow,*
>
> *Downto these dusty fields."*

He sprinkled the water from the well in a bucket around the yard, then he took a mug of beer, lifted it up, put it in front of his mouth, and said:

"Ukko's toast!" And then he took a good swig of the beer.

Everyone did the same, including Meinbald, Dietrich, Ulf, and Magnus.

The devout atmosphere was immediately released when the beer kegs were emptied. A happy gabble started to fill the air. It felt as if the narrow-mindedness and curmudgeon from the minds of Tavastian people had been washed down into the digestive system in one fell swoop along with the beer. Kaukomieli sat down next to Meinbald.

"Listen, my son-in-law, since you are German and come from further away, I feel that I have to tell you a little background about why we continue this hundreds of years old tradition. Listen, we sing a lot of songs, which are often sung at parties like this - today, however, we didn't sing them, because I wanted to follow a short formula, when I knew that we would have a more worthy company here than ourselves- that is, you and your men. But listen when I tell you how farming came about at the beginning of time and how we explain to ourselves the incomprehensible works of the creator."

Kaukomieli told the mythical story of Sampo's robbery as a shortened version. At the end, the Sampo broke into pieces at sea, and when the pieces finally landed, they brought farming skills, money and prosperity to humanity.

"What is that Sampo, what kind of widget is it?" Meinbald asked, already a little tipsy himself.

"Well, listen Mielivalta, it's a very mysterious widget, but I guess it was a bit like that mill that grinds grain on the banks of river Hiidenjoki."

"What, do you have a watermill here? I thought they were the latest gadgets even in Germany."

"Yes, the first mills were put in some rapids already a hundred to two hundred years ago. They were adopted here from Sweden or Norway. Secondly, some have compared Sampo to the salt mills used on the shores of the Väinö Sea, they wash the sea water and evaporate the water from the salt. But Sampo's whole point is that it's inexplicable, it's not from this world, Mielivalta. We humans need people like that, just like Jesus' miracles, there is no need to explain them either. Now let's take Ukko's toast, part two", Kaukomieli signaled to Matti, who rushed to the place with a leather flagon and a wooden cup. He removed the cap from the flagon and poured the clear liquid into the pot.

"Take this Mielivalta, and give it to the men also, so that your thoughts will brighten and your mind will rise", Kaukomieli ordered and smiled like the sun.

The men drank the moonshine grinning down. Intoxication hit the consciousness like an iron nail. The evening was warm and long, the guests of the village had already left a long time ago, when Meinbald and the men finally got to the guest house for the night. He dreamt of Sampo, Pohjola and Väinö, the colourful cover of Sampo was spinning in his head. In the morning, he thought it was best to take a dip in Hiidenjoki for a swim just to clear his head.

At the breakfast table, Dietrich opened his verbal treasure chest:

"Lord Dominus I have a request for you. The construction of the castle requires a lot of attention from me, and I think it is of the utmost importance that I do my job well. That's why I ask you to give the post of tax collector to Knight Berlholt, he could very well focus on tax matters, which, frankly, I am not capable of at all."

"Well, that's a good proposal, it's fine for me, if it's fine for you, Herr Berlholt?"

"Yes, it works well for me, through my wife I have already gotten to know the people here a lot and I believe that I will get along well with them, even if my task is to take part of their harvest and assets to the crown", Berlholt answered.

The matter was then settled, Meinbald returned to Turku and the men got back to the castle from Niemenpää after breakfast.

Turku

Meinbald wrote a letter of resignation to Grand Master Konrad, because he considered that he could not follow the rules of the knightly brotherhood and he had decided to stay permanently in the north. Grandmaster "Cockroach" answered him, asking that they'd still keep in touch, because the Pope and the Dominican monks needed a good administrator in the new area.

He received recognition from the Grand Master and special status as the northernmost country master of the Order of the Red Star and Cross, approved by the Pope. He thanked Konrad in his reply letter, even though he felt disgust in his stomach at the thought of dealing with Cockroach.

So now, at the age of 33, he was the land marshal responsible for the affairs of the Swedish king's Eastland, Capitaneus Finlandesis, and the northernmost country master of the Bohemian Order. And he had a spouse from Satakunta and Tavastia and two children, a boy and a girl.

"Not a bad achievement for such an orphan weakling", he thought.

Chapter XIII
Crusade to Narva

In Rusko, Turku, the first of June, AD 1255

Elin gave birth to another daughter in 1255. She was baptized Tuulikki. Meinbald was so happy to had already been blessed with two healthy daughters. Elin held the little ones in her arms, glowing with happiness.

She said, "Oh, my dear husband, don't we have cute girls? Yes, we have been blessed with happiness, and they will not lack anything in their lives."

"And when they grow up to become beauties like their mother, I can choose the greatest and richest spouses for them," he replied to Elin.

"Oh, my husband, you don't know the will of Tavastian women. They choose themselves, not you. You only think so because you are allowed to think so," Elin rejoiced.

The year progressed peacefully, summer, autumn, winter, taking care of children and doing everyday chores. Until one rainy afternoon, a messenger brings a message to Meinbald. The message was from Earl Birger, and in it he obliged him to collect and equip a significant army from Finland and Tavast land, to join the knights and men-at-arms sent by Birger's son Valdemar to Turku, and to sail in a joint fleet to the mouth of the Narva River. There they should disembark and join the army of the Danes and Teutonic Knights to support his crusade against the Novgorodians. They should free the peoples of Vadja, Inger land, and also Karelia from false faith, and make them true Christians.

Vironmaa, AD 1256

Dietrich von Kyvel, a vassal of the Bishop of Riga since 1245, was one of the largest landowners in Estonia, alongside the King of Denmark. He was a very influential man who was in direct contact with the Pope and, in the summer of 1256, together with the Danes and the Swedes, organized a crusade to Vadjamaa.

Vadja belonged to the Novgorod principality. Whereas Earl Birger is considered the founder of Stockholm, Dietrich is considered the founder of the city of Narva; the deputy governor of Denmark's Estland; the head of the vassal league there; and also the commander-in-chief of the Narva Crusade. Dietrich had a half-brother, Otto von Lüneburg; they shared a mother but have different fathers.

The brothers' estates were located near Vadja and Ingerland. These vassals of the Reval Diocese and the Riga Archdiocese had asked Pope Alexander IV for an order to appoint a bishop for those pagan peoples who wanted to become Christians (Vadjaians, Ingers, and Karelians) and who lived near their manors. In his letter on March 19, 1255, the Pope gives the Archbishop of Riga, Albert Suerbeer, permission to appoint a bishop for them. Dietrich, Otto, and their third brother, Heinrich, worked very closely together during those years.

King Kristoffer I of Denmark had formally inherited the power of the Estonian region from his father, but as a strong local leader, Dietrich led all practical actions in Estonia during those troubled times. Kristoffer had his hands full in his heartland of Skåne, where he had an ongoing power struggle with the Archbishop of Lund. He was also on good terms with the rising Earl of Sweden.

At Kristoffer's request, Birger agreed to send several military divisions to Estonia. Of course, he did not do this completely unsolicited, but he knew how to act in accordance with the times and with diplomatic wisdom. Later, Birger also acted as a peace mediator between the Bishop of Lund and the kings of Norway and Denmark.

The first of June, AD 1256, on the Narva River

Dietrich von Kyvel led the provincial army, which he had collected from Estonia and partly already from the Vadja region; in addition, he had a few Sword Knights and Danish soldiers. Dietrich had received two bishops from Albert Suerbeer, although they had still remained in their home parishes in Germany.

Meinbald led the Germans, Tavastians, and Finns, who had joined together with the Swedish force led by the knight Kettil.

"It's good that that grouchy John Teet is there, because he has experience in cooperation with the Knights of Livonia and the Danes," he considered.

"Yes, and of course Dietrich Balk; his uncle was the Prussian Landmaster of the Teutonic Knights when the Livonian Knighthood was incorporated into the Teutonic Knights twenty years ago. This uncle, Herman, became the first Landmaster of the Teutonic Knights in Livonia."

Matti led the Pirkka warriors and Tavastian forces from Satakunta, Fridrik the Finns, and Meinbald commanded the army detachment as field marshal. Otto von Lüneburg served as a field marshal of the Livonian Order.

Teet and Fridrik acted as the commanders of the cavalry. After having conferred with Dietrich von Kyvel, Otto and Kettil, Meinbald briefly shared the common battle plan, "John Teet, you attack the left flank. Fridrik, you take the right flank. The Danes, Livonians, and Estonians attack from the middle with their cavalry, followed by theirs and our infantry. Matti, I'm coming with your Pirkka riders; we'll join the attacking group in the middle in the second wave. Questions?"

The professionals had no questions; they got down to business. Grouping up for the attack was soon complete, and visual contact with the enemy's vanguard was achieved after advancing only under half a mile.

Dietrich blew his horn, and the cavalry broke into a gallop. They spreat out on the flanks so they could hit a wider enemy group. The enemy section was not very wide; it seemed to have a depth of only three to four ranks.

Meinbald noticed, while riding with Matti in the second step of the middle group, that the Livonian troop looked really small, just one flag, six riders.

The Danish group was just as small; luckily Matti and he had come to reinforce, he thought. Their onslaught sent the Novgorodians into a state of terror and near paralysis. When they hit the center, most of the vanguard fled out to the flanks, making room for the center.

The pincer movement of the flanks prevented the fleeing

troops from getting away, and fierce, close fighting was encountered right at their main objective. Matti rode in together with Meinbald's troops, and his men from Pirkka fought bravely and relentlessly.

Magnus and Ulf followed the horsemen again as the spearheads of the infantry; they struck like lightning, or Thor with his hammer, mowing down the enemies.

Matti turned his horse toward the left flank, where he saw the Swedes fighting hard against the enemy. He arrived just in time to knock down the horseman who was threatening Kettil's life. Kettil was saved at the very last moment from a certain, fatal sword strike.

All in all, the attack of the troops made a deep impact among the Novgorodians. They had been poorly armed; seeing the superiority of the attackers, they finally laid down their weapons and surrendered. Dozens of prisoners of war were taken.

Kettil came to Matti and Magnus after the fight, put his hand on Magnus's shoulder, and said, "Garper, you beat the enemy like a foreign pig!"

"What is he saying?" Magnus asked Matti, who he knew could interpret.

Matti interpreted, and Magnus laughed. "After all, they are pigs, pig dogs, Schweinehunde!"

Everyone laughed out loud, releasing the stress of the battle from their bodies. Kettil profusely thanked Matti for saving his life.

"It's nothing, Kettil; I just did my best, and you would certainly have done the same if things had been the other way around," Matti stated, quite modestly.

At the evening campfire, Kettil told Matti about his sister, Malin. Matti said that he definitely wanted to meet Malin after the trip. Kettil stated that Matti, as an honorable Birka warrior, would be a great groom for his sister, and he promised to act as a spokesman to Father Bengt.

"Is she prettier than you?" Matti asked, and so they get another round of laughter in the middle of the chaos of the battlefield.

Meinbald went to the command tent for consultation with Dietrich, Otto, Herman, and Kettil. Dietrich began the negotiations by saying,

"Gentlemen, it went well. We didn't lose many men. We captured all the surviving Novgorodian outpost troops. Our fortifiers are now starting work on the fortification, for we must have a strong foothold on this east side of the Narva River to hold our position against the Novgorodians."

"Herr Otto, you lead the troops of the Livonian Order here, but you only have six horsemen? When will you bring your reinforcements across the river?" Meinbald inquired.

"Herr Meinbald, I can't say that yet. It depends on the outcome of this negotiation."

"Now I don't understand, aren't you ready to take over and keep the lands for yourself?"

"We do not have any information about what has been agreed about the occupied land. We have already presented, some time ago, that we want a third of the countries. How much do you want?"

Meinbald couldn't believe his ears. Weren't these things agreed in advance? He had never seen such an improvised, poorly planned operation before, and now this, the pinnacle of it all. He was holding back his surprise and said, "I have no information about it. I ask the will of our Swedish king." He translated the question into Swedish for Kettil.

"Lord Birger wants us to join all the regions to the Swedish kingdom. He has not given me any authority to hand over a piece to anyone else. This is the will of our King Valdemar."

Meinbald translated the answer, knowing it will dismay the others as much as him.

"If you take everything, there's no point in us participating in the whole campaign! Why did we even come with this small department!?" says Otto, under provocation.

"We thought that you were aware of the territorial claim of the Livonian Knights," Dietrich explained, a little more diplomatically. "The previous Danish king, Valdemar II, and the knights agreed in Stensby in 1238 that one-third of the new pagan territories belonged to the knights; two-thirds remained in Denmark. If we don't get the support of Livonia in keeping the new territory, we will have to get much more support from the Kingdom of Sweden in the future. And I don't see that here I would take any unreasonable risks on behalf of a king unknown to me, who has already announced in advance that he is not ready to give up even a piece of the land that we would have conquered for him. Do you understand, Herr Marshal Meinbald? If you don't believe what we are telling you about these past deals that were made long ago, just ask your knight Dietrich. His uncle, Hermann, was the country master of the Knights of Livonia, and he himself was arranging the matter in Stensby, Zealand."

Meinbald sank deeper and deeper into despair. Dark thoughts flooded his mind:

"This can't be this crazy! Birger must have unknowingly screwed me and my men, but also poor Kettil, who was only sent here to bring bad news and impossible wishes. Von Kyvel seemed to be aware of the demands, but he was apparently not aware of the terms on which Sweden and Denmark had agreed on the arms aid.

Or, knowing Birger, maybe even Denmark hasn't been aware, damn it, what a mixed soup came out of this crusade. I shouldn't have left here in the first place, but it's too late to regret it now."

"Exactly, I understand very well. I suggest that we now take a break from the negotiations and look at the situation again in the morning, after sleeping overnight," he said succinctly.

This was done. Dietrich, Herman, and Otto stayed in the tent in their dismay, while Meinbald and Kettil returned among their troops with the same feelings.

"Kettil, this is a really messy and dangerous situation. Do you understand? If we cannot agree on the division of the land, we cannot defend ourselves against the Novgorodians when they come, with our own troops alone. Our maintenance route is too long, difficult, and laborious, and, besides, it is easy to interrupt. We have a wide body of water behind us, so we can't retreat, and no half-finished wooden equipment will hold the enemy back for long."

"Yes, you are absolutely right, Meinbald. We didn't have enough advance knowledge of what was going on here, and now it seems that Dietrich and Otto themselves have been preparing this operation for a long time. We are in the wrong place; our victory today came far too easily, and we will be lost if we stay here waiting for the Novgorodians without the support of the Livonians. It seems to me that the Pope has given permission both in Sweden and here to go to holy war, but has not understood anything about the conflicting interests of our kingdoms here. King Kristian of Denmark is not interested in this territorial conquest at all, and it shouldn't be of interest to our Valdemar or father Birger either. I will explain the situation to them when we get home."

"It's great that we agree! In the morning, we announce that we are withdrawing and going to protect our own territories from the future wrath of the Novgorodians. We can be sure that this border violation by us will not go unretaliated by them. Of course, I want to talk to Brother Dietrich, but he will probably confirm that von Kyvel is telling the truth."

Meinbald marched straight to Dietrich Balk's quarters.

"Brother Dietrich, we have a problematic situation, to which you can bring a little additional light," he opened. "Can you say whether your uncle, Hermann, has had negotiations with the King of Denmark regarding the ownership of the new lands?"

"Herr Marshal, I do remember that he was in Denmark years ago to negotiate. We were still in active correspondence at that time. After all, he was in Acre when he joined the German Brotherhood and later encouraged me to join this holy path. Why do you ask?"

"Now it seems that your uncle and the Danish king agreed, eighteen years ago, that one-third of the newly conquered pagan land belongs to the Knights of Livonia, and two-thirds belongs to Denmark. The King of Sweden could not have known this, maybe not the new King of Denmark either, but here they still stick to that agreement."

"It means that we don't have a united front force, so we have unknowingly arrived in a very dangerous situation!" exclaimed Dietrich.

"Yes, that's exactly what it means. Thank you, Dietrich, for confirming what Herr von Kyvel told us. We must leave here in the morning and withdraw without raising a finger against the Novgorodians. This war that is starting here is not our war, but, because of the border conflict we have caused, we must quickly return to protect our own country from a future retaliatory attack."

Meinbald walked back to Dietrich von Kyvel's command post in the evening to tell them that they would withdraw in the morning.

"It's a wise decision, Herr Meinbald. We will continue here with the support of Livonian brothers. Thanks for your help so far."

"I suggest, Herr Dietrich, that we maintain communication in the future, in case we can inform each other of the enemy's movements. I would like to take one of your messengers on our trip in the morning. We will take him to my command post in Tavastia and thus teach the message route while we retreat."

"Excellent suggestion. I will send you my best messenger, who also knows the language of the Tavastian people."

At the Narva River, June 30, AD 1256

Dietrich von Kyvel continued fortification work and guerilla warfare in the Vatja region. When the Swedes left, Otto managed to negotiate additional troops from the Livonian Knights in exchange for a third of the conquered land. He enticed the mercenaries of the detachment led by John Teet to stay by offering them a decent share of the loot.

Aleksander Nevski was away from Novgorod, but after he returned, he finally learned about the border skirmish and their defeat in Narva. He decided to gather his forces for a revenge attack. When Alexander's troops finally arrived in November near the Narva River, where the hostilities had taken place, they saw that a fortress has been started on their side but then left unfinished. The fortress was set on fire.

Some locals and Ingers told them that Dietrich's forces had retreated to their side of the river, but the Sveans, Finns, and Tavastians fled the place earlier. After hearing this, Alexander headed his troops to Karelia together with the metropolitan, with the obvious intention of recruiting the Karelians to join him in the revenge expedition.

At the Koprye fortress, Aleksander made the decision to attack both Tavastland and Sweden. He sent his sub-commanders and messengers from the fortress to take word to all the Karelian chiefs of the fifth part of Vatja who were loyal to him. The metropolitan and some of the Novgorodian men return from Koprye back to Novgorod.

Meinbald received information about the strong troops seen in Narva from Dietrich von Kyvel's messenger and was happy that they were able to save their entire force from a futile, hopeless battle and were able to return intact, ready for the coming counterattack. He had divided the men into the forts on the coast of the Gulf of Finland and the river estuaries in such a way that each fort had one knight, five Tavastian horsemen, and about twenty infantrymen. In Tavastia, inland, the fortresses were filled with Pirkka horsemen and peasants from Tavastland, who only had little time to be given short combat training by the fort's commander.

It had been agreed that, when the enemy approached, the signal fires were to be lit immediately; and, when they were seen from the forts, half of the crew was immediately sent to the lit signal. The chain of fires thus signaled the direction of the enemy's approach, and the men at the ends of the chain turn off the bonfire when they had sent an auxiliary force.

In this way, the entire eastern border of Tavastia, following the natural terrain barriers formed by Lake Päijänne and its tributaries, was as well protected as possible. The coast guard also patroled the Gulf of Finland on skidboats throughout the summer season, trying to spot all unknown fleets and report their approach as early as possible.

They were waiting for what was to come and where the enemy would be seen first. They were ready. Summer turned to autumn; the crew was trained hard in every fort. Nothing was heard from anywhere, and some of the men had already started to think that Novgorod would not come. However, he was sure that they would. He invited the chiefs of all the fortresses to gather at Tavastehus Castle. In two days everyone was there: Fridrik, Kort, Dietrich, Lydeke, Matti, and Antero.

"Gentlemen, I have thought about this situation and concluded that although the defense posture is favorable and good for us, it is not yet good enough. So, we're going to attack across Päijänne with one-third of our men!"

"What did you say?" Matti asked, wondering if he understood correctly.

"I think the Romans already said in their time that attack is the best defense, and that is still the case today," Meinbald explained. "We advance to the area of Vatja fifth, where there are only scattered small villages, and free that area from the taxation power of the Novgorodians. This is not a crusade; we are not converting anyone there. We just take over that country and start collecting taxes for Sweden, and those who agree to this get to live. Those who do not agree are allowed to go to Novgorod or lose their lives."

"Matti, you and your Pirkka warriors will take the northern offensive line from the northern end of Päijänne to the east. If you don't encounter any enemies, you hook to the south until you make contact with the enemy or you encounter the advancing troops in the middle groove. In the middle course, Kort, you push from the south end of Päijänne to the northeast. Fridrik's southern group advances along the coast as far as it can go. On the Karelian Isthmus you continue to Lake Laatokka, if you can."

"When you encounter an enemy, you immediately send me a message by pigeon. We keep in touch with all progress-makers. I will give further instructions as the situation progresses. Lydeke, you lead the defense forces staying in Turku. Antero, you lead Kokemäki. And Dietrich, you stay here in Tavastehus Castle."

"I'm taking one Hundred troop with me, which I'm keeping as a reserve. We initially follow the middle attack furrow about half a day's journey behind. We leave tomorrow morning to advance towards Päijänne. Fridrik, you return to the fortress at the mouth of Kukinjoki, where you assemble your coastal group. The actual advance to the offensive direction begins at the same time, at dawn on the fifteenth of September, without a separate order. Do you have any questions?"

"No, no, this is clear," all the captains repeated.

Everyone had understood the order and, as professionals, were ready to fulfill their heavy duty. Returning to the fortresses, Dietrich, Antero, and Lydeke began to organize supply wagons for the attacking troops. The fortresses distributed the soldiers' rations directly from the collected tax barrels, this was exactly what the crown collected the taxes for, the men thought unanimously. Lydeke delivered part of the cargo from Turku immediately to the Raseborg fortress.

The Northern Shores of the Gulf of Finland, December AD 1256

The sea was still thawed, but the freezing winds gave a strong reason to assume that the enemy could no longer sail from the sea. The coastal forces, which were smaller than the one-third that was attacking, withdrew to strengthen the inland forts; only small outposts were left to bide their time and take care of the operation of the supply chain.

Fridrik's southern invasion force had advanced along the coast to the east without encountering any notable resistance. Most of the small villages had received them kindly. Only one village, five days after crossing Kymijoki, objected to the change of tax owner. The village elder, a cattle herder, began to protest loudly, when one of Fridrik's younger horsemen lost his temper and snapped the big man's neck with one swift stroke of his sword. The result was horror among the villagers, women crying and wailing, but also a very quick descent of the people to their knees, showing obedience to the new masters.

The villagers, in their distress, would have given the soldiers, they thought were Swedes, half of their food supplies, but Fridrik wanted to show humanity and good Christianity by taking only a quarter with them. Advancing in full military gear was already very exhausting even without fighting, so the men's daily rations were quite large. Now that they were already in the Gulf of Vyborg, the entire northern coast of the Gulf of Finland had been secured for Sweden.

Lake Saimaa

Kort and his troops had progressed equally efficiently from the south shore of Päijänne all the way to Saimaa. The terrain of their advance had been full of watercourses and swamps, sometimes to be crossed, sometimes to be bypassed. It had been thawing until the beginning of December, so the waterways had not frozen yet. For a few days now, it had started to feel like the more severe frosts had begun to grow ice layers in the marshes and lakes.

Rautavaara

Matti had taken the soldiers of Pirkka as far north as Rautavaara. The Laplanders they had run into did not really find any understanding of why they should start paying taxes to the Swedish king when the Prince of Novgorod had granted them tax exemption. The Pirkka warriors had been just as cruel as the Germans and had threatened to kill if the Laplander did not agree to submit to taxation. Even more effective threat than killing had been that the man's reindeer would be slaughtered and the meat taken away, or the carcasses entangled in the swamp.

They had not encountered Novgorodians, so Matti turned their direction directly towards the south as agreed. They hadn't needed to kill anyone yet, except for a couple of reindeer for dinner, of course.

"Christmas is approaching; it's damn dark here. You can't even see a horse moving," Matti's cavalrymen muttered from time to time. They continued, without enemy sightings, first past Koli; then they passed Kontiolahti and continued south.

In Joensuu, the Karelian army attacked them with a surprise strike from the east. One of Matti's horsemen was captured when the Karelians overturned the horse and took the man with them, retreating to the east. Matti didn't chase too far, because he was aiming to the south, as he had been ordered. He thought that the Karelians wouldn't go north but south or continue east, so he didn't fear they would go around their back. As a precaution, however, he ordered the rear end of his marching section to make occasional stops and short patrols to the rear.

Saimaa, January AD 1257

Kort's section met the enemy advancing from east to west at Savonlinna, south of Kyrönsalmi, at a point where you could cross the Saimaa waterway along a narrow isthmus. A fierce skirmish ensued; neither side was able to immediately deploy their troops due to the narrow ground surrounded by water. The ice was still so thin that men who got out to try hooking through it stomp their feet through the ice, luckily right on the shore. The top men of Kort fought bravely on the isthmus, knocking down many Karelians, but after each fall, a fresh line-up of new men came on with new enthusiasm. The Karelians had a clear number superiority, and they also knew how to use the terrain to their advantage much better than Kort's German troops.

Kort and his men were, little by little being outnumbered in the narrows, but just then Matti and his horsemen rushed to the rescue to attack the rear of the Karelian troops right flank. They scattered the enemy forces by riding through them and killing almost every one of them.

Before the attack, Matti had ordered his men to equip themselves with heavy steel armor, so the already almost fearless Pirkka-men were now "immortal" young heroes in their own opinion. Birger had acquired a fleet of armor imported from Germany to distribute to the best troops of the Eastern Army.

Helmets, breastplates, shin guards, and steel shoes aroused great wonder at the beginning, especially among the Pirkka warriors, but now they themselves experienced how superior the new military technology was compared to the old ring shirts and leather equipment.

The self-confidence of these young men was at its peak, just before it turned into arrogance. One Karelian soldier found a weak point in the armor of Matti's best warrior, Jalomieli, and managed to kill him by stabbing him directly in the heart with his spear.

When the troop saw what happened, humility returned to the men, and they took no more extra risks. The men attacked, besieging the Karelian section, and, in the end, no one from this small section survived. The Karelians in the front turned when they saw the reserve behind them destroyed and rushed back towards their certain destruction. Matti commanded his strike force to rush directly towards this retreating force, and he ordered his rear force to attack the rear end of the enemy group he had cut off.

Kort's forces noticed the dispersion of the enemy and the relaxation of the attack pressure, starting to push across the isthmus. Karelian men and Novgorodians fell under the avalanche; panic spreat and made the enemies defenseless.

When the fighting finally stopped, the men took off their helmets, letting their sweaty faces and hair cool in the biting winter wind. Steam rose from the troops until they had cooled enough so that it was time to remove the heavy armor and change into lighter leather clothing.

Kort sent Meinbald a message with a pigeon, telling him that he had made contact with the enemy and with Matti's forces. The enemy had been beaten together, and their intention was to turn southward next, unless the commander ordered otherwise.

After the night at the camp, the journey continued again. Now Kort's and Matti's men formed a fairly invincible force, marching south toward the Gulf of Finland. Meinbald sent approval of the intention by carrier pigeon, with the information that he and his reserve troops had already turned south the night before and were now approximately half a day ahead of them on their way to the Gulf of Finland.

The reason was that the main forces of Novgorod had been spotted by Fridrik's scouts in Kattilainen, advancing from the east toward Vehkalahti. Meinbald's own troops advanced as a fast-march section from the west side; he ordered Kort and Matti to advance in two parallel sections on the east side of the waterways, making sure there was no enemy in the area.

The Karelian Coast of the Gulf of Finland

Fridrik's forces had ended up in a fierce struggle with the enemy. Despite excellent intelligence, the enemy managed to surprise them with cavalry, and the skilled Tatar horsemen kidnapped a couple of men taking them with them.

After a while, Novgorod seemed to come crashing down on them with force. Fridrik wondered what would have happened to them in Narva if they had stayed there with the river behind them, and soon realized that they were now in a very similar situation, still in the Vadja region. They had crossed the Kymi River just a couple of hours earlier, and now the Novgorod forces were closing in.

Fridrik's knights were able to quickly regroup and attack the enemy's vanguard. They captured one horseman, and the rest of the vanguard retreated. The retreat seemed suspiciously like a Tatar trick to Fridrik, and he ordered his troops to halt instead of giving chase.

Prince Aleksander Nevski observed the situation from a distance. He ordered his elite troops to hook north and strike from behind Fridrik's detachment. The attack from the north succeeded, and Fridrik was caught in the middle of a battle in which his forces had to commit to two fronts. He sent a message by pigeon to Meinbald, asking him to quickly send all necessary reinforcements, as the main force of the Novgorodians was estimated to be four to five times his own fighting strength. After sending the message, Fridrik ordered his detachment to form into two companies to defend both fronts.

To get in touch with Klaus, whom he has appointed as the commander of the rearguard, he sent a messenger on horseback to hook through the north with a verbal order. Fridrik's main forces had to retreat to almost a hedgehog defense near the coast. The situation looked very bad. The sea was not frozen, they have no ships or boats to save the troops from certain destruction.

But then, again a miracle happened: Meinbald arrived just in time with his reserve to save Fridrik's troops from the pinnacle. He also knew that Matti, Kort, and their troops were following right on his heels. Combat contact with the main body of the enemy had now been obtained, and it was time to concentrate all strike power against it.

Meinbald's forces met Fridrik's forces in the midst of the greatest battle these latitudes have seen. Fridrik had sent him, by pigeon, the intelligence he had received from a couple of captured Karelians, that Aleksander Nevski himself was actually commanding the Novgorod forces.

Meinbald led his men in the front line to attack Nevski from the side. He forgot the teachings of the commanders of the order, according to which the Marshal leads the battle from behind, and did not stay to command from the rear. After all, it was Fridrik who was to be saved, so he rode at the head of the cavalry and charged straight into the enemy. He slammed his lance into the first incoming horseman, then drew his sword and charged forward, dealing deadly blows to the infantry men-at-arms. He advanced about twenty meters in an instant and knocked down three soldiers, causing great confusion in the enemy force. Fridrik and Otto followed a little further behind and widened the stroke, Fridrik to the left and Otto to the right. Meinbald had directed the attack straight toward Aleksander's command troop, which he had picked out by the crested helmets of the bodyguard about a hundred meters deep in the line. Infantry fell with every blow, and the disarray only worsened when the Novgorodians realized that they were being attacked with force. The infantry started to move away from Meinbald, leaving more space for the advance.

Aleksander saw what was happening on the flank and ordered his bodyguards to attack these rushing "Swedes." Meinbald, taking advantage of the space, had pushed forward in a rush, making a head start on Otto and Fridrik. Fridrik watched the development with concern. Meinbald confronted the first man of the bodyguard and parried his sword thrust, riding right past him.

The horse saw the oncoming guards in a line and slowed, intending to stop. He realized he had made a mistake and that he was now perhaps in the worst trouble of his life.

The Novgorodians besieged and isolated him from the others. The infantry gathered tightly around him. They drove two spears into the side of his horse, which fell with a gurgle, and in a moment he found himself lying helpless on the ground.

He struggled to get off the horse, but he had one leg still caught in the stirrup when Aleksander himself rode up. The bodyguards made room for their commander. Aleksander raised his sword to cut off his head, but Fridrik had noticed the danger and charged through the ring of blockers, knocking Aleksander over with his horse. He only succeeded in toppling Aleksander, not harming the man or even the horse.

Aleksander quickly got up from the ground and struck at the prone Meinbald, who managed to roll aside and bring up his left arm to catch the blow. Using the left forearm to block protected him to the extent that the strike through the chainmail crushed the elbow, but did not sever the limb.

The sword fell from his hand. He snatched it up with his right hand and stood up. A couple of Aleksander's lieutenants arrived and dismounted, as did Fridrik and Otto, who had reached the scene. Otto, a skilled swordsman, dropped one of the sub-leaders in an instant; Fridrik struggled with the other as an equal, fiercely exchanging blows.

As the initiative shifted away from the Novgorodians, Aleksander was confused and abandoned his intention to kill Meinbald. He backed off, likely waiting for his lieutenants to finish these threatening front men.

Fridrik kicked his opponent, taking him down, and drove his sword into the man's chest. Meinbald advanced, sword now firmly in his right hand, without fear, directly toward Aleksander, who fled, mounted again, and galloped away.

The commander of the Tatar forces saw Aleksander retreating and shouted the order to withdraw. The Novgorodians pulled out of the battle. Karelians followed them, shouting:

"Roman believers! Lord Aleksander of Vadja and Novgorod has decided that we're leaving. Do not ever again enter Vadja, you have here enough space and woods! And Swedes, you will still regret and experience Vadja's anger, believe it!"

Meinbald was no longer hearing the last cries, because he had passed out from the pain after the clash. Fridrik and Otto stayed to tend him, and Fridrik commanded the knights to pursue.

"The infantry may advance a maximum of one hundred meters and remain there in defense," he ordered. Fridrik took the whole army under his command and saw to it that not a single brother was left on the field. Meinbald's horse had to be put out of its misery. The torturous stuttering and gurgling stopped when a loyal friend sent the steed to horse-heaven.

The Knight-Brothers had a field hospital in the steep backcountry. Fridrik and Otto made a stretcher and carried the still-unconscious Meinbald back. In the field hospital, the wound on his arm was cleaned and bandaged, and the entire forearm was splinted as best as possible. Matti also heard that Meinbald had been wounded, so he came to see him. Fridrik had been there as well to check on the commander's condition. Matti told Fridrik that he will take care of his brother-in-law in his home.

"Okay, Matti. I am sure you take care of him like your brother. He's like a brother to me, besides being our commander. I am now acting as the commander on this expedition while he is out of the game, wounded. Tell him, when he wakes, that we are keeping our reserves here on the border of the new land we conquered, and that we have nothing to worry about here."

Fridrik and Kort grouped the troops on the west side of the Kymijoki for defense in case the Tatars made another diversionary retreat and returned again. They counted the north as secured, because the cold, dark midwinter and biting frost in the east made an enemy attack practically impossible.

Niemenpää, in the heart of Tavastia, February AD 1257

After a week, Matti's Pirkka warriors accompanied Meinbald to Niemenpää. The journey had been long and arduous, as his wound had become inflamed and raised a fever. However, Matti had made sure that he ate at least a little and drank enough. Getting water in the bitter cold had not been easy either, because the kettles froze and they had to stop from time to time to thaw them over a campfire.

Elin ran to meet him when she realized her husband was in that death cart. Kaukomieli and Kyllikki had also come to the yard to receive the convoy.

"Oh, Matti, how did he do? Does he still have life in him, and will he survive?" Elin cried to her brother, inconsolable.

"Dear sister, he is a strong man; he survived Aleksander Nevski's attack, and he survived our difficult frost to come home to you. I think he can survive your cooking, too," Matti winked, giving Elin a little spark of hope.

"Thank you, my brother, for bringing him home. Let's quickly take him inside the house. Mother! Get the bed ready in the cabin and wood in the oven so we can warm him up."

Matti ordered his four warriors to carry the stretcher inside. When the wives took command indoors, Matti and Kaukomieli stayed in the yard to exchange words.

"My son, tell me now, man to man, how did it go?" Kaukomieli asked.

"Meinbald's plan was good; we cleared the entire northern Vadja, which now pays taxes to us, not to the Russians. I was in the far north. I easily got the Lapps to pay tax, and then we turned south, joined Meinbald's and Kort's forces, and arrived, in the middle of a fierce battle, to Fridrik's aid on the Karelian coast. There, for Meinbald, it went badly; Aleksander's men surrounded him and knocked him to the ground. Aleksander himself was about to kill him, but Fridrik and Otto came to the rescue. By a hair's breadth they did not finish him."

"What do you think, Matti, will he survive?"

"It's not in our hands, Father, but there is hope. You just have to pray, and if you still know great spells, using them here wouldn't be too bad," Matti answered.

"After all, we have our own home seer here; yes, he will fix him. Even if you had brought the man in pieces, he would have bundled him together like Lemminkäinen's mother bundled her son," Kaukomieli stated. "Come on, boy; let's go to the house and let your men go to the barn, the mill, and the sauna to make themselves at home. Firewood, heat, and we have beer, too! Now the wars have been fought again, and we enjoy peace."

Matti felt comfortable being at home. Now they would truly start recovering from the trials of war. The defense of Tavastland was successful, but they lost several men, and Meinbald almost lost his life. Among Meinbald's men, knight Rheinhold was captured and disappeared. Pirkka warrior Pekka, from Matti's group, was also kidnapped. They had either been taken all the way to Novgorod or killed. The Swedish knights Stigulf and Björn also suffered the same harsh fate. But they saw Aleksander himself run away when Mielivalta did not back down but turned right on him.

The Gulf of Finland, May AD 1257

When the ice had left from the sea, the main troops of the Karelians sailed along the Gulf of Finland directly to Stockholm, making a harsh extermination expedition there. Several Swedes were killed, and a few were kidnapped and taken away.

King Valdemar was enraged by the Karelian attack, but Father Birger finally calmed him. Birger was skilled in diplomacy and told his son that, in fact, they had avoided a war against Denmark, because the crusade they sent did not head out to conquer the territories they were ordered to, but returned to defend the East.

Birger admitted that it was a wrong decision on his part to send a crusader force to Narva, even though King Kristoffer of Denmark had asked him for help. Either Kristoffer did not know about the land distribution of conquered territories agreed by his father, Valdemar the Conqueror, or, if he did, he had tried to use Sweden's reason to declare war against Sweden.

"And this Herr Meinbald, my former son-in-law, never ceases to surprise us. Instead of merely defending, he attacked the fifth part of Vadja from the east and brought us a huge area of new land with his victory! After all, this is an excellent result that should be rewarded royally," Birger explained to his son.

Niemenpää

Valdemar rewarded the commander of the Finnish forces, Meinbald, and his top men with the king's greatest approvals. They received lands from the king as gifts, lands suitable for establishing large family mansions on the coast. Meinbald had spent the whole spring recovering in Niemenpää. He had been very weak for a long time, because the wound on his left hand was weeping, keeping a high fever. However, Elin's and Kyllikki's tireless care, prayers, and perhaps even the spells of Kaukomieli's home seer gradually began to help and bring strength back to the man. The wound healed, and the fever subsided.

Fridrik and his men held a defensive camp at the fortress site they named "The Lock of Karelia." Three wooden forts were built near the west bank of Kymijoki to provide security for the troops. Meinbald conveyed, with a dove, the glad tidings to Fridrik of his recovery and of the king's prize lands, which awaited the brothers when the situation wouls allow them to detach themselves from the defenses for the holidays.

Meinbald already started to plan how he will rotate the commanders in the fortresses and then arrange free time in the summer for Fridrik, Otto, Kort, and others. The responsibility had to weigh heavily on the brothers' shoulders; maintaining constant vigilance and patrolling around Kymijoki was known to wear on men's nerves.

Birger and Valdemar, meanwhile, planned how to make administration work smoothly between Eastland and Stockholm. Effective military administration requires, above all, well-functioning communication. Therefore, the leading military commanders in Eastland had to be placed as close as possible to the route that runs through Åland to Turku.

In the summer, pigeons could convey quick messages across the sea, but in the winter the birds must be kept in their flocks in order to stay alive. However, the enemy from the east could move nimbly across inland waterways in winter, so in winter there had to also be the ability to send messages across the sea to Stockholm and from there to Eastland. This means that a chain of messenger couriers must be established to get the message through even in the middle of the darkest and coldest heart of winter. The freezing of the sea makes it possible to cross by sled or ski, so the message would travel in summer and in winter, but not during autumn storms or the thaw of spring.

Taivassalo was named in the king's letter as the most appropriate area for military commanders, because the navy had also used Taivassalo's Helsinginranta as a base.

Meinbald chose for himself an area of land named Iso-Särkilä in Taivassalo, on the shore of Särkilahti bay. The whole of Taivassalo seemed to him a very attractive place to live; the proximity of the sea fascinated him, and there was enough cultivated land, more than enough to support even a large family.

Fridrik, Meinbald's childhood friend and fateful companion from Bohemia, naturally chose his own farm very close, less than ten miles away. While acting as deputy marshal and muster, he had always carried a horn, so he chose a horn as his shield emblem. Kort, originally from Bitzen near the Alps and a member of the clergy of the cross-brothers, loyal to the Pope, took the character known by his nickname, Bock, on his shield. He got Aasamaa as his farm, because the Church, under the guidance of the Dominicans, considered it important that all places referring to past pagan deities be inhabited by Christian priests. "Aasa" meant viking-age deity.

Klas, from Brandenburg in the Flemish province, chose explosive metal balls for his shield, the kind that the Tatars threw on the battlefield. Otto, the swordsman, of course took the sword as his sign, or actually, two crossed swords. Ulf had similar straightforward logic; he chose an axe as his sign. Lydeke, "the Teen," a scribe-savvy administrator, chose a bird-headed monk, which puzzled the others. However, Lydeke explained that without pigeons, war would not lead to a time of peace so effectively. Lydeke was also appointed lord of Hakoinen Fortress. Finch, or Gödecke from Vienna, Austria, did not see it worth the effort to make such shield selections, but he was happy to settle on a good farm in Taivassalo. Dietrich "Balk," a big man and a carpenter, took beams on his shield. Magnus Garper chose a stone wall, depicting fortification work, for his coat of arms.

Meinbald was happy to have all his closest battle-mates as neighbors in Taivassalo. Regarding the coat of arms, he decided to choose the same line as Finch for the time being; he had managed without it and still did well. However, he paused to think: what was the point of repeatedly attacking the Christians of Novgorod?

To him, the whole crusading spiel was beginning to feel like an annoying eyesore and even an outright lie. He confessed his thoughts to Kort, who, as the brotherhood's priest, was always available for confessions. Kort knew exactly how to make him believe that they were on the right track. After all, as a priest, he had gotten to know, e.g., the works of St Augustine.

"Brother Meinbald, we all have doubts sometimes; it's part of being human. But when it comes to waging war, your conscience must be completely clear. Saint Augustine, already eight hundred years ago, wrote very clear definitions of what constitutes a just war, and believe me when I say that those definitions absolutely apply to the wars we're fighting here. Besides, our entire department has received its orders from the Pope himself, as have our brothers-in-arms. We must obey this command, and we cannot refuse to use weapons against those who are considered infidels."

"And what about the witchcraft that still prevails here?" he asked. "That, too, is something we must continue to fight against."

Around that time, a Dominican priest named Thomas Aquinas, five years younger than Meinbald and traveling between Rome and Paris, had accepted the Byzantine view on sexual relations between demons and humans. He believed that witches could fly with the help of the devil, create illusions, and summon storms through weather magic. Finnish witches were "known to raise storms on the Baltic Sea" and cause shipwrecks. Such practices, he maintained, had to be stopped once and for all.

For years, Thomas worked on his treatise *Summa contra gentiles*, intended as a handbook for missionaries, and he believed that heretics deserved the death penalty. Kort, Meinbald, and all the crusader knights were still blissfully unaware of the rigid views of this rising Dominican leader in Italy. Here, in the northern reaches of Europe, they still relied on the old teachings of Augustine.

After the discussion, Meinbald decided to remain in his post as the commander of the Order's regional division and to write to Cockroach in Prague. In his letter, he expressed that he felt a great responsibility—not only for the members of the brotherhood but especially for all those who were being captured and taken to Novgorod.

Cockroach's reply was evasive, full of polite turns of phrase, without addressing the fate of those taken to Novgorod. He merely wrote that the Brotherhood of the Red Star and the Cross had moved to a location by Judith's Bridge in Prague. The bridge was named after Judith of Thuringia, the grandmother of Mother Agnes, and it was the first stone bridge ever built in Central Europe.

"There's no point expecting any help from Cockroach's direction on matters of the northern front," he remarked to Elin after reading the letter.

"At least the King of Sweden has some genuine interest in the affairs of this region and in defending its people."

"You and your endless letters to Cockroach and your war matters," Elin replied with a teasing tone. "You're fully recovered now, my dear husband—so perhaps, just once, you could raise that *softer spear* of yours in my direction?"

He didn't need a clearer hint. He grabbed his wife by the hips, squeezed her breasts, kissed her on the mouth, and asked:

"Shall we go to the sauna right now?"

"I thought you'd never get it," Elin sighed. "Let's go!"

Impatiently, they slipped across the yard to Niemenpää's sauna, where they engaged in a passionate battle. Some time later, Elin returned from the sauna, smiling, her cheeks flushed. Mother Kyllikki asked playfully if the steam had been good, and Elin only smiled mischievously in return. A little later, he returned as well, whistling cheerfully as he sat back down at his desk.

Meanwhile, Dietrich von Kyvel and Meinbald had also been corresponding, keeping each other informed about the ongoing battles against Novgorod. Meinbald wrote that he had been wounded and had lost men. He asked Dietrich to stay alert and to send word immediately if any of the captured men were found in Novgorodian prisons. He was also interested in reports of any bodies discovered that might belong to Finns, Swedes, or Germans.

Von Kyvel replied that he had brought up the matter with Burkhard von Hornhausen, the newly appointed Master of the Order in Livonia. Burkhard had instructed all his knights operating in the area to search for and report any possible prisoners or the remains of fallen men.

A New Bishop and a New Beginning

At the beginning of the following year, Bishop Bero passed away. His successor was another Swede by birth, Ragvald.

The lives of Meinbald and Elin now revolved around their family, for in March, Elin gave birth to another daughter—right there in the sauna at Niemenpää. Once the little one had been safely welcomed into the world in Tavastia, the family moved together to Turku, where the new bishop Ragvald baptized Marshal Meinbald's daughter, giving her the name Kyllikki.

Meanwhile, King Valdemar, following in his father's footsteps, had launched a major migration movement toward the Eastern Lands. Families were encouraged to settle in these new territories; new colonies were being founded along the coastal areas of Uusimaa.

"The new lands must be settled with Swedish-speaking people—both military and peasant families," said Birger to his son Valdemar. "As for the Church, the priests still have more than enough work here in the mother country, so let the Germans take care of the Church and trade over there."

Meinbald brought his eldest son, Magnus, to the monastic school on Kaskistenmäki Hill in Turku, where, in addition to Dominican brothers, there were also a few nuns. The boy began his schooling when he was six years old.

Elin now visited the monastery every week—both to see Magnus and to pray for forgiveness for sins that she herself did not have, but which, she was quite sure, her husband had more than enough of.

Meinbald and Elin spent part of each year—the summer months—in Särkilahti, Taivassalo, where they traveled by a small "uisko" boat, which could swiftly carry them up the Aura River as far as Koroinen or even Vanhalinna in Lieto. During the winters, they lived mostly in Rusko, though each February they made a sleigh journey to Niemenpää in Tavastia.

After spending a few days enjoying the hospitality of Kyllikki and Kaukomieli, they set off to visit Matti. Their horses pulled a long sleigh caravan across the frozen lakes and rivers—past Tavastehus Castle, through the Vanaja trading post, farther north past Sääksmäki, and finally to Laukko in Vesilahti, where Matti had settled down.

Kaukomieli was visibly pleased to spend time in Laukko with both his son and his son-in-law. The men reminisced about their first meeting ten years earlier and all that had followed since. Matti, proud of his accomplishments, showed them the log cabin he had built and remarked with a secretive smile that perhaps, before long, a mistress of the house might be found for it as well.

Chapter XIV
Departure to Lapland

At Taivasalo, June AD 1258

After Meinbald had fully recovered from his wound, Matti dropped by Taivassalo to lure him on a trip to Lapland. Matti was still a bachelor, but he had visited Sweden several times to meet Kettil's little sister, Malin. He was once again coming from Skåne.

"If it suits Elin, then I'll be happy to go, Matti. I have heard many stories from you and your father about that wonderful land of witches, so I must finally experience it with my own eyes."

"Well, dear sister, isn't this an agreed matter? Will you let your husband come with me to Lapland? I promise to bring him back stronger than ever. We can bring some reindeer-antler extract for the storeroom when we return, so you can enjoy a new pace and a harder ride when he comes back to you," Matti teased.

"Listen, my brother, know that my husband's vigor has not yet faded, and I don't need any reindeer magic in our bedchamber. But take him to Lapland; a trip to the wilderness will surely do you both good."

Nothing else was needed, the matter was agreed.

Matti went to Vesilahti to gather his gear for Lapland, and Meinbald arranged for them and their luggage to board a merchant ship arriving in a week. It would sail along the Gulf of Bothnia to the mouth of the river Kemijoki. On the way, the ship stopped at the mouth of the Kokemäenjoki, because Meinbald wanted to check the state of the fortress. Antero received them as castle master. The meeting was very warm, and humid.

"My old brother-in-arms, our commander, " Antero began formally, then quickly getting to the point. "Let's enjoy our time together, so that this doesn't turn into mere idleness and empty talks. Come, a cold barrel has just been brought up from the cellar. We must empty it."

"You're the one who knows how to show hospitality and leave out all the useless phrases, Antero," Matti said with a smile.

"Matti, my brother, you know me too well. I don't like talk; I'm a man of action."

"You're right, Antero, I'll sign that too," Meinbald added. "You're such an exceptionally good and efficient patrolman that I think you're a little wasted here at the mouth of Kokemäenjoki. I would like to move you to Åland, because it is a much more central place, where a creator and visionary will be needed. The coast guard needs a vigilant leader there."

"Well, you don't cultivate fancy phrases either, you always go straight to the point," Antero laughed. The brothers raised their beer mugs and sealed the thought with a smile.

In Keminmaa there was fur trading and exchange of salt barrels for full barrels of salmon, but Matti noted they would not linger here, the journey just began from now. The men took the horses with the load and they rode to Tornionjoki. There, at a hidden spot Matti knew, a nimble three-seater rowing boat was waiting. Matti was known everywhere here; he was clearly respected among northern men. He secured a very experienced Sámi man to be their guide, a man he had traveled with in the north before.

"I'll take you along the fairway to the north. How far is the trip this time?" Aslak asked simply.

"We continue from here up the river all the way to Kiruna and beyond. Then we hike across the fells to Kilpisjärvi and back down from there."

"I hope you like river trips, Meinbald, because you'll have enough for all the days to come. We'll go all the way to Norway," Matti said.

"I like river trips. I have sailed quite a lot along the big rivers in the south, Elbe, Spree, and Vltava. But I've never been this far north before. How much farther can you go?"

"We'll go so far that the sea will meet us. And you'll see fells along the way. We'll leave the horses in this cove; they won't do well where we're going. We'll catch fish, salmon and grayling. The headwaters of this Väylä flow far away into wide, pathless fell country. There we'll leave the boat and move on foot to the high ridges, just a few days' walk. All that's left now is to go, hep!"

In its lower reaches, the river ran wide and flowed through forest. For long distances it slid in mild backwaters and rapids through the villages, turning to roaring whitewater in places. They passed these rapids either by swimming the gear and lining the boat along the shore upstream, or by portaging it overland.

Then, on the next stretch of rapids, they launched again, rowing the calm eddies to the following carry. Sometimes they tried their hooks, and quite often one of them, Matti or Meinbald, landed a fish. A couple of times a day they lighted the campfire, fried, and eat the catch. Matti had brought a bag of salt for the journey; to Meinbald, nothing tasted better than slightly salted grayling, except maybe slightly salted salmon. Only now did he notice the cross-bow among Matti's gear.

"Do you mean we'll find salmon so big we have to kill them by shooting?" he asked, a little mischievous.

"Listen, brother-in-law, you'll see we still need that on this trip," Matti answered enigmatically. "I should have told you to bring a bow in addition to the spear, but we'll get by with just one. And we both have swords, without them it would feel a bit naked, even here in Lapland," he laughed.

So the men continued up the river. At Pello they stopped to fish properly. The catch was so plentiful that Matti declared there was no need to fish again before Kilpisjärvi: "We'll salt these and eat them along the way."

The trail branched shortly before Pajala. At the fork in the river, Matti explained, "We'll come back by the right-hand branch; now we take the left." They spent the night in Pajala and continued along the river again: Nurmasuanto, Kuokso, then Jukkasjärvi, called "Laxforsen" by the Swedes ("Salmon Rapid"), and not for nothing. As they carried the boat along the shore, the rapids showed salmon rising, seeking ever cooler waters for spawning. But there already was another kind of fisherman there.

"A honey-palm," Matti whispered, raising his hand to halt the men and drawing out the cross-bow.

Now Meinbald understood what the bow was for, not a giant salmon, but a bear. The beast waded above the falls, scooping fish while standing on the rocks. It had already eaten one and now tried to seize another.

"Meinbald, take the spear. We may need it if I don't hit cleanly."

They creep into range, still hidden. Bear cannot hear them for the thunder of the rapids. Matti took aim and shot; the short bolt drove precisely into the bear's neck. The beast roared once, rearing on its hind legs, then slumping onto the stones of the shore. It did not die at once, so Meinbald rushed forward and ended the animal's pain by thrusting his spear into its heart.

"We'll get good meat from this honey-palm," Matti said as they skinned the bear.

The boat got heavier; the bearskin and the neatly boned meat added real weight when they later hauled the craft upstream.

"Let's row a little farther into the next bay," Matti adviced. "There's a wilderness hut, an eräpirtti, where we can keep a decent feast, so we don't have to drag extra weight the whole way."

At the eräpirtti, three stout packs of bear meat will last them several evenings; there is plenty and no need to waste it. The bear's head, dragged along as well, was set at the head of the table like a place of honor. Over beer and hard liquor, listening to the songs of the Lapland man and sometimes joining in, Meinbald felt he had found a primal contact with this receding northern world. He felt something similar at the Ukonvakkas hosted by Kaukomieli, when he had heard of Sampo's birth and drank the pontikka Matti had poured into his mug. He could not resist reminding Matti of that night, and it became the theme of their talk for the whole evening.

Kaukomieli himself has often been here in Lapland," Matti began. "Even as a child, my father sometimes took me with him to visit Lapland. From him, I learned all the fishing spots, customs, and tricks."

"Your father is a good man, Matti, and a very skilled chief. I noticed that the first time I met him. But he could be enigmatic to begin with. Only after touring Tavast land with him all summer did I understand that he was actually the one who led the war events in Tavastia, not me, and not Birger."

"Birger, that devil… that's a hell of a man," Matti cursed, taking a sip of booze, grinning.

"That man's thirst for power is completely insatiable and, moreover, a vicious circle. He hides his cruelty behind his smile. A man who coldly cuts off heads, like Birger, is cruel and hard no matter how he smiles. And Birger is the real king of Sweden; the Valdemar boy was chosen for that role only to carry out his father's will."

"Skull to the tree!" Matti suddenly shouted.

"What?"

"Well, now we're going to raise that 'Otso Otavainen' to the branches, come on!" Matti explained, grabbing the bear's head as he headed out the door into the yard.

They marched to a scraggly fir tree in the yard. "Now, brother-in-law, lift us, me and the teddy bear, on your shoulders." With a wobble, Meinbald rose from his crouch with Matti on his shoulders. They took care not to fall and soak themselves on the ground; Matti steadied himself on a branch, standing on Meinbald's shoulders, and reaching toward the top of the fir. They didn't go all the way up, but at about three meters they found the final resting place for the bear they had shot. The bear's head was left in the fir to reach toward Otava, the Bid Dipper stars.

"Listen, Meinbald, let's go inside. I want to tell you something starry-eyed," says Matti, after they had stared respectfully for a moment at the skull gazing toward the Great Bear.

Inside, Matti opened his "verbal coffin":

"My brother Meinbald, my sister's husband, listen: I'm absolutely terrified because I'm facing a big change. I'm going to be a father too! Malin told me, the last time we met, that we will have a child later this year."

"Oh, Matti, that's great news! I already suspected as much, since you've been so often in Skåne. Are you getting married soon?"

"I guess I must. But yes, I love Malin so much! She is the light of my life, Meinbald. I'm going to be a father! Can you believe it?"

"Well yes, I can, and as I said, I even expected it a little. Becoming a father is a big thing for a man, just as becoming a mother is for a woman. Here, Matti, we are at these bear-feasts at the same time as your rite of passage into fatherhood. Let's have Ukko's toast for that!"

The evening ended in pious spirits, and through rest and sleep Matti passed from boy to man.

Wilderness trekking while carrying a boat grew heavy at times. There were ridges in the streams; stopping and a little fishing gave strength to continue. The men trusted Aslak's guidance, and when he told to stop somewhere, that is what they did. The party continued its hike along the right side of the hilly region ahead toward the river leading to Kilpisjärvi. The fish stocks began to run low, but it was enough, because the woodsmen also grilled bear meat, which still tasted good with salt.

The gentlemen stopped camping at Kilpisjärvi. The Laplander built a hut, and Matti set up the campfire.

"Please, Aslak, tell us how did that fell Saana come to be?" Matti asked. "I'll translate into Swedish, so he'll understand too."

The man nodded and started:

"The old ones say there was a great wedding at fell Halti. It had to be great, because Lapland was the land of giants. Pältsa was the surly rival suitor of Saana. Both giants sought the hand of the beautiful maiden Malla. Saana won Malla as his own, but Pältsa came uninvited to the wedding, bringing with him the wretched northern wizards of the Arctic Ocean. The magic of those wizards got out of hand, raising a huge ice-avalanche that covered all the giants. The wedding guests fled; lake Kilpisjärvi was born from the tears of Malla and her mother. Pältsa tried to escape back to his homestead, but could not outrun the avalanche; he was buried up to his ears in ice, only his head left showing. At last, millennia later, the ice masses melted and revealed the giants, frozen in place. The clothes of the Lapps who fled were torn by the storm and strewn over slopes, plateaus, and valleys. Every autumn the same splendor of color floods the fells in crimson, reminding us of these long-ago wedding feasts.”

Meinbald still loved stories, and something in this one spoke to him, the magic of Lapland. “It’s like the tale of Frederick Barbarossa sealed in a mountain and letting a raven fly as a sign. Frederick lives in a mountain, but Saana is a mountain, a petrified giant.”

The next morning, they continued from near Saana, from Kilpisjärvi, born of Malla’s tears, towards Norway, to Kuohkimajärvi, from Kuohkimajärvi to Kolttajärvi, sometimes carrying the boat, then rowing along Breiddalselva to Koutajärvi. Along a small fell stream they descended to a fjord that thrusted inland from the Norwegian Sea. Meinbald and Matti admired the majestic landscape. The mountain walls rose straight from the sea, leaving a long fjord between them.

“Matti, I have never seen such a fairy-tale place,” he sighed, admiring and a little awed.

“This is Norway, and these villages on both sides of the fjord are old Viking villages. Even here in the north, the sea has been used for at least six hundred years.”

Down the fjord they rowed toward the open sea, but guided by Aslak, they turned to a coastal village about mid-fjord. A crowd came to greet them kindly as they tied up the boat at the pier. Matti offered bear meat to the village elder.

“Här, var så god, det er björn-kött, mycket bra! Jag er Matts Faravidsson; han er Meinbald, Capitaneus Finlandensis.”

“Ah-ha, Faravidsson? So you are the son of Far-sighted?”

“Yes”

Meinbald could already follow; after all, he had heard and spoken Swedish for ten years. He decided to be bold and introduced himself in Swedish:

"Jag är Meinbald; jag är gift med Matts syster, Elin. Så Faravid är också min fader."

"Meinbald, a strange name, neither Finnish nor Swedish?"

"No, it's a Germanic name, though not a saint's. I am very much a Christian; I'm the Land Marshal of the Order of the Bohemian Red Star and Cross here in the north."

"From Bohemia? You're the first I've met from there. Be welcome here in Skibotn! I am Odvar, the village elder. And hello to you too, Aslak, you've brought us special guests this time!"

"Det gjør jeg nok," Aslak replied briefly.

From the village, they turned back toward the fells along the small river. Often the men had to push the boat over rock-studded shallows, but now the load was lighter after a well-enjoyed meal. Besides, they left all the bear meat to the villagers; the meat salted by Matti proved a popular change from the usual fish diet.

After a couple of days' ascent, they came to a wonderful waterfall on Rovijoki. It was good to rest, frying grayling and enjoying. Then on again, first to Siilasjärvi, and next they reached Kilpisjärvi. They did not stop there this time, but went down-river: Kummavuopio, Keinovuopio, Saarikoski. Before Karesuvanto, they passed the point where they had first come ashore on the way up. Jatuninniemi was a good place to spend the night; a hut and a campfire were again made there.

"What is a 'jatuni' anyway?" Meinbald asked Aslak in Finnish, ever curious.

"It is an ancient giant, like Saana, Malla, and Pältsa," Aslak answered. "There used to be many here, but over the years the witches have bewitched them away. If you see a maze laid out in stones, that is a witch's garden. Those ancient giants have been driven there; perhaps they cannot get out. There is one jatuni-garden on Saana's high roof as well."

"And to be honest, we have a lot of them," Matti added. "Especially on the coasts and in the southern archipelago, there are those mazes here and there. Giants were apparently here hundreds of years ago, living here even before the ice melted away."

"Well, if they lived here, I suppose you've seen one at some point? Or at least their bones?" asked Meinbald, skeptical of the tale.

"Well, you just heard me tell you," Aslak replied with a sly wink. "Because they've all been driven into the mazes. There's no residue left, nor even after a sudden search!" He took a good pull from the bottle. The men burst out laughing and moved on to other talk.

In the morning, they quickly decamped and continued downhill towards the sea. The journey went swiftly: Sotkaniva, Saivomuotka, Sonkamuotka, Kätkesuanto, every bend of the river had its own name and its own story, as did every creek. Meinbald did not have to listen to the tales when the steeper rapids appeared; even Aslak fell silent while they carried the boat along the bank.

At Lake Muonionjärvi, the men stopped to fish and, after a good haul, made camp for the night. Fresh fish over the campfire tasted good again. The remaining beer and liquor tasted good, too; the men decided this was the time to finish the lot, better to travel lighter the rest of the way.

Matti opened up about his time in Sweden and reflected on what he had learned from his father, Kaukomieli. He said he loved Finland and swores they would never become Swedes, no matter how hard they pushed westward. But the Novgorodians, "the Russians," as the Swedes called them, he could not and would not understand.

"Damn it, they come, they rape, they rob, I can't make sense of it," he growled. "And the traces they leave, filth and wreckage. Houses and barns burned. Everything smashed. If they only took valuables or animals, but no, the bastards destroy everything. Nothing of the lowest behavior is foreign to them. Liars and cheats, that's what they are. They used to be gentler, more reasonable, but under the Tatars they've gone mad. Just kill them all, that's what I think every time I see them. Karelians and some Lapps must be out of their heads, when they bow them. The Karelians could be converted; they just took on the god of the Eastern Church. And how is it that their god is the same as ours, and yet they still ride to attack innocent homes? The devil take it."

Meinbald nodded slowly. "Matti, you know, I thought the same when I came here. And I thought it even more when we left for Narva. Innocent people there too, what the hell were we doing there?" He let the question hang.

Aslak, who had listened in silence, cleared his throat and answered Matti's barb about the Lapps.

"Aye, I understand," he says. "You saw us Lapps turn fierce when we met the Russians. But think on it a little from our side. The Russians have long let the Lapps be, in the north and east; they've not pressed us with tax beyond measure. Then the men of Pirkka came from the south to collect tribute and drove us farther and farther north, long before you Swedes were thick in these parts.

"You speak Swedish and say you love Finland, but out here you are the Swede, and the Birkarl. Maybe you don't sail abroad to plunder like the old Vikings, but in your own land your work can look much the same to us. Don't take the worst of it to heart. I don't say this to shame you. You serve king and crown, not just your father. I say it friendly, so you might understand us a little, and learn to see us Lapps, and the Russians, and the Karelians, more squarely in your sight."

Matti sat quiet a long time, thoughtful. At last he said, "Thank you, Aslak, my friend, for speaking straight. This is what I was missing, plain talk. I knew none of it as you've said it. Thanks… and sorry for being such a fool."

They passed the bottle around and let their thoughts run freely. Among friends, they could speak without trimming their words.

"This was the anger speaking in me, I know," Matti said. "But believe me, brothers, the hatred has roots. I'd rather take our way from the west than from the east. Listen: I have clear plans with Malin. We'll be betrothed and married; we'll have a firstborn son, and I want him to grow into a great man in Sweden. I have sat on the courts in Satakunta; my son will sit in the courts of Uppland."

"Wouldn't you want him at the king's court first, as page, like you and your father were raised?" Meinbald asked.

"True. First he must be a page, to learn manners as I did. But then, Uppland."

"Why there?"

"It's an old land of the mighty, and close to Turku and Satakunta besides. My son will not remain a vassal in the East; he will go west, where the king keeps his court and needs his best men. You and I, Meinbald, we are the shield-wall against the East. We stop Ivan long before he reaches the wealth of the West. The tax silver is counted in the West; here, we scratch to get by."

"Wise words," Meinbald said. "You've marked the power of the Bjälbo house well. Your future brother-in-law, Kettil, is already a great man and very near to King Valdemar. Be sure, he will marry his children into Bjälbo family. Why should you not do the same? I daresay it would please your wife-to-be Malin."

"How about you, Meinbald? You were married to Hildegard of the Bjälbo family, and when you were widowed, you wed my sister. Didn't you ever think to take another wife from the same house?"

"Oh, Matti, Elin and I fell in love. When such a wind takes you, you don't reckon up the hoard of power or the tally of mammon. You go, you trust your heart, and your heart's mate."

"True enough. So it is with Malin and me, heart first," Matti smiled. "But listen, now that we've turned homeward, remember this: we must come to Lapland again. In summer the nights are so bright the sun never sets. In autumn, the darkness returns and the fells blaze with color. And in winter, you can see and hear the northern lights! You must see them, Brother Meinbald."

"Well, that's an agreed matter. I'll be happy to come with you again, Matti. This has been the best trip of my life so far, and we're not even close to home yet."

The journey continued down to Pello, where they camped on a large island in the middle of Väylä.

"Hey Aslak, do you know if Noita (the Witch) is at this time of year here in Pello or is she at home in Saukoriipi?"

"Yes, she's here now, where the travelers are. She makes a small fortune here in the summer and then in the winter, she lives in her cabin in Saukkoriipi, when no one goes anywhere."

"Well, makes sense, you keep the fire in the camp, and we'll go by boat to see what's going on with her."

"I might like it. I'll drink some booze while I'm waiting here," Aslak replied.

The men jump into a boat and row south across river to Jolmanpää. The witch has set up her reception on the southern shore of Jolmanputaa.

"Hello, Matti!" Noita greeted when she saw them come ashore. "Let's go further," the old seer said and beckoned them to her hut. Inside the house, the air was slightly smoky, bones and metal bells were hanging on chains.

"Could you predict for both of us what awaits us in life next year and beyond?" Matti asked. "I'll pay, and I won't charge any tax from you at all this time, so you're just telling it like you see it, and you're not embellishing at all, you hear?"

"Well, that's fine," the witch replied and took out her drum. She beat the drum, danced, and began to sink into a trance. The men were both listening to the drum, which started to feel very hypnotic for them too.

"Well, this is a completely new experience," Meinbald told himself.

After hearing their prediction, the men returned to the island. In the morning, Aslak noticds that neither of them was talking about yesterday's predictions. It was a bit strange to Aslak; usually, the travelers got excited and talked whatsoever. However, Aslak didn't ask anything but continued to guide them back to Tornio, where they should get the same day.

"I wonder how the horses are doing?" Matti started small talk.

After returning home, Meinbald told Elin the happy news too: "Matti is having a son! The witch had seen that it will be a boy, and not just any boy, but a big man! And it is said that boys only get better by the generations. Matti's grandson will also do great things. And I heard that also we will have a boy next!"

"Well, what did that witch say about our child, this boy? Doesn't that make a great man?" Elin asked.

He was silent for a moment before he replied: "Yes, he will become a great man, and they are still good friends as adults, Matti's firstborn and this future child of ours. Which, by the way, hasn't been even started yet. Wife, come here, so I can hug you again!"

"You didn't hug those Lapland women there, did you?" Elin mades sure jokingly.

"Well, no. I saved my juice for you, come here now. After all, some work has to be done here before the witches' predictions can come true." And so, Elin hugged her husband, who went into action.

In December, Matti and Malin's son was born in Skåne, Sweden. The christening was celebrated at the end of January when the sea was already frozen. Therefore, party guests invited from the East could reach the sleigh along the winter road through Åland. Elin and Meinbald travelled there as godparents, Kaukomieli and Kyllikki to see not only their new daughter-in-law but also their grandchild for the first time.

In Bolstaholm, Åland, the sleigh party stopped to greet Antero, who had moved there from the Kokemajoki fortress. Antero had taken his commander Meinbald's wish into account and set up halfway to protect the most important military communication channel in the kingdom and to patrol the route in case of dangers facing the travelers. He was very happy and surprised to see the company, and especially his old king and his consorts. After hearing the destination of the travelers and the purpose of the trip, Antero wished Matti all the luck and warmest greetings. He said that he himself had set his eyes on a certain farmer's daughter who had moved to this area from Sweden.

The group's journey continued the next day across the ice to the Swedish side, from where they continued day trips south towards Skåne.

After arriving in Skåne, Matti finally introduced the new future relatives to each other: "This is my fiancée Malin Bengtsdotter; she is knight Kettil's sister."

"Nice to meet you, Malin! I can hardly wait to welcome you to the family!" Elin flirted with her best Swedish.

"It's really a pleasure to meet you, finally! I have heard so many good things about you from Matts that the joy is really on my side," Malin answered politely, her beautiful smile revealing that she was genuinely happy. "And you don't have to wait long, because we're getting married today. Matti proposed, I agreed, and so we thought that now that everyone is there, including the priest, why not celebrate our wedding at the same time?"

"Oh, what a happy surprise! We didn't know anything about this when we left the East," exclaims Elin.

The boy was baptized as Knut Matsson, and immediately after the baptism, the priest conducted the ordination of Matti and Malin. After that, an intimate wedding party was celebrated, and the new relatives got to know each other. The men already knew each other; Malin's brother Kettil and father Bengt were familiar men to both Meinbald and Kaukomieli. Malin's mother Gertrud and Matti's mother Kyllikki, on the other hand, had not met each other before, so they had plenty of new stories to share and acquaintances to make.

After the wedding, the day of returning to home followed. Malin wanted to stay in East Götaland to take care of Knut, where her parents were closer to to help. Kaukomieli was sorry when he couldn't get his grandson to Satakunta but accepted his fate. However, Matti traveled with them to Finland because he had official duties there. In the future, he often went to Lapland to collect taxes and spent most of his free time in East Götaland.

Chapter XV
The King's and Bishop's Men

Turku, AD 1259

Dietrich Von Kyvel died in 1259. Meinbald had kept in touch with him by letter and even visited him once after the failed expedition to Narva, mainly on a learning trip to learn how Dietrich acted under the Danish king. He had been very critical based on what he saw and heard on the trip.

"Estonian vassal Dietrich is dead. His son is a *hundsfott*, a future pirate who stalks Hanseatic ships", he told Elin.

"You would think that a man as great as Dietrich would have taken care of his offspring better", Meinbald stated and continued: "Had he done that, there would be now a big funeral organized for him, and I would also respectfully go to bury him. Instead, now I'll just read this message I got and continue without further ceremony on with my life. It's still a pity, as he was a very accomplished man."

He decided to continue the inquiry after the brothers-in-arms lost in the battle by writing a letter directly to the country master of the Livonian Order, Burkhard von Hornhausen. He was receiving his orders from the Grand Master of the Teutonic Knights, just as Meinbald received his orders from Cockroach.

"In practice, I mostly only take orders from the power council or the king", he thought. *"Albert Suerbeer, who acts as the archbishop of Livonia, seems to be in charge of the biggest power in Livonia, because Denmark and Sweden have alternated the power of the crown there",* he concluded.

Hornhausen replied to his letter in about a month. He regretted that he had no news for him regarding the missing, but remembered to admire Meinbald's perseverance and hopefulness. According to Hornhausen, the prisoners had most likely been taken to Novgorod, but he promised to report if any observations were made about them.

King Kristoffer I of Denmark also died on May 29, 1259, and a rumor soon spreat that he might have been poisoned. Soon after these unofficial messages, Meinbald and Elin received much happier official news: They got an invitation to a royal wedding! Birger's son, King Valdemar, married the Danish princess, Sophia, in the summer of 1260.

A very grand program had been planned for the wedding, there would be a multi-day event full of tournaments, dances, competitions and theater and poetry performances. Birger, who had sent the invitation, also asked Meinbald to nominate the "Knight of Eastland" to the tournament. For a moment, he thought about naming brother Fridrik, but then he had second thoughts.

"After all, it's a wedding, the knights there are the king's men, young people, so I should also take a young man of a similar age with us", he thought out to Elin. "And you also have to make sure that this youngster doesn't win the tournaments, but lets the king's favorite win."

Elin, Meinbald and a young knight named Albert, with their

squire, travelled by ship to Norrköping, and from there on horseback via Linköping to Öninge on the shores of Vättern, where the wedding feast was organized. Matti had also received an invitation, after all he had spent his time at both Erik's and Valdemar's courts as a page from 1248 to 1253. However, Matti had now traveled to the place by a different route, as he had picked up his new bride Malin from his homestead in Kråkerum, Skåneland, as a companion to the wedding. The meeting of the four at Öninge church was warm and joyful.

"Hey, my brother Matti and his beautiful wife Malin", nice to see you!

"As well, dear sister! And my favorite brother-in-law Meinbald, what a happy meeting we have here!", Matti greeted them.

"It's nice to see you, Matti, here", exclaimed Meinbald in his joy.

After cheerfully greeting each other, they walked into the church together and head to the same pew to sit, there was still room in the back.

Archbishop Jakob Erlandsen of Lund would perform the royal consecration. He began the festivities by reading aloud the letter of absolution granted by Pope Alexander IV himself:

"We, Pope Alexander IV, the representative on earth of our Lord Jesus Christ, the only son of God, hereby grant, on the first day of March in the year 1259, to His Majesty, King Valdemar I of Sweden, and to His Highness, Sophia, daughter of Eric, King of Denmark, exemption from the ecclesiastical rule, which would prevent them from being united through the holy matrimony of our Lord. We grant this release with the great motivation that the Swedes and Danes would be better able to fight against the neighboring pagans through this marriage."

"Did he just say against the neighboring pagans?! After all, here in North there is no one but Christians anymore. And now with the Pope's special permission, these little cousins are marrying each other", Elin protested, but in Finnish so that only Meinbald and Matti could understand. She was absolutely sure that they were the only Finns who had "Made it" to the place to witness this, according to the standards of the time, consanguineous initiation into marriage. They had all sat down in the back pew of the main nave of the undecorated wooden church.

"You also seem to know the royal family relationships very well, my dear wife", Meinbald noticed. "Your father's lessons?"

"Yes, our dear old father, he has taught me, just like Matti, that you have to know all the people in power and their families in order to get along with them at all", Elin answered.

After the long wedding ceremony, the party moved out of the church and moved in a procession to the place of celebration, the field where the knights and squires had formed a tournament field. Young Albert, with his squire, had also found his place here.

The royal wedding couple stepped into the royal enclosure in the middle of the field. Valdemar, his younger brothers Magnus and Bengt, and his father Birger together with his new fiancée were sitting in the shed. The crowd surrounded the field.

It was only here at her own wedding that Sophia found out that her future mother-in-law was the widow of her father's, late Erik "Ploughpenny's" brother, Abel, who had been considered the murderer: Birger Jarl was engaged to the Danish queen Mechtild of Holstein (Matilda in Swedish).

According to popular rumors, both Abel and Mechtild were considered the murderers of Sophia's father. Erik Ploughpenny had been taken by Abel's men and beheaded in Schleswig in 1250. Abel had only been crowned the next king of Denmark after he had sworn that he had nothing to do with his brother's murder. Among the people, however, he was still considered the organizer of the murder.

Birger was the main opponent of this king Abel, who had died during the crusade against the Frisians. Birger's thirst for revenge was only quenched by Abel's sudden death. Or maybe it was still a little off, and part of Birger's motives were still some kind of revenge when he had planned to marry his married widow, Mechtild.

The main motive, of course, was the unification of the royal houses of Denmark and Sweden. After all, Birger had already declared it in his letter to the Pope as his heavenly wish. If the expansion and consolidation of the kingdoms of Valdemar and his brothers required it, he was ready to marry—even that "Old Bitch," who seemed to take delight in shocking his young niece's world by appearing at her wedding unannounced.

From his seat, Meinbald scanned the stands and noticed familiar faces. First, his eyes caught John Teet, who, as always, had placed himself at the foot of Birger's royal enclosure. Fortunately, on the other side of the grandstand, he spotted more pleasant company.

"Hey, Svantepolk is sitting over there! I've known him since I first came to Finland," Meinbald shouted.

"Yes," Matti nodded, "I remember him too."

"Wasn't he quite close with Lydeke?"

"Indeed. They became friends during the battles at Sääksmäki. Svante was just a young squire then, but now he seems to have a rather high-born lady by his side."

"Let's go greet them!" Meinbald huffed, already making his way toward the couple.

Svantepolk's face lit up at the sight of Meinbald and Matti. He greeted them warmly and immediately inquired about Lydeke, wondering if he still flied pigeons with the same skill he did twenty years ago.

As a man of etiquette, Svantepolk quickly introduced his wife:

"Here is my wife, Lady Benedicta, who, like so many other noble guests here, also descend from the Bjälbo family. She is the daughter of Folke, grandson of Birger Brosa."

"An honor to meet you, Your Ladyship," Meinbald replied gracefully.

"Allow me to present my own company. This is my wife, Elin Faravidsdotter, of an old Finnish noble family from Eastland. And this is her brother, Matts Faravidsson, the famed Eastern warrior, and his wife, Malin Bengtsdotter, of a noble Skanian line. Elin and I have three children. Tell me, Svantepolk, has our Lord been merciful to you as well—has He blessed you with family?"

"Indeed," Svantepolk replied joyfully. "We have three wonderful children—and more on the way!"

Lady Benedicta, clearly delighted with the company, added her own tale:

"I was actually kidnapped from Vreta Monastery by Filip

Petterson, who took me into exile in Norway. After hiding there, we returned to Sweden—but Filip was killed during the rebellion at Herrevadsbro in 1251. Later, I met Svantepolk, who had just returned from Eastland, and we married the following year. We have been very happy since. Svante is not originally from Sweden, you see—his family roots lie in Denmark and Pomerania. My own mother, Benedikte Ebbesdatter, came from the Danish Galen family.”

“You were taken from a monastery? How wild!” Elin exclaimed, half in disbelief, half in amusement. “We’ve not seen such things in Eastland—though brides are sometimes spirited away from weddings!”

The ladies soon found themselves deep in conversation about their children, while the men drifted naturally toward talk of military campaigns and fortifications. None of them paid much attention to the tournament, finding it too theatrical for men who had experienced real war.

In the midst of the chatter, Meinbald paused, eyes narrowing as he studied a young man across the crowd.

“That boy… he’s the very image of Karl! Karl died only a few years ago—this must be his son.”

He excused himself and approached the lady beside the youth.

“Pardon me, madam. I couldn’t help but notice your son—he bears the likeness of someone I once knew. Are you, by chance, the widow of Karl Karlsson?”

“I am Ingeborg Pedersdotter, and yes—Karl was my husband. And you are?”

“Meinbald, *Capitaneus Finlandensis*, Marshal of Eastland,” he replied, bowing slightly. "Your husband and I served together when we helped Lord Birger conquer Tavastia for King Erik."

"Ah! I have heard many good things about you, Sir Meinbald," said Ingeborg warmly. "Karl often spoke of your deeds—how you organized the field hospital and supply lines for the northern campaign. It is truly a pleasure to meet you. Are you here alone?"

"Not at all," he smiled. "My wife, Lady Elin, and her brother Matts are here with me, along with his wife, Lady Malin. We come from Eastland and don't know many here—would you and your son care to join us? Karl was a fine man, and I'd be honored to share his memory with you."

"Thank you kindly, we would love to," Ingeborg replied. "Wouldn't you, Ulvar?"

"Indeed, Mother," the boy replied eagerly. "It's wonderful to meet someone who knew Father."

"And what about you, young Ulvar?" Meinbald asked with a smile. "Have you decided whether you'll follow in your father's footsteps?"

"Yes," Ulvar answered proudly. "I'll study in Stockholm and become a knight and horseman, just as he was."

"Splendid! Come, let me introduce you to our company," Meinbald stated, guiding them back.

Svantepolk, Benedicta, Elin, Matti, and Malin greeted the newcomers warmly. Meinbald spared no praise for Karl's memory, and both Svantepolk and Matti nodded in agreement, remembering their fallen comrade.

By then, the serving tables had opened, and the group moved together to the banquet. The wedding meal unfolded amid cheerful talk and the clinking of cups.

As the wine began to take effect, laughter grew louder, the tone of conversation softened, and the formality of titles quietly faded away.

Svantepolk told Mats and Meinbald, "My grandmother, Helena, had an extramarital affair with Denmark's Valdemar the Conqueror. However, the relationship ended when the king married Dagmar of Bohemia in 1205. Helena returned to the lands of her own father, Earl Guttorm, in Sweden, together with my little father Knut. So my father was Valdemar's bastard child. In time, he received the Duchy of Estonia from Valdemar, but he was later ousted by his official half-brothers. They gave Knut land from southern Blekinge as a consolation."

"The world is small, Svante", stated Meinbald. "I was raised, fed and guided into the knighthood by Dagmar of Bohemia's sister, mother Agnes! Dagmar died in childbirth, and their son Valdemar the Young died young. To think that we too have such a connection: without Dagmar of Bohemia, you could be even the next king of Denmark, without her elder sister, I would be an orphan tradesman's son in Bohemia, if I were even alive. Isn't it amazing how this life throws us? Without us being able to do anything about it?"

"It's really amazing", the group responded in many voices.

The summer evening was getting dark, the tournaments had already ended some time ago, and the knights had returned to their hosts. Albert had also joined the party and got to eat. The crowd began to retreat to the nightstand. This was how

Meinbald's party also broke up, and they thanked each other for the happy company and hobbled to their lodgings. In the morning, the wedding party was offered a festive breakfast, and after that, they were expected to go home peacefully.

Meinbald, Matti and Malin had hardly been able to leave Öninge for their journey home when their peace of travel was unexpectedly interrupted. Meinbald's, Elin's, Albert's and the squire's path was interrupted by a horse-drawn cart that had been driven diagonally behind a bend in the cart path. Albert stopped his horse first and approached the carriage on foot after getting off his horse.

Two men emerged from behind the carriages, swords in hand, threatening Albert. The armor bearer came right after him to level the punts; he also pulled out his sword just like Albert. Elin and Meinbald rode a little behind them and got their horses stopped a little further back. More men emerged from the bushes on both sides of the cart path to surround them. Meinbald did not dismount, but drew his sword and shouted:

"Miserable bandits, how dare you attack the party coming from the king's wedding!"

He turned his horse back and charged directly at the men who were now on the cart path behind. Meinbald's sword slashed one through the head, and the other was crushed under the horse. At the same time, Albert and the squire attack the two men in front. After a while of fighting, they were also finished. The rest of the men took notice of the unexpected counterattack, started using their feet under, disappearing into the forest.

Meinbald left with a shocked Elin back to Öning, telling Albert that they would wait here until he came back with the bailiff.

"Our trip home is just getting a little longer, this is quite the wild west compared to the East", he told his wife.

In Öninge, they are walked by John Teet, who just rushed past them strangely fast after recognizing them.

"What a bummer", Meinbald just thought, and didn't stop to think about it any deeper. *"Now we have to find that bailiff"*.

Birger was a man who tended to execute his plans. So, Holstein's Mechthild, Matilda in Swedish, widow of Abel, the late king of Denmark, married him in 1261 after first making an agreement with the Archbishop of Lund. By agreeing to Birger, Matilda had to break her monastic vows, as she had been forced to flee to a convent after her husband's murder. In the same year, Birger and Bishop Karl of Västerås gave a letter of trade privilege to Hamburg, which allowed German merchants to settle in several cities in the Kingdom of Sweden. That's when German burghers began to settle in Stockholm and other cities of the Swedish Empire.

"Now that Birger has married that Danish widow queen, he has a bottomless desire to expand his power! Elin bursted out to Meinbald when she read the information about Malin's letter to her.

"Well, I did marry you too, Meinbald laughed. You, too, are the daughter of the great king of Satakunta, a Princess! If your brother Matti's son Knut doesn't want to rule Eastland, our firstborn son will become the next vassal king of Satakunta. Have you thought about that? And I preferred you even after I had already married Birger's daughter, may her soul rest in peace!"

"Well, it's not the same thing, my dear husband, we fell in love and for love you married Hildegard too, and you've never wanted power, have you?"

"Well, no, my love, no, I'm just teasing you. When I follow the news from the world, even what has happened in Denmark, I wouldn't want to be king, neither myself nor my children. In Sweden and Denmark, the kings have to fear for their lives and the lives of their children every day. Now think, after the death of Valdemar the Conqueror of Denmark, each of his four eldest sons has become king and met his death: Valdemar the Younger, Eerik Plughpenny, Abel and Kristoffer. And what about Svantepolk's father, Knut? He was a duke of Estonia, but was deposed by the half-brothers, giving him some land as consolation, which he then left to Svante.

The pursuit of the crown has mainly resulted in nothing but death and sorrow. Here in our country, the church offers good, stable careers to priests who may one day become bishops, but the crown only offers stability to merchants and peasants as long as they pay their taxes.

The soldiers of the crown and the church, whose job it is to keep evil away, are allowed to fight, and when they fight evil, there is stability in the whole country again. I don't want any power, but stability, and for that, I am ready to fight whenever necessary. And tax collection, after all, is also an exercise of power, but you see, dear Elin, I have arranged that too, primarily for the sake of stability."

"Yes, yes, my dear Mielivalta, yes, yes. My brother Matti taxes the Lapps with his Pirkka men and drives them further and further north. Think, when you came to the country, they were still in Vesilahti. Now the wretched Lapps have already had to flee all the way north, up to Torniojokilaakso."

"Why did "Those wretched" let the Novgorodians and Karelians into the country? Why didn't they join us, who brought the Western church order here? Is that brother Russian somehow a better master when he allows them to raise their huge herds of reindeer, roam around the forests and not pay any taxes to their princes?"

"Calm down, my man, Matti does agree with you, but you men always want war, and you never see the good in others."

"Well, it's easier for a soldier to act when he sees only evil in his enemy. If you see the good in the enemy in battle, it will paralyze you, and you will not be able to hit him, and so you will be knocked to the ground. I've seen this many times, Elin. My hard training as a knight has made sure that on the battlefield, I don't see good in the other side, but pure evil."

"Well, my dear husband, tax collection and fighting are completely different things now, I guess you admit that?"

"Yes, well, I'm just a flawed person too, and prone to making mistakes", Meinbald snapped, realizing that it wasn't worth going out with his wife now. "Errare humanum est".

Matti was visiting Turku from Vesilahti to settle Pirkka taxes, this time with some good salted fish and many barrels of salmon. Matti gave the fish barrels to Lydeke's appointed assisting bailiff, who received them.

"Oh yes, do you have salt barrels for sale here?" Matti asked.

"Yes, we can sell you a barrel for money", bailiff answered.

"Salt used to be brought from Northland from the Väinöjoki, from where it was also taken to the south along the silver road, but nowadays it is brought by Hansa ships from Lüpek, from the German salt mines. How much does a German salt barrel cost?"

After paying the taxes and the salt shops, Matti planned to stop by to see Meinbald and his sister Elin in Taivassalo, when his convoy was caught and asked back for help, to the bank of Aurajoki.

"The Danes attacked, Matti! They took the fully loaded tax backlogs from the Swedes! Come back with your men, the Danes demand discipline right from the father's hand."

Matti and his men turned back to Aurajoki, and they see how the boats manned by the Danes were leaving the pier. Matti got off his horse like a flash, jumped nearby to the debris still attached to the shore, grabbed the loose rigging pole of the boat in his hands and pushed the Danes overboard with it. One by one, they clambered over the side of the boat.

"Resolve your arguments or have your boats broken!" Exclaimed Matti and nimbly jumped onto the next boat. One quick circular movement with the wooden pole, and there were more Danes swimming in the river again. In the third boat, they just watched what was happening now with mouths open.

Matti picked up speed, pushed the rigging pole to the bottom of the water and managed to jump into the third barge with its help. Pole itself stuck at the bottom, but Matti grabbed his sword. He had to strike only the first man to death; the others surrendered and handed over their weapons.

Matti had managed to save the entire tax payload with his quick action. Most Danes could swim and survived, being captured on shore. Matti brought the two surrendered men of the third boat to the shore. Word of these events traveled with the bailiff towards Stockholm, where the king's bailiff gratefully accepted the taxes.

In no time at all, Matti noticed that he had risen to the favor of King Valdemar: He would receive lands that he already had anyway, namely Niemenpää in Janakkala and Laukko in Vesilahti's Hinsala. But now his ownings were based on his letter, also confirmed with the official seal of the King of Sweden.

"Now, Matti, it's bad for anyone to try and take your lands from you; even the Russians will have to fight with the Swedish king's troops first", Meinbald sneers, when Matti is visiting them with Malin. Both of them know who he means: Meinbald's own Finnish army and therefore also Matti's own Hundred.

Matti took Malin to Vesilahti to get to know Laukko. They were clearly in a hurry, and they didn't stay, even though Elin offered them a place to stay for the night in Särkilä's shed. When Matti and Malin had left, Meinbald grabbed Elin in his arms and asked: "Could the nanny be with the girls for a while now, so that the parents had some time for themselves again?" Elin looked deeply into her husband's eyes and nodded.

"Go to the granary, I'll come right after you, after I first tell the maid that she can do without us for a while."

In Heaven, the fifteenth of January, AD 1263

Elin and Meinbald's firstborn son was born in 1263. Meinbald was happy, and he wanted the child to be christened Mielivalta. The Finnish priest, Father Mikael, was a bit reserved about this and even tried to suggest that they should use a Christian name known from the Bible.

Meinbald stated to the priest:

"If my Christian parents were able to baptize me as Meinbald, I guess I can continue their tradition by baptizing my firstborn son with a plain Finnish name, which means the same as my Upper Saxon name. Isn't it so, priest?"

Father Mikael was surprised when Meinbald answered directly in Finnish and understood from the strained tone of voice that he agrees, and so the child was christened Mielivalta. And it wasn't even difficult, after all.

In the spring of the following year, merchants of Hansa sailing east of Neva brought with them news that Aleksander Nevski had died. He had been 43 years old when he had died in November.

"He was my age", Meinbald thought thoughtfully after hearing the news. Alexander had been in the Golden Horde for a long time mediating the tax revolt of the Novgorodians and, after being there for a year, received the Khan's forgiveness and release to participate in the Mongol campaigns, in which they would have had to shed the blood of Christians on the side of the pagans.

"There was a brave man in it, who did not bow before the Swedes, nor the Germans, nor even the Mongols. After all, we had quite a lot in common", he says with a grin to Elin, holding little Mielivalta in his arms.

"Oh, my dear husband, you too are brave and unyielding, but don't you bend to the bosom of the earth just yet, like

Alexander. You go ahead and live at least another 40 summers, will you, my husband, Elin cood and took Mielivalta to feed him.

In the evening, Meinbald told his children an evening fairy tale, which he had developed after hearing a touching saint's story from Asser. They were all in the room, ready to be covered up in their beds to sleep.

"Children, now I will tell you the story of Saint Nicholas, who was born in 280 in Myra, Byzantium. At that time, Christians were still being persecuted because Emperor Constantine had not yet converted Rome to Christianity. Nikolaus' father was a prosperous merchant who dreamed that his son would follow in his footsteps. However, his mother wanted her son to become a priest. They taught Nicholas to share everything he had with those most in need."

"At that time, a terrible plague was spreading, and Nikolaus' parents, being Christians, took care of the sick. Unfortunately, they both contracted the disease and died. Nikolaus inherited all his parents' property and distributed it to the poor. Then he became a monk, and later, after visiting the Holy Land, he also became a bishop. The persecution of Christians continued, and St. Nicholas was also arrested and imprisoned for almost 30 years. Only when Emperor Constantine came to power did he order Nicholas to be released. "

"At that time, Nikolaus was already an old man with a white beard. He returned to his hometown in Myra just as Christmas was being celebrated. All Christians celebrate not only the birth of Christ but also his arrival. Once Nikolaus heard of a poor man who had three daughters but could not afford a dowry. So these daughters would not get married. To remedy this, St.

Nicholas went to the man's home at night without anyone seeing him and placed a bag of coins in each of the daughters' socks that were drying in front of the fireplace. So everyone got married. But you know, my daughter, what is most exciting? Well, when time left Nicholas, he did as many other saints have done after him. He closed in on the mountain. And you know, I've seen that mountain – it's here in the north, in Lapland! The name of that place is Korvatunturi. And every Christmas Eve, St. Nicholas comes and gives gifts to children, because he loves children. If you're really kind, like St. Nicholas, you can even see him in his red bun on eve."

"Could he come already on the first night? Why only at Christmas?" Asked Mielikki, who had just turned ten.

"Yes, I would like to see him so much that I won't sleep at all next night", continued Tuulikki.

"If they don't sleep, I don't either", said the youngest of the daughters, five-year-old Kyllikki. "Will he come next night, will he, father?"

"Oh, girls, Christmas is still more than half a year away, and as I said, in order for him to come with presents at Christmas, you have to go to bed nicely at night and be very nice children during the day as well."

"Father, I, too, will become a bishop, like Nikolaus", says Maunu. "I want to give gifts and help the poor just like him when I have a white beard."

"Well, that's a very good goal, Maunu, very good. Now to bed, kids!"

News of Birger Jaarl's death arrived from the west across the sea to Finland in 1266. Meinbald travelled to Stockholm for the funeral. Elin stayed at home to take care of the children.

King Valdemar wanted to make sure that the leader of eastern military affairs was still loyal to him. Forty-six-year-old Meinbald found it somewhat amusing that he had to swear his loyalty to the under-thirty Valdemar, but he wisely swallowed his laughter and made the necessary reassurance.

"I thank you for your loyalty", Valdemar thanked him. "My father, my brothers, and I still have time to meet the Pope's legate in Kalmar in the summer. At that time, our respected father Birger praised you profusely, and they say you are a master of the papal order and skilled not only as a soldier but also as a merchant. My brothers and I are lucky to have such a skilled man in the East."

In the same year, the Swede Kettil was named bishop in Eastland after the death of Bishop Ragvaldi.

In Niemenpää, the thirtieth of July, AD 1269

Kaukomieli died at the end of July 1269, aged 69. He was to be buried in Kaukola, Sastamala, in the burial place of his father's side of the family. The heads of the family, the "Kaleva kings," had been buried there for hundreds of years. Meinbald had lost his father-in-law, Elin and Matti their father. Kaukomieli was the last king of Satakunta, so the whole province lost its supreme protector; there was a land sorrow in Tavastia and Satakunta. Kaukomieli's widow, Elin's mother Kyllikki, moved with Elin and Meinbald to live in Taivassalo. Antero also arrived from Åland to participate in the funeral of his king. He, too, was clearly deeply saddened by the loss of his former king, but Antero had some good news to share:

"In my old days, I have found happiness. I married Ingegerd, the daughter of a Swedish house settled in Geta, and we are about to have a family addition. Just imagine, I, who have managed to live on my own for more than half a century, suddenly become a father too!" Antero shared with Matti and continued: "Would you and Malin become godparents of our first child? It would be a great honor for us."

"Well, of course, it's our honor, brother Antero", Matti replied happily.

The baby boy would be born at the end of August and will be named Andris at the baptism of the Lord.

King Valdemar appointed Matti as the bailiff for Kokemäenjoki castle. It was a formality that was made from Meinbald's suggestion. Matti now worked as the chief and lawman of the entire Satakunta, because he knew Finnish law, which was still followed in the region.

Swedish jurisprudence had reached the coast, the church had brought its own canon law, and these different guidelines and practices were all followed side by side in the country.

The Niemenpää farm, which Matti had already officially received from King Valdemar, was a centuries-old *moisio* that had been cultivated by his maternal ancestors. Matti saw that he himself did not have time to devote himself to farming or livestock breeding, so he decided to ask Elin and Meinbald for advice on what to do.

"Listen, Matti, don't you worry, we Saxons have already solved this farm management issue centuries ago: You just appoint yourself a farm manager who will cultivate the farm for you. The profit belongs to you, and then you pay the farm manager and his family a salary for it. That's how it works."

"It's a good thing, Meinbald, that you belong to our family, such a clever man!" Matti answered with relief. "I would like to appoint one of your men as my farm manager. Meinbald, is that okay with you?"

"Depends on who you're thinking of."

"Hero-Magnus, the man the Swedes call 'Garper.' He was with you at the spring sowing and also at Ukko's feast, remember? He fights bravely and also dares to order men to work in the fields. Wouldn't he be a good farm manager for Niemenpää?"

Meinbald looked into Elin's eyes, who nodded at him with a smile.

"Matti, you're a precise and clear-headed man. This is an agreed-upon matter."

"I'm sure he'll get excited about it, but you can ask him yourself. We can't assign him to this important task; this has to be about his own will."

Matti and Magnus talked, and the matter was agreed upon in no time. Magnus "Garper" started as a farm manager in Niemenpää and moved to the farm with his family within the same week. Magnus was married to Kirsti, a Tavastian maiden, so they were happy to move to the center of Tavast land.

A Surprise Wedding in Sweden, 1274 AD

Matti's son Knut Matsson married Ingeborg, Ulf's daughter. Knut was only sixteen, and Ingeborg was only fifteen. Ingeborg's mother, Katarina, was the daughter of Karl Lejonbalk. Her father was Ulf Karlsson, who was already well-known to Matti. He knew Ulf's late father, Karl, from the time of the conquest of Tavastia. Ulf belonged to the Bjälbo family; his grandfather was Carl the Deaf.

Knut had made Ingeborg pregnant, and a healthy baby boy would be born before the wedding in early summer. The situation was a bit "torn from the joints" because the time and the church rules were strict, but Matti got Knut to take his responsibility, acknowledge the child, and he also got the church fathers inclined not to pass judgments of shame, as long as the young people got married immediately. The boy was christened Torgils.

At the wedding, Ingeborg's mother, Katarina Karlsdotter Lejonbalk, told Matti and Malin the story of her own family, "My own mother, Ulvhild, is from an old Saxon family. After coming to Sweden via Denmark two hundred years ago, they adopted a coat of arms with deer antlers and a French lily on their shield."

"My mother's grandfather was a very cruel man. He lived with his family on the island of Saxholmen, where a stone castle had been built. The father of the family, infamous for his cruelty, bullied his entire household, but especially his wife. However, he got his rightful punishment when his wife escaped with her lover over the Ölmeviken ice on Christmas morning on a horse. The horse was shod backward, so it looked as if no one had left the castle for anything, and the simple master had not realised the trick. Before leaving, the wife had set the castle on fire and thrown the key into the castle yard."

Ulvhild was an old but very noble grandmother, proudly married to her husband, Karl Ingeborgarson Lejonbalk. There were other guests from the Hjornthorn family at the wedding, and they were all proud of their Saxon roots.

Filip Törnesson Hjornthorn (Deer Antler), Knut's new relative, was the first lawman appointed by the king in Närke. He had been appointed a couple of years ago. He wished the young couple a lot of happiness and warmly welcomed Knut to the family. He clearly had the gift of speech, which he had practiced in his role as a lawman.

The bride's father, Ulf Karlsson, also told Matti, Malin, and Knut about his family, "My grandfather, Carl the Deaf, was hard of hearing and thus earned the nickname 'Deaf.' The brothers Carl, Magnus Minnesköld, and Birger Brosa were all typical men of the Bjälbo family, full of ambition and, moreover, ruthless, greedy men. This had meant that even within the family, power had been fought mercilessly from one male generation to another. My cousin Karl, son of Ulf Fase, started the Folkunga rebellion together with Knut Magnusson and Filip Knutsson. However, he did not participate in the Battle of Herrevadsbro but voluntarily went into exile and joined the Knights of Livonia. He fell in Courland in the battle of the Teutonic Knights in 1260. He bequeathed several of his estates here in Sweden to the Teutonic Knights."

Matti can't help but remember Ulf's father, Karl Karlsson:

"My father, Kaukomieli, and your father, Karl, were good friends. They became friends even before Birger led his troops to Tavastia and completely conquered the East for Sweden."

Ulf Karlsson took Knut under his protection with Matti's persistent help and introduced him to the king as well. Knut seemed to be quite fond of the work of Lawman. Father Matti had worked as a lawman in Ylä Satakunta, and Knut had learned a lot of the things involved in the work by following him since he was a little boy.

Finnish law followed very similar principles to Swedish law. Therefore, he got along easily in Närke as Filip's apprentice and often even got to visit the island of Alsnö with him during the summers, when King Magnus delt with legislative matters in his summer residence. Magnus noticed the young man's abilities and wanted to build his administrative machinery on talented men.

Chapter XVI
Return to Bohemia

In Taivassalo, AD 1275

Meinbald turned 55 and decided to take Maunu, Elin, and Mielivalta with him to Bohemia. However, Elin talked him down because she didn't want to go with small children and she was even a little offended that Meinbald would take his son but not his daughters on the trip.

"No such madness," she said. "Go alone if you want. I understand you want to see your home and your sister again."

Meinbald was a little disappointed, of course. He didn't want to go alone. After going to see his son Maunu, he still told Elin's opinion, but asked Maunu if he would be going with him.

Maunu answered immediately, "Dad, I'm actually really happy to go with you! You see, the Dominican brothers have already told me that in order to gain enough additional experience and learning, I should apply outside of Finland and Sweden to study towards the Baccalaureus degree. After that, even a Master's degree could be within my reach, and I could return to Finland to a good position."

In Prague, AD 1275:

Meinbald left for Bohemia in June and took Maunu with him. When they arrived in Prague, Meinbald marveled aloud at the change he was seeing, "This was just a village nuisance when I left here thirty years ago. Now there are huge, magnificent stone buildings built here. The village has indeed grown! I don't recognize the roads here, and I can't navigate without the help of the locals."

After asking for directions to a convent in Prague, he finally found his sister, who was still in the convent. The reunion of the siblings was very warm. Maunu is very happy to finally meet his aunt, whom his father has often told him about.

"Kunigunde! Do you still know me?" Meinbald asked.

"I would know you anywhere," the sister answered and hugged her brother warmly. "But who is this young gentleman who looks just like you when you left here on your travels?"

"He is my son, Magnus, the wisest ecclesiastic in Finland."

"Magnus, come here to hug your aunt!" Kunigunde said and scooped Magnus into her embrace.

"Meinbald, let's go see Sister Agnes. She is already old, but when she heard that you were coming, she asked immediately to come and see her, because she still wants to see what kind of gentleman you have grown from the rascal she saved.'"

And so, the three of them walked to a room at the end of a long corridor, where Sister Agnes received them.

"Sister Agnes! Do you still know me? I'm Meinbald, remember? You saved me and my sister, this Kunigunde here, from certain death and offered us not only the salvation of that moment, but the salvation of the rest of our lives, offering food, drink, clothes, a roof over our heads, and a new direction and purpose for our lives."

"Meinbald, of course I know you. You are still the same little boy, even though you already have gray hair. You are like my own son to me that I never had, come here so I can hug you!"

Kunigunde also took Meinbald and Magnus to see the Grandmaster. The Grandmaster had been Merbot since 1260 from Ratibor.

"Meinbald, it's nice to finally see you again! You probably don't remember me, but we were together fighting the Mongols with King Wenceslaus in Klodsko."

"Merbot! I remember you, even though it's been 20 years. It's really great to see you again!"

Merbot praised profusely that Meinbald had cooperated despite the fact that he had to leave the active leadership of the brotherhood. As a sign of his semi-official status as still the brotherhood's "Caretaker of Northern Affairs," Meinbald received the brotherhood's seal and permission to use it as his own in Finland.

Meinbald introduced his son Maunu and praised how talented he was and how he had progressed in Turku's Dominican monastery school, so that, actually, he could no longer find a new doctrine or teacher in the whole of the North. But they were now looking for a good enough post-graduate study place for Maunu here in Prague. The Grand Master promised to immediately contact a Franciscan brother he knew, who was in correspondence with the University of Paris about students.

"Together with Bologna, the University of Paris is one of the most admired places of higher education in Europe. There are complete programs of study in the arts and sciences. When they hear your recommendations, they will take you in immediately, and you can teach wherever you want after you graduate. You were also lucky, the university has just expanded its nationes division so that they accept students in their Anglo-German nationes in addition to our brothers from Eastern Europe, but also promising students from Scandinavia!"

After hearing Merbot's praises, it was clear to Maunu himself that he had found his future place of study. Only in Paris would he gain enough additional experience and learn Latin and German so that he could later qualify for an important position in Finland.

"Father, this is a very attractive offer, but I'm afraid I can't accept it. I have no idea how much it costs to live in Paris, and where I can get enough money to study."

Before Meinbald could say anything, Grand Master Merbot opened his verbal casket, "Maunu, your father has expanded the world ruled by the Pope in the North to Finland, beating out the heretics of the East and thereby enabling considerable additional income for our entire church organization. The least I can do to show my appreciation for him and the achievements he fought for us is to show you hospitality now and in the future whenever you visit here in Prague. In addition, I would like to direct an annual sum from our tax-cooperative funds to you, Meinbald's firstborn son, with which you will do well in Paris. Do you understand that this is the least I can do and that you and your father are always very welcome guests of the Brotherhood of the Red Star and Cross?"

Meinbald was just as surprised by Grandmaster Merbot's words as Maunu, and together they bursted into joyful laughter, thanking the Grandmaster. Kunigunde also joined in with a tear of joy. "My nephew will become a great master, and who knows what kind of church prince!"

Together, they all enjoyed a festive dinner and drank a few beers. In Prague, beer was in its glory. Sister Agnes also came to dinner, and they all had a great time reminiscing. Of course, Maunu couldn't remember the past, but he was very happy to listen to all the stories and events that had happened to his father and aunt in Prague. Agnes still loved to tell stories, and when she realized that Meinbald's son was really heading for an ecclesiastical career, she decided to tell one more story.

"Magnus, I want to tell you this story in particular, which I have not told Meinbald and Kunigunde before. The story is completely true, like all my stories, and it tells about a man whose birth name was Vojtech, who later adopted the name Adalbert, a staunch man of the church. He became the second bishop of Prague. He was born in 952 in the fortress of Libice, belonging to one of the ruling families of Bohemia, the Slavnik clan. His father was Prince Slavnik, and his mother was Stretislava, one of the Premyslides. Having previously spent more than 10 years in the Church's doctrine in Magdeburg, its first bishop, also named Adalbert, was his apprentice. When the bishop died, Adalbert returned to Bohemia, where he was ordained a priest by Dietmar, the first bishop of Prague. After Dietmar's death, despite his young age, Adalbert was elected bishop of Prague in AD 982. Adalbert tried to make necessary reforms in Prague, where polygamy and deep-rooted pagan beliefs still prevailed. He faced strong opposition, and in six years, his preaching made little progress. The Slavnik family also opposed the then Prince Boleslaus, who belonged to the Premyslides, and did not support him in the ill-fated war against Poland."

"In 988, Adalbert left the episcopate behind and traveled to Rome with his brother. Five years later, after living as a hermit in a monastery, the Pope sent him back to Prague at the request of Boleslaus."

"In 995, Duke Boleslaus II of Bohemia captured Libice and annexed it to Prague. They killed Adalbert's parents and five brothers. Adalbert and his half-brother, Radim, the future Archbishop of Poland, Gaudentius, survived by fleeing into exile in Poland. Strackvas, who was chosen as his successor, died unexpectedly during the consecration liturgy, and the Pope then urged Adalbert to return to his episcopate. However, he considered the request impossible in the situation and asked to become an itinerant preacher."

"Adalbert traveled to Hungary, baptized the royal family there, and then left for Poland, where Duke Boleslaus I welcomed him and made him bishop of Gniezno. However, Adalbert did not settle here either but went on a missionary journey among the pagans living in Prussia."

"Boleslaus I sent soldiers after him. They traveled along the coast of the Baltic Sea all the way to Gdansk, from where Boleslaus's soldiers escorted them to the Polish border. From there, they continued their mission on their own, together with Radim and the Polish Benedict-Bogusza. They also had with them an interpreter who knew the language of the heathens."

"When they arrived among the Gentiles, they converted some of them at first, but mostly they met with angry opposition. The chief of one of the villages hit Adalbert on the head with an oar, and they had to flee across the river to escape the life-threatening situation that had arisen."

"At the next place where they tried to preach, they were met with an equally angry reception, the locals striking the ground with their sticks and shouting, hoping for their death. A similar reception was at Truso's marketplace."

"On 23 April 997, after mass, when Adalbert and his companions were lying in the grass eating their lunch, they were attacked. A pagan priest named Sicco was the first to strike Adalbert, and the others followed. They disconnected Adalbert's head from the body. After he died, they attached it to the end of a pole and went home."

"King Boleslaus I of Poland bought Adalbert's body from the Prussians, paying for it the body's weight in gold. A few years after his martyrdom, Adalbert was canonized as Saint Adalbert of Prague."

"Adalbert's remains are kept in Gniezno. It was not until 1127 that his head was found and also delivered to Gniezno. Boleslaus I presented Adalbert's hands to the Holy Roman Emperor Otto III in 1000. "

"Duke Bretislav I of Bohemia looted Adalbert's bones in 1039 and took them to Prague. However, the Poles said that Bretislav's men had taken the wrong bones, namely Radim of Gaudentius's carcass. Thus, both Prague and Gniezno have a shrine where the relics of St. Adalbert are said to be kept."

Magnus listened carefully to the story and thought about its lessons.

"Thank you, Mother Agnes, for telling this horrible story. It makes me think about my own future career and what I want to leave for posterity. At least I don't want my head to be removed from my body after I die, as happened to Adalbert, or my bones to be disputed between the princes of different earthly kingdoms."

"Oh, child, you will become a great and mighty, wise church prince! Believe me, I have the gift of a seer," Agnes said very calmly.

"Note that even among the church's own priests, Adalbert faced opposition, and it made him give up his duties as a bishop. Bishops used to be at the forefront, like Adalbert, converting pagan nations, but now that there are no longer whole nations to convert, we should focus on converting our own citizens, because there are still many false beliefs among us. This work is endless but very rewarding," concluded Agnes with her wise words.

Meinbald had also listened, as he always did when Agnes opened her verbal coffin.

"Amazing story. Amazing that he always left and had time to visit so many places. And what happened to him over there in Prussia… cruel fate. Fortunately, I did not know this story when I left for Finland."

The next morning, Meinbald said goodbye to his son, who promised to be worthy of his father's expectations and to work hard.

"I know, Maunu, that you will make me very proud. Goodbye, my son, remember to come back when you are wise enough for the top job in Finland."

"Goodbye, Dad. Please also send my greetings to the sisters, to Miclivalta and to Elin. I remember them fondly here, and when I return, I will immediately come to see you and them."

After leaving his son in his temporary home and saying goodbye to his sister in the monastery, Meinbald admired the bustle of Prague for a while but felt that he already longed for peace. Sitting next to the market alone with a beer mug, he finally realized that his home was in Finland, because his family, all his descendants, would grow and influence Finland.

"Or in Eastland, as the Swedes call it. Turku is just a village, but a growing number of German burghers are flowing there on the ships of the Hanseatic League."

Meinbald still spoke his mother tongue, German, but he had learned not only Latin but also Swedish. He even spoke Finnish in a way that Mielivalta could understand. He confessed to himself that he was quite talented in different languages. He also knew some Russian, having learned a few words from prisoners of war, Christians whom he initially thought were pagans.

"However, I didn't cut their heads off, like these princes and royals, Birger too. There must be something in power that corrupts the human mind," Meinbald thought.

Then he woke up from his dark thoughts and spoke to himself in a low voice, "You poor bastard, you don't know anyone else here except Agnes and Kunigunde, this place doesn't need you, nobody here needs you."

"Go home, there," Meinbald says to himself in a Karelian manner and sips the beer mug empty with a grin. "Now, to the river ship and towards Lübeck."

On the way back, while stopping in Lübeck at a harbor cabin, Meinbald heard that Birger's son, Magnus, who was next in line of succession, had gone into exile in Denmark with the intention of bringing several Hundreds of Danish and German mercenaries from there to take over the power for himself. There were a couple of dozen German mercenaries in the harbor waiting for shipping. They would be on the same ship that Meinbald bought his return trip on.

From the beginning, he actively talked with the Germans to find out what the troops' intentions were. Many did not even know which city they were going to, even though they were on a ship headed for Stockholm.

Instead, when Meinbald found the group's commander, he managed to learn that this little group was going to meet the Swedish marshal.

Meinbald hurried to Turku, quickly changing ships in Visby, and did not want to stop in Stockholm. This was not his war, but a question of power within Sweden, a possibly very nasty showdown between brothers, where the stake was the kingdom and the lives of many people. He thought that it was necessary to be prepared for the fact that the noise in question might cause movement in the direction of Finland as well.

In Turku, June AD 1275

After reaching Turku, Meinbald did not delay but ordered all the castle commanders under his command to raise their level of readiness. Everyone received an instruction letter with the same content the next day; in Kokemäki Castle, Matti; in Tavastehus Castle, the fortress master Dietrich Balk; in Aarborch, Brother Gödecke Fincke; Brother Otto Swerdh in Raasepori; Brother Fridrik Horn at Porvoo Fortress; Brother Kort Bitzer in Rapola.

Lydeke Diekn was responsible for the garrison of the Turku fortress and the military economy of the entire country. Brother Herman, who had received the nickname Agricola for organizing farming and cattle breeding, was the master of accommodation for the garrisons of the whole country. In addition, Magnus Garper worked as master of arms in Turku. With them, Meinbald reviewed the war situation in the Turku Fortress camp every day.

The situational picture was built on the basis of messages arriving from different fortresses. It was naturally very calm in the Finnish fortresses, but from Stockholm, on the other hand, more and more varied messages were starting to arrive from day to day.

At first, the messages were to the effect that King Valdemar and his troops were going to march from victory to victory south towards the territories controlled by Denmark. Then came in information that progress had stopped.

On Midsummer, Valdemar's peasant army met Magnus's forces at Hova, which was only about three days' riding distance from Stockholm. Later, at the end of June, another message arrived, the message which turns out to be much darker, according to which Valdemar's peasant army had been completely destroyed. Magnus had defeated Valdemar with the help of hudred Danish foot soldiers and seven hundred German mercenaries, and Valdemar had fled to Norway.

Meinbald left for Stockholm without delay. The new king had to be seen soon. Lydeke remained responsible for the defense of the entire country together with Herman. In Stockholm, Meinbald found Björn Näf, who escorted him inland along the Mälaren to meet Magnus at the old fortress of Hovgården.

"Lord Magnus, I came as soon as I heard the news. You have beaten your brother, so I want to tell you that your grace need not be worried about Eastland. The whole of Eastland shows its loyalty to you. I, as your humble servant, came to show my loyalty to you."

"I will gladly accept your loyalty. Nice to see you, Herr Meinbald. Both my father, Birger, and my teacher, Björn, have spoken a lot about you. You have handled eastern military affairs in an exemplary manner. It's amazing to hear that you speak Swedish so well. Are you German?"

"Your Grace, yes, I was born in Germany. I spent my childhood in Bohemia, but I have already spent almost half of my life here, and Swedish is one of our family's home languages, because my wife and children speak Swedish. In fact, my eldest son is not only your first namesake, but also your cousin, for his mother was Hildegard, may her soul rest in peace."

"That's right, Bero married you, now I remember! Listen, Meinbald, we sons of Bjälbo, like our father, have not been too strict about monogamy. My brother Valdemark, yes, despite everything, he is still my brother; he, too, has brought his own sister-in-law as his lover here from Denmark. Yes, and I… what exactly brings you to my speech?"

"Your father, Birger, may his soul rest in peace, gave me great authority to use my own independent judgment in arranging Finnish fiscal and military affairs. I now want to discuss with you, the future king of Sweden, how you want to manage the administration of Eastland in the future."

"Yes, I've heard so many good things about you, Meinbald, that I'm going to give you a completely free hand for the time being regarding Finland's military activities. It is enough that you swear your allegiance to me, and that you will never raise your arms from the East against your king."

"I gladly swear it, my lord Magnus."

"I thank you. When it comes to taxation, the church's laws and practices are followed. Reforms are coming to Crown taxation, but I am quite sure that you will be happy to implement them when the time comes."

In July, Magnus was elected king at Mora Meadow and was crowned the following year in Uppsala.

Southern Sweden and Skåne, AD 1275

After Valdemar's exile, Magnus's relationship with Denmark's king Erik Klipping deteriorated. Erik Klipping made an alliance with Valdemar and formally demanded 6,000 silver marks from Magnus as payment for his previous help. Magnus' forces attacked Halland and Skåne but retreated when confronted by the Danish army. The Danes, on the other hand, attacked Småland the following year. The Swedes defeated the Danes at the Battle of Ettak, but the Danes made another foray into West Gotland. In 1278, a peace was concluded, in which Magnus's debt was reduced to 4,000 silver marks.

Magnus had to surrender the southern part of the kingdom to Valdemar in 1277, but managed to get it back two years later. Some of the great men of the kingdom also rebelled against him, and it was not until 1280, when Magnus had the leaders of the rebellion executed, that the situation calmed down. Meinbald and his men did not take part in these rumblings, but they closely watched over the security of Eastland and collected taxes.

Collecting taxes for the king was new in the entire Swedish kingdom, and it seemed to strangely calm the people's earlier bubbling and the previously very sensitive transition to war. It unified the people because it removed the conflicts of interest between the big men in collecting taxes.

Valdemar and Queen Sofia had six children. Five of the children were daughters who were married either to princes or kings, and one of the daughters was sent to a monastery as a nun. The only son, Erik, was only three years old. Meinbald had had very little direct contact with Valdemar, but he had nevertheless paid attention when he heard that the middle one of his daughters, Rikissa, was married to the Duke of Great Poland, Przemysl II.

The duke's name made Meinbald ask his knight brothers about it, and Kort knew to tell him that this duke was the posthumously born child of the Silesian princess Elisabeth. Elisabeth, on the other hand, was the daughter of Henry II the Pious and Anna of Bohemia, i.e., Agnes's sister.

"These royals are either fighting each other or marrying their daughters to each other's children. Peaceful coexistence seems to be possible only by doing this. Even in Rikissa's case, the duke from Poland had not even made it to the wedding ceremony himself, but sent his representative to Sweden for the event," Kort had concluded his explanation.

Lydeke and Herman had organized knight training in Eastland, and members of the Orders of Teutonic knighths and St. John's had also been brought in as trainers. John Teet was also said to have been involved, surprisingly often and with pleasure, enthusiastically bringing forward the battle practices adopted by the Knights Templar. A fortified barracks area had been built on the castle island of Turku, where knights and squires lived together.

Meinbald was very pleased with this for many reasons. He knew that Magnus's court was preparing a new rule involving tax exemption. Getting this desired freedom would require equipping the cavalry. Meinbald had learned about it, of course, from Matti's son Knut, who had been trained to become a knight and a lawyer in Sweden while growing up. He had also heard the same message from Karl's son, Ulf, and so he willingly arranged his son, Mielivalta, to knight training.

East Götaland, AD 1276

King Magnus appointed Ulf Karlsson Ulv to the Lord High Steward (*riksdrots* in Swedish). This was a completely new position in Sweden; the Lord High Steward was the closest official to the king and was responsible for the kingdom's finances and legal affairs. The title and function of Earl were buried with Birger ten years ago.

Magnus and Helvig from Holstein got married on 11.11.1276. Helvig was one of the younger children in a large group of siblings. The marriage between her and King Magnus was not the only connection between the counts of Holstein and the Nordic countries. Helvig's aunt Mechtild, widow of King Abel of Denmark (d. 1252), remarried in 1261 to Magnus's father, Earl Birger (d. 1266). Barely a year before Helvig's own wedding, her brother Gerhard had married Ingeborg, daughter of the deposed King Valdemar.

Helvig founded the Gray Brothers monastery in Stockholm and later many other churches and monasteries. She participated in the consecration of bishops and the installation of relics, for example, at St. Erik's Mass in 1277. The Swedish kingdom could not have had a better queen than her. She was a noble, loyal, and peace-loving mother figure.

In the spring of 1288, almost twelve years after the wedding, Magnus received papal permission to continue his marriage with Helvig, despite the fact that he had previously been engaged to Helvig's sister-in-law, Sofia, and had also had an affair with another sister. Thus, it was said that Magnus had entered into this marriage to prevent the King of Denmark from getting help from his stepmother against him.

Count Gerhard must have received 600 marks a year from Magnus. During the rebellion against Magnus in 1278, Skara was attacked by the rebels, who attacked Helvig and his father. Helvig managed to escape to the monastery, but Gerhard was captured.

Helvig's coronation was held in Söderköping on July 29, 1281. All the notables of the kingdom were invited, including Meinbald, Elin, Matti, and Malin.

When meeting the royal couple, Meinbald recounted his own background, including his orphanhood and his mother, Agnes, to Helvig and Magnus. This especially stuck in Helvig's mind.

Chapter XVII
Law, Order and Privileges

Adelsö, an island in Mälaren, 30 September AD 1280

The deciduous trees were still green, even though the nights had started to cool down already in August. King Magnus often stayed in Alsnö castle during the summer seasons. He had built Sweden's first brick castle in place of the old fortress at Hovgården. In the summer residency, I got some distance from the administrative machinery that is crowded in Stockholm. Now, Magnus had invited Sir Meinbald of the Eastern land to go through the current administrative reform.

Meinbald had immediately jumped on the next ship leaving for Stockholm in Taivassalo's harbour Helsinginranta. The ferryman already knew him well; he had sailed this distance so often before that he no longer needed to show any travel documents.

Along with the letter of order, he had received his own copy of the new rules drawn up in Alsnö, which the king wanted to discuss with him. Alsnö's rules were written in the form of an open royal letter. Now that Meinbald got to the ship by the familiar route, he had time to read the letter in more detail.

In article one, it was said that for a long time, there had been a strange behavior where traveling magnates and their retinues raped peasants without doing justice to themselves. They had emptied their barns and did not hesitate to visit the poor person's house to take food without paying, and thus ate up the poor person's hard-earned food stocks in an instant. The article stipulated that there must be a judge in each district who will assign the travelers a place to stay with a farmer, to whom monetary compensation must be paid for the stay. The amount of the fine was determined by the person who opposes the judge's decision. If a farmer refused to receive a guest, he must be fined three marks. If the judge could not order a suitable lodging, he was sentenced to pay six marks, two to the traveler, two to the king, and two to the district. If a traveler raped a farmer and didn't pay him, it counted as robbery.

After that, the culprit had one month to pay a fine of 40 marks; otherwise, he will be condemned as an outlaw throughout the kingdom. It was generally clarified that hospitality included an obligation from which only the king and the bishops' own farms and the farms owned by knights and squires in the king's service were exempt.

The first provision of the second article delt with the punishment of someone who kills someone else, in the victim's own yard or in a third party's yard. Such a murderer is sentenced to banishment. He loses all his earthly possessions and is declared an outlaw throughout the kingdom, meaning that anyone can kill him without cause if found within the kingdom's borders.

The property is divided into three equal parts belonging to the claimant, the king and the county. However, if a settlement has been reached, the claimant can ask the king to allow the perpetrator to redeem the legal protection with 40 marks of money, which goes to the king. The article imposed the same punishment on anyone who kills or injures someone in a church or court, who violates an agreement made, maims or rapes someone, or arrests a man for another act.

The third article declares that: "...we free all the men of our men and our dear brother Bengt and all their miners and peasants and all who are in their place free from all royal right. Also, all the archbishop's men and all the bishops. We also desire that all men serving on horseback have the same freedom..."

Meinbald thought about this point for a moment. The first reaction was that, well, he doesn't have to pay taxes to the king anymore, but then a doubt creeped into his mind about how sustainable this would be for the administration in the future and how much discord this would cause.

"Well, that's how it's been decided," Meinbald thought and continued to study the letter to the end:

"The bishops were there: Jakob, Archbishop of Uppsala, Bishop Anund of Strängnäs, Bishop Kettil of Finland, Bishop Assur of Växjö. There were knights there: first, our brother Benedikt Birgersson, then Herr Ulvar Karlsson, Herr Benedikt Magnusson, lawyer in East Götaland, Magnus Jonsson, Svantepolk Knutsson, Ulvar Holmgersson, Anund Haraldsson, lawyer in Södermanland, Knut Mattiesson, governor, lawyer in Närke, Rörik Algotsson, Karl Haraldsson, Torsten Hunvidsson, Bened Hunvidsson Jonsson, Ragnvald the fox, Ragnvald Ingesson, Brynjolf Botillarson. There and present were Herr Peter Erlandsson, Bishop of Västerås, our Chancellor Herr Benedikt Johansson Ängel, Archdeacon of Uppsala, priest Andreas Andreasson, and priest Jon in Strängnäs."

"I see, wise men in their great wisdom. Fortunately, Knut and Ulv Karlsson were also there, because I do already know their father," Meinbald thought and wrapped the letter back in the tube where it had been delivered to him. King Magnus had appointed Ulv Karlsson as his Lord High Steward four years ago. Since then, "Ulvar" had been one of Magnus's most important men.

After sailing during the day, they arrived in Stockholm, where the ship docked at its standard location at the cog pier. At night, Meinbald walked towards the monastery of the gray brothers, which offered a place for travelers to sleep. On the island of Stockholm, he noted how many buildings were under construction, and the city was being built. Some buildings were already ready, the most visible of which was the Church of St. Nicholas, which was completed just last summer.

The building of a stone wall around the city had started, as had the castle started rising in the northern part of the island. After reaching the monk's bridge leading to the Gray Friars' monastery island, Meinbald looked north towards St. George's hospital. It was completed a couple of summers ago, and now the sick, the lepers and the poor were treated there as well as the rich. The trip continued in the morning to Mälaren on a smaller boat.

They reached the island of Alsnö very quickly. King Magnus received his guests in his study, which was located at the back of the castle behind several halls.

Magnus wanted to go through all the neede changes in Eastland directly together with Meinbald. Ulvar had recommended to the king that this be done and that the king appointed Meinbald as the top organizer of legal affairs in

Eastland. And that's not all. The king confirmed that Knut, Matti's son, was to be the next Lord High Steward in the Swedish kingdom after Ulvar. "Here's quite a bit of news to take to Matti, Malin and Elin", Meinbald thought to himself after hearing a happy surprise from King Magnus.

After finishing all things, the king warmly wished Meinbald a safe journey home.

****

In Turku, Finland, AD 1282

Although meeting the king on Alsnö island felt a temporary, even a very meaningless moment, with time it became a part of a grander historical development. Its meaning is visible still today. Peasants had been treated badly. Powerful men had used forced labor to feed their private armies. Magnus now forbidded the general forced labor of peasants and gave knights and men-at-arms tax exemption. That's how the nobility was born, and King Magnus earned the nickname "Ladonlukko", "the Barnlock", from the people. Meinbald considerd this development very good, because in his opinion, people should always be given value, even enemies, so why not the people of one's own country?

"My own country, funny, but this feels very much like my own," Meinbald thinks to himself.

Magnus the Barnlock also established a new governing body called the Power Council. A representative was invited from each region of the kingdom to this council of the king's advisers and closest men. Meinbald received an invitation for the Eastern region. Eastern bishop Kettil also received an invitation, thus both the secular and spiritual leadership of the regions were represented in the council. The council met in Stockholm at regular times, so Meinbald got to travel together with Bishop Kettil to Stockholm often enough. However, they often agreed that only the other would represent the East with his personal presence.

Meinbald used the fraternity's star and cross seal stamp he had received when sealing letters, even outside of fraternity affairs. Otto had now been named Grandmaster. He kept in touch with Meinbald less often because he had never met him. The members of the fraternity who had stayed in Finland were all old, married men, and they didn't really need to keep in touch with Prague anymore.

Meinbald thought that it was good to keep it active with a little effort, and so sometimes he only wrote a short report to Otto, in which he told that there was really nothing burning to talk about in the North, Christian peace prevailed, and sometimes there was enough from the tax tithes to pay a small contribution to the brotherhood.

Meinbald had received a tax exemption for Särkilahti from King Magnus as a thank you for his loyalty, because Mielivalta served as a horseman in the king's troops. King Magnus the Barnlock, Birger's son, had now established a state of rule in the country. Every landowner who equipped a horse got a tax exemption. The king's men and nobles who had received this freedom began to identify themselves as knights or free lords.

As a land marshal appointed by the king, *Capitaneus Finlandensis*, meant that Meinbald now also had to think about what kind of coat of arms he would take for his shield and seal. The star and cross would naturally be the suggestion of many old knight brothers, but Meinbald did not want to take the brotherhood's symbol on his own shield. Besides, Teet had already decided to carry a star and a cross on his coat of arms, even though the cross was the slanted Cross of Andreas.

Meinbald thought feverishly and finally came up with an idea: in the future, he would have an outstretched, armored right hand as a symbol of cooperation. It suited the merchant's son well. Shields and seals had to be equipped with this hand pattern.

Fridrik had served as a field marshal, and as a rallying officer, he always carried a horn, so he had already chosen a horn as his coat of arms. Kort's coat of arms was a buck—his unwavering faith helped him and his brothers-in-arms push through every situation. Herman, a farmer and a soldier, took care of bread and livestock, so his coat of arms was a plow.

Of course, Otto's coat of arms was a sword—he knew that he was the most skilled swordsman in the group. Lydeke, the group's scribe and a very skilled administrator, had flown pigeons and practiced asceticism as a monk. His view of the coat of arms reflected this: it was a human figure with a bird's head in a monk's robe. Ulf's coat of arms was more straightforwardly an axe.

Asser, who had also joined the group very closely, now chose a star and crescent as his coat of arms.

"What is your idea behind your choice?" asked Lydeke, who was clearly interested in abstract things.

"The star is the sign of the Virgin Mary. I came here North through land of St Mary. The crescent moon, on the other hand, is the symbol of my hometown, Constantinople. The Latin Empire conquered the western part of Constantinople in the Fourth Crusade, after first plundering and destroying the city. The churches of Western Rome and Eastern Rome separated because of this. Here, on the edge of the earth, where the churches of East and West meet at the last border, I believe that we can build a peaceful coexistence."

"Are you Asser Byzantine? And yet you have fought with us against the Byzantine Karelians and Novgorodians?" Meinbald asked, confused.

"I don't know who is right, who is wrong—East or West. I'm Asser; it's Hebrew, and it means *happy*. I am happy that here I have found brothers in arms and in spirit, and I am happy that we can bring peace and order to these heathens. And if someone does not want to receive this peace and order, but sows the opposite, I can very happily let him die. That's why I chose the star and the moon."

****

A fortified house was being built as a home for Bishop Johannes in Kuusisto. At first, the fortress was made of wood. Meinbald visited the bishop for consultations from time to time, not only in Koroinen on the banks of the Aura River, but also at his place in Kuusisto. While visiting Kuusisto, he stated aloud to the bishop, "Being made of wood, this can burn a little too easily if the unbelievers attack again."

Saying this, he instilled a constant fear of fire in the Polish-born bishop and offered his help.

"I can send word to Germany; they have long known how to build stone castles there, if a good, free master could be found to build a stone fortress for you."

Of course, there was much more need for stonemasons in Turku, because at the mouth of Aurajoki, on an island in the estuary, a stone castle and a new home church for the bishop would also be built from stone. This new church was referred to in Latin as *Domus*, i.e., the home church of the bishop, but at some point it was mistakenly translated into Finnish as "cathedral of Doom." With this designation, the nation was perhaps better suited to an obedient and self-sacrificing mind.

Meinbald lived the glory days of his local power, blissfully ignorant of the fact that power always and forever arouses envy, competition, and fighting. This dream of happiness ended very suddenly. One fine September day, armed men rushed through the door of his mansion to arrest him. The men were commanded by an old acquaintance, Asser. He ordered his men to lift the chained man onto the horse waiting in the yard. Elin was horrified and shocked, and Meinbald himself was stunned.

"Asser, what does this mean? Why do you come to my house and put me in chains? Who gave you your orders?" Meinbald asked.

"Brother Meinbald, I have orders from His Highness King Magnus to take you to Turku Castle Island to await your sentencing."

"Sentencing? For what?" Meinbald asked with cloudy eyes.

"You know—don't act confused. I never would have believed that from you, Meinbald. The king's messenger brought us a letter of command yesterday. It tells how you have plotted against the king and the church and sought the crown for yourself. We are all really disappointed in you; you have failed all your brothers."

"What the hell am I being accused of? I have never done anything against the king; on the contrary, I have always fought for him and the church!"

"Save your explanation for the hangman, Meinbald. Of course, if you want, you'll have time to let out a few more screams before your neck snaps."

The horsemen galloped off, taking Meinbald with them and leaving Elin howling in terror in her yard.

****

Paris, 1275 - 1280

Meinbald's firstborn son, Magnus, studied in Paris from 1275 to 1278. He was the only student from Eastland at the University of Paris, but some other Scandinavians had also been admitted to the German-English department. In Paris, Magnus met, among others, Swedish Andreas And, who had started his own studies only a couple of years before him.

The first time they met was at a lecture where Andreas was a teacher. However, they also partly attended the same lectures, studying in the same German-English class in the 'Natione'. Somehow, they felt like they were the neighbor's boys, coming from similar circumstances, both far from home and in a completely foreign culture. As the years went by, they both noticed that this culture didn't feel so foreign anymore; the home country instead had started to seem a little more foreign to them.

After his graduation, Magnus teached at the University of Paris for a couple of years and then returned to Finland in 1280. Andreas had already returned to Sweden a couple of years earlier.

As a learned master who was allowed to teach wherever he wanted, Magnus has no trouble getting into the favor of Bishop Johannes, and he acted as the bishop's appointed supervisor for the construction work of both the new Cathedral and the new bishop's palace to be built in Kuusisto. Acting as a chaplain in the Koroinen church was a fitting activity in addition to that. He also went to the monastery school to teach future apprentice priests.

****

Turku, September AD 1281

Meinbald woke up in a stone dungeon built on Turku's Castle Island. He had been thrown here yesterday to await his official sentence. Only barely drinkable water and hard bread were available as refreshments.

"If only I could somehow get a word to Fridrik." That was his first thought; it was what he'd been thinking about all night long. However, he had come to the conclusion that they probably also had taken Fridrik and everyone else from his brotherhood. If they didn't, he still had hope. Fridrik, Lydeke or Kort — one of those three could still save him. The king had obviously been fed some willow-rope stories about us here in Finland. Asser didn't know what; he just took orders as orders."

Elin did not stay idle waiting for her husband's fate the day before. As soon as the biggest shock had eased a little, she had come to the same conclusion as her husband and galloped away on her horse to the neighbour, Fridrik Horn. After knocking on the oak door of the seemingly empty mansion, Elin was finally relieved when she saw a familiar man open the door himself.

"Fridrik! You're luck they haven't picked you up yet," Elin exclaimed in greeting, then bursted into inconsolable tears.

"What has happened, dear neighbour? Who—and why—would someone pick me up?" Fridrik asked. "Wife, will you bring us a glass of wine soon to calm Elin down?"

"Fridrik, now is not the time even for a glass. The armed men just came to us; they fetched Meinbald and took him to Turku Castle Island to be killed."

"My God! Now I understand your trouble. Since I haven't been picked up yet, let's go inside and make a quick plan. Meinbald and I have been men of quick action since childhood."

Inside Fridrik's manor, Elin recounted the morning's events. Fridrik would like to rush immediately to save his friend, but he restrained himself. There was something so peculiar here that he needed to think a little.

"If no one has picked me up yet, it could be that there is a plot behind this to get us all out of the game. Now that wouldn't be unusual at all. Asser has told us about the age-old intrigues and murders of Byzantium. And now he is himself implementing one of those here in Finland. I have never really trusted Asser to begin with, and for that matter, his commander, John Teet."

"They are just turncoats running after money and power."

"I will immediately send word to Kort. He will probably be the last to be sought, as he is under the protection of the Church, and King Magnus wants to be on good terms with the Church. Kort, if anyone, could quickly reach the archbishop and the king and clear up this misunderstanding. Not Meinbald—none of us have done anything to deserve this. On the contrary! The king has always been grateful to us, and so has the Church. Elin, how much do you know about your husband's enemies?"

"As far as I know, my husband doesn't have any here. It is impossible to argue with him even at home."

"I thought you would say that. However, along each journey, you come across men and situations that leave you scratching your head. Has your husband ever talked about John Teet?"

"I have never heard that name."

"Teet is a former Knight Templar; he came to Tavast land with the mercenary army. Asser was one of his mercenaries. I'll bet my head that he has a hand in this."

After receiving Fridrik's message by pigeon, Kort did not delay but immediately set sail from Aasaamaa towards Stockholm. He was, like Fridrik, convinced that John Teet had his dirty fingers in this incomprehensible accusation.

Kort was not only a physically strong fighter, but also a giant of spirit. He, too, had seen and experienced tough battles and was fully aware that not all battles stayed on the battlefields. They also took place all the time in hidden chambers, in the dark, both inside the Church and in secular homes, mansions, and castles.

Before leaving, he sent a reply to Fridrik, urging him to remain calm and that he should not under any circumstances attack Turku Castle Island—except at the last desperate moment, if he saw the commander they admired being brought to the scaffold. Kort was absolutely certain that Asser's men were hiding around the island, waiting for the attackers.

****

Elin visited her husband every day. As an elderly woman, she wasn't perceived as a threat by the guards, and she was already old enough that she did not have to worry about her own safety and integrity. Tears rolled down both of their cheeks when they finally saw each other. The dungeon was in the basement of a brick stone tower, through a hole in the roof, the prisoners were lowered down and from the same hole they were also fed. They met once a day by the same roof opening. They exchanged a few warm words at first, but mostly they just stared at each other in silence.

Some days, Elin brought greetings from Maunu, whom he had visited at the Cathedral construction site. When it was time for Elin to leave, when the guard came to pick her up, she sent her husband a flying kiss and said, "See you again tomorrow, my love! This gave Meinbald more strength and faith, but on the other hand, it also somehow felt more and more inconsolable day after day."

****

Fridrik had gathered the men of the brotherhood and drawn up a plan to free their commander. Kort and Fridrik exchanged pigeon messages daily, so they all had a clear understanding of how the situation was progressing. All the brothers and their men were aware that it was a conspiracy, and direct contact with the enemy had to be avoided for the time being. Reconnaissance around the fortress island was done at night, and Asser's camps were revealed quite easily. Lydeke was on the castle island itself in the capacity of head of the knight school; he was kept up to date with the help of a messenger. Using a carrier pigeon would have been too big a risk.

Kort met the Archbishop in Stockholm and after explaining the situation to him he finally managed to secure an audience to the king.

"Your Grace, on the way here, I saw your fleet in the archipelago sea of Turku. In my opinion, you have been misled regarding the officers of Eastland. Unless I am completely mistaken, you must have heard some alarming claims from Mr. John Teet?"

"Herr Kort—that is your name, right? I have indeed made the decision, based on the intelligence provided by Mr. Teet, that the top military leadership in Eastland must be immediately replaced by men loyal to us. John Teet is in charge of the landing operation; he is one of my trusted men in the Baltic Sea. After landing on Helsinginranta and Aurajoki, the troops are to clear all military targets and execute those who do not agree to accept their new commander. But how did you get here? No ship was supposed to even reach Åland."

"Your Grace, I left directly from my home in Aasamaa and thus got past the blockades. Allow me to explain my understanding of the true state of things and what I, as a man of the Church, consider to be the truth."

Kort laid out his understanding of the whole conspiracy and finally convinced King Magnus. King had already written the cancellation of his order letter and was planing to send it by pigeon to Turku, when Kort had a better idea.

"Give me that cancellation letter, Your Grace. I see to it that our brothers, faithful to you, would receive it and be relieved. Instead, write a new warrant in which you order John Teet and

Asser the Byzantine to be wanted throughout the kingdom. Distribute that letter to all provinces—and be the first to send one directly to Asser in Turku by pigeon."

"Directly to Asser the Byzantine, but according to you he is a double-faced traitor, like his master Teet?" King wondered.

"Trust me, your Grace. Show them directly, that you cannot be fooled anymore. I am pretty sure, that this is the fastest, easiest and the only way to snap the necks of the conspiritors who have acted against you."

"I like you, father Kort, where did you say you are from?"

"I came here from Bohemia, but originally my family comes from Bitzen, north of Alps, Your Grace."

***

In Finland, the fleet led by Teet carried out landings in several places at the same time. Teet, an experienced naval commander, had chosen strategic landing sites so skillfully that it posed no difficulty for them to advance on land with their cavalry and armed men from different directions toward Turku. There was practically no resistance; the soldiers were free to advance in their gleaming armor and plumed helmets. Because Asser's men controlled the mouth of the Aura River and the castle-island, Teet decided to glide in at his leisure aboard his command ship all the way up to the castle-island itself.

There he would take command of Finland, read aloud the accusations he had invented against the man he hated, Meinbald the Bohemian, and then, following "his king's order," carry out the execution of the man condemned to death under aggravating circumstances. After all, treason was the gravest of crimes imaginable against the crown.

Elin saw Teet and Asser together on the castle-island when she was leaving her visit to Meinbald. There was also a third man with them whose features Elin could not recognize and whose origins she could not place.

"That plumed-helmeted man must be the rival my husband told Fridrik about," she thought as she hurried away from the castle-island. There was no time to remain and get recognized here. Earlier Elin had already sent word to Mielivalta that he should keep a low profile and, at the same time, secretly report the happenings on the castle-island to his mother every day whenever she came to visit his father.

Under no circumstances were these men to learn that the two of them were mother and son. For the same reason Elin had forbidden Mauno from coming to the castle-island, even though as a clergyman he would surely have been allowed to see his father.

The first detachments of Teet's landing forces met one another at Koroinen. After assembling, the troops waited for further orders from their commander. Some units had not reached the rendezvous because they had landed at Taivassalo's Helsinginranta and had begun clearing the commander's area house by house, manor by manor, with the aim of capturing or executing all commanders loyal to Meinbald. But at every door they were told the same sort of story: "The master of the house, Lord Dominus Lydeke, is on official duty on the castle-island," or "Lord Dominus Otto is guarding Tavastehus Castle," "Lord Dominus Klaus is taking care of arms procurement in Estonia." Unfortunately for this lynch mob, they drew blanks at every Taivassalo manor because none of the masters were at home. This frustrated them and enraged the attack forces. A few houses were simply set alight out of spite.

Elin relayed word of Asser's meeting with the man she suspected to be Teet to Fridrik, who had himself already suspected a landing and had sent carrier pigeons to all the important garrisons asking every man to march at once to Turku to free their commander and the appointed ruler. Within a couple of days Fridrik received word that the marches had begun. Troops from Hakoinen, Ratzeborg, Arborg, Tavastehus and Sääksenmäki were all already moving south — and, of course, the men of Pirkka as well.

Having received this information, Fridrik decided to launch an attack on Teet's combined main force, since it was necessary to engage it before it could disperse and attack the region's various fortresses. They had already begun constructing siege machines, so their intent to besiege castles was clear. Fridrik had capable young men who had undergone knightly training and eager young squires, all ready to defend their country against the invaders. Fridrik himself focused, as usual, on maintaining the overall picture and moving the troops. He took his command post on the highest hill, from which he could observe well where Teet's detachments were moving.

"Clerk, send a message to Lydeke on the castle-island. Now we must take a risk and use a pigeon, because Teet is probably already there. Knowing his ruthlessness, he is ready to execute the moment he gets the chance. Lydeke must act immediately."

***

Meinbald got occasional horror images in his mind when, after moments of confusion, it became clear to him where he was being held.

"This is Castle Island, where Mielivalta is also in knight training! If I am killed here by the king's orders, it is quite certain that Mielivalta will be killed after me. This is how those in power work—this was Birger's way of working. The Barnlock is not an apple that fell far from the tree. Tomorrow, I will tell Elin to take the boy away from here under some pretext. Maunu should also stay away. Maybe they could escape together to a monastery in the west—perhaps as far as Norway."

Mielivalta, as well as all the other knights, had, of course, heard who was being kept in the dungeon. He was deeply upset. His own father—the man he had known all his life—did not deserve such treatment. His fellow knight trainees were understanding and sympathetic toward Mielivalta, because even to them, the vague accusations leveled against their legendary supreme commander sounded unbelievable.

Lydeke, as the head of the school, had come to tell him that it would be best for Mielivalta to stay safely away from his father, so that none of Asser's men would get any hint of their kinship. He also hinted that help was on the way; for now, they simply had to wait patiently for the right moment to raise their weapons against Asser and his troops. They agreed that Mielivalta could leave the castle camp to join Fridrik's forces, who would soon be approaching the fortress.

∗

Matti rode with the Pirkka warriors at full gallop toward Turku. He had received a message brought by a carrier pigeon from Fridrik to the Kokemäki manor, and after reading it, he immediately ordered his men to depart. The same was done by Magnus Garper and Otto Svärd, who set out from Tavastehus. Klaus Fläming and his troops were already very close to Turku, as they were coming from Ratzeburg along the coastal road of Uusimaa.

Some of the forces under Fridrik's command attacked Teet's main troops, who had encamped at Koroinen. Other detachments struck simultaneously at the guard camps Asser had stationed along the banks of the Aura River.

In the castle courtyard, Lydeke saw a pigeon land in the camp's message loft. He sensed that it would be wise for him to be the first to read the message before Asser's men could get their hands on it. Approaching the young squire who tended the pigeons, he said casually:

"I'm expecting an important letter — let me read that message that just arrived... Yes, this is the one I was waiting for. Good. Now, squire, listen carefully: Lord Asser's men have received reinforcements in their landing, but they are now engaged in battle with my fellow knights' troops. Even your friends are already taking part in that fight. Your duty now is to manage the communications and spread the word to all the squires in the camp that, from this moment on, we are to fight against all of Lord Asser's forces. Our struggle is supported by strong troops along the riverbanks, and reinforcements are arriving to aid us at any moment. Do you understand, young squire?"

"Yes, my lord dominus, I understand and will spread the word at once. From now on, I will deliver all incoming messages directly to you, Dominus Lydeke."

"Excellent, young man, excellent. Now, take up arms and defend justice against wrongdoing!"

With his sword in hand, Lydeke set off straight toward the castle's main fortifications, where he believed Asser and Teet were plotting their next move. He knew he had to act before the sounds of battle from the nearby shores would alert Teet and make him rush to pronounce the summary judgment he so eagerly desired.

Lydeke, deeply respected as a father figure by the knight trainees, was quickly joined by armed trainees — young knights he had guided and instructed for many years.

From the hill known as Vartiovuori, Fridrik observed the movements and battles of the troops. He had only half a company of cavalry as guards for his command post. Eventually, after confirming that the forces he had sent to Koroinen were gaining the upper hand in the opening phase of the battle, he decided that they were now needed at the castle. Meinbald was being held there, and his life was still in grave danger.

"We just need to strike hard and keep the enemy tied up until reinforcements arrive," he muttered half aloud as they galloped down from Vartiovuori toward Turku Castle Island.

Klaus arrived at Koroinen with his cavalry and crushed Teet's landing troops. Fridrik's detachment had already been in some trouble and was beginning to lose ground, but now they regained momentum. The arrival of Matti and the Pirkka warriors a short while later brought even more energy to the battlefield, as they rode in just moments after Klaus's troops. Otto and Magnus, meanwhile, headed to Taivassalo with their men to bring order to the forces that had been spreading destruction there.

***

On the castle island, Lydeke and the squires found Teet and Asser in a wooden headquarters behind the fortifications. The men did not flinch nor surrender when they were confronted — instead, both drew their swords and, shouting for alarm, attacked Lydeke and the group of squires.

Lydeke found himself face-to-face with Teet, who, it seemed, recognized him only then — an old comrade-in-arms from years past. The squires focused on surrounding Asser and guarding the doorway in case reinforcements arrived.

In the heat of the sword fight, Teet managed to corner Lydeke. But one of the squires' armed men saved the situation by shooting Teet with a crossbow. The bolt pierced Teet's chainmail and embedded itself in his arm.

***

Fridrik and his cavalry had already defeated Asser's riverbank guards. As soon as the battle was won, Fridrik sent an advance detachment across the Aura River on rafts, aiming to establish a bridgehead on the shore of the castle island. The stone wall built along the island's northern shore made the attempt difficult, as a rain of arrows was unleashed upon the men crossing. The vanguard shielded themselves beneath their shields but pressed on determinedly. The following troops found the crossing somewhat easier, and Fridrik ordered that siege engines captured from Teet's landing forces — including a siege tower, two ballistae, and three catapults — be brought over on the rafts.

***

Meanwhile, inside the walls, Lydeke and the squires captured Teet and Asser. In the headquarters there was a small cell built for prisoner interrogations. The two villains were locked inside, and three squires stayed behind to guard them while Lydeke, with six squires, went to the walls to strike at the rear of Asser's men.

Teet and Asser had been in contact with the Prince of Novgorod and had received from him a promise of eight ships full of men. The Novgorodian fleet was waiting for a signal. Commander of the Novgorodian vanguard, Yuri, had arrived with Teet's own ship along with a few men. In the early hours of the morning, he had fired a flaming arrow into the sky — the agreed-upon signal for the rest of the fleet to sail freely up the Aura River toward the inland.

At dawn, the Novgorodians had already reached the mouth of the river with their ships. Some had advanced to Kuusisto, made a swift landing, and begun to move inland, laying havoc to the countryside. Livestock were slaughtered, and all wooden buildings were burned. Matti received a notice of this from the bishop's messenger. The Pirkka warriors withdrew from the battle at Koroinen — now turning clearly in their favor — and headed south to confront the Russians.

Around the castle island, full-scale siege warfare was underway. The ballistae wounded many of Asser's and Teet's men who were shooting crossbows from the walls. The catapults hurled glowing iron and fiery pots at the castle's defenders. The besiegers worked tirelessly, digging without rest, and soon the siege tower was brought closer to the fortress.

Fridrik, knowing that his childhood friend and commander was imprisoned in the castle dungeon, decided that the fortress had to be taken by a sudden assault over the ramparts. These traitors had to be punished — as a warning to others.

"Whoever is the first to climb into the castle shall have all the horses there — and Asser as his slave! As for Teet, we'll hoist him above all others, hanging him from the highest branch!"

This proposal suited the devout warriors of Eastland perfectly. They made their vows of offering to the Lord and the Holy Virgin, and thus the assault began immediately after the morning mass.

Inside the castle, however, the defenders had other plans. They lit great fires and opened a large breach at the top of the fortifications. Through the opening, they rolled down flaming cartwheels aimed at the siege tower. The attackers, though, quickly managed to extinguish the burning wheels and the fires they caused. Meanwhile, another assault group piled wood beneath the drawbridge and set it ablaze. Some of the castle's defenders rushed out through the gate to meet the attackers head-on.

Mielivalta, who had joined Fridrik's forces as soon as he reached the shore, seized a torch and was the first to climb up the tower toward the wall. His fellow squire, Peder, followed right behind, and together they swiftly reached the battlements. Seeing this, the other soldiers hurried after them. Each man helped his comrade up into the fortress, while others forced their way through the opening from which the defenders had hurled the fiery wheels. The first men over the wall cleared space for those who followed, driving the defenders from the fortifications with sword and spear.

Matti and the Pirkka men launched a cavalry charge against the marching column of Novgorodians. After the initial strike, they dismounted and cut down with swords and spears all who were within reach, then took up crossbows to shoot down the fleeing survivors. Klaus Fleming's cavalry arrived just in time to surround the retreating enemy. The Novgorodians had clearly come prepared only for raiding, not for facing a fully equipped army — and so, confronted by such a force, they fell into chaos and disorder, making it easy for the defenders to strike them down.

***

In the morning, at the time of the rooster's crowing, Meinbald woke up and heard distant sounds outside, which he recognized as the call of battle. It stirred him. After a long time, adrenaline flooded his veins, his heart beated faster, and his eyes sharpened. Approaching steps and shouts were heard, and finally, the hatch in the roof opened.

"Are you still alive, my brother?" a familiar voice called.

"Fridrik! Here I am, strong in soul and body."

After climbing up the rope ladder, Meinbald joyfully embraced his longtime brother and neighbor.

"I knew you would come, though I didn't know how long it would take. Now even the jokes are starting to make me laugh. But what about Asser?"

"Hanged himself like Judas Iscariot. I didn't see any silver coins, but John Teet's ambitions and scheming could be found behind it. The gentlemen had exchanged letters, and that Pole hadn't burned them. Asser had received a letter from the king yesterday—the one Kort had asked to be sent. After reading that he was wanted together with Teet, Asser ended up hanging himself this morning when the rooster crowed. There's some symbolism in that, don't you think?"

"I believe so. What of Teet—any word?"

"According to Lydeke, Teet managed to escape from the squires while wounded. He fled aboard his ship — most likely to Estonia. I doubt he will ever return to the Kingdom of Sweden. And if he does, he'll end up at the gallows without delay. Lydeke and the squires have joined my men, and together they're right now striking down the Russian troops that landed by the castle."

The battle near the castle raged fiercely for a while longer, until all the Novgorodians and mercenaries were defeated. Those who were lightly wounded and surrendered were taken prisoner — the rest were slain without mercy.

***

Matti, Klaus and Otto, with their seasoned warriors, beated the Novgorodians and the mercenary bands that had advanced from the west, driving the remnants from the land. One Novgorodian fleeing party finally escaped on a single ship that had landed at Kuusisto. Most of the mercenaries laid down their arms and were fully prepared to join the defenders' side, only awaiting provisions and daily pay as compensation from their new commander.

The Novgorodian commander Yuri and the other Novgorodians captured after the fighting were locked in the castle dungeon to await further proceedings.

"I see the most sensible course of action is to exchange these captured Novgorodians for the prisoners of war they took from us," Meinbald said after pondering the matter. "To be honest, my loyalty to Ladonlukko is being severely tested. The man is a relative, for God's sake, and yet he gave the order to exchange us without batting an eye!" Meinbald exclaimed.

"Let's exchange the prisoners, that's a good idea," Fridrik agreed.

"Perhaps we should exchange something else as well," Magnus Garper, who had arrived at the castle from Taivassalo, added.

"What do you mean?"

"Maybe the Bishop of Finland should seize power from the crown. We could make this a church state, like in Livonia. The bishop would lead us directly under the papal authority, and you, Dominus Meinbald, would govern the temporal affairs — with no ties to the untrustworthy King of Sweden."

Meinbald was silent for a long time. He thought, feverishly trying to resolve the gnawing, long-grown conflict within him. The king — the son of his former father-in-law — had attacked him and his sons. What would stop Barnlock from doing the same again in the future if they now simply let it pass? The Church would easily be on their side; Kort and he could count on papal support if they wished. But then another thought struck him like a hammer. Kort would be in mortal danger if they followed Magnus's suggested course. Kort was at Barnlock's court, as a guest. He would become a hostage — and very soon headless, executed — if they threatened to split Barnlock's realm. No. They could not tread that path lightly.

"Magnus, I remind you that our brotherhood — which both I and your quiet comrade-in-arms Otto represent — follows the Rule of Saint Augustine, and those rules are very clear in forbidding rebellion against secular authority. If you now suggest that I should represent that same authority here in Eastland as the bishop's vassal, then I would have to receive the blessing for that power directly from the Pope himself. Yet the Pope granted this authority over Eastland to the King of Sweden thirty years ago."

"If you, my brothers-in-arms, truly wish it, I am ready to devote myself to this demanding task — but only on the condition that I have your full support. For I know well that Barnlock would not take such a step lightly. It would most likely mean a new, greater war within the Swedish realm. Is that what we truly desire? Barnlock has used mercenaries before — he can buy German and Scottish warriors with silver, and he would not even need to send his best troops against us if he wished to save them for a campaign against Denmark, for instance."

A deep silence followed. Meinbald urged each of his brothers to speak their mind. All of his closest men — Fridrik, Lydeke, Herman, and Gödeke — opposed the idea of a civil war. Even Otto, who had previously supported Magnus's proposal, withdrew his backing. Each knight-brother had to wrestle with his conscience and face his own inner Jacob's struggle. Was it the deliberate breaking of St. Augustine's rule that restrained them from grasping this chance for independence — or did the papal dispensation that had allowed Meinbald to take a wife in Finland still weigh on the scales, even thirty years later? Was Birger's binding so enduring after all?

Whatever the reason, in the end the forces of Eastland remained loyal to the king — the very same king who had been willing to have them slaughtered without a blink. To the king who had believed the tall tales of a Scottish mercenary without seeking any explanation from the commanders of his own eastern forces. That single moment of decision did not only shape its own time; it also pointed to the course future events would take. Eastland would remain under the Swedish crown for centuries to come.

Once the decision had been spoken aloud, Fridrik immediately handed over command of the defensive forces to his friend, briefing him with soldierly precision on everything he had learned about the invaders. Throughout the day, they updated their situational reports at the castle with messages brought by carrier pigeons.

As evening fell, Fridrik finally began to feel a weariness he had not allowed himself to acknowledge for many days. The situation was at last completely settled, the war was won, the invaders defeated. Messages from Matti, Otto, and Klaus confirmed the victory. Together, Fridrik and Meinbald sent a pigeon-borne message of good news to Kort at the royal court, ensuring that the king's favor would remain with them. They were careful to mention the fact that Teet, acting behind the king's back, had invited the Novgorodian fleet — evidently with the intention of placing his own future vassal state under the tribute of the Grand Prince of Novgorod.

"What now, O admired commander?" Fridrik asked, looking Meinbald in the eyes, the fatigue in his own unhidden.

"We go on as before, as friends and neighbors, Fridrik. Once more, I owe you my life."

"That suits me. Do come visit, once you and Elin have had time to recover from this ordeal."

"We will, thank you for the invitation! Elin visited me every day while I was held captive — but I miss her so terribly that, if you'll forgive me, I'll depart for Taivassalo at once."

"We'll give you a ride — I figured home would soon be calling. But surely you have a moment to speak with your son first?"

Mielivalta stood in the castle yard, before the tower door, waiting for his father. Meinbald and Mielivalta embraced warmly, though a bit restrainedly under the watchful eyes around them.

"You'll come visit your mother soon, won't you?"

"I will, Father — and you as well. I'm so glad you're free again, my lord."

"Glad to be free in a free land, my boy! Now, watch how your old father greets his rescuers!"

Clearing his throat, Meinbald raised his voice to address the men in the courtyard.

"Dear brothers-in-arms and loyal men of Finland! This adventure has ended well for us — my deepest thanks to you, my saviors! Had those scoundrels succeeded in their schemes, we would all be gone, and they would now hold the reins of power. But things turned out otherwise! Now I go to greet my faithful wife, yet within a week you are all welcome here on the Castle Island for a grand feast, whose bounty I shall offer you from my own purse in gratitude for your loyalty and bravery! The Crown is thankful to you as well, for all of Swedish Eastland still stands under the same steadfast defense — the same that has guarded it these thirty years. In that time, our castles have turned to stone, and our men's grip to iron against all invaders!"

Lydeke, Gödeke, and Herman joined Fridrik in leading their men in a rousing cheer for their commander. As night fell, the boats began to glide toward Taivassalo.

***

Elin greeted her husband joyfully at the Särkilahti pier.

"My beloved, you came home alive after all."

"Aye, it was an ordeal that knocked the wind out of me. My own men — Asser and his followers — had plotted with John Teet and sought to end us all. But it turned out otherwise, my love, otherwise indeed! Had you not acted swiftly when they came for me, Fridrik and I would never have set foot in Taivassalo again — we'd have been brought here our feet first. It was that close."

"Come now to the sauna. I'll wash you clean of the dungeon's dust and that dreadful stench. Then you'll have supper and rest in your own bed again."

Asser left behind a wife, three sons, and two daughters in Tavastia. The boys were taken to Turku for knightly training, and the daughters were sent to a convent.

Turku, AD 1283

Turku – Stockholm, AD 1284

Sad news came from Bohemia, which touched Meinbald deeply: Sister Agnes had died the previous year. Kunigunde wrote in her letter:

"My dear brother,

It is with a heavy heart that I have to tell you that our dear benefactor — our foster mother on earth, Sister Agnes — has fallen asleep. She was the only person, after our own parents, who always gave her all for us. We are forever indebted to her, even in the afterlife, where she has now passed on. God will bless us for a long time here on earth.

That is why it took me so long to write to you. Know that she remembered you until her last moment. I know because I was there when she was anointed for her last journey. She whispered to me in her shaky voice, 'Keep in touch with your brother; you still have each other. I am waiting for you on the other side, with your and my own parents.'

Oh, my brother, I know these words, when they reach you, will cause shivers — but I so hope that one day we could still see each other here on earth. Come and visit Prague again!

Wishing you health,

Your sister Kunigunde — weakling."

Meinbald weeped after reading the letter. He decided to visit Prague once more, even though he was now an old and wizened sixty-three-year-old soldier. This time, he took Elin and Mielivalta with him. It was time to show the boy where his father had come from. Magnus had also seen Prague and often spoken of it to Mielivalta.

Their departure was organized quickly, as ships left for Lübeck every week during the summer season. The journey could have been described as slow and arduous, but Meinbald maintained a calm and reflective state of mind. From Lübeck, horse-drawn carts carried them swiftly — Meinbald, with the help of Lübeck's church authorities, had arranged for them to travel with the mail convoy going directly to Bohemia.

Arriving in great Prague, Elin and Mielivalta's eyes glowed with wonder at the splendor and the teeming crowds. Kunigunde was grateful and overjoyed to see her brother — and even more so, his family. Together they spent a memorable week in Prague: sometimes dining together, sometimes attending services in St. Vitus Church, and sometimes visiting Agnes's grave.

At the grave, Kunigunde told Meinbald:

"Agnes was so happy when you came here, and she was still able to see you, my brother. A couple of weeks after you had left, she began to tell of a dream in which she had seen you and me together in St. Clara's Monastery in Sweden. She spoke of it several times, clearly believing she could see into the future. Even on her deathbed, Agnes told me that this was the miracle she had been waiting for all her life — and that she would die happy, having experienced a true miracle."

"Oh, Kunigunde," Meinbald replied, "she had the gift of foresight in her family, and in her own life she was able to influence our future. So why wouldn't she be able to do so even after her death?"

"Do you think so, Meinbald? Could it be true?"

"I believe that no one can know the future for sure, but it can be influenced. And I have a good relationship with the King of Sweden. When I tell him what Agnes has accomplished here in Prague, I am certain that Agnes's dream will come true."

"Oh, it would be wonderful if I could come to Sweden! Then we could see each other more often, my dear brother. I miss my family, and since I cannot have one of my own in this earthly life, I long for yours. My dear brother, do what you can to make Agnes's dream come true!"

The week flew by, and their return journey began — this time by riverboat down the Vltava.

"Thank you, my husband, for bringing us here," said Elin as they slid under the Judith Bridge toward Dresden for the last time.

"Thank you for coming. This place means so much to me; I grew up here. But the last time I came, without you, I had no reason to stay and felt out of place. Now that you've been with me, I feel much more at peace."

"Home is where the heart says it is, my husband. Where does your heart say home is now that we're all together?"

"Yes — it's in Taivassalo, my dear wife. That's where my heart says my home is. That's where we'll return, and that's where we'll grow old together."

"And in Taivassalo, Mielivalta will grow into a great man and a great soldier, following in his father's footsteps. Isn't that right, Mielivalta?"

"Dear Mother," Mielivalta answered, "I have been educated as a knight of the Swedish Empire, and now, here in Prague, I've come to understand that although my father has brought many blessings to us in the North, we ourselves must defend what we hold dear — what we call home. For me, that is Finland and Taivassalo. The King brings the framework of earthly power, and the Bishop brings the framework of heavenly power, but soldiers — knights and infantry alike — form the hard instrument of that power, keeping enemy forces at bay."

"Well said, my son. That's the way it is," Meinbald concluded.

Turku – Stockholm, AD 1284

The following summer, King Magnus appointed his brother Bengt Birgersson as Duke of Finland. In a letter to Meinbald, the King wrote that there was no need for new loyalty banners or changes to the tax system, as his royal servants would continue to manage the collection and allocation of revenues from the East "just as before."

However, he hinted in his letter that Meinbald, Maunu, and Mielivalta would be welcome to receive him for an audience in Stockholm. Thus, Meinbald and his sons visited the King a week later.

King Magnus greeted them warmly — almost like relatives, if one could say such a thing of the men of the Bjälbo family — and introduced them to his brother Bengt. Magnus, in royal fashion, remarked aloud that he hoped they would become very close partners. Bengt, like Meinbald's son Maunu, had also received a priestly education. Gregers, visiting from Västmanland, was also present.

"Meinbald, do you still remember me?" Gregers asked, somewhat unexpectedly.

"Of course I remember. Welcome, Herr Gregers. And is this your son?"

"Yes, this is Magnus. He will first serve as a squire and later be raised to knighthood. Could he study with you in Eastland? I think it would be a fine continuation of tradition."

"Of course, I will arrange it, Herr Gregers. You can rely on me," Meinbald replied.

"My son Mielivalta has attended knight training in Turku; he'll gladly tell him everything he can learn there."

"The gentlemen are welcome to the castle ballroom for dinner this evening," the King invited his guests.

At dinner, Meinbald sat beside the King, with Maunu next to him and Duke Bengt on the opposite side. King Magnus the Barnlock stated:

"Herr Meinbald, we must agree on one practical matter related to taxation in the East. My brother Bengt needs a greater income from his fief of Eastland, and the common people cannot bear any heavier burden. Do you agree with me?"

"Yes, absolutely — the nation's tax burden cannot be increased further."

"Good. Then surely you understand that we must find another way to raise revenues. Therefore, this is what we shall do: I will grant Duke Bengt a manor called Harviala, in the village of Janakkala. In that same village lies a stud farm named Niemenpää, owned by your brother-in-law Matts. Matts must relinquish ownership, but he still holds Laukko in Vesilahti as his fief — where, as we understand, he resides."

"Your Grace, it is true that Matts lives at Laukko, but he also receives income directly from Niemenpää, which has been in his family for centuries — perhaps even millennia."

"Yes, Herr Meinbald, and from now on, those revenues shall belong to Duke Bengt of Finland, not to your brother-in-law Matts. Do you understand?" the King asked, without a hint of threat in his tone.

"And you, Herr Meinbald, will see to it that no hostility arises from Matts toward us or the Duke. The Swedish realm always arranges its affairs in the best way — does it not, Herr Meinbald?"

Meinbald had not expected this. Inside, he seethed with rage, but outwardly, he maintained perfect composure.

"Well, if Your Majesty has decided thus, then so it shall be. However, I ask two things of you."

"Yes, Herr Meinbald — *Capitain Finlandensis*?" Magnus the Barnlock inquires.

"I present my wishes to Your Majesty and to you, Lord Duke. First, let Magnus Garper — the farm manager appointed by Matts, the Master of Arms of the East — continue his work and reside on the estate. And if your aim is to expand the farm, let him handle all practical matters independently, without interference. This way, I can guarantee the highest possible yield. I would imagine, Lord Bengt, Duke of Finland, that you have no plans to move to the poor Eastland?"

"Your wish is wise," Bengt replied. "Indeed, I have no intention of settling in the East. The growing kingdom of uniting Svea demands my attention here, near my King. I have also heard that the German Brotherhood has expanded its holdings here in our homeland. As a man of the Church, I wish to ensure that the tensions seen in Estonia and Livonia — between the Brotherhood, the Bishop, and Denmark — do not arise here."

"Did you have another wish, Herr Meinbald?" asked King Magnus.

"Yes, Your Grace. As you know, my brother knights and I are graduates of the Hospital and Convent of Prague. My sister and I were under the special protection of the late royal of Bohemia, Agnes Přemyslid, founder and abbess of St. Clara's Monastery. We owe her so much that I feel compelled to ensure that even here, in the Kingdom of Sweden, the poorest and most needy may have a place where they can be cared for. It was Mother Agnes's last wish.

Therefore, I ask that Your Grace establish a Monastery of St. Clara here in Stockholm, where nuns can serve our Lord and tend to the sick and helpless. The hospital needs capable sisters; though the monastery of the Grey Brothers you founded is a fine beginning, I can assure you that when you learn what Mother Agnes accomplished in Prague — as a king's daughter who gave herself to the monastic life — you will wish your own daughter to have a place where she may practice such charity and service.

The Prague monastery founded by Agnes was the first St. Clara's north of the Alps — and now you have the chance to establish the next, before Denmark does. Moreover, my sister Kunigunde would be the perfect choice as the monastery's first abbess. She was taught by Agnes since childhood and would gladly come here to spread the holy teachings of Clara and Agnes, and to care for the poor and the sick."

"Excellent!" exclaimed the King. "The matter is settled. We shall speak further of the details later. My wife, Queen Helvig, is most enthusiastic about monastic foundations; she has already established several new ones in our realm. One more — the Monastery of St. Clara you describe, right in the heart of Stockholm, sounds like a noble undertaking. I already have land in mind for it, Herr Meinbald.

Now that we have agreed on these fine matters, let us continue our dinner and enjoy the dessert that is about to be served!"

In their excitement, the royals at the high table failed to notice that their guests had lost their appetites — and left their plates almost untouched.

****

After dinner, Meinbald and his two sons retired to the guest chamber. Meinbald's son Maunu turned to his father, "Father, that was a surprising move by the king and the duke — they'll take Niemenpää from Matti. Did you expect that?"

"My son," Meinbald replied, "I have been on journey with these Swedes for more than thirty years. The Bjälbo family has surprised me more than once. They surprised me again today."

"Father, you didn't look angry at all — how do you keep so calm?"

"I was boiling inside. But remember this, Maunu: in the presence of those in power, never show your feelings. If you are angry, keep it inside and strike later when no one is looking. Yes, I was furious, but you seemed calm as well?"

"I must have inherited that from you. But poor Matti — and poor Mother — how are you going to tell them?"

"I have no fixed plan yet, but I'm an old fox; I trust things will turn out. Don't worry now. When we get to Finland, we will decide what to do. For now, let us assume it will all work out."

Back at Taivassalo, Meinbald told Elin the news as soon as they returned. She bursted into tears.

"Oh, Matti! Niemenpää has been in our mother's family since time immemorial. How can those Birger's sons be so cruel?" she cried.

"My dear, I am speechless. Their insolence staggers me. Yet I am their appointed steward in Finland — I must carry this news and face your and Matti's anger."

"Oh, my husband, this is not your fault."

"Perhaps not, but I must tell Matti in a way that will not send him gathering the forces of Satakunta for revenge. This kind of a trick could feel a far worse insult than any wrong done by Ivans of Novgorod. After all, Matti and I have defended those layabouts and hudswots before against the Novgorods!"

Maunu, who had been silent, spoke up. "Father — remember what the king said: 'The Swedish realm arranges things in the best way.' If the king believes that, isn't it our part, as loyal subjects, to make it true?"

"There is a truth in that reasoning," Meinbald answered, "but I'm still unsure how we could do that?"

"Well," Maunu continued, "Matti will lose mainly the income. He's left the farm management to Magnus Garper; the practical running has already been done by him. What if we arrange compensation — some other source of revenue — and let Matti keep honor and access to the farm? He can visit, but the income would go elsewhere. That way, no public shame or blood feud arises."

"And Magnus Garper must be told that his lord is changing," Mielivalta added.

"True. As for compensation, I will speak with King Magnus. I think the king will allow Matti to retain half of the Lapland taxes as compensation."

"Excellent, Father! If Matti keeps that revenue, even financial harm won't touch him. The king will agree — otherwise he removes the incentive for the very man who brings him northern taxes."

Meinbald smiled with relief and pride. The plan seemed viable.

A week later, Matti learned of the arrangement and accepted it even more easily than expected.

"You have turned this around for me!" Matti said. "You kindred men, what have I done to deserve such help? Truth be told, keeping Niemenpää was a burden. Even with Magnus in charge, I worried constantly. Now I am free — as light as a bird. I would gladly share part of this with your sons if the king consents."

"Matti, you are fair — let it be so," Meinbald replied.

Meinbald sent pigeons to the king and arranged the details: Matti would receive four-tenths of the Lapland tax, from which he will give one-tenth to each of his sons. Because Meinbald remained responsible for tax collection across Finland, the king ordered that Meinbald and Elin may live at Niemenpää, now designated a Crown estate. Magnus Garper was directed to build a larger house and remain as farm manager.

Meinbald also pressed his second request — the foundation of St. Clara's Monastery in Stockholm — and recommended his sister Kunigunde as a capable first abbess. He included her address for the Queen.

Not waiting for a reply, Meinbald wrote at once to Kunigunde with the good news and urged her to prepare to travel: "I can hardly wait for our reunion, dear sister!"

A week later a royal reply arrived: King Magnus confirmed that Queen Helvig had welcomed the idea and written to Kunigunde in Prague, promising to cover her travel expenses and inviting her to come as soon as possible to arrange the foundation of the monastery.

****

1285 — The Power of the Church and the East

In the year of our Lord 1285, Duke Bengt of Finland was also appointed Bishop of Linköping.

The Church's strong grip and its entanglement with secular power thus continued to shape the North.

As bishop, Bengt extended his influence over Gotland, an island of vital importance to trade and the Crown's maritime reach.

By bringing Finland Proper, Tavastia, and Satakunta under Swedish taxation, the realm had more than quintupled its number of tax-paying farms, or *hooks*.

Eastland was becoming the granary of the kingdom — and with that, the royal court's attention turned increasingly toward securing the trade routes that sustained Sweden's growing power.

Stockholm, Summer 1285

That same year, Abbess Kunigunde began her journey from Prague to Lübeck, and from there by Hanseatic cog to Stockholm.

She wrote ahead to Queen Helvig and, of course, to her brother Meinbald, who now travelled with Elin to meet her. They waited at the harbor when Kunigunde's ship finally docked.

Brother and sister embraced warmly. Together with Elin, they made their way to the royal castle, where Queen Helvig welcomed them graciously.

"My husband, King Magnus," said Helvig, "has made it possible to build the monastery and mill through generous donations of land.

Now that the buildings are ready and the first of the sisters has arrived, the Order of St. Clara may begin its service without delay.

Should you, Mother Kunigunde, have any concerns or questions, you may always speak directly to me."

That evening, the queen held a dinner in their honor. They spoke at length about the future of the new monastery and the paths that had led each of them here — all agreeing that this was no coincidence, but a design written long ago.

Both Meinbald and Kunigunde knew in their hearts that Mother Agnes had foretold it: this was the destiny their faith had prepared.

In the years that followed, Meinbald and Elin often visited Stockholm, bringing one of their sons or daughters each time to see their beloved aunt.

Kunigunde delighted in these visits, questioning each child about their lives before launching into the stories she so loved to tell.

Stockholm, A.D. 1286

In the spring of 1286, Knut, son of Matti, and his wife Ingeborg, were blessed with a daughter.

At her baptism in the newly built Church of St. Nicholas, the child was received into the Christian congregation and named Birgitta.

The ceremony was grand and joyful. Matti, Malin, Meinbald, Elin, Mielivalta, and Kunigunde were all present.

The little Birgitta was calm and cheerful in her mother's arms. Matti's pride was plain for all to see — the baptism of his granddaughter in the kingdom's capital was an honor not lightly granted.

Torgils, now twelve, answered his grandfather's questions about his knightly training with boyish excitement, amusing everyone at the table.

St. Clara's Monastery — 1288 – 1289

The construction of St. Clara's Monastery was completed in 1288, and the church was consecrated the following year with great ceremony.

During the dedication celebrations, King Magnus performed Sweden's first knighting ceremony. He began by knighting his eldest son, Birger, who had recently turned eight.

Then followed older knights, many trained in the barracks of Turku Castle.

Among the guests, Matti felt special pride as he watched his descendant Knut, now the royal *Riksdrots* (Lord High Steward), and Torgils, Matti's fourteen-year-old grandson, receive the accolade. King Magnus knew well how to bind faith and chivalry together under his rule.

Kunigunde, now installed as the first Abbess of St. Clara, received high honors from both the bishop and the king. Overcome with joy, she thought of Mother Agnes, surely watching from heaven.

"What a miracle," she whispered.

Meinbald met his sister's gaze and smiled — he was thinking the very same.

That same day, Svante, aged sixty-two, was also knighted at last. His old friend Lydeke, a dignified gentleman of sixty-seven, approached with Meinbald, now sixty-eight, to congratulate him.

"Thank you, my good friends," Svante said. "But to tell the truth, this knighthood warms me less than it once would have. At my age, one worries most for one's children.

My daughters are mostly well, but my Ingrid was kidnapped from her convent two years ago — and I have heard nothing since.

Wild times, these. It is the third generation of my family to suffer such a fate. Would you believe it?"

Lydeke and Meinbald looked at him in disbelief. "Three generations?" they exclaimed.

"Yes, it is true. The old Germanic custom of bride-abduction still haunts this land. In 1210, Helena, the only daughter of the deposed King Sverker II, was taken from Vreta Abbey by the young nobleman Sune Folkesson, son of an earl. They married and had two daughters — the elder wed King Erik XI in 1244. The younger, my late wife Benedicte, was herself abducted from Vreta by Laurens Pedersson, the *lagman* of East Gotland. He sought to unite the lines of King Erik the Saint and the Sverkers to claim the crown. However it went, we found peace together and were blessed with six daughters and one son. My daughter Ingrid, like her sisters Katarina and Ingegärd, was placed at Vreta for schooling. The two elder became nuns, but Ingrid was betrothed to the Danish marshal David Torstensson — until Folke Algotsson carried her off to Norway two years ago."

Lydeke shook his head. "It sounds like something out of a Saxon legend!"

"A legend, perhaps — but a serious matter to King Magnus. He declared Folke an outlaw and confiscated his property. Folke's kin faced harsh judgment under the new *Peace Laws*. His father Algot, former *lagman* of Västergötland, and his brother Rörik were imprisoned; the bishop Brynolf, another brother, fled to Alvastra Monastery and swore loyalty to the king. The harshest punishment fell on Karl Algotsson, accused of plotting the abduction. He tried to flee to Norway but was captured and beheaded on Lindön in Lake Vänern earlier this year."

The news of the case spread across the kingdom — just as King Magnus intended.

It was a warning that the new laws of peace must be obeyed, and that women, especially those under the Church's protection, must be safe from violence.

To affirm this, Magnus and Helvig placed their six-year-old daughter Rikissa into St. Clara's Monastery, a living symbol of their vow to secure peace within the cloisters of Sweden.

****

Knut Mattsson, the firstborn son of Mat and Malin, served as *lagman* of the province of Närke and as *riksdrots* of the entire kingdom — a position he had received from the king in 1280.

Knut was the second man in Sweden to hold that title; before him, it had belonged only to Ulf Karlsson. As *riksdrots*, Knut was responsible not only for the financial affairs of the realm but also for its legal matters. Thus, it fell upon him to deal with this latest conflict as well.

He uncovered the plans behind the unrest and succeeded in capturing some of the conspirators, striving to restore peace to the kingdom. Yet the king's opponents could not be driven from their hiding places. Instead, they struck back — and Knut was violently slain in a nighttime ambush in Stockholm in September 1289.

For Matti and Malin, this was a crushing blow. Elin and Meinbald, as the nearest kin and Knut's godparents, shared deeply in their grief but could do little. It was impossible to make sense of such a loss. Why did this have to happen?

Matti and Meinbald spoke man to man. Meinbald's own son, Mielivalta, had been born five years after Knut. Despite the difference in age, the cousins had always been close, and Mielivalta had admired Knut's courage, sense of justice, and strength.

"Knut was such a powerful young man, and his whole life was ahead of him…" Meinbald's voice broke. "Now Torgils, his firstborn, is only fifteen. He still has to grow into a man — and I know what that means, having been orphaned myself. I had my sister Kunigunde, Mother Agnes, and the whole Brotherhood of the Red Star and Cross to guide me. We must make sure that Torgils finds such support around him, too, Matti. You and I — we've always managed things together, and we will again."

"I know what goes through that young man's mind," Matti whispered. "He has a fierce stubbornness and fire that must soon be guided into the right path. Meinbald, help me talk sense into him — he must not fall into a cycle of revenge. Torgils must pour all that energy into his training, into becoming the man he was meant to be. Otherwise, in his anger, he could do something irreversible that would destroy his own path to greatness."

"Of course I'll help," said Meinbald. "Let's talk to him at once."

Together they took young Torgils aside for a warm but serious talk. Afterwards, Meinbald said quietly:

"He took it well. Torgils seems very mature for his age. Matti — he will become a great man. Do you remember what your Lapland witch told you thirty years ago?"

"Of course I remember," Matti said, managing a small laugh, though the worry still lingered in his eyes.

"It was a great journey, my brother," Meinbald said. "I'm glad that we took it while we were still young."

Torgils devoted himself fully to his knightly training, showing exceptional skill in leading troops during practice battles. King Magnus remained personally interested in the young man's progress — after all, Torgils was a relative, and he was also godfather to King Magnus's and Helvig's younger son, Valdemar.

As the grandson of Matti, Torgils was also tied by blood to the Bjälbo dynasty through his grandmother Kristina, the half-sister of Jarl Birger. He grew up alternating between the hard military training of Eastland and the disciplined service of Stockholm's royal court — just as Matti, and even Kaukomieli before him, had done in their youth.

Gotland, 1288

King Magnus and his brother, Bishop Bengt, concluded a trade agreement with Visby. German wall-builders were allowed to fortify the city with a stone wall for its protection. The local peasants, however, resented being cut off from the lively trade and soon rose in rebellion.

King Magnus, ever the strategist, did not need to send troops. Instead, he persuaded the Visby council and the German masters that they must treat the Gotland peasants more fairly — or face consequences from the crown itself. He also urged the peasants to write to him directly if they were dissatisfied with their treatment.

When Meinbald heard of this through the bishop, he immediately grasped the king's true purpose: Stockholm's marketplace would grow immensely from such centralization of trade.

"Turku must not be left in Stockholm's shadow," Meinbald said to Elin. "Our merchants must build direct connections of their own — to Visby, Gdańsk, and Lübeck. I will write at once to my old friend Johannes Blankenfeldt in Berlin. His son is now mayor and may well be interested in trading — not only with me and Mielivalta, but with all our merchants in the East."

Chapter XVIII
East and West, War and Peace

Turku, AD 1290

The following spring, Meinbald and Hildegard's son Maunu was appointed bishop. Meinbald and Elin, Mielikki, Tuulikki, Kyllikki, Mielivalta, Matti and their families had all been invited to the consecration ceremony at the church in Koroinen. Kunigunde had also been invited; she, too, would come to Turku and spend a whole week with her brother in Taivassalo as a guest of honor. Matti and his family also stayed in Taivassalo's Särkilahti, where Meinbald and Elin had built a large log main building and sheds, a stable and a barn in the yard.

The whole party sailed to Turku together on a long river boat, rowing up the Aurajoki river.

"Do you remember Matti, when you beat the Danes here with a boat mast?" Meinbald asked as they rowed past the old marina.

"Well, I remember, I'm still a spry boy in mind and body! Of course, you're very high-spirited too, for such an old man," said Matti with a grin.

"I don't need to be much cooler than this anymore, when Mielivalta is a ready cavalry soldier and a skilled swordsman," sighed Meinbald, satisfied with his life, before realizing that he shouldn't have turned the knife in Matti's hurt soul. He changed the subject to keep the mood lighter.

"My sister Kunigunde, will you tell us a funny story about your years in Prague?" Meinbald asks, and Kuni, who had seen mainly the poor and sick during her time in Prague, understood very well his brother's purpose. She has adopted stories from Agnes, which could always be told in appropriate places. Now she chose one of the funniest ones from her repertoire; it was about a chronically ill person named Roman, who was always hurt, and everything happened while he was in the monastery hospital. Roman was kind-hearted but unlucky.

The crew listened to the story told slowly by Kunigunde in clear German, and she did manage to raise everyone's mood, causing bursts of laughter and even tears of joy.

Their rowers rowed the church boat all the way to Unikankare, and the boat could be moored almost next to the steps of the church. Mielikki, Tuulikki and Kyllikki and their families were already waiting for them at the church. Meinbald and Elin greeted their children, sons-in-law and grandchildren warmly.

"Today we are talking about peace, and we are not discussing military matters," he says to his sons-in-law, each of whom was in the cavalry service and had thus earned freedom from taxes.

The party entered the church and walked down the long aisle to sit in exact order, Meinbald and Elin in the front pew, Mielivalta, sons-in-law and daughters in the second row.

"Kunigunde, you also belong here in the front seat. Come over here next to me," Meinbald said to his sister, who had been left a little lost in her seat.

During the consecration ceremony, Meinbald returned in his mind to the mass where the founding of the Order of the Red Star and Cross had been celebrated under the leadership of the Bishop of Prague. At that time, he had been very proud of his brothers and moved by Sister Agnes's speech.

Now he was extremely proud of his sons and got emotional when he thought about their journey so far. At the mass, a hymn familiar to Meinbald from his time in Prague was sung, but this time only in Latin. Church Slav was not used in Turku.

> *"O Domine, miserere*
>
> *O Domine, miserere,*
>
> *Iesu Christe, miserere,*
>
> *Salus es totius mundi,*
>
> *salva nos et percipe,*
>
> *o Domine, voces nostras;*
>
> *da cunctis, o Domine,*
>
> *panem, pacem terrae;*
>
> *panem, pacem terrae.*
>
> *Kyrie eleison!"*

"Adalbert's anthem, I haven't heard it in decades," he whispered to his sister.

"Exactly, it's been a while, then you were knighted and your brotherhood received its holy mission from Agnes," she whispered back.

They looked at each other, and neither could help but notice the twinkle in the other's eye.

After the ceremony, a warm family party was held in the party house near the church. The party was not ceremonial, but mainly consisted of socializing, laughter, giggles, and old stories over a festive meal. Kunigunde felt so happy because everyone took turns getting to know her better. Mielikki, Tuulikki, and Kyllikki all also spoke German, much to Kunigunde's surprise.

King Magnus the Barnlock died in December. Birger Magnusson, who had already been confirmed as the heir to power at the age of four, was a minor, so Torgils Knutsson, Magnus's confidant, acted as the guardian ruler.

Torgils had focused all his strength and energy on becoming a knight and had worked hard trying to push the storms and poisons of anger roaring in his mind to the background. Now his efforts were rewarded — now was his moment to shine and rule the entire Swedish kingdom.

Bishop Maunu of Finland was in close contact with Bishop Bengt of Linköping, who was also the Duke of Finland.

In 1291, Bengt died. He never visited Finland himself, but he supported the equipping of his duchy with his own funds, so much so that he even went into debt for his support. For example, the construction of the bishop's castle in Kuusisto and the construction of the Cathedral required capital, which was not available in the poor Eastland. Nor could the tax burden be increased on the poor people.

Both son Maunu and father Meinbald also followed Bengt's example and financed the fortification and construction works themselves. However, Meinbald, as an old tradesman, knew how to be on his guard — e.g., with the Hanseatic League, the merchants, the stonecutters, and the master masons — and avoided over-indebtedness.

And Bengt certainly didn't go completely bankrupt either, because in his will he assigned 840 marks worth of silver to the Turku Cathedral, to be used, among other things, to set up an altar.

Maunu gratefully accepted the funds to fulfill Bengt's last wish.

***

Turku, June AD 1292

Maunu did not need to be idle as a new bishop, and in addition to ecclesiastical duties, secular matters also needed his attention. As the long and cold spring began to finally turn into summer, Novgorod attacked Tavastia again.

Information about this attack arrived in Turku by a carrier pigeon. However, the message was hastily written and did not provide enough information about where the troops had been seen and in which direction they were heading. Judging from the message, its author might no longer be alive to receive a reply, but nevertheless, more information was asked.

The central task of the bishop was to protect his congregation; the bishop's staff not only symbolized the spiritual shepherd. Maunu was involved in the Eastern Defense Council, which Meinbald called together after hearing about the matter. The bishop had his own horsemen, and Maunu suggested that he would take and leave for Tavastia with his troops as soon as possible. However, Meinbald added:

"Maunu, as the bishop of Finland, you are responsible for the security of the various parishes in all of Finland, and what if Novgorod sends additional troops, even here to Turku? I have a pretty sure idea that it won't be long before they start to be seen on the coasts here as well. If they can get up past the castle island from the mouth of Aurajoki, they can sail all the way to your bishop's seat, Koroinen. I suggest that messages be sent to Tavastehus Castle garrison, Ylä-Satakunta and Kokemäki Castle with pigeons, commanding that they send reconnaissance troops to patrol and keep us closely informed of where enemy contact is found. If the Novgorodians have forgotten to respect the might of the Pirkkas, you can be sure that they will be slain. My friend, my brother-in-law, my brother-in-arms Matti, is still leading the Pirkka clan; he has never been beaten."

"Father, you speak wise words, and luckily, your iron experience is on our side," said Maunu approvingly.

"Mielivalta, you should quickly assemble a strong strike group of the king's cavalry, take them to Tavastia yourself to make sure that there is additional strength if it is needed. As a marshal, you lead your troops and choose your deputy marshal before you march. I'll stay here in Turku to take care of the local defense. I'm already too old a man to gallop after Russ. Well, my son, go and do as you must; you will be fine."

***

Mielivalta led his two-hundred-man cavalry division at full gallop to Tavastia. The horses were changed to rested ones at the turnpike, which was halfway through the journey. At the castle, he got the information that no signals had been lit in the east or in the south, so the Novgorodians had used the northern route. Then the fires were lit from the north, so Mielivalta rode to Sääksmäki to the Rapola Castle mountain. There was no enemy in sight there either, so the journey continued straight away towards Vesilahti, again with fresh horses. When they reached Vesilahti, they saw how Novgorodians and Karelians had gathered around Matti's Laukko estates.

***

Matti and some of his Pirkka men had gone on a tax trip to the north. In the wilderness near Ruovesi, they met familiar Lapps who told them that Novgorod had once again come on a raid.

"Their leader is the giant-sized Pohto, and he has told me boldly that he wants to challenge the hero of Pirkka people to a duel. The Karelians are striking westward to expand Novgorod's domain."

Matti spent the night with the Lapps in the camp, intending to go back to Laukko early in the morning, where they said Pohto was heading. Matti asked the witch traveling with the Laplanders to predict how he would fare when he met that giant from the east. The witch saw Matti as victorious and predicted death for Pohto. This was enough for Matti; he confidently returned to Laukko.

Mielivalta and Matti met on the road leading to Laukko. Laukko's main building and the troops surrounding it could already be seen over the fields. They rode together to the meet the chief of the Novgorodians. Chief Pohto was a giant over two meters tall, a head taller than the others. He had a three-headed eagle pendant around his neck and iron wrist guards on his wrists. He spoke the Karelian language, so there was no need for an interpreter.

"Yes, we came by the Grand Duke's orders to see if you are a man worth of your fame. Grand Duke will control the taxes here in the future, and they say you are the biggest tax collector

~ 338 ~

here. Will you hand over the taxes to the Grand Duke in the future, or will you fight swords with me together?"

Pohto was challenging Matti to a "holmgång", a duel in an island. This would save bloodshed. The Novgorodians were certain to win, and so were the Pirkkas. Mielivalta told his men to be alert and ready to attack as soon as the opponent started to move.

Matti and Pohto were rowing to the island of Sarvu in front of Laukko, each in their own boat. After landing, they settle in a small clearing near the beach. Matti kicked Pohto's boat off the shore and said:

"One of us doesn't need a boat anymore, because only the winner returns from this island."

The men settled into a sword position. According to old Viking traditions, the challenger Pohto started with the first strike; his sword was also longer. Matti barely parried the blow with his own sword, but the blow was so strong that Pohto's blade slided along Matti's sword into his hand, cutting off the index and middle fingers. Matti didn't have time to feel the pain, but still he would have liked to howl in pain. Instead of howling, he unleashed an energy wave from the shock by bouncing on one leg.

"That's why it looks like a crow, right? That's how you danced," laughed Pohto out loud.

Then Matti grabbed his sword that fell from his hand to the ground in his left hand and leaped towards Pohto. With the force of surprise, he slashed the latter's head with his sword and shouted in his rage, "I still fly like a crane, you vassal of Russian robbers!"

Pohto didn't have time to react; his head fell to the ground with a thud and rolled downhill towards Lake Pyhäjärvi. A moment later, his big, headless body fell to the ground after a couple of missteps. Blood was still gushing from Pohto's neck when Matti left the body where it was. He just grabbed Pohto's head from the beach with him in the boat and rowed back from the island towards Laukko's shore.

Only after a few rowing strokes did he slowly start to feel pain in his right hand. As he looked at his missing fingers, he realized that he didn't have much time until the pain would become so great that he would lose his ability to function. The blood splashing from the fingertip also started to slip the oar, so that it was difficult to hold the grip. However, he got close to the shore, where he, standing in the boat, raised Pohto's head so high that all the Novgorodians surely saw that their chieftain had been defeated.

The Novgorodians immediately began to retreat in confusion. They couldn't possibly expect their big, sane hero commander to lose to that little brat. The shock spreaded among them, and in an instant, it turned into panic. Mielivalta commanded his men to charge, and they struck mercilessly at the Novgorodians, killing every single one they could catch. Matti commanded the Pirkka warriors to join the chase.

Matti himself walked up to Malin, held out his hand to her, and grimaced once more in pain. The pain was now really starting to kick in as the adrenaline disappeared from his system.

"My dear wife, use all your skills in healing and bandaging so that you can keep your husband alive and happy here."

"Oh Matti, you're my hero, and not just mine, but all of us. Yes, I'll make a man out of you, don't worry. I bundled you up like Lemminkäinen's mother did her son."

Malin tied Matti's hand with her own cloth and took him to rest inside.

When Matti's hand had been bandaged and medicated with herbs, he returned to the yard and received big cheers from the people who were still there. Matti decided to deviate from his habits and said a few words in public, for once, when there was something worth saying.

"I won in an honest duel. We will never submit to Russian rule. We will bury Pohto on that battlefield, and let it be called Pohto's island from now on, so that it will always remind us of our freedom!"

***

The news of Matti's great heroic work spreaded among the people like wildfire and quickly reached the king's court. Torgils was proud of his grandfather, and with good reason. He was preparing a military expedition to Karelia in the name of the minor Birger king.

The participation of the Karelians in the plundering expeditions orchestrated by Novgorod had to be stopped, and for that, a permanent foothold had to be obtained for the collection of taxes on the Karelian Isthmus. Käkisalmi and Suomenvedenpohja must be cleared from Novgorod so that the conditions in the border region could be calmed down.

Taxation for the Swedish crown would certainly calm the Karelians, which in turn gave better conditions to also calm the entire Hanseatic trade route to the east.

This time, the Church and the Crown were investing enormously together in equipping the fleet, and the Hanseatic

League was of course also involved as a protector of its own interests. The wooden fortress in Suomenvedenpohja, held by the Karelians, was to be conquered and upgraded into a stone monument—a symbol of Swedish power and a permanent lock of Karelia.

The launchers and the occupying forces of the first attack wave were already being concentrated at the mouth of Kymijoki, from where the fleet would then in time, set sail towards Suomenvedenpohja. Cavalry and armed men had been grouped along the Kymijoki branch to wait for the order to attack.

Even the stonemasons and master masons had already been reserved so that they could be loaded onto the ship for the second wave, when the soldiers from Uppland and Eastland, transported in the fleet of the first wave, had done their work and calmed down the castle construction site.

In Eastland, AD 1293–1295

Mielivalta also participated in the war expedition led by Torgils Knutsson along the Gulf of Finland to the east. Torgils, "Torkkeli Nuutinpoika" as the Finns called him, "Tyrgils" by the Germans and Latin-speaking monks, was still very young, only nineteen years old, but already fully capable of acting as the leader of the expedition and the state marshal.

Mielivalta was thirty years old and also in good spirits. Of course, it still bothered him a lot that his cousin Knut, whom he had always admired since he was a child, was now gone. But since Torgils, Knut's son, was ready to go and strike against the Novgorodians, so was he—if for nothing else, at least he regarded that that's what he owed to Knut.

The Novgorodians could be quickly evicted from western Karelia from harassing the Karelians. The main goal and biggest achievement of the whole trip was that the construction of the castle could be started according to the plans. The name for the castle had already been decided—it described its main purpose of protecting trade routes: Viaborg, "the castle on the way".

The minor King Birger rewarded Mielivalta, who had been elevated to the king's favor for his bravery during the expedition. He received land from Tavastia—Lammi's Vanhakartano, Gammelgård, which was transferred to Mielivalta's homestead from the crown. He found his young bride Aino in Tavastia, a Tavastian peasant house. Meinbald was, of course, very proud of his son.

In Stockholm

The power council, which held the real power, was led by Torgils Knutsson. Like Magnus, Torkkeli continued on a line favoring the Germans and the Hanseatic League, and this aroused a schism among his internal political opponents.

War success in the east, however, kept Torkkeli as the unchallenged number one in the kingdom. A very powerful duchy had been built from the East, and now the whole kingdom was led by a young man who had his family roots there.

In 1294, the Swedes attacked further east and conquered Käkisalmi castle. Mielivalta finally got a well-deserved vacation and met with Aino in Tavastian town of Vanaja. Meinbald was busy taking care of the kingdom's connections and matters with Lübeck's merchants and the German churchmen. He was mostly based in Taivassalo's Suur-Särkilä.

Mielivalta fell while defending the Käkisalmi fortress, when Novgorod recaptured the fortress in 1295. He had only lived to be thirty-two years old.

Mielivalta's cavalry comrades took his body with them when they retreated from Käkisalmi. The rules of knight education were well internalized—no comrade in arms was left on the field.

Mielivalta got a military funeral, where his own brother, Bishop Maunu, acted as the master of the funeral ceremony, when he was blessed to rest in the grave under the floor of the Koroinen church. A new cathedral was already under construction in Unikankare.

Meinbald and Elin were now, in their turn, broken by grief. However, Mielivalta's newborn firstborn son brought them some comfort, as well as the fact that Mielivalta's spouse Aino named the boy not only the Christian Peter, but also Mielivalta, a name known in Tavastia.

In the coming years, Elin and Meinbald started spending more of their time in Niemenpää, since it was close to the younger Mielivalta and Aino. Matti and Malin also understood very firsthand how Meinbald and Elin felt, because they had experienced the same grief six years earlier when their own firstborn son Knut had died.

In Stockholm, AD 1296

Knut's son Torgils married Birgitta, daughter of the late King Magnus, in 1296. He had been the head of the guardian government of the minor King Birger, and thus the true ruler of Sweden, for six years now, since Magnus the Barnlock had died.

By marrying the king's daughter, he strongly associated himself with the top of the list of crown aspirants. Torgils might not have been dead serious about wanting the crown, but he also didn't understand that sometimes how things look was more important than how they really were. In political circles, his moves were noted precisely as a quest for power.

Aino and Peter Mielivalta

Aino spent most of time with Peder Mielivalta at her mother's place in Vanaja, and they also often visited Elin and Meinbald in Niemenpää during the summer when the waterways were open.

Along the waterways, you could also reach Vesilahti Laukko, where grandmother Elin's brother Matts was spending his old age. One summer, Meinbald took the whole group on boat to Laukko, saying that they and Matti hadn't had time to go through all their old war memories this summer yet.

Aino, little Mielivalta, Elin, and Meinbald enjoyed an exciting but comfortably peaceful trip to the lake. The landscape varied from the narrow bed of Hiidenjoki to a growing series of increasingly wider and longer lake ridges, then to a narrow bed past Mierola and Lepaa and across the wide Vanajanselkä, until again, after a couple of smaller ridges, they proceeded to a narrow bed called Hiidenvuolle.

They still descended through the rapids of Kuokkala and continued along the small ridge of Pyhäjärvi to the long Toutonen, and from there through the narrows to Laukonselkä. Matti's Laukko could already be seen there, behind the island of Pohto.

Malin and Matti come to the pier to receive them when they saw the expected boat approaching. The reunion was warm; the sauna was also warm. It was already evening when they arrived, so after a sauna, a swim, and an evening snack, the whole group was ready for the night. Then in the morning, they talked and spent the whole day together.

Matti was sixty-five years old, but still, due to his growing tough reputation, quite an unstoppable hero. It didn't even slow him down that he had to learn to get by almost single-handedly.

Matti loved it when he was asked once again to tell how he had actually won Pohto, who had been considered invincible, on the island right there in front of Laukko. Mati and Malin were visited by magicians, composers of poetry and songs, and just curious people who wanted to meet a living legend.

The Lapps stayed away because Matti and his Pirkka guard had driven them far to the north and taxed them for years, so that they would rather just tell their stories about Matti from a distance.

Matti's wife, Malin was the daughter of Bengt Bielke, the sister of knight Kettil. They also had grandchildren visiting them. The oldest of the surviving sons, Matts, was thirty-five years old; he already had a couple of children: seven-year-old Jakob and five-year-old Elin. Matti's and Malin's next son, Johan, had also already had his first child, Paul, who was a toddler.

Meinbald enjoyed the children's laughter and the knowledge that Peder Mielivalta will be able to grow up while maintaining good contact with his little cousins. Meinbald was so moved that he found himself rubbing tears from the corners of his eyes while watching his relatives' children play.

After the warm summer day and summer night they spent in

Lauko, they enjoyed a hearty breakfast and then wished a warm farewell to Matti "Kurki" (Crane) and his offspring as they letf for home.

The boat slowly sailed past the island of Pohto, proceeding along Laukonselkä through narrow Hinsalansalmi. The Naulinkari island in front caught their attention.

Elin told them: "There, on Naulinkari, Kirmu-Karmu and his men crucified the Lord of the Veil almost a hundred years ago. The first missionary of these regions languished there until he was rescued by local Christians."

They continued rowing quietly in their thoughts to Sakaselkä, past the tip of cape Kaakilanniemi and then between Linkokari and the cape, leaving a juniper shore and continuing along Toutosenselkä towards Lempäälä church bay.

***

Ringshult, AD 1299

Nils Sigridsson wanted to finalize his will because he felt that he was already very close to his death. He called, among others, Svantepolk and Torgils as witnesses to his will.

Nils had visited the Holy Land since he'd been a warrior during the crusade to Tavastia. As a close man of the men of the Bjälbo family—Birger, Valdemar, and Magnus—he had accumulated quite a considerable fortune, which included several farms and cattle, gold, silver, money, and even slaves.

Now Nils wanted to free his slaves in his will, but of course, only after he died. He also wanted to redeem his place in heaven, and so many monasteries received a donation from the funds left by him.

Nils said, "I want to be buried next to my beloved wife in Askeby monastery. Twenty silver marks will be paid to the monastery for that good. I also brought that little golden cross with me from the Holy Land. I want to donate it to Gårdsby church in Värend.

"I donate my farm in Linköping to Linköping Cathedral, my farm in Värend to Växjö Cathedral's building funds. I want to bequeath three marks of pure silver to the cathedral of Nidaros, when it seems that I will no longer be able to visit the grave of St. Olav there before my death.

"In addition, one silver mark will go to each monastery and hospital in the area of the bishopric of Linköping, as well as to the Dominican monastery in Sigtuna and the Franciscan monastery in Stockholm. In addition, three marks of money for the Torpa church in Ydre."

During his life, Nils had done a lot of business with the merchants of Söderköping and Visby, as well as Lübeck. So he also left a lot of his property to several merchants in the mentioned cities. Most of these were debt settlements, but there were certainly a few donations as well.

Nils continued, "All these donations of mine have already been recorded in my will by the scribe. Now read it in peace, and after that, I ask you to confirm my last will with your valuable seals, distilled gentlemen of rank. The bishop and dean of Linköping will then act as executors of my will.

"Torgils, I want to say something else to you. Svantepolk, excuse me, I want to say a few more words to this young man before I leave this time for eternity."

Svante said goodbye to his old friend and then left Nils and Torgils alone.

Nils spoke again, with a fragile voice: "Torgils, your grandmother's brother Kettil asked me as his last wish to tell you how your grandfather Matts saved him from a certain death in the East half a century ago. Without Matts, Kettil's children would never have been born, my son-in-law Ture wouldn't have existed either, and I wouldn't have my wonderful grandsons Bengt, Sten, and Nils, who I see now one day doing great things with you, Torgils."

"Mattis-farfar has never told me about this," said Torgils, a little surprised.

"That's why I'm telling you now, because I knew he wouldn't. Mattis is very modest—perhaps too modest. But Torgils, you are destined for a great task. You have already conquered Karelia; you have already founded Viaborg Castle. Be that as it may, you still go to establish the castle of the Land Crown on the Neva, but remember that your higher mission is to finally secure an agreement between the sons of Magnus the Barnlock, so that Sweden can unite and take its rightful place in this world."

"Swear to me, for the sake of Kettil's memory, my son-in-law Ture and my grandchildren, that you will do everything you can to promote reconciliation between the royal sons."

"Sir Nils, Dominus, I swear," says Torgils. "I will leave no stone unturned to make this wish of you and Dominus Kettil come true."

"Thank you, Herr Torgils Knutsson. Now I can pass from here to eternity in peace, because I know that you are a man of your word, just like your father Knut was and your grandfather Mattis still is. Thank you, son. Always remember that blood is thicker than water. Farewell now, and call my house priest here to give me the last anointing."

Torgils said goodbye to the dying old man, and when he left, he called the priest to perform absolution and the last anointing for him.

Turku, AD 1300

By the Pope's decision, the year 1300 had been defined in advance as a holy year, and it meant a great celebration in the Christian denomination. A lot of pilgrims traveled to Rome at that time. A few pilgrims might also have left Finland from the edge of the world.

Bishop Maunu decided that the new church in Unikankare will be consecrated this jubilee year as the bishop's new home church, i.e., a new cathedral. Turku was planned to be expanded in such a way that a city began to be built around the church, so it was also necessary to move the episcopal seat to where the wider congregation would meet in the future.

Following the old Catholic tradition, Maunu set the consecration celebrations to be two days, so the Turku cathedral would be consecrated on June 16 and 17, AD 1300. At that time, Unikankare church was still a wooden church— only its nave was made of stone. However, it would now become the main church, not only of the Diocese of Turku, but also of the whole of Finland.

Maunu had completed ten years in the office of the bishop. He had been able to participate in many things together with the Finns and Swedes—with the people, the clergy, the soldiers, as well as the royals.

Theology still fascinated him in a certain way, even though he had been able to state that the activities of a bishop are much more mundane and worldly than he had initially felt before he took office. The Church of Finland was very independent, even though the archbishop sat in Sweden. It suited Maunu well.

He corresponded with Kunigunde and visited her at St. Clara's monastery almost every time he visited Stockholm. Kunigunde was very much like how he remembered Agnes. It's funny that he still remembered that abbess who passed away a long time ago and compared the aunt-abbess to her in his mind.

But those stories—Agnes was happy to tell them, and Kuni had also absorbed at least enough of them for her own and others' pleasure.

Maunu loved stories and storytelling. He had often forgotten time passing in his talks with Kuni for such a long time that he was late for the ship. If he had not been the bishop of Finland, he would often have been left to tell the story where the ship raised its anchor and headed towards Åland and the East.

Now, however, an inferior priest from the traveling party always had to hurry by boat and run to St. Clara's monastery to pick up the bishop. Once, when this had happened, Maunu had just heard a repeat from Kuni about the fate of Adalbert.

After all, he went on a mission to Prussia and lost his head on that trip. And his bones were fought for, sold, and eventually ended up in two different cities. A saint's story—that's what it was, a grim one.

"Well, we in Finland also have our own saint with his own story—Bishop Henrik. Lalli killed Bishop Henrik just as Sicco had killed Bishop Adalbert."

"Bishop Henrik's bones!" Maunu exclaims out loud after thinking about it on the boat trip home.

"What does your grace mean?" asks the chaplain traveling in Maunu's entourage.

"Just that we have a real national treasure in Nousiainen. We have to move the remains of Henrik to our new cathedral, which is being completed."

"And then nothing is said about this to the Swedish government, did you hear? I don't want Henry's bones to become merchandise that kings buy themselves into heaven with. Those bones belong to the entire poor people of this poor country of ours. It is enough that the crown takes its share of the grain and other products of the land—they are not entitled to anything on top of it. The bones of saints can heal the sick and bring luck in war against the persecutor."

After saying the words aloud, Maunu realized that he had to write a letter to Kunigunde right away, and he did so immediately. The ship stopped in the port of Mariehamn; Maunu gave a letter to the ship boy to take to another ship, which was leaving for Stockholm.

"What did you write in the letter, Your Grace?" the chaplain asked.

"I wrote to my aunt, the abbess, that she knows how to keep Adalbert's story to herself in Sweden. If anyone from Bjälbo got the slightest hint that you could trade bishop's bones and even buy a place in the kingdom of heaven, you can be sure that I, too, would be able to get rid of my bones in no time."

"This is how I wrote, and I believe that my aunt Kunigunde

knows how to keep her mouth shut in this regard. She is a fierce storyteller, so let her tell other stories to the people of the crown."

The chaplain nodded in understanding to his bishop, silently thinking in his mind, "Oh, my lord, are things like that taught in the theological faculty over there in Paris—the bone trade and the protection of relics..."

Maunu, on the other hand, remained silent in his thoughts to concentrate on another, even more important, point that had popped into his mind.

"I have heard the story of Lalli and Bishop Henrik from Kaukomieli already as a child. Laurentius was the chief who hosted Köyliö's *moisio*. Bishop Henrik came to collect taxes from the area. His party left Laurentius', or Lalli's house after enjoying the hospitality, and did not pay hostess Gertrud for the night, as had already been the custom at that time.

"When Laurentius, after returning home, heard from Gertrud what had happened, he took his Schläger from the wall and went after the bishop. Lalli caught up with the bishop's party on the ice of the lake and beheaded him with a sword."

Maunu connected the events to the stories of martyrs he had heard during his studies and understood why a similar story was needed in Finland.

"I have to go to the Dominican monastery as soon as we return to Turku. They get to create a saint's story about Henrik there. Let Lalli become a scoundrel, Bishop Henrik a saint."

The Consecration of Turku Cathedral

The dedication celebrations of the Turku Cathedral were unprecedented. Many people gathered in Turku to watch the celebration. People and market stalls also crowded around the church.

The wooden church hall was full when Bishop Maunu I solemnly consecrated the church by sprinkling holy water on different parts of the church to be blessed.

As beautiful Latin hymns played, the church people could admire the multi-colored mystical atmosphere of the land under the summer sun as the daylight filtered through the bright stained glass windows.

Meinbald and Elin were invited to their familiar places in the front row, with their daughters and their families. Matti and Malin, with their families, had also traveled from Vesilahti.

Meinbald looked behind him to see if any of his familiar knights could still join this most important church ceremony in Eastland. In a way, this symbolized a certain endpoint for the work they had done to bring Finland under the influence of the Church of Western Rome.

"The ranks of my brothers have thinned. There sits brother Fridrik with his family; there, on the other side, I see Lydeke. I don't see others."

The church's second altar of saints was the altar of the Virgin Mary, the mother of Jesus and the giver of the Son of God. She is considered the saint of all mankind.

In addition, each church got its own patron saint. On the second dedication day, St. Henrik was made the patron saint of the church, and at the same time, Henrik's relics were carried to the church.

According to the Catholic faith, the sanctity of a saint remained even after death in his remains. Prayer to the saint had to be done at the saint's altars.

Since the regular congregation could not enter the part of the church dedicated to the saint, during the coming holidays, Henrik's relic box would be carried in a procession around the church, when the parishioners could also touch it.

A patron saint was needed right away in the following winter, which turned out to be unprecedentedly cold. This was followed by a rainy and cool summer, when the grain harvest became practically unsustainably small.

The famine worsened among the entire Swedish people. On the eastern side, the poor people persevered with what little they had left from the previous harvest.

Maunu saw the plight of the people, and after talking with his father, they decided that taxation should not be done at all.

"Every household must have its emergency provisions — who knows what trials may still come our way?"

∗∗∗

To these cautious and uncertain times, we now leave Meinbald, whose journey you have been following from Eastern Europe to the North, from his childhood through youth and adulthood, all the way into old age.

With him came armies to Finland the likes of which the land had never before seen. They represented the most advanced military technology and expertise of the 13th century. From their descendants in Finland—the eastern lands of Sweden—arose a warrior nobility, whose duty it was to fight for the king and to serve in the administrative offices of the crown.

Behind these events, the historical forces and developments of the era reveal a deeper story of their time. Church and state operated then in close interaction; bishops and the king's governors wielded broad local authority as they dealt with the great questions of the nation's fate.

After the brotherhood of Meinbald, the lives of the Finns and the Swedes alike continued to be shaped by the long dialogue between war and peace. Altogether, the 14th century and the centuries that followed brought at least the following recorded armed conflicts into the history books concerning the Finnish lands:

Recorded Armed Conflicts Affecting the Finnish Region

1311 – Novgorod attacked Tavastehus Castle; later that same year, a retaliatory raid was carried out to the Neva River.

1313 – King Birger's forces attacked the fortress of lake Ladoga.

1318 – Novgorodian troops attacked the Turku region: the church, town, and the bishop's castle of Kuusisto were burned, though Turku Castle withstood the assault.

1322 – The commander of Vyborg Castle attempted to seize Käkisalmi, but failed.

1322 – Grand Prince Yuri of Novgorod launched an attack against Vyborg Castle.

1323 – The Treaty of Nöteborg (Pähkinäsaari) established the so-called "Eternal Peace."

1337–1338 – Swedish troops from Vyborg captured Käkisalmi.

1348 – Under King Magnus Eriksson, Swedish forces captured Oreshek (Pähkinälinna) and gained control of the Neva River.

1349 – Novgorodians retook Pähkinälinna.

1350 – A new campaign against Novgorod.

1351 – Novgorodians retaliated by burning Vyborg.

1377 – Novgorodian forces attacked the mouth of the Oulujoki River, devastating the region.

1411 – The commander of Vyborg Castle raided the Käkisalmi area; in revenge, Russian forces burned the town of Vyborg that same year.

1415 – Russian raiders carried out plundering and destruction in the Oulu region.

1430s onward – For about half a century, records note at least five Russian raids into Northern Ostrobothnia, as well as a Karelian raid into Savonia in the late 1460s.

1479 – Karelian raiding expedition into Ostrobothnia.

1480 – Erik Axelsson, together with the Teutonic Order, attacked territories belonging to Novgorod.

1495–1496 – Russian forces attacked from Kola, following the Kemijoki River into Ostrobothnia, as well as into Western Karelia, Savonia, and Häme (Tavastia).

1497 – The Peace of Novgorod.

1499 – Russian incursions into the Olavinlinna region and Northern Ostrobothnia.

1520s onward – Border skirmishes and raids between Savonians and Karelians.

1555 – King Gustav Vasa's Russian War, marked by mutual raids and guerrilla warfare.

1557 – The Peace of Novgorod.

1570–1573 – The Russo-Swedish War, the beginning of the "Long Wrath" (lasting 25 years), with raids on both sides.

1577 – The second phase of the Nordic War after a long truce;
again, devastating raids on both sides.

1595 – The Treaty of Täyssinä.

1600 – The Polish War.

1610 – The Ingrian War.

1617 – The Treaty of Stolbova.

1618 – The Thirty Years' War begins: Sweden, now a Great
Power, fights in Germany and Bohemia.

1629 – The Treaty of Altmark.

1648 – The Peace of Westphalia.

1655–1661 – The Northern War.

1674–1679 – The Scanian War.

1700–1721 – The Great Northern War.

1721 – The Treaty of Nystad (Uusikaupunki).

1741–1743 – The War of the Hats, also known as the Lesser
Wrath.

1743 – The Treaty of Turku.

1756–1763 – The Seven Years' War, including the Pomeranian
War.

1788 – King Gustav III's War, including the Liikkala Note and
the Anjala Conspiracy.

1790 – The Treaty of Värälä.

1808 – The Finnish War: Sweden loses Finland to Russia.

1809 – The Treaty of Fredrikshamn (Hamina).

1809–1917 – Finland under Russian rule.

1830–1831 – The Polish Uprising.

1853–1856 – The Crimean War.

1877–1878 – The Russo-Turkish War.

1918 – The War of Independence / Finnish Civil War.

1939 – The Winter War.

1940 – The Moscow Peace Treaty.

1941 – The Continuation War: Finland and Germany jointly attacked the Soviet Union as part of Operation Barbarossa.

1944 – The Moscow Armistice.

1944 – The Lapland War, in which Finland, under Soviet demand, drove its former German allies from its territory.

1947 – The Paris Peace Treaty, which ushered in the longest uninterrupted period of peace in Finland's recorded history.

Epilogue

Agnes of Bohemia was canonized as a saint only in 1989 by Pope John Paul II. However, even in her own time, she was regarded as a saint.

Magnus I, Magnus II Tavast, and Magnus III Särkilahti were among the most prominent Finnish bishops of the Middle Ages. All had studied in Paris or Prague.

Meinbald's grandson, Peter Mielivalta, held Lammi Old Manor as his home estate but was also active in Taivassalo. He served, among other things, as commander of the garrison at Tavastehus Castle, and was known to the Swedes as Peder Tavast. He was a knight of the nobility, and his surviving daughters were married into other noble families, such as the Djäkn and Ingesson lineages.

Olof Pedersson, or Olavi Pietarinpoika, continued along the path laid by Meinbald in the third generation. He fought in the king's armies and, as a reward for his service, received a charter of nobility granting him exemption from taxes in 1410.

Olof's son, Nils Olavsson, was a squire who still owned Iso-Särkilä Manor and the Tammisto estate. He served as the King's Judge in Finland and was also a member of the Council of the Realm, for he was among those who signed, at Kalmar in 1441, the peace treaty between Sweden and Norway.

Nils Olavsson's son, Bishop Magnus III Särkilahti, studied in Paris and, in 1466, obtained the office of Dean of Turku Cathedral, which carried the rank of count. In 1488, Magnus signed, as Sweden's representative, a treaty in Tallinn establishing perpetual peace with the Livonian Order. He also decreed that church services were to be held in the language of the people. Magnus personally financed Finland's defense against the Russians in 1495, which led him into great financial difficulty. As a result, Iso-Särkilä Manor passed in 1498 to Nikolaus Särkilahti, the mayor of Turku, who was married to Magnus's sister Martha.

Martha and her hot-tempered husband Nikolaus — known as "Angry Niku" — had a clerical son, Peter Särkilahti, who became the first representative of Luther's Reformation in Finland. He scandalized his contemporaries when he returned from his studies in Wittenberg, for he brought a wife with him — something no priest in Catholic Sweden of that time was permitted to do, as they were bound to live in celibacy. The Stiernkors family of soldiers and clergymen, descended from this line, kept the symbols of the star and cross in their seals well into the 17th century.

Stories about Matti Kurki still live on as legends, though his ancestry, life, and death remain shrouded in the mists of history. Matti Kurki was active in the late 13th century, during the time of the northern crusades. His descendants later rose to prominence in Swedish state affairs — as councillors of the realm, judges, military commanders, and even bishops throughout the 14th to 17th centuries. The Svärd and the Kurki families, as well as the later Kurck family, proudly carried on the legacy of Matti Kurki. Yet some have argued that he was an entirely fictional character.

In reflecting on what is true and what is invented, in this book or in life in general, one may recall the words of Saint Augustine, and turn inward — for, as he said, truth resides within the human soul:

"Seek, therefore, the place where the true light of reason is kindled.

For to what else would every good user of reason aspire, if not to truth?"